Susan R. Sloan is a former trial attorney who brings the full scope of her experience to the subject of violence against women. She lives in the Pacific North-West and is currently at work on her next novel.

GUILT BY ASSOCIATION

SUSAN R. SLOAN

WARNER BOOKS

A *Warner* Book

First published in Great Britain in 1994
by Little, Brown and Company

This edition published by Warner Books in 1995

A CIP catalogue record for this book
is available from the British Library.

ISBN 0 7515 1444 6

Typeset by Solidus (Bristol) Limited
Printed and bound in Great Britain by
Clays Ltd, St Ives plc

Warner Books
A Division of
Little, Brown and Company (UK)
Brettenham House
Lancaster Place
London WC2E 7EN

I would be more than remiss if I did not acknowledge some of the people who helped make this book a reality.

I wish to thank Lieutenant Mike Pera and Sergeant Angela Martin of the San Francisco Police Department, Sexual Assault Division, and members of the San Francisco Rape Treatment Center, for their invaluable input.

My sincere appreciation goes to Dr. Susan Pendergrass for her expertise, to Susan E. Klein for her research and observations, and to Janine Asch and the library staff of Half Moon Bay, California, for their assistance.

I am indebted to my agent, Esther Newberg, for being one in seventy-eight, and to my editor, Jamie Raab, for creating more out of less.

I am particularly grateful to Linda Stenn for her many contributions, to Howard Schage for his continuing support, and to my little group of readers who kept me going when I was ready to quit.

And my deepest gratitude goes to Sally Sondheim for her unflagging faith in me – and her eagle eye.

For Pamela,
who was there from the beginning,
and got the body up front.

And for Virginia,
who never stopped believing in me.
I know she's smiling.

DECEMBER 22, 1962

I t was cold – the kind of cold, at once heavy and bitter and penetrating, that was so characteristic of New York City in winter. There hadn't been much snow to speak of, only a brief flurry now and again that powdered the sidewalks and dusted the rooftops and then disappeared, as if by sleight of hand, leaving people to wonder whether they had really seen anything at all.

It was three days before Christmas, and Manhattan could not have been described as anything but bleak. Temperatures lurked in the low twenties and skies were filled with sullen clouds that never managed to do more than glower by day and threaten by night.

Margaret Westfield was not used to being awake at six o'clock on a Saturday morning, much less dressed and out. But she had a week's vacation from her job as an assistant bookkeeper for a Seventh Avenue clothier, and she was taking advantage of the time off to spend the holidays with her family in Rhode Island. She wanted to give Brandy, her frisky golden retriever, a good run in Central Park before relegating him to the cramped back seat of her Volkswagen beetle for the three-hour journey to Providence.

Only rich people and crazy people kept automobiles in Manhattan, Margaret knew, but her father had ignored her protests.

'It's just my way of making sure that you'll always have a way to get back home to us,' he said when he handed her the keys.

He knew she had gone to New York to get away from the family or, more precisely, away from the embarrassment of being thirty-three years old and the only one of his eight children who was still unmarried. But he had no intention of abandoning her.

'If traffic's not too bad, we'll be there in time for lunch,' she told Brandy as they crossed Fifth Avenue and entered the park.

It was too early for most New Yorkers to be up and about, and Margaret found herself alone on the path she and the dog usually took to the pretty little lake in the green oasis that ran down the middle of the concrete city. After several yards, she stopped and, reaching down, unsnapped Brandy's sturdy leather leash. The retriever bounded on ahead of her and was soon out of sight.

Margaret pulled her knit cap down over her short brown hair, buttoned her navy pea jacket over her stocky figure and started after him. She wasn't concerned. They took this same route every day and she knew Brandy wouldn't go any farther than East Drive, where he would sit on his haunches, with his tongue hanging out and his tail wagging, waiting for her to catch up so they could begin their game of fetch with the ratty tennis ball she always carried in her pocket. Even in the middle of winter, he couldn't wait to plunge into the lake's icy water. But when she reached the road, the dog was nowhere in sight.

'Brandy?' she called. 'Come on, boy. We haven't got all day.'

There was no response. Margaret frowned, peering up and down the road in the pre-dawn gloom. The four-year-old retriever was impeccably trained, responding to her voice commands almost before the words were out of her mouth, and next to his breakfast and dinner, there was nothing in the world he liked better than his morning play.

Margaret crossed the road and continued along the walk toward the lake, looking in all directions, calling for the dog every fifteen or twenty steps. She was well beyond the boathouse before she heard a faint whimpering sound.

'Brandy, where are you?' she shouted.

This time she received a short urgent bark in response which came from somewhere off to the right. Margaret spotted a narrow path and turned quickly onto it, hurrying along for several hundred yards while it twisted and turned and the retriever's woofs and whimpers grew louder. Around one last corner, the path abruptly widened into a small clearing. The dog was about forty feet away, barely visible, with his rump exposed and the rest of him buried beneath a clump of bushes.

'Brandy, you come out of there,' Margaret ordered. She hoped he hadn't cornered some small animal in the brambles. She had never known him to go after a park creature before, but she supposed there was always a first time.

The retriever looked over at her, gave another short urgent bark, and turned back to the bushes, making no attempt to obey her command. Margaret was totally bewildered. He had never behaved like this before. Sighing, she reached for the leash she had slung over her shoulder and started toward him.

When she was thirty feet away, she realized that, in between his cries and yelps, he was indeed working at something he had found. The last thing she ever allowed him to do was pick up strange food.

'Brandy, no,' she demanded at twenty feet. 'Whatever it is, you leave it alone.'

When she was ten feet away, Margaret stopped dead in her tracks. In the gray dark, she saw a human foot in a black satin pump. Margaret gasped. The body of a girl lay half-hidden under the bushes. Whatever clothes she might have worn were shredded beyond recognition, she was covered with angry-looking bruises, and her skin had a bluish tinge to it. Brandy was crouched on top of her, licking at her face.

'Oh my God,' Margaret murmured, now frightened, inching closer, one hesitant step at a time.

The girl's face was swollen and caked with frozen blood, and ugly purple marks showed on her throat. There was something unnatural about the way one leg was positioned but Margaret didn't dwell on it. She was sure the girl was dead, yet when she mustered up enough courage to push her fingers against the purple neck, she felt a feeble, thready pulse.

'She's still alive, Brandy,' Margaret cried. 'She's not dead – she's still alive. We have to do something.' She tried to think. 'Keep her warm, that's it. We have to keep her warm.'

She pulled off her pea jacket and laid it over the part of the girl's body that the dog wasn't already covering. She didn't have any idea how long the girl had been lying there, or how close she was to freezing to death, but she knew the temperature was low enough to numb her own body in just the few seconds since she had shed her coat.

'Brandy, *stay*,' Margaret ordered the retriever. 'I'm going to find help.'

With the bitter cold urging her on, Margaret ran as fast as she could back up the twisting path, past the boathouse, across the deserted East Drive, and out to Fifth Avenue. She knew it was still too early for much traffic, but she prayed that there would be someone about at this hour. She ran into the middle of the road and stopped the first vehicle that came along.

'What's the matter with you, lady?' the irate taxi driver yelled, slamming down hard on his brakes and skidding to a stop. 'You wanna get us both killed?'

'Help,' Margaret cried. 'Oh, help me, please. There's a girl back there. I think she's been beaten up and she may be almost frozen to death. Please, get a doctor, get a policeman – get somebody.'

'Okay, lady, okay,' the cabby said in a more reasonable voice. 'Calm down. There's a police station right up the road. Just tell me where to bring 'em.'

'It's back there,' Margaret told him, quickly pointing out the direction.

'Yeah, yeah, okay, they'll be able to figure out where that is.' He reached into the back of his cab and pulled up a car blanket. 'Here,' he said. 'It's not much, but maybe it'll help till I can get someone to you.'

Margaret took the blanket and quickly retraced her steps to the clearing and the clump of bushes where her retriever was right where she had left him.

'We have to keep her warm awhile longer, Brandy,' she said. 'Until help comes.'

She picked up her coat and put it back on, jumping up and down a few times until she grew warm inside of it. The last thing in the world Margaret wanted to do was get near the girl. Even the thought of blood was enough to make her queasy, but she suppressed the surge of nausea and forced herself to crawl into the bushes, lie down on the ground as close beside the broken body as she could get, and drape the blanket carefully over all of them. Brandy stirred a little beneath the unfamiliar cover but stayed where he was.

The stench of waste was awful. Margaret shut her eyes and swallowed hard and, searching her mind for anything that might distract her, began to think about the Christmas tree that her family would be trimming tonight.

Unlike any other in the neighborhood, the West-field tree would be hung with garlands and ornaments that her mother and sisters spent weeks creating, each one hand-fashioned and unique. It was a tradition that had been passed down through generations of West-fields, but Margaret had never really cared that much about it, until now. Now it seemed like the most important thing in the world, and for the first time since she had moved from Providence to New York, she couldn't wait to get home.

She didn't know if the girl she held in her arms could hear her, but she began to talk aloud, about that tree and about her family, and about all the silly, crazy, happy moments they had shared down through the years, one thought leading to another, in a soft, soothing voice.

They stayed there like that for almost half an hour – the girl, the woman and the dog, until the cabby appeared, bursting into the clearing with a burly policeman and two white-uniformed medics in his wake.

PART ONE
1962

We believe no evil till the evil's done.

— *Jean de La Fontaine*

one

Karen Kern left the subway at Columbus Circle, deciding on impulse to walk the rest of the way to the Hartmans' West Side apartment.

Office Christmas parties, held on Friday by companies that would be closed on Monday, were ending. Cabbies, cold and irritable, leaned on their horns as they inched around the clogged intersection. Salvation Army Santas in stuffed red suits clanged their bells from every corner, and the tantalizing odor of roasting chestnuts hung in the air.

Karen didn't mind that there was no snow. She had just come down from Ithaca, where almost three feet of it had fallen in forty-eight hours, disrupting traffic, causing accidents, and canceling classes at Cornell University, where she was a junior. She didn't mind the cold, either, although the black cashmere coat wrapped tightly around her slender figure gave little real protection.

Dodging taxis, donating a quarter to the nearest Santa, and skirting knots of tipsy secretaries with a smile, Karen threaded her way through the intersection and headed north along Central Park West. It was December 21, 1962. She was young and healthy, and she had never been happier.

Even in the murky glow of the streetlights, it was clear that her face was too long for classic beauty, her nose too small, her cheekbones too prominent. But her dark Jackie-Kennedy-styled hair gleamed, her blue-gray eyes sparkled, and a pair of impish dimples framed her full lips. Her slim feet in black satin pumps barely touched the pavement.

Her mother might have been devastated when Karen was rejected by Radcliffe, where she would have mingled freely with Harvard men, and refused even to apply to Smith or Mount Holyoke, which were well within striking distance of Yale, but Karen was delighted with her choice. She loved Cornell, with its picture-postcard setting, grand Gothic campus, and amiable atmosphere. Besides, her father was a graduate of the university's dental school, which didn't exactly leave her mother in much of a position to protest.

'Don't waste time with undergraduates,' Beverly Kern had advised. 'Concentrate on the men in the professional schools.'

For a month or so, Karen made a halfhearted effort to comply, ever conscious of her mother's social set, in which success was measured by the number of doctors or dentists or, at the very least, lawyers brought into the fold. It was the direction in which sons were pushed and the end to which every parent of a marriageable daughter openly aspired. But then Karen met Peter Bauer, and her mother's exhortations flew right out of her head.

The very thought of the senior engineering student was enough to deepen her dimples and warm her heart on this frigid night, and she had thought of little else for weeks. After two years of dating, she and Peter had gotten pinned, in one of those incredibly romantic ceremonies, and were already talking about getting officially engaged come summer.

She could still remember how special she felt, standing on the porch of her sorority house, surrounded by all her sisters, grinning from ear to ear, while the men from Peter's fraternity serenaded her. And at the moment when he actually fastened his fraternity pin to her pink angora sweater, she was profoundly sorry for every other girl in the world.

Karen sighed in the chill Manhattan night, watching her breath frost in front of her, and wishing Peter were here beside her instead of in Bangor, Maine, spending Christmas with his family. Despite her mother's importunings, Peter was everything Karen had ever wanted, ever hoped to find in a man, from his quick mind and generous nature to his short crop of sandy hair, warm brown eyes and soft lips that hardly needed an excuse to curl into a grin.

'At least we'll spend New Year's together,' he'd told her when they hugged good-bye at the Ithaca train station. 'I'll see you on the thirtieth.'

Nine days and counting, Karen thought with anticipation. Still, she couldn't suppress a small stab of disappointment because she would have so enjoyed the chance to show him off at the party Jill and Andy Hartman were throwing tonight.

At Seventy-seventh Street, she turned west.

Although Great Neck, the upper-income suburb jutting out into Long Island Sound where Karen had been born and raised, was no more than half an hour's train ride from Manhattan, the very last thing the

Cornell coed had planned to do on the Friday before Christmas was come into the city. But here she was, dressed in her finest and on her way to her best friend's party. Her best friend who had returned from her sophomore year at Northwestern ten pounds overweight and two months pregnant.

What a mess that had been – Jill disgraced, Andy dragged back from his summer abroad, Jill's parents trying in vain to put a good face on everything. No one bothered to mention the option of a back-alley butcher. Instead, there was a hushed, rushed little civil ceremony that was promptly predated six months. Jill's father, a prominent New York attorney, pulled some strings to get Andy transferred from Northwestern to the law school at Columbia. Of course, Jill had to quit college.

Karen could just imagine what her own parents would do were she to get herself into such a predicament. The very thought of her mother's wails and screeches brought her stomach to the edge of revolt. She said a silent prayer of thanks for Peter, who had made a few attempts to get her to go all the way with him, in the back seat of his green Pontiac after they had drunk too much sour-tasting beer, but had never pressed her past a certain point.

Perhaps it was going out of style nowadays, but Karen still believed in the value of virginity and the importance of saving herself for her wedding night. Besides, her mother had certainly warned her often enough about the perils of promiscuity.

'Men might date tramps, but they marry virgins,' Beverly Kern would state bluntly, hammering her message home at every opportunity. 'Would you go into a store and pay top price for used merchandise?'

Karen had to admit she wouldn't.

'And God forbid you got pregnant,' her mother always continued. 'How could we ever hold up our heads in this town again? The tongues would never stop wagging.'

Just the notion of humiliating her family in such a way was enough to make Karen break into a cold sweat. So each time she found herself getting high on beer in the back seat of the Pontiac, a prudent little voice, which always sounded remarkably like her mother's, would begin to echo very clearly in her ear. It was more than enough to keep her resolve firm and her legs crossed.

Karen felt awful for Jill having to quit college, for having to marry so inopportunely, and for having a baby when she was still practically a baby herself. She knew Jill had dreamed of going to Paris after college, of living in a quaint little garret on the Left Bank, painting surrealistic versions of the Eiffel Tower, and hobnobbing with expatriate artists for a year or so, until her graduation money ran out.

For herself, Karen had no such lofty ambitions. While she intended to earn a degree in English at Cornell, a career did not really figure into her future. In fact, there wasn't any fantasy in her head that didn't ultimately end in getting married and having children – a whole houseful of children. Especially since she had met Peter. And while such a goal might have seemed dull or old-fashioned to some, she could hardly wait for the day when, as she pictured it, she would walk down the aisle and begin her real life.

Karen knew a few girls at Cornell who planned to pursue careers after graduation, but her mother had always dismissed a vocation as something to fall back on only in the case of early widowhood, and dismissed Karen's schoolmates as girls who, lacking enough marketable assets to make good marriages, were simply making the best of unfortunate circumstances.

Moreover, Beverly Kern was convinced that anyone with Andy Hartman's good looks and other attributes, having been forced into marriage, would probably divorce Jill at the earliest possible moment, thus ruining her forever.

By the time Karen reached the corner of West End Avenue and Seventy-seventh Street, it was after eight o'clock. The brick building in front of her, which rose twelve stories and occupied almost half the block, was, like so many that lined the streets of Manhattan, a once-elegant structure that was past its prime. In the dreary December night, it appeared more gray than red.

A doorman in maroon livery ushered her in out of the cold and across a softly lit lobby so ornately appointed that Karen imagined it might have been lifted from a palace like Versailles.

'At last,' Jill Hartman exclaimed when the elevator deposited Karen on the eighth floor and she made her way to Apartment G. 'I was beginning to think you'd changed your mind about coming.'

'And miss a good party?' Karen laughed. 'You know me better than that.'

Jill was now eight months pregnant and she looked absolutely radiant. Her long, honey-colored hair glistened, her hazel eyes danced, and her face glowed. This party was her final fling, as she described it, before the baby burst onto the scene.

'Well, come on in,' she cried. 'There are scads of great-looking guys here that ought to keep you from pining for Peter for at least one evening. I'd take you around and introduce you, but the truth is, they're mostly friends of Andy's. I hardly know any of them.' She took her guest's coat and purse and waddled off down the hallway. 'Don't be shy,' she tossed over her shoulder. 'Just jump right in.'

Karen chuckled. Always bright and bubbly, she was anything but shy. So she fluffed out her hair and smoothed down her skirt and looked around. The apartment was truly fabulous, boasting large, airy, cream-colored rooms with high ceilings and intricately carved moldings. Crystal sconces graced the walls, velvet curtains framed windows that overlooked the Hudson River, and those floors that weren't buried beneath thick carpeting were highly polished parquet.

With insolent indifference, the Hartmans had taken this glorious setting and filled it with Danish modern furniture. A makeshift bar sat at one end of the living room, while an assortment of spindly teak sofas and chairs upholstered in ugly brown tweed occupied the other. Across the foyer, a stick-legged dining table sagged under an extravagant buffet supper. The throaty voice of Nat King Cole drifted out of an elaborate hi-fi system that Andy had installed, completing the incongruity.

The crush of guests who filled the apartment were split pretty evenly between the bar and the buffet. Karen wasn't much of a drinker, so she turned toward the dining room. She was in the process of filling a plate with creamed chicken, shrimp curry, and a variety of salads that must have taken Jill a month to prepare, when someone brushed up against her, jostling her elbow, and she felt warm breath tickle her ear.

'You must've just arrived,' a husky voice whispered, 'or I would certainly have noticed you were missing.'

It was so unexpected that Karen promptly spilled macaroni and mayonnaise down the front of her favorite black party dress.

'You're right, I did just get here,' she managed to say, although at the moment she felt more like grinding her high heel into the stranger's foot. 'But now you'll have to excuse me.'

She set her plate back on the table, and, without so much as a glance in his direction, fled down the hall to the bathroom where she stood in front of the mirror and stared in dismay at the oily stain that had quickly spread across the expensive satin.

'Damn,' she muttered, snatching a towel off the bar and beginning to dab at the mess.

'What's the matter?' Jill asked from the doorway.

With a sigh, Karen turned around.

'Good heavens,' her friend cried. 'What happened?'

'Some would-be Don Juan tried to whisper a sweet nothing in my ear as I was helping myself to the macaroni salad.'

'Cornstarch,' Jill said, vanishing and returning faster than Karen would have believed possible, given her friend's present condition, with a box of powdery white stuff, which she proceeded to sprinkle liberally over the black satin. 'Who whispered in your ear?' she asked as the two of them waited for the cornstarch to soak up the oil.

'I don't know,' Karen replied. 'I didn't stop for the formalities.'

'Well, go find out,' Jill suggested when the home remedy had worked its miracle. 'And spill some cocktail sauce down his shirt.'

'Now that's an idea,' Karen chuckled. But she skipped the buffet this time and went to the bar instead, busying herself with a bottle of root beer.

'I'm sorry about your dress,' the voice said from behind her. 'I'd be happy to buy you a new one.'

'That's all right,' Karen told him, wondering whether root beer would do as much damage as cocktail sauce. 'Most of the stain actually came right out, and I think a good cleaning will take care of the rest. But I appreciate the offer.'

She turned around then and looked up into a pair of aquamarine eyes so arresting that she was left with only a fleeting impression of what the rest of him was like.

'It's a beautiful dress,' he said, and Karen actually felt his blue-green glance travel from the rise of her bosom to the turn of her ankle.

'Why thank you, kind sir,' she responded lightly. In fact, it *was* a beautiful dress, a graceful, scoop-necked concoction with a tight bodice and a flattering tulip skirt.

'I'm Bob,' he said with a seductive smile that lit up his face, a very handsome face she now saw, with straight brows, a thick fringe of eyelashes, a thin nose, sculpted mouth, and a small black mole on his right cheek that may have marred perfection but suited him absolutely. The whole was set off by a lot of dark hair that apparently curled too much for his liking, judging by the amount of Brylcreem he had used.

'I'm Karen,' she replied.

'Well, Karen,' he said as though he were actually caressing the name, 'there's no doubt that you're the most attractive woman here tonight.'

She knew it was a line, but he delivered it so well that she couldn't stop a little shiver from skidding down her spine. Bob was taller than Peter, who was far from short, and, where Peter was lean and trim from hours on the tennis courts, Bob was broad and muscular like a football player. She noted that his slacks were sharply creased, his cuffs, peeking from beneath a navy blazer, were fastened with expensive gold links, his tie was modestly striped, and his loafers were polished to a high gloss.

He was obviously quite stuck on himself, but Karen had handled this type before, and she didn't feel she would be betraying Peter any if she let a handsome stranger pay her a compliment or two.

'I think you have exceptionally good taste,' she said, smiling back.

He touched his Scotch highball to her bottle of root beer. 'Well then, here's to getting to know you better,' he said softly.

The party circled around them. Karen was at her best in crowds, moving in and out of various groups with such grace and ease that a professor once observed that she would be a real asset to an ambitious politician. She was included in a conversation about the truth behind the Cuban missile crisis, took part in a discussion of James Meredith and the future of integration, and joined a circle speculating about the future of a shaggy-haired quartet from Liverpool who went by the name of some insect.

The comfortable cloak of Camelot – that invisible sense of security and innocence and well-being – rested gently over everyone.

Karen would have enjoyed spending more time with several of the people she met, but Bob seemed always at her elbow, distracting her. At some point, he took charge of the drinks, pouring her root beer into a tall glass and adding a little something extra when he thought she wasn't looking. Karen grimaced a bit at the unpleasant combination of Hire's and Scotch, but didn't object. Bob was so attractive and he was being so considerate and, although she knew it was all just harmless flirtation, it made her feel terrific when, several times, she caught the envious glances of some of the other young women.

It's only for tonight, girls, she thought with a self-satisfied smile. Tomorrow, he's all yours.

Bob, as it turned out, was a friend of a friend of one of Andy's former roommates from Northwestern. He told her he was a born-and-bred California boy and had graduated from Stanford.

'Palm trees, sunshine and tequila,' he summed up for her with a nostalgic sigh. 'It was a glorious four-year-long party.'

'Oh, I'm sure of that,' Karen said, laughing.

'But now that I'm at Harvard Law,' he added with a grimace, 'all I get to do is study, study and study. Have to keep the old nose to the grindstone, you know, fourteen hours a day, seven days a week. Would you believe that this is the first real party I've been to in almost a year and a half?'

'Poor baby,' Karen consoled. Another lawyer, she thought with an inner chuckle. He was going to make some girl's parents very happy one day.

'No joke,' he assured her. 'I came down from Cambridge the day before yesterday and I have no intention of going back until I'm partied out.'

'Good luck,' Karen told him.

'You know, Cornell's not all that far from Harvard,'

he commented at one point during the evening, although Ithaca was in fact hundreds of miles from Cambridge. 'Maybe I'll look you up sometime.'

It was on the tip of her tongue to tell him about Peter, but she reasoned his remark was merely party talk and not to be taken seriously, and anyway, she was enjoying the attention too much to relinquish it so soon.

'Let's see, that should be in another year and a half, right?' she quipped.

'Oh, I just might make an exception in your case,' he countered, flashing a dazzling smile.

It was two o'clock before she realized it, and the party was winding down. About a dozen guests remained, wandering around, looking as though they couldn't remember where they were supposed to go. Andy had gotten drunk and passed out on one of the spindly brown tweed sofas. Jill was clearing away the debris.

'Let me help,' Karen offered.

'I'm not doing any heavy cleaning up now,' her friend replied. 'I'm just stashing the leftovers in the fridge. Everything else can wait until tomorrow. Look, it's really late. Do you want to stay over? I'm sure we can find an extra sofa.'

'Thanks, but I'm all set up with my aunt and uncle.'

Edna and Harry Kern lived on East Seventy-sixth Street, across Central Park. Over the years, Karen had occupied their flowery guest room whenever she stayed late in the city. The arrangement was quite convenient. She kept a change of clothes, a pair of pajamas, and a toothbrush in a dresser drawer, and Uncle Harry would leave an extra key with the night doorman so that Karen could let herself in without disturbing them.

'Then you'd better get going or you won't be able to find a cab,' Jill told her.

'It was very nice meeting you,' Karen said to Bob as he helped her on with her coat. 'I had fun.'

'The evening doesn't have to end, does it?' he asked. 'It's still early. There's bound to be a club or two that's open.'

'Thank you very much,' she replied, 'but it's pretty late by my clock and I have to get crosstown.'

'Are you sure I can't change your mind?'

'I'm afraid not. I'm staying with relatives. They're kind of old-fashioned and if I don't show up pretty soon they're apt to send the police out looking for me.'

She knew that Aunt Edna and Uncle Harry had been sound asleep for hours by now, but he didn't. Had circumstances been different, she might have said yes to his invitation. But the party was over and Peter would be coming down in a few days, and that was the way it was.

'Then let me help you find a cab,' he offered. 'I don't like the idea of you wandering the streets alone at this hour.'

She smiled because he really was very nice. 'Thanks,' she said, 'but the doorman will take care of that.'

'Well then, the least you can do is let me accompany you down in the elevator,' he persisted.

'Why not?' she agreed carelessly.

They said their good-byes and departed. When they reached the lobby, however, the doorman was no-where in sight.

'Maybe he had to go to the john,' Bob suggested.

'Perhaps he's on a coffee break.'

They stood around for ten minutes or so, but the doorman did not reappear.

'Look, let me get you a cab,' Bob said. 'I have to find one for myself, anyway.'

Karen shrugged. 'Okay.'

The temperature had dipped down into the teens by the time they emerged from the apartment building and began their hunt for a taxi, walking east, past the Museum of Natural History complex, on their way to Central Park West. The streets were almost deserted at this hour and the sound of their shoes on the pavement echoed off the rows of dark, frowning buildings.

When they reached the edge of the park, they stood on the sidewalk, Karen stamping her feet and rubbing her hands together to ward off the cold, while Bob searched up and down the street for a cab.

'One's bound to come along sooner or later,' he said reasonably.

Karen chuckled. 'With a little luck, before we die of frostbite.' She was glad now for the warmth of the alcohol he had added to her root beer.

They waited fifteen minutes.

'Maybe we should walk down to Columbus Circle,' Karen suggested. 'We might have a better chance there.'

'I have a better idea,' Bob said. 'Why don't we just walk across the park?'

It was an option she would never have considered, going into the park at night. There were a number of stories about how dangerous it had become.

'Look,' she said, 'you've really been very nice, but I can't ask you to go out of your way like that.'

'Sure you can. Where do your relatives live?'

'On East Seventy-sixth Street,' she told him. 'Between Park and Lexington.'

'It happens that I'm staying with friends on Seventy-fourth and Third,' Bob said. 'So you see, it's hardly out of my way at all.'

'Well, in that case …' She was still a bit hesitant but then not all that anxious to have him walk off and leave her alone. Besides, she supposed this nice broad-shouldered man could protect her from just about any kind of hobgoblin they might encounter. 'I guess it would be all right.'

They crossed into Central Park, following the pedestrian paths, Bob's hand firmly on her elbow, steering her this way and that – to the right, to the left, over a little bridge, then to the right again, until the sights and sounds of the city were far behind them. It was dark and eerie here, and ominously quiet. No voices broke the silence, no moon shone down through the thick clouds to light their way. Spidery branches reached out for them like gnarled black fingers against the grim gray sky.

'I haven't the faintest idea where we are,' Karen admitted after they had been twisting and turning from one path to another for some time.

'That's okay,' he said. 'I know the way.'

He directed her along as though he really did know where he was going and, because she didn't exactly have much of a choice, Karen followed. She remembered him saying that he was from the West Coast and had been locked up at Harvard for the past year and a half.

'How do you know which way to go?' she asked.

'I came this way earlier,' he replied smoothly. 'The

people I'm staying with gave me directions.'

'Oh,' she murmured.

'Trust me,' he said with a smile in his voice.

They walked on, even as the path got narrower and the underbrush thicker.

'It's so dark,' Karen observed, 'I can't even tell what direction we're going in.'

'It's easy,' he said. 'Hear the water? That's the lake. As long as that sound is to our right, we're heading east.'

Karen listened intently but she couldn't figure out from which side the faint slap-slap was coming, and she had a sudden wish that she had dropped bread crumbs in their wake.

'Are we heading for the Seventy-ninth Street Transverse?'

'No,' he told her. 'I don't know that way. But this way comes out right at Seventy-sixth Street.'

'I hope so,' Karen said. 'My teeth are beginning to chatter.'

'Are you cold?' he asked. 'Well, I can certainly take care of that.' He opened his heavy overcoat and pulled her inside, wrapping it around them both. 'There, is this better?'

His unexpected body warmth did help, but he was holding her too close and too tight and it made her uncomfortable.

'That's all right,' Karen told him. 'We can't have that much farther to go. I can make it.' She tried to move a step away from him but he wouldn't release her. 'I'm okay,' she assured him. 'Honestly.'

'Don't be silly,' he insisted, moving her along beside him. 'What would your relatives say if I brought you home frozen solid?'

'Well …'

She was just about to concede the point when he added in a husky voice, 'Besides, this feels nice.'

Karen stopped short. 'Please,' she said politely yet firmly, 'I appreciate your good intentions, but I really would feel more comfortable if you let me go now.'

'What if I don't want to?' he teased, tightening his grip even more.

Despite the numbing cold, she felt a little spurt of apprehension sprint down her spine.

'Look, you're a very nice person,' she replied, choosing her words with great care, 'but I wouldn't want you to get the wrong idea. You see, I'm engaged to be married.'

Karen rarely lied to anyone, but she felt that, under the circumstances, this slight exaggeration of the truth was justifiable.

'If you're so engaged,' he snapped, 'why do you go around flaunting yourself in front of other men?'

'I wasn't doing anything of the kind,' she retorted.

'Oh yes, you were. And I didn't waste a whole evening for nothing.'

Before she could stop him, he had turned her to him and was kissing her, his tongue pushing its way into her mouth, his hand beginning to grope beneath her coat.

'Stop it,' she sputtered, trying to twist out of his grasp. But he was much too strong and held her easily.

'You can cut the act now,' he said, laughing.

'This isn't any act,' she protested, struggling against him, 'and you're not very funny. Now let go of me this instant.'

Perhaps it was the amount of liquor he had consumed or maybe it was the stress of his law studies, she didn't know, but something inside of him seemed to snap.

'Shut up,' he snarled and slapped her across the face with such force that she fell backward against a clump of brambly bushes.

'What do you think you're doing?' she cried, realizing, too late, that something had gone very, very wrong.

'I'm going to give you exactly what you've been asking for,' he said, tossing aside his heavy coat.

'I wasn't asking for anything,' she insisted, scrambling to her feet. 'I was having a good time at a party – just like everyone else.'

He laughed harshly. 'Don't you think I can recognize a come-on when I see it? That dress alone was all it took.'

'You're crazy,' she shouted, before considering the effect her words might have, and turned for the path.

He reached out and grabbed her by the hair, yanking her back so hard that she lost her footing and fell against him. Then he pulled her right arm behind her back, twisting until, with excruciating pain, she felt it snap.

'Crazy? You think I'm crazy?' he snarled in her ear. 'Well, you're going to be crazy about me by the time I finish with you.'

Whirling her around, he knocked her to the ground with one swift punch in the stomach. Karen lay where she was, gasping for breath, unable to get up, as disbelief turned to fear. Even as she wondered what would come next, she felt the toe of his shoe slam into her rib cage. When she tried to roll aside, he caught her in the small of the back, and when she tried to wriggle in another direction, he kicked her in the abdomen. Wherever she turned, the polished loafer was waiting for her, smashing into her, over and over and over again.

'Please,' she whimpered.

'That's right, beg,' he hissed. 'Tell me how sorry you are you made me angry. Tell me how much you want me to do it to you.'

He straddled her then, threw open her coat and started to claw at her dress, the expensive satin shredding as though it were made of tissue paper. He reached for her bra, yanking it off with a skin-cutting snap. He ripped her garter belt in half, and the delicate silk panties her mother always insisted she wear came apart in his fingers.

She felt his hands sliding down her body, over her breasts, along her thighs, between her legs – places not even Peter had yet been allowed to explore. And following his hands were his teeth, marking her skin in a gruesome trail of his own design.

When she thought she could take no more, he suddenly stopped. But it was only to fumble at the front of his trousers. Then, without further preparation, he shoved himself deep inside that most private part of her.

Karen screamed. She had never known pain like that before. It was as though she had been split in two by a red-hot knife, starting at her thighs and shooting up into her chest. Immediately, one hand closed over her mouth and the other clamped around her throat – cutting off her shriek, and her air.

'I didn't say scream,' he snarled. 'I said beg.'

But she couldn't utter a word, she couldn't move, she couldn't even breathe. She couldn't do anything but lie there as he stabbed at her, again and again and again. Tears streamed from her eyes and her lungs began to burn. She didn't want to believe that such a thing could be happening to her, when she had always been so careful, but the agony she felt assured her that it was.

It was then she knew she was going to die, that he could not let her live, and she prayed it would be quick.

Soon enough, the world around her began to blur, her eyes fluttered. Sights and sounds seemed to fade and she felt herself rising, strangely weightless, higher and higher and higher still, until she was floating above the sinister gray clouds in a soothing white light, where everything was beautiful and no harm could reach her. She thought that being dead was not so bad, after all.

When she opened her eyes, the first thing she saw was the sullen sky. He was gone – his hands no longer closing off her mouth and throat – and the cold had almost numbed her to the pain. She sucked in great gulps of icy air and wondered where the peculiar rasping sound she heard was coming from. She couldn't believe she had survived and she was just beginning a silent prayer of thanks when his face loomed above her.

'Did you like that?' he crooned. 'Come on, tell me how much. I bet you never had it so good before.'

Karen turned her head away.

He slammed her across the face with the back of his hand. 'Tell me,' he barked.

She opened her mouth, but nothing came out except a throaty hiss.

He began to caress her roughly. With every ounce of strength she had left, she moaned and tried to move away, but he was there to stop her.

'Where do you think you're going?' he sneered. 'I'm not through with you yet. On the contrary, I'm just getting warmed up.'

Karen stared at him with revulsion, wondering how she could ever have thought him attractive.

'No more,' she managed to croak.

'The hell you say,' he laughed. 'I have to make up for all those monkish months I spent learning the law, and right now you're the only game around.'

With that, he shoved her over onto her stomach, pushed her legs apart, and forced himself into that place where such an invasion had heretofore been unthinkable.

The shriek that began in Karen's throat died in a mouthful of dirt. As agonizing as the other had been, this was infinitely worse – a battering ram, tearing, plundering, punishing, destroying everything in its path.

For an unspeakable length of time, he rode her like a bull, stripping her of every last shred of dignity, working himself into a mindless frenzy until, with a final grunt, he exploded from the inside. So dazed was she that she hardly felt him withdraw, and could not have said whether it was seconds or minutes or even hours later.

Bodily fluids oozed out of every part of her, visible evidence of a life that was slipping away. She scarcely noticed when he rolled her onto her back.

'Now that was even better,' he said with obvious relish. 'With a little practice, you could be quite good at this.'

Her only response was a raspy breath.

He reached down and pulled her head up by a

handful of hair, causing her to wince in pain from a dozen different places.

'I bet I know how you want it next,' he purred in her ear. 'Sure I do. In fact, I bet you love it that way just as much as I do..I bet you're going to be real good at it, too, aren't you?'

Her eyes were glazed, she could barely see him. She had no idea what he had in mind, but it didn't matter – she knew she couldn't stop him. He would do what he wanted and then he would be done and she would be dead, and that was all right. She couldn't imagine living after this, anyway.

He still had her by the hair and now she felt him tighten his grip. Before she quite understood what he meant to do, he had risen up on his knees and thrust himself deep into her mouth.

'Show me how good you are at this, bitch,' he cried hoarsely. 'Show me how much you appreciate what I'm doing for you.'

Karen couldn't help herself – she gagged and, as she did, her teeth reflexively snapped shut.

Bob squealed in rage and yanked himself free of her. 'I'll teach you to play games like that with me,' he howled and his right fist crashed into her face, shattering her jaw.

After that, Karen knew nothing.

two

Dr. Stanley Waschkowski was in the last year of his residency at Manhattan Hospital. A tall, gaunt man, with thinning brown hair, inquisitive dark eyes and a persistent five-o'clock shadow, he had the pallor of one who spends too much time indoors among the sick and dying. In four years, he had been exposed to almost every possible kind of illness and injury – one advantage of big-city training he would have missed in the small New Hampshire town he called home – and he prided himself on having achieved the emotional separation that a physician needed in order to survive.

'If you give up a piece of yourself to every patient you can't help,' a doctor he greatly admired had once told him, 'pretty soon you'll have nothing left to give to those you can.'

Waschkowski had learned the value of that advice even before he completed his internship. So well, in fact, that he was now frequently referred to, behind his back, as the 'Old Stone Man' by some of the younger residents. He didn't mind. In fact, he was rather proud of the sobriquet, knowing what it had cost him to earn it.

But as he watched an emergency room nurse cut away what clothing remained on the brutalized young woman before him, anger filled his dark eyes, and the iron clamp that held his emotions in check slipped a notch.

'God, she's hardly more than a child,' he murmured.

Waschkowski had two young daughters of his own. The thought of anything like this ever happening to one of them was enough to make him forget his Hippocratic oath.

'Okay, we have respiratory distress,' he told the intern who had summoned him. 'Prep her for a tracheotomy.'

He looked down at the girl as she lay there, bruised and bloody, barely able to breathe, depending on him to help her. He set his jaw and began his grim work.

'Tell me what you can, as soon as you can, Doc,' the corpulent policeman who had accompanied the ambulance said. Despite his age and obvious experience, the officer looked a little green.

'Take a seat, Sergeant,' the doctor said. 'Have a cup of coffee. This might take a while.'

An hour later, a weary Waschkowski emerged from the tiny cubicle with blood splattered on his white coat. 'Do you have any ID on her?' he asked the policeman.

'Yeah,' the officer replied.

'Call,' the doctor said. 'Get someone down here. We need a consent.'

Henry 'Tug' McCluskey was less than six months from retirement. He had put in thirty tough years on the New York City police force, playing it straight and clean right down the line, which hadn't always been easy. His living room wall was lined with commendations, his dress uniform was covered with medals, and his gold watch was waiting for him. In spite of that, he hadn't been able to protect that poor girl.

From one end of Manhattan Island to the other, he had seen more than his share of gunshot wounds, stabbings, mutilations, strangulations and beatings, but in thirty years he had never gotten used to it. Every one of those brutal crimes had taken its toll on him, but none had been as bad as the sight of Karen Kern's broken, bleeding body lying there under a bush.

Sitting in the hospital emergency room on a cold Saturday morning three days before Christmas, he knew he would have traded his commendations, his medals, his gold watch and even his pension, come to that, for five minutes alone in a room with the bastard who had done that to her.

Tug had been raised to respect women, and in turn had taught his four sons to do the same. He was known around town as 'the Gentleman Cop,' even by the hookers he used to roust over on Eighth Avenue. There was no doubt in his mind that, whatever this girl might have done to provoke such violence, she didn't deserve what she had received.

The sergeant hefted his bulk out of his chair and shuffled to the bank of telephones along the far wall of the emergency room to do the part of his job that he disliked the most. Keeping his voice as calm and unemotional as he could, he suggested to the woman at the other end of the line that she get to the hospital as quickly as possible.

'No, ma'am,' he sighed. 'I'm afraid I don't have any of the details yet. But I'm sure the doctors will be able to tell you everything when you get here.'

Although he had to have the results of the medical examination for his report, Tug McCluskey didn't need any know-it-all resident to tell him that Karen Kern had been raped and beaten half to death. But there was no point in telling the parents such a thing over the telephone. There would be time enough for them to hear that when they reached the hospital.

three

Leo and Beverly Kern paced the length of Manhattan Hospital's third floor corridor – a spare little man with rimless spectacles and trousers pulled over his pajamas, and a buxom woman in bright-blue eye shadow and a full-length mink coat – passing each other wordlessly at the midpoint on their way to opposite ends.

Beverly's high heels click-clacked against the stained gray linoleum, sounding sharply out of place in the subdued and sterile atmosphere. Not in all her forty-five years had there been a circumstance so dire that she could not first take the time to attend to her appearance. It was an edict that had been unchallenged in her family for generations – never to leave home without the appropriate outfit and clean underwear.

Leo fussed and fumed as Beverly took the time to shed her nightgown for a stylish woolen dress and camouflage her sags and wrinkles with a varied assortment of cosmetics, but in fact barely fifteen minutes passed before they were in the garage, revving up the engine of the big black Buick and speeding out of Great Neck.

Now, as they paced and waited, it seemed a lifetime ago that they were awakened by the telephone call, but it was actually little more than six hours.

'What could be taking so long?' Beverly grumbled when she had tapped her way up and down the corridor for perhaps the hundredth time.

'There are some things you can't hurry,' Leo responded mildly, 'and surgery is one of them. You wouldn't want them to rush, and risk making a mistake, now would you?'

'No, of course not,' Beverly conceded. 'It's just the waiting – it's so hard.'

Orderlies had wheeled Karen off to the operating room at nine-thirty. It was now two forty-five.

'Your daughter has been badly hurt,' Dr. Waschkowski told them when they hurried into the emergency room, having abandoned the Buick in the hospital parking lot. They had encountered very little traffic and no highway patrol cars on the Long Island Expressway at that early Saturday hour, and had reached midtown Manhattan in a record twenty-seven minutes.

'What happened?' Beverly demanded.

'Apparently, she was the victim of an assault.'

'An assault?' Beverly cried in dismay. 'What are you talking about? There must be some mistake. She was at a party last night. At the home of her best friend.'

'She was found in Central Park at approximately six-thirty this morning,' Tug McCluskey told them. 'I got to the scene a little before seven o'clock.'

He didn't want to tell these frightened parents what he found when he and the two medics followed the cab driver into the clearing.

'I brought your daughter here,' he said instead.

'What was she doing in Central Park?'

'We don't know that, ma'am,' McCluskey said.

'What about her injuries?' Leo asked.

'My preliminary examination indicates that she sustained multiple contusions and fractures and there are signs of abdominal bleeding,' Waschkowski replied. 'We've done a tracheotomy to give her a clear breathing passage.'

'Is she in a lot of pain?'

'No,' he assured them. 'She's unconscious.'

'Dear God,' Beverly gasped.

'That's not unusual in these cases,' the doctor was quick to explain. 'She's had a considerable shock to her system. Aside from the trauma due to injury, we estimate that she was exposed to temperatures well below freezing for several hours.'

'Why would anyone do such a thing?' Leo pondered aloud. 'It couldn't have been a robbery. She wasn't wearing any expensive jewelry. She wasn't carrying much money.'

Waschkowski cleared his throat and shifted from one foot to the other. Next to losing a patient, this was the part he most hated about being a doctor.

'We – uh – don't think the beating was necessarily her assailant's primary intent,' he said as gently as he could, having found evidence of semen in her vagina, her mouth and her rectum. 'She's been raped.'

Beverly cried out and sagged against Leo. Of all the things that could happen to one's child, this was a mother's worst nightmare.

'My baby,' she wailed, 'my baby.' Then she straightened up. 'I want her to have the best possible care,' she said firmly. 'And I want her in the best possible facility.'

'Manhattan Hospital *is* the best possible facility,' Leo told her.

'Then I want top doctors in charge of her treatment,' she retorted. 'No offense, Dr. Waschkowski, but I won't entrust my little girl to a resident. I want the best.'

'I've already taken the liberty of calling in a number of specialists,' Waschkowski assured her. 'There's an oral surgeon, an orthopedist, a urologist, a neurologist and a gynecologist standing by, all highly respected in their fields, and all in agreement that surgery should begin as soon as possible.'

'Of course,' Leo said.

'Well, if they say so …' Beverly muttered.

'One of you will have to sign the necessary papers.'

Leo had gone to do that and Beverly had stayed, waiting for the occasional glimpse she could get into the small white cubicle where nurses and technicians were preparing Karen for the operation to come.

'Your daughter's going to be fine, ma'am,' Tug McCluskey tried to soothe her. 'I've seen a lot worse pull through.'

'Thank you,' Beverly murmured.

Tug cleared his throat, much the same as Waschkowski had earlier. 'I just wanted to say, ma'am,' he added, 'how sorry I am.'

'That's very kind of you.'

'What I mean is, I've got granddaughters of my own, you see, and well, if I ever find the guy who did this to your little girl, I might just kill him.'

'Ohhh,' Beverly groaned, turning away. The thought of all these people knowing what had happened to her baby was almost more than she could bear.

Medical personnel bustled in and out of Karen's cubicle in a constant stream, while Beverly waited helplessly outside. Then, in twos and threes, they emerged, discussing what they had seen in brief sentences peppered with technical terms that were difficult for Beverly to understand.

But, she thought now, pausing outside the doors to the surgical suite, she didn't understand much of anything at all, except that Karen had left home at six-thirty yesterday evening to go to her best friend's party, and twelve hours later had been found unconscious in Central Park. Her bright, pretty, well-behaved daughter – after all the times Beverly had warned her not to have anything to do with strangers, how could this awful thing have happened?

'Maybe we should telephone Jill,' Leo interrupted her.

'What for?' Beverly replied. 'Surely you don't think the Hartmans had anything to do with this, do you?'

'No, of course not,' he murmured. 'I just thought Jill might know something that would help us figure this whole thing out.'

'What's there to figure out?' Beverly moaned, looking down on her husband's shiny bald head. 'It's all painfully clear, wouldn't you say?'

'But shouldn't we at least …?'

'Why don't we wait a bit,' Beverly said. 'There'll be time to talk to Jill. It's bad enough that the police are already involved. Until Karen herself can tell us exactly what happened, the last thing we need is more publicity.'

Leo nodded slowly. 'I guess I didn't think of that.'

He was a myopic little man who, at the age of twenty-six, had traded one mother for another without ever knowing the difference.

They brought Karen out of surgery at twenty minutes to four. An exhausted Stanley Waschkowski met the Kerns in the recovery room.

'She came through just fine,' he told them. 'There was more internal damage than anticipated, but we're confident we were able to take care of everything.'

Later, he thought, when they were stronger, he would give them the details, but they were in no emotional condition to listen now.

'She's going to be pretty uncomfortable for a while,' he said. 'But in time she'll be up and about again, and all this will be nothing more than a bad dream.'

'Is she awake?' Beverly asked.

'No, not yet.'

'Can I see her?'

'Why don't you wait an hour or so, until we move her into the special care unit. She may be awake by then.'

'She needs special care?' Leo asked.

'In cases like this, where there's been severe trauma, we don't take chances,' Waschkowski replied. Your daughter was unconscious when she was admitted. That might be the result of shock, or it might be an indication of some kind of intercranial pressure buildup. We want to watch her closely for a possible kidney involvement as well. With constant monitoring, we'll be on hand to detect any problem and act immediately.'

By ten o'clock in the evening, Karen was running a fever of 105 degrees.

'What is it?' Beverly cried.

'Pneumonia,' Dr. Waschkowski said. 'We had hoped to avoid it but it wasn't unexpected, given her condition.'

'Is it critical?' Leo wanted to know.

'At this point, unfortunately, everything is critical.' The senior resident sighed. 'But we've started her on a program of penicillin, aspirin suppositories, and alcohol baths, and that should help fight the infection. The good news is, so far, there's been no indication of any abnormal cranial pressure or kidney failure.'

Around midnight, the exhausted Kerns were persuaded to leave the hospital.

'There's really nothing you can do, even if she does regain consciousness,' Waschkowski assured them. 'And it may be as much as seventy-two hours before we know if we've beaten the pneumonia. I'm going to be here all night, and I'll call you immediately if there's any change.'

'No matter what the time?' Beverly asked.

'No matter what the time,' he promised.

They went to Edna and Harry Kern's spacious apartment on Seventy-sixth Street. Despite the hour, Leo's brother and his wife were still wide awake.

'We didn't even realize that Karen wasn't here until we got your call,' Edna sobbed. 'We left the key and went to sleep, just like we always do.'

'Don't blame yourself,' Leo said. 'You had no way of knowing this would happen.'

'Of course you didn't,' Beverly added, and making the only possible decision, as far as she could see, she planted her foot firmly on the first rung of the ladder of lies that she would climb in the weeks and months and lifetime to follow. 'How could anyone possibly have known there would be such a terrible ... accident?'

four

At first there were no days or hours or minutes, no way of measuring time or distance. There were no thoughts, no feelings, no recognition, just the murky black of nothingness that cradled her body and wrapped itself protectively around her mind.

Then the darkness began to give way to a thick gray fog, layer on top of layer, roiling around her, tangible, almost touchable, relentlessly propelling her toward unwanted sight, lurking just beyond her mind's grasp.

In the end, despite every ounce of resistance she could muster, awareness overtook her. It began with the voices. She could hear them through the fog – soft, urgent, too low for her to catch the words, annoying. Next came the smells, unfamiliar and unpleasant, that stung her nose with each laborious breath. And finally, there was the realization of pain, and with it, the last agonizing thrust into the harsh light of reality and horror.

Karen opened her eyes.

She was lying in a bed that was not her own, in a
place she had never seen before. Shards of bright
sunlight slanted through a large window in the opposite wall. Unknown people in white hovered around
her. Everywhere she looked, there was white – the
gown that clothed her, the sheets that covered her, the
pockmarked ceiling tiles above her. She wanted to ask
where she was, she wanted to tell someone about the
pain, but she couldn't seem to move her mouth or
produce anything but a curious gurgling sound.

'Julie, go get Dr. Waschkowski,' a lady with gray hair
pulled back into a bun instructed the aide beside her.
'I think she's awake.'

'Yes, ma'am.' A petite strawberry blonde with enormous china-blue eyes dashed from the room and the
gray-haired lady leaned over the bed and smiled. Wisps
of hair had come free of her bun and drifted around
her kindly face.

'You're quite safe,' she said in a reassuring voice that
floated gently over Karen. 'You're in the special care
unit at Manhattan Hospital. You were brought here
after your, uh, after your accident. Now, you're not to
worry about a thing. The doctor will be right along
and he'll answer all the questions I know you must
have.'

Karen tried again to say something and again failed.
She tried to raise her right arm to see if she could feel
what was holding her throbbing head immobile, but
the arm was encased in something white and heavy.
She looked out of the corner of her eye at her other
arm. It was anchored to a white board, palm up, with
a needle protruding from a vein in her wrist. Tubes
and wires seemed to be coming out of every part of

her. Karen's eyes widened fearfully. She wanted to scream, but as before, only a gurgle escaped.

'Now, now,' the lady in white soothed. 'You just relax, dear. Don't try to talk. You're going to be just fine. Trust me, all this paraphernalia looks much scarier than it really is.'

Rose Thackery had been a nurse for forty-one years. She wasn't sure she could think of anything much scarier than what had happened to this poor girl.

Karen shut her eyes as tears began to ooze out the sides and drip onto her pillow. The pain came from everywhere, her head, her eye, her nose, her mouth, her chest, her arms, her abdomen, her leg. It hurt to move, it hurt to lie still, it hurt to breathe. She dimly remembered being in Central Park with Bob, but that had been at night, and now it was day, and she didn't know what had happened in between. She hoped the nice gray-haired lady had called her aunt and uncle. She didn't want them to worry that she wasn't there for breakfast.

'Karen?' a voice asked. 'Karen, can you hear me?'

She opened her eyes again. The sunlight was gone. It was dark outside the window. A tall man stood beside the bed. In the shadows, he looked like Bob. Karen gasped and began to thrash about. This time, she knew she had to get away from him, and that gave her the strength to ignore the sharp pains that attacked her from every corner.

The Bob-man said something over his shoulder and a woman in white hurried over and handed him something. He leaned down and, flinging aside the bedclothes, plunged a long needle into Karen's hip.

A peaceful warmth flooded through her. She was dancing in a lush meadow and the scent of wildflowers filled her nostrils. The sun was hot on her face.

'Karen?' the voice said again. 'Can you hear me?'

She didn't want to answer. She wanted to stay and play in the meadow.

'Karen, I want you to wake up now.'

The meadow began to slip away, the vibrant greens and the sky-blues fading into colorlessness, the sweet fragrance of flowers and grass turning sour, like disinfectant. She awoke reluctantly. The white world of agony greeted her.

A man stood at the foot of the bed. He had kind brown eyes, a large hooked nose and a warm smile, and the sun picked bronze highlights out of his thinning hair. His hands were long and slender and his fingernails were neatly trimmed. He looked as if he might play the piano.

'Hello,' the man said. 'I'm Dr. Waschkowski.'

Of course, a doctor, not a piano player, Karen thought. She gurgled painfully.

'No, don't try to talk,' he told her. 'Your upper lip is stitched, your jaw is wired and you have a tube in your throat that's helping you to breathe.'

Karen stared at him.

'I know that sounds pretty frightening, but the truth is, things usually sound worse than they are.' His smile broadened reassuringly.

Karen tried to smile back, but couldn't.

'No, you can't smile with your mouth just yet,' the doctor told her, 'but I can see it in your eyes. So I'd like you to do something, sort of play a little game with me, okay? I'll ask you some questions, and you answer me by blinking your eyes. Once for yes and twice for no. Do you understand?'

Karen blinked once.

'Good,' he said. 'Okay, here we go. Is your name Karen Kern?'

Blink.

'Are you twenty years old?'

Blink.

'Do you live in Port Washington?'

Blink. Blink.

'Good girl.' Waschkowski smiled and moved around to the side of the bed. 'Do you remember being in Central Park?' he asked gently.

Karen's eyes filled with tears. Blink.

'All right,' he said with an encouraging nod, 'you've told me everything I need to know for now. As your doctor, I prescribe more rest. We can talk again tomorrow.'

He made a move to go but Karen, using all her strength, raised her right arm in its heavy cast to stop him.

'Don't be afraid,' he said kindly. 'You're going to be just fine. I'm an excellent doctor and I would never let a slip of a girl like you make a liar out of me.'

Blink. Blink.

'Is the pain very bad?'

Blink.

'Up until now, we couldn't give you anything for it, because we didn't want to mask any symptoms. But now that you're fully awake, I'll have one of the nurses give you a shot.' He made another move to go, but again she stopped him. 'Is there something else?'

Blink.

Waschkowski sighed. 'Let me guess. You want to know what all this stuff connected to you is about?'

Blink.

'Why don't you rest for a while and then we can have

a long talk about that later?'

Blink. Blink.

'Okay,' he said with resignation, pulling a chair up to the bed and sitting down on it straddle-style. 'I can tell you're not going to let me get away with anything. Well, let's see. Do you want to start at the bottom and work up, or start at the top and work down?'

Karen blinked once, then twice, then once again.

'Serves me right,' Waschkowski laughed. 'Okay, we'll start at the top.'

One by one, he cataloged her injuries, mentioning the black eye that would be tender for a time and the broken nose they had set and the split lip they had sutured, and then pointing out each of the tubes and wires, telling her in simple terms what it was and why it was there. The enormity of it might have over-whelmed her had he not been careful to maintain a calm, almost matter-of-fact, attitude.

'You have a fractured jaw,' he began. 'We've wired it shut and immobilized your head with a splint. It should be as good as new in a month or so, but until then, your ability to talk and eat will be restricted.'

She could remember Bob's fist crashing into her face.

'Along with that, you have a crushed larynx, which means you *really* can't talk for a while. Think of it as having a very sore throat. We did a procedure we call a tracheotomy, which is a big word that means we put a little hole in your windpipe to help you breathe more easily.'

She remembered Bob's hand closing around her throat.

'Moving on,' Waschkowski said, as though he were a docent describing masterpieces in a museum, 'we have several cracked ribs, which we simply taped up because modern science hasn't yet provided us with a better way of mending them.'

She could feel the toe of Bob's shoe smashing into her over and over again.

He pointed to a tube emerging from the side of her rib cage. 'Now this little beauty is what we call a chest tube. We put that in because one of your ribs went and poked a hole in your right lung. Think of your lung as something like a balloon, and then picture what happens when you stick a pin in that balloon.'

Waschkowski saw her eyes widen. 'Fortunately, a hole in a lung isn't something to worry about these days,' he went on smoothly. 'The tube will drain the fluid out of your chest cavity and then your lung will reinflate, just like that balloon again, and most likely heal all by itself.'

He was so casual about it that Karen supposed having a hole in a lung wasn't such a big deal, after all.

'I bet you can pretty much figure out what the cast on your arm is for.'

Blink.

'I thought so. It was a clean fracture, easy to set. You'll probably have signatures from the entire staff on that cast by the time it comes off.'

She remembered falling out of a big maple tree and breaking her arm when she was eight. She had worn a cast for six weeks. 'I told you so,' her mother's voice echoed.

'Next,' Waschkowski continued, 'we have some discomfort in the abdomen, right?'

Blink.

'That's because we had to open you up inside and fix a few things. Do you know what a spleen is?'

There was a pause before Karen blinked once, then twice.

'Yes and no,' Waschkowski interpreted. 'Well, that's okay. It doesn't really matter, because you don't have one anymore. It was ruptured, so we took it out. Luckily, you can live to a very ripe old age without it.'

He opened his mouth to tell her about the uterus, about how torn it was, about how they had tried to repair it, but failed.

'You also lost a fair share of blood along the way,' he said instead. There would be time enough later, when she was stronger, physically and emotionally, to tell her she would never have children. 'So we gave you a couple of pints of healthy new A positive to fill up those veins again. And last, but not least, we have a smashed kneecap. Now I happen to like the symmetry of it,' he joked, 'seeing as it's your right arm that's busted and your left kneecap that's smashed. But you might prefer to be lopsided.'

Blink. Blink.

'Ah, good,' he said with a grin. 'You obviously share my sense of artistic proportion. We put a splint on the leg, which will immobilize it until we can operate. There's an orthopedic specialist waiting in the wings who'll tackle the job when you're a bit stronger.'

He told her about the pneumonia next, again as though it were an everyday occurrence rather than a potential killer, and about the IV dripping nourishment and antibiotics into her system, and about the sinister-looking machine that monitored her heartbeat and the cuff on her arm that allowed the nurses to take her blood pressure.

Finally, he told her about Margaret Westfield and her dog Brandy.

'Animals have excellent instincts,' he said.

When she was four years old, Karen was bitten by a neighbor's Rottweiler and had since been somewhat wary of dogs. How ironic, she thought, that she might now owe her life to one.

'Your parents are here,' Waschkowski said at the conclusion of his monologue. 'They've been here right from the start, of course, and they've really been keeping us on our toes for the past eight days.'

Karen had listened to the recitation of her injuries with relative calm, but now her eyes opened so wide they threatened to engulf her entire face. Eight days? She had lost eight days? How was that possible? And much worse, in that time, how many strangers had looked at her, examined her, and discovered the awful things that Bob had done to her? It was humiliating to realize what they had seen.

She began to agonize over what they must have thought of her as she lay unconscious and unable to explain. They must have thought her stupid, at best, to get herself in such a situation. At worst, cheap and common. Tears welled up in her eyes again. Even her mother and father knew, before she had a chance to prepare them. Above all, Karen prayed she wasn't pregnant. *Anything but that,* she silently begged a God she didn't know if she still believed in.

At that moment, all she wanted was to rip the tubes and wires from her body and crawl, if she had to, into a hot shower bath, to burn off the layers of skin that the monster in the night had touched, to scrub away all evidence of his existence. Even as she struggled to get her mind around the enormity of her ordeal, she knew that she would never be completely clean again. The tears rolled down her cheeks.

Waschkowski's heart turned over. 'Look,' he said, 'I'm not going to tell you that you haven't had a rough deal here. You have. Rougher than anyone deserves. But you're a strong young woman. The fact that you've made it this far proves that, and you're going to make it the rest of the way. It may take a little time, but you're going to be just fine. In all the weeks and months ahead, you remember that I told you so – and that I'm never wrong.'

He had a sincere face and kind eyes and Karen wanted so much to believe him.

As a doctor, Stanley Waschkowski knew, perhaps better than most, how badly a body could be ravaged by an unexpected injury or a debilitating disease. He had learned how to set bones and treat infections with a reasonable expectation of success. But he had never, in all his years of schooling and practice, been called upon to treat a damaged soul.

five

Karen slept a great deal after that. Deep, dark, pain-free slumber that blotted out reality and hastened the healing. It was so much easier not to have to think and not to have to feel and not to have to remember. She wished it might go on forever.

She would lie in oblivion until the nightmares came to jolt her back into consciousness, and then she would stare up at the reassuring pocked ceiling and around at her cocoon of white night curtains and listen to the soft noises of the special care nurses at work until the panic ebbed and her heart stopped its erratic pounding and she could close her eyes and float back into forgetfulness. She had no concept of hours or days. Her only indicator was that sometimes it was light outside the window when she awakened and sometimes it was dark.

Once, when she opened her eyes, her parents were there. She wanted to smile and tell them not to worry about her, but her wired jaw wouldn't cooperate, and nothing more than the now familiar gurgle made its way past her throat.

'Hello, darling,' Beverly cooed. 'Daddy and I are right here and we're making sure you get the best possible care.'

Gurgle.

'Don't try to talk, sweetheart. You just rest. That nice Dr. Waschkowski says the more you rest, the quicker you'll be all well again.'

Karen needed no encouragement. She drifted off, almost immediately, eager to return to nonexistence. Another time she awakened, Peter was sitting in a chair beside the bed.

'Hi, honey,' he said gently. 'Happy 1963.'

Dimly, she remembered that he was coming down from Maine to spend New Year's with her and that they were going to live happily ever after. But she had slept through New Year's and there was no happily ever after in her nightmares.

By the end of a month, she had been moved out of the special care unit and into a private room at the other end of the third floor.

Here, the walls were painted a surprising pastel-peach color with a broad band, the exact shade of ripe raspberries, circling the room just above eye level. Curtains striped in peach, raspberry, forest green and gray framed the window. Two upholstered chairs, which stood like bedside sentinels, matched the curtains. Except for one swath from the door to the bed, the institutional linoleum that covered most of the hospital's floors had been replaced by a dove-gray carpet. A framed Monet print hung over the bed, a Renoir accented the opposite wall.

'This whole wing was redecorated last year,' Julie van der Meer, the aide, told her. 'The designer convinced the administrator that recovering patients would re-cover faster if they were surrounded by cheerful colors and a touch of class.'

The special care unit was located in the relatively quiet rear of the building, but this room looked right out onto busy First Avenue. Now, Karen was treated to the drone of traffic, night and day, and the indiscriminate intrusions of squealing brakes and honking horns and angry voices.

Sometimes in the late hours of the night, as she waited for sleep, she would think about the people in those cars and buses and taxis and trucks and wonder where their lives were taking them. It was her first reconnection with the outside world.

The day Karen was able to take her first real food – a chocolate milk shake, from a flexible straw inserted in the corner of her mouth – everyone celebrated. It tasted delicious and she drank almost all of it. She had lost fifteen pounds since entering the hospital, and the doctors were anxious to get some of that weight back on her slender frame.

Now that she was no longer attached to all the tubes and wires, the staff began to fuss over her, bringing nourishing drinks at all hours, sponge-bathing her sometimes twice a day, combing her hair before her parents arrived, giving her muscle-stimulating massages. Karen could see how proud they were of their handiwork, having put the bits and pieces of her back together again. But she was so totally unfamiliar to herself that it was as though they had worked without a pattern and gotten it all wrong. She wished they would stop fussing and go away.

Her parents came to see her almost every day, her father unutterably sad, her mother artificially cheerful. They encouraged her to finish all her liquids and to exercise her arms and legs as though they actually believed that was all that was necessary to make her whole again. Occasionally her younger sister Laura came with them and tried her best not to stare.

And, of course, there was Peter, who sat beside her for hours on end, holding her hand and telling her funny little stories and smiling at her with his warm brown eyes, until the winter recess was over and he had to return to Cornell.

'I'll call you,' he said. 'You get someone to hold the phone for you and then tell me that you're hearing what I'm saying. Of course, you'd better not let anyone else hear what I say,' he added with an impish grin. 'That might be very embarrassing.'

Karen wondered what could possibly be embarrassing to a staff of professionals who had seen and heard every single thing there was to see and hear about her since the moment she had been brought in out of the Central Park bushes.

On her thirty-fourth day in the hospital, she said her first word.

It was early afternoon and her mother sat in one of the striped chairs beside the bed, knitting. She was wearing a black suit over her matronly figure, and had on too much rouge.

'To cover my hospital pallor,' she said with a chuckle.

Her hair was swept stylishly up on top of her head and her eyelashes were coated with an extra layer of black mascara. It occurred to Karen that her mother had been wearing a lot of black lately and it was not a particularly becoming color.

On the day Karen was moved to the private room, flowers had begun to arrive. They came from friends and relatives all over the country, from neighbors, and even from her father's patients, until the combined fragrances of roses, chrysanthemums, tulips, gladiolas and delphinium almost succeeded in disguising the acrid smell of disinfectant. As soon as one bouquet began to wilt, another appeared to take its place. When there was no space left, Beverly would pluck the sender's card from the arrangement and direct an aide to take it down to the charity wards.

In addition to the flowers, dozens of cards came in the mail. Beverly would perch her eyeglasses on the end of her nose and read some of the clever ones aloud. Later, she would reply to all of them, thanking each one, in Karen's name, for the good wishes. She had also sent a heartfelt note of thanks to Margaret Westfield.

On this day, Beverly had just finished with the mail when Julie van der Meer brought in a huge vase of roses.

'I believe this is the third bouquet from Jill and Andy,' Beverly said after a quick glance at the card. 'I beg your pardon,' she amended, scanning the whole message. 'This one is from Jill and Andy – and *Rebecca Karen*, born January twenty-third, seven pounds, two ounces, twenty-one inches, ten fingers, ten toes, all perfect.' Beverly put the card on top of the pile and resumed her knitting. 'A girl. How nice. How sweet to name her after you.'

Jill wanted to come to the hospital to see Karen, but Beverly put her off, as she put off everyone else except Peter, and that was only out of necessity. She explained that just the immediate family was allowed to visit, which was true – Beverly had issued those instructions herself. So the cards and flowers had come instead.

'Shall I take these down to the ward?' Julie asked, the roses still in her hands.

'No, not these, dear,' Beverly replied. 'I think we'll find a place for them here.'

Beverly knit two and purled one. Julie looked for a place to set the vase. Karen looked from one to the other.

'Ba-by,' she said.

It was a half whisper, half groan, hoarse and wheezy, but it was most definitely a word, not a gurgle.

Beverly dropped a whole row of stitches. 'Did you hear that?' she asked, turning to Julie. 'She spoke. I think she said *baby*. Did you hear?'

'I heard,' Julie replied with a broad grin and hurried off to spread the news.

Beverly jumped out of her chair and leaned over the bed. 'That's right, darling,' she encouraged, speaking slowly and distinctly as though her daughter might be hard of hearing or mentally retarded. 'Ba-by. Jill's had her ba-by. Can you say it a-gain?'

'No,' Karen wheezed with an inward smile, wondering whether her mother actually thought she had lost her mind along with her voice.

But Beverly missed the sarcasm. She was much too busy laughing and crying and jumping up and down all at the same time. Her little girl had spoken. In all the weeks of having to sit by and watch the mending process inch its way along, this was what she had been waiting for, praying for – proof that the damage to Karen's body had not affected her brain. Broken bones could be explained, but what could be said about a broken mind?

She had spent countless sleepless nights listening to Leo's staccato snoring and contemplating the possibility of her daughter's emerging from this disaster little more than a vegetable, unable to think or do for herself. Injury aside, minds had been known to crack under a lot less stress than Karen had endured.

It didn't matter that both Dr. Waschkowski and the neurologist had told her, over and over again, that there were no indications of any brain damage. What did doctors know anyway? As long as there was even the slightest chance that they could be wrong, Beverly would wait, hoping for the best, but preparing for the worst.

There would be no question of keeping Karen at home, if it came to that, she was quick to realize. The town gossips would have a never-ending field day with it, and there was Leo's dental practice to consider, not to mention Laura. And now, with one little word, Karen had erased all her mother's fears.

'Sweetheart, it's so good to hear your voice again,' she cried, the tears of joy running down her over-rouged cheeks, tracking her mascara with them. 'I was beginning to think I never would.'

'No-such-luck,' Karen rasped.

'Now, don't overdo it,' Beverly instructed. 'We can't have you wearing out your vocal cords the very first time.'

'I-want-to-tell-you …' Karen croaked, letting the sentence dangle.

'I know, dear, but not now,' her mother said hastily.

The last thing Beverly wanted to hear from her sweet, innocent daughter, she realized, were the gory details of what a madman had done to her. It would be so much easier to believe there really had been an accident.

'You need your rest,' she said. 'We've waited this long, we can wait a little longer. Right now, I'm going to go call your father and tell him the wonderful news.' She gathered up her knitting and prepared to flee. 'When you're a little stronger, the three of us will sit down and have a nice chat.'

A nice chat, Karen thought. How like her mother to put a Hans Christian Andersen face on an Edgar Allan Poe tale. She didn't know anyone who could do it better.

'What do you say, darling? Isn't that the best plan?'

It was difficult enough to challenge Beverly when Karen was well. Now it was impossible. She blinked once, out of habit.

SIX

The word spread like a brushfire, whipping down the hospital corridors.

'She spoke,' one joyfully told another.

'That's wonderful,' came the response.

Doctors, nurses, technicians and aides whom Karen hardly knew were suddenly stopping by to exchange greetings. People she didn't know at all were pausing at her door to give her a friendly smile and a thumbs-up sign. Everyone, it seemed, wanted to be a part of her success.

'I understand you had something to say today,' Dr. Waschkowski said that evening, a big grin covering his dear homely face.

Karen looked up, her throat sore from responding to the steady stream of well-wishers.

'Too-much,' she wheezed.

'I guess what they say is true – you can't keep a woman quiet for long.'

'Fuh-ny,' Karen said.

'Here,' he said, bending over her. 'Let me teach you how to talk through that tube in your throat.' When he had shown her how to place her fingers over the little air hole, he sat down in one of the striped chairs. 'So,' he asked, 'what do you have to say to me, after all this time?'

There had been a measure of protection in her silence, an excuse for not having to participate, not having to communicate. Karen had gotten used to the idea of listening and observing, used to hiding behind the simplicity of one blink or two. She thought about all the questions everyone would now want to ask and the explanations she would be expected to give.

'I want to go back to blinking,' she said.

Sergeant Tug McCluskey arrived the next day accompanied by a thin man with a pinched face, horn-rimmed glasses and a dark-blue suit.

'I don't expect you'd have any way of remembering me,' Tug said kindly, 'but I was there. I mean, I was one of the ones who ... who found you.'

Karen nodded as best she could. The burly policeman had small blue eyes, a prominent nose, and a weathered face, and the jacket of his uniform pulled a little too tightly across his girth.

The other man cleared his throat. 'I'm Michael Haller,' he said. 'Investigator for the district attorney's office.'

Karen shifted her attention. Almost skeletally thin, the investigator's dark suit hung poorly on him, reminding her of a hastily assembled scarecrow. His starched white collar was at least two sizes too big and he had the smallest hands Karen had ever seen on a man. His thick horn-rimmed glasses kept sliding down his nose, and every few seconds he would reach up with his right pinky finger and push them back.

'Now that you're able to talk,' he was saying in a brisk impersonal voice, 'I'd like you to tell us what happened.'

Karen looked at him in dismay. She had spent a lot of time thinking about what she would say to her family and her friends, framing the words carefully, but she never realized she would have to talk to the police.

'Is this really necessary?' she replied, pressing her fingers over the tracheotomy tube as Waschkowski had taught her to do.

'I'm afraid so,' Haller replied, fishing a pad and pen from his jacket pocket. 'You see, the way it works is, Sergeant McCluskey here files a report, and then my office investigates.'

'I see,' Karen conceded. 'What is it you need to know?'

'Do you remember the events of the night in question?'

'Yes,' she replied, thinking how pompous he sounded.

'Why don't you tell us about it?'

She looked from one to the other, wondering whether she could suddenly develop amnesia, but she didn't suppose they would go away until they'd gotten what they'd come for, so she took a deep breath.

'His name was Bob.'

'He told you his name?'

'Yes. At the party.'

The two men exchanged glances.

'Maybe you should start at the beginning,' the policeman suggested.

Karen shut her eyes as images she didn't want to see flooded her mind, images she didn't want to share with these strangers. It took almost an hour for the whole story to come out, in bits and pieces and tears. By the time Haller ran out of questions, Karen's mind was numb, her throat ached, her sheets were damp with perspiration, and her pillow was soaked with tears.

'Why did he do such an awful thing?' she rasped. 'Why?'

Tug sighed. 'There doesn't always have to be a reason,' he admitted. 'There are a lot of psychos wandering around.'

'He didn't seem like a psycho.'

'Some of them don't, until something sets them off.'

'I can't promise that we'll get this guy,' Haller said, returning his pad and pen to his pocket. 'These kinds of cases are difficult at best, and we don't have very much to work with.'

'But don't you worry about that right now,' Tug told her. 'You just concentrate on getting well, and leave the rest to us.'

The scarecrow was already halfway out the door.

Karen blinked, but the significance was lost on the two officers. She watched silently as they left. Maybe it was the way they probed for every tiny detail, almost like voyeurs, going over and over the same ground, but it was as though they had raped her all over again – coldly and callously violating the fragile sense of self she needed so desperately to protect.

She took a small measure of comfort in knowing

that, after this, telling her parents and her friends and Peter would be easy.

'Don't you think you were a little hard on her?' Tug asked as he walked with Haller down the front steps of the hospital.

'It's how you get at the truth,' the investigator said with a shrug.

'So, what do you think?'

The investigator shook his head in disgust and sighed. 'It'll never get to court,' he said.

'You don't think you can find him?'

'Oh, I'll probably find him, if I look hard enough, if his name really is Bob, if he really does go to Harvard. But what's the point?'

'Jesus, Haller,' Tug protested. 'He shouldn't get away with what he did to that girl.'

'Come on, Sergeant, don't go getting soft this late in the game. She knew him, for God's sake. They were partying, they were drinking. She went for a walk with him. At two o'clock in the morning. For all I know, she could have been a willing partner and things just got a little out of hand.'

'You didn't see her the way I did, dumped under those bushes,' the veteran policeman replied. 'I don't think you can call that a little out of hand.'

'So maybe she teased him, led him on a bit and then, when it was too late, changed her mind and went virginal on him, and he lost his temper. That kind of thing happens all the time, you know. Women say no when they mean yes, and yes when they mean no, and who knows what they really want?'

'I don't think so.' Tug shook his head. 'I think it happened exactly the way she said it did.'

'You may be right, Sergeant,' Haller said with another shrug, 'and I'll follow through on the investigation because that's what I get paid to do, and because maybe I feel a little sorry for her, too, all beat up like that. But take my word for it, the DA won't prosecute. You know as well as I do these cases are tough enough to prove even when there are half a dozen eyewitnesses, a ton of physical evidence, and we're dealing with a known offender. But a guy from Harvard Law School? Jesus, he could represent himself and still make mincemeat out of that girl.'

'He shouldn't walk,' Tug insisted.

'Maybe not,' Haller agreed, pushing his glasses up his nose and reaching for his car keys. 'But in the end, it'll be her word against his.'

'If it was one of my granddaughters lying there, looking like that, I'd rip the balls off the bastard.'

Haller sighed again. 'If she were my granddaughter,' he said, 'I'd tell her to go home and forget it – and be more careful the next time.'

seven

By Saturday afternoon, Karen had forgiven the policemen. She reasoned they probably didn't realize they were being offensive. More likely, it was their way of being polite, deliberately trying not to show any emotion as she plodded through her grim recitation.

Still, there was the feeling that they hadn't believed her that kept nagging at her, that they thought her in some way responsible for what Bob had done. But of course that was absurd – she had tried everything she could to stop him. Karen decided that it was only because the policemen were strangers and knew nothing about her values or her upbringing that they had cross-examined her in such a harsh way.

She sipped the last of her afternoon shake as she waited for her parents to arrive, knowing that, even though she would have to tell her grim story again, this time she would be talking to the people who knew her best and loved her and would, above all, understand.

'Hi, sweetheart,' Beverly cooed shortly before four o'clock.

The black was gone. Her mother was wearing a bright-red suit with a cropped jacket and a flattering A-line skirt that Karen had never seen before, and she had been to the beauty parlor. Her hair was perfectly coiffed and her nails gleamed with red polish.

'How's my girl?' Leo asked, looking rather drab beside his flamboyant wife as he took the seat farthest from his daughter.

'Better,' Karen told him. It wouldn't matter if it were true or not; she knew it was what he needed to hear.

'That's good.' He nodded, satisfied.

Leo Kern was the kind of man who found it easier not to see ugliness in the world around him. He spent his days in a sterile stainless-steel cocoon, where defects could be fixed, as if by magic, decay could be drilled out of existence, and discoloration could be polished to gleaming purity. He left his wife to deal with the harsh realities of raising a family, and Karen sometimes felt he was more involved with the lives of his patients than with the lives of his daughters.

'What is that you're doing with your fingers?' her mother asked.

'Closing the hole,' Karen told her. 'So I can talk.'

'And is that what you've been doing since Thursday – talking up a storm?'

'I guess,' Karen answered. 'The police came to see me.'

'The police?' Beverly echoed sharply. 'What for?'

'They're investigating what happened.'

Her parents exchanged a glance that was too quick for Karen to catch.

'What did you tell them?' Beverly asked.

'I told them everything I could remember.'

Beverly settled herself in her chair. 'Well then, I guess maybe you'd better tell us, too.'

Karen took a moment to search for the right words, the right phrases that would convey the facts of that night to her parents without the horror. The last thing she wanted was to upset them unnecessarily.

'You went to Jill's party,' Beverly prompted.

'Yes,' Karen said. 'I went to Jill's party. And right after I got there, I met a friend of a friend of Andy's former roommate, named Bob, from Harvard Law School. I don't know what his last name is – he never told me, but he seemed very nice and he was attentive, and we sort of spent the evening together.'

'Well, that doesn't sound so bad,' Beverly commented.

'That part wasn't,' Karen agreed with an uncustomary hint of bitterness in her voice. 'When the party was over, Bob offered to help me get a cab to Aunt Edna's. It was pretty late, after two o'clock, and I thought that would be all right. We waited and waited but we couldn't find a cab, so then he suggested that we walk across the park.'

'A nice young man from Harvard Law School offered to escort you across Central Park at two o'clock in the morning?' Beverly summarized.

'That's right.'

'Well, I guess that explains how you got there, although God knows why you would go into such a dangerous place in the middle of the night, even if you were with a friend of a friend of Andy's former roommate.'

'It was cold,' Karen told her. 'Walking seemed like a better idea than standing around.'

'So, you were in the park. Then what happened?'

Karen took a deep breath. 'He attacked me.'

'Who attacked you?' Beverly asked, looking blank.

'Bob did. He made a pass. I tried to stop him, but he wouldn't let me go.'

Beverly stared at her daughter with a combination of dismay and disbelief. 'You were, you were … damaged' – she couldn't even bring herself to say the right word – 'by a Harvard Law student?'

'Yes.'

'It was someone you knew?'

'Yes.'

'Why?' Beverly cried.

'Why what?'

'Why would the young man behave like that? What did you do?'

'What do you mean, what did I do?' Karen replied. 'I didn't do anything.'

'Well, there must be something you're not telling us,' Beverly said flatly. 'Nice young men from Harvard don't go around taking advantage of innocent girls for no reason.'

'Well, this one did,' Karen retorted.

'Oh my God,' her mother muttered, springing up, almost knocking over her chair.

'What's the matter?' Karen asked.

Beverly looked to Leo for support, but Leo was looking at the crease in his trousers with a very pained expression on his face.

'I thought we were talking about some maniac. I thought some very sick stranger grabbed you off the street, and you couldn't defend yourself.'

'I couldn't defend myself,' Karen insisted. 'He was too strong.'

'I just don't understand you at all,' Beverly snapped. 'You keep telling us you're madly in love with Peter Bauer. So why on earth would you take up with someone else like that?'

'I didn't take up with him,' Karen protested, tears filling her eyes, forgetting for the moment that Peter Bauer had never fit into her mother's narrow category of acceptable suitors. 'He said he was taking me to Aunt Edna's. That's all. I believed him.'

'And you're sure you didn't lead him on in some way, or give him any reason to expect that you might be receptive to his advances?'

'No.'

'You didn't lean up against him, say, in a manner that he might have misconstrued?'

Karen remembered Bob pulling her inside his coat when she complained of the cold, but that had been his idea, not hers.

'It wasn't like that,' she cried, the tears now flowing freely down her cheeks. 'I didn't do anything wrong.'

'Oh, darling,' Beverly said hastily, grabbing a tissue and dabbing at her daughter's eyes. 'Now don't get yourself into a tizzy. Nobody said you meant to do anything wrong. It's just that sometimes we don't realize how our actions might appear to another person. The way we smile, perhaps, or the way we stand or the way we say things. It's so easy to be misinterpreted.'

'I was just having a good time,' Karen sobbed.

'Of course you were.' Her mother relented. 'Just like anyone else at a party would. You had no way of knowing that this Bob person would take it so seriously.'

'No,' Karen mumbled. This wasn't going at all the way she had thought it would. First the police, and now her parents. She was suddenly very confused.

'I don't mean to distress you,' her mother added, 'but your father and I just can't understand how you could have gotten yourself into such a situation, how you could have been so, so … careless.'

Leo had yet to say a word.

'Neither do I,' Karen sobbed, letting go of the tube to cover her face with her hands.

After a moment, Beverly sat back down in her chair, crossed her legs at the ankles and clasped her hands together in her lap.

'Yes, well, I think we have a pretty clear idea of what took place and we're not going to dwell on it any longer,' she said firmly. 'You'll soon be well again, and I think it's time that we consider this … unfortunate incident over and done, and get on with the rest of our lives.'

Over and done, Karen thought wistfully. Could it really be over and done with a snap of her mother's fingers?

'Do you think so?' she asked.

'Yes, I do,' her mother affirmed. 'I can tell how terribly upset talking about the whole thing is making you, and I don't see any reason to put you through the painful ordeal of repeating this story again. After all, it's none of anyone's business.'

'The police know,' Karen reminded her. 'I told them everything. They're going to find Bob and arrest him and make him pay for what he did.'

'Your father will take care of that,' Beverly said

smoothly. 'The last thing we're going to do is let anyone drag you into some sordid courtroom and smear your name all over the newspapers.'

'But I'll have to testify,' said Karen. 'I want to. I want to see him convicted and put in jail.'

'You'll do nothing of the kind,' her mother declared. 'You're not going to have anything more to do with this whole unpleasant mess. From now on, we'll simply tell anyone who asks that you were taken to the hospital because ... because of an accident.'

'An accident?'

'Yes.' Beverly declared. She studied a speck of lint on her red jacket. 'Actually, that's pretty much what we've been telling people anyway.'

Karen looked from her mother to her father and back to her mother again. 'You told people I had an accident?'

'We weren't very specific about anything, of course. After all, we didn't really know anything. We just sort of intimated that it was an accident. There wasn't any reason to go into the gruesome details.'

'What kind of accident did I have?'

Beverly hesitated a moment. 'I think we'll make it an automobile accident,' she decided. 'That's the most logical choice, isn't it? I mean, considering how damaged you were, we can't very well say you fell out of a tree, now can we?'

Karen's head suddenly began to hurt. 'But that's a lie,' she said.

'Well, if it is, it's only to save you, save us, from a lot of humiliating gossip.' Beverly's full lower lip began to quiver. 'Isn't it enough that we have to know what went on, does the rest of Great Neck have to know, too? We're respected members of the community. There's never been a hint of scandal in our family. Think what it would do to your father's practice if this ever came out.'

'Now, Mother.' Leo spoke up for the first time.

'And think of your sister,' Beverly went on, as thought he hadn't. 'If you go around broadcasting all the ugly facts, people might start asking what you had in mind when you went strolling in Central Park in the middle of the night with a young man you hardly knew.'

'But the people here know there wasn't any automobile accident,' Karen argued, wondering dimly what this had to do with sixteen-year-old Laura.

'Maybe they do and maybe they don't,' Beverly declared. 'Besides, hospital records can be sealed or something, and then we can do whatever's necessary to prevent anyone else from finding out.'

'What about Peter?'

'The time for worrying about Peter was before you went walking in Central Park, I should think,' her mother replied tartly. 'But of course we'll have to tell him the same thing as everyone else.'

'I can't lie to him,' Karen objected.

'Of course you can,' Beverly snapped. 'What chance do you think you'll have to make a decent marriage, to him or to anyone else, if you repeat this dreadful story? Do you really want to ruin the rest of your life? Because that's exactly what will happen if you ever tell anybody what you told us.'

Karen's head was throbbing and she began to pray for the oblivion that had always come to ease her pain to come now and swallow her up forever.

'It's not fair,' she said.

'Fair?' her mother pounced. 'You think it would be

fair to stand up and tell the whole world what you did?'

'What *I* did?' Karen echoed. 'You mean, what *he* did, don't you?'

'Whatever,' Beverly replied, picking the piece of lint off her jacket.

'You're my parents,' Karen whispered. 'You're supposed to love me. I thought you'd be on *my* side.'

'Of course we love you,' said Beverly. 'Of course we're on your side. That's why we're willing to go to such lengths to protect you.'

'No,' Karen accused. 'You think this was all my fault. You don't think he ought to be punished – you think I should. You think I flirted with him and teased him and then enticed him into the park. You think I asked him to do this to me, don't you?'

'I don't think anything of the kind,' Beverly retorted. 'I think there was probably a terrible misunderstanding somewhere along the way and he took advantage of you. Maybe he should be punished for that, but not at the expense of this family's reputation.'

Suddenly Karen couldn't seem to catch her breath. Her right leg was in spasm, her face turned beet-red, her whole body began to heave, and she was clawing at the wires that fastened her jaw.

'Oh my God, what's wrong?' Beverly shrieked.

Leo sprang up and grabbed for his daughter's hand before she could do any serious damage to herself. 'Get a nurse in here,' he told his wife.

Beverly rushed for the door. 'She can't breathe,' she shouted into the corridor. 'Do something.'

Rose Thackery came running. After one look she turned on her heel, returning seconds later with a hypodermic. She hurried to the bed, almost knocking Leo aside.

'Karen,' she said firmly, 'calm down now. You're having a little anxiety attack, that's all. It's nothing to worry about.'

She stuck the needle deep into Karen's hip. Then she took hold of her patient's hand. 'Listen to me,' she said soothingly. 'You're all right. You're safe. Nothing bad is going to happen to you.'

Karen stared at the kind face through the flood of gasps and tears – a face that had always meant comfort and acceptance and good humor, and heard the soft words that had never been anything but supportive.

The panic began to subside.

'Just take a nice deep breath,' the nurse encouraged. 'Come on, just one.'

Slowly, Karen began to draw air into her lungs, and when she could hold no more, she let it all out.

'Now another.'

Karen obeyed. By the third breath, the spasm in her leg had eased and her face was returning to its natural color.

'She's all right now,' Rose Thackery assured the Kerns. 'Do you know what caused this? Did one of you say something to upset her?'

'Certainly not,' Beverly retorted. 'Why on earth would either of us say anything to upset her?'

eight

It was dark outside the window. The draperies had not been drawn and night shadows moved in all directions. A cloud scudded across the moon, a newspaper was swept up in a sudden gust, a taxi slid along a slippery street.

The weary swing shift had departed, the grumpy graveyard shift had arrived. Most of the patients on the third floor of Manhattan Hospital had been asleep for hours.

Karen lay in her bed, wide awake despite her evening sedative, her head pounding even after two doses of aspirin. Try as she would, she couldn't get her mother's words out of her mind. The thing she had feared the most had happened. She had disgraced herself and her family. So much so that her mother was willing to tell a terrible lie rather than have anyone know the truth.

But what *was* the truth? That was the question Karen

struggled to answer in the dark hours before dawn. Had she in some way prompted her own misfortune, as the police had more or less intimated, and her mother seemed so ready to believe?

For the thousandth time, she began to replay that long, harrowing night in her mind, from the moment she spilled mayonnaise down the front of her dress to the instant Bob's fist smashed into her jaw and the world had gone black. She went over every action, every gesture, every smile, every giggle, every word she could remember, but it had all been harmless party flirting to her.

Was it possible that Bob had seen an invitation in her behavior she hadn't meant to be there? Read some signal she hadn't realized she had given? Yes, she had been flattered by his attentions, but had that made her appear easy? Did casual flirting mean she had agreed to have sex? Had she really brought all this on herself?

Two men she didn't know and two people she had known her whole life apparently thought so. Karen groaned aloud in the darkness and wished she could ask for more aspirin. But it was barely half an hour since she had had the last ones.

If only she hadn't thought Bob so attractive. If only she hadn't enjoyed the envious looks of the other girls at Jill's party. If only she had insisted that they wait for the doorman to hail a cab. If only she hadn't worn her favorite black dress. If only she had stayed at home in the first place. Her head throbbed with all the if-onlys that might have kept her from ending up, with her clothes and her life in tatters, under a clump of bushes in Central Park.

Was it only two months ago that Karen had believed there was nothing worse than getting pregnant and having to marry a man you didn't love? It seemed a lifetime ago. How could she have been so naive? Why, compared to the Kerns, Jill's family would be considered fortunate. Next to Karen, Jill had everything.

A small light began to flicker in the darkness of her soul because there was one thing Jill didn't have, and that made all the difference – she didn't have Peter Bauer.

Strong, devoted Peter, who called on the telephone twice a week and sent funny little cards and big bouquets of her favorite yellow roses. No matter how bad things got, Karen could still take courage from the knowledge that Peter was there for her, and that alone was enough to ease the pounding in her head and let the gray curtain of sleep steal over her.

Michael Haller came back two weeks later, wearing the same baggy suit. Tug McCluskey was not with him.

'I found Bob,' he said without social preamble. It was on the tip of his tongue to fill in the last name for her, but he decided there was really no point unless, of course, she asked. 'He was exactly where you said he would be.'

'Did you arrest him?'

'We couldn't really do that.'

'Why not?'

Haller pushed his eyeglasses back up his nose. 'Because we have no proof that he committed any crime.'

'Look at me,' Karen cried. 'You can see for yourself what he did. Isn't that proof enough?'

'Yes, well, the thing is,' Haller replied, studying his scuffed shoes, 'the young man doesn't exactly corroborate your story. Actually, he says it was your idea to walk across the park and that it was *you* who came on to *him.*'

The fact that this Bob had been so easy to find, in plain sight at Harvard Law School, had more or less clinched things in Haller's mind. A man bent on rape didn't normally go around telling his victim where to find him.

Karen stared at the investigator. Part of her was outraged, but part of her, she realized, had almost expected it. The conspiracy, as she now thought of it, was complete.

'He said I asked for it? He said I wanted him to do this to me?'

'He said he didn't do anything – other than accommodate you, that is,' Haller told her. 'He said he simply had sex with you and afterward, when he wanted to leave, you refused to go with him.'

'Did you believe him?' she asked dully.

'He seemed sincere.'

'Did you believe him?'

'It doesn't matter what I believe,' Haller declared in his own defense. 'It's what a jury would believe, if this were to go to trial. We have no real evidence here, no eyewitness, just your word against his and, from everything my investigation has turned up so far, he's a straight-A student from a prominent San Francisco family who's never been in any trouble.'

'Neither have I,' Karen reminded him.

Haller shifted uneasily. 'I know that,' he replied. 'But in cases like these, the burden of proof is on the state. And the reality is that juries just don't convict fine upstanding young men from prominent families of rape without a great deal more evidence than we have here.'

'You mean they'd say I made it all up? That *I* seduced *him* and then went off into Central Park by myself, looking for more, and lured some stranger into the bushes, and begged him to rape me and beat me half to death, and then tried to blame some nice innocent guy who didn't do anything but try to take me home?'

'It could go down like that,' Haller said.

'Even if that's not what happened?'

'Look, if it were up to me, I'd lock the bastard up and throw away the key,' he told her, because he didn't need her anger and he had a perfect out. 'But it's up to the DA, and the DA doesn't go to trial unless he thinks he can win. He just doesn't think he can win this one.'

In fact, the wily politician had all but laughed Haller out of his office.

'You mean, winning is all that matters – not what's true or what's right?'

'Okay, I'll give you that.' The scarecrow sighed. 'But I never said anything about justice. I'm only saying it's the system.'

A justice system that didn't have anything to do with justice? Karen pondered his statement in genuine confusion. It had never occurred to her that truth could be meaningless if no one chose to believe it. Or that lies could be accepted because of expediency, because they were more comfortable to live with.

'Did my father come to see you?' she asked.

'Yes, he did,' Haller said. 'As a matter of fact, both your parents did.'

'Did they tell you that they wanted you to stop this investigation?'

'If they did,' Haller replied, 'it's because they don't

want you going through any more pain, and I happen to think they're right. You're a nice kid. You have no idea what a clever defense attorney would do to you in open court. Trust me, by the time he was finished, he'd have the jury believing you weren't much better than a two-dollar hooker off Eighth Avenue. If you want my advice, forget all about it. You won't get any satisfaction in a courtroom.'

'Thank you for coming,' Karen said.

If the police thought her a liar, if her parents thought her a tease, if a jury would think her a whore, what was the point of protesting any further?

'I'm sorry,' Michael Haller said, annoyed because his words sounded so hollow and inadequate.

'So am I,' she replied.

'No one deserves to be hurt as badly as you were hurt,' he added, to make up for some of it. 'I hope you get well soon.'

The conversation was over. He turned to leave, noting that she hadn't asked for Bob's last name. It was just as well.

Karen shut her eyes so that she wouldn't have to watch him go. Oddly enough, it seemed to be the broken bones and bloody bruises that disturbed people more than anything else. It was almost as though, if they could focus on them, they wouldn't have to deal with what had really happened to her.

nine

Karen was discharged from Manhattan Hospital on the eighth of May. Her jaw had healed, as had her arm. Two more sessions in surgery had reconstructed her smashed left kneecap. Physical therapy two times a day was helping her to regain muscle tone and she had learned how to walk again with the aid of crutches.

The hole in her throat, where the tracheotomy tube had been, was now a small red bump. The hole in her side, where the chest tube had been, was now a little wrinkle of skin between two ribs that she could reach around and feel with her fingers.

Driving home in her father's roomy Buick was almost like seeing the world for the first time. Winter had come and gone during her months in the hospital and spring had burst across Long Island. Karen drank it in.

The mighty maple trees and graceful elms that she

last remembered being naked and gnarled were now dressed in bright new greenery. Tired lawns had been transformed into lush carpets, and everywhere, it seemed, azaleas and rhododendron were in bloom. Little gray sparrows and red-breasted robins hopped from branch to branch, singing of sunshine.

When Leo turned onto Knightsbridge Road, Karen craned her neck for a first glimpse of the circular driveway that fronted the stately brick colonial where she had lived her entire life.

'The cherry blossoms waited for you,' her mother said, as the Buick slid beneath a row of delicate pink petals that were usually gone with April.

Karen sighed happily. It looked exactly as she had hoped it would: the burgeoning trees, the curving beds of begonias and impatiens and peonies that her mother so carefully cultivated, the thick blanket of grass, the neat hedges that separated them from their neighbors. It was good to know that some things never changed.

From the outside, the house looked just the same as it always had. Although Karen had gotten used to the quiet hustle of the hospital's third floor, the constant stream of white uniforms that passed by her door, the ministering routine that never varied, and her wonderful mechanical bed with its infinite positions, it hadn't been home.

Home was like a pair of old slippers that you could snuggle into and be totally comfortable, and it didn't matter how you looked or what you said or even what you did, because you were loved and accepted. But coming home this time was different, because she was different, and the spacious colonial on Knightsbridge Road felt both familiar and strange as she crept back to it and pulled the walls in around her.

At first she hobbled from room to room, learning to negotiate on her crutches, needing to reacquaint herself with everything that had always signified stability and security – the polished mahogany banister she had slid down as a child, the Persian rugs and Duncan Phyfe furniture that seemed lost in the huge living room, the flowered wallpapers and heavy brocade draperies, the Meissen lamps, the Dresden porcelain, the Revere silver, her father's books overflowing the shelves in the library, her sister's Elvis Presley albums and, last but not least, her own room that hadn't been changed since high school, with the moiré curtains, the profusion of yellow ribbons and rosebuds that climbed up and down the walls, the white oak furniture, the cluttered desk, and the cork bulletin board that told the story of her girlhood.

The first night, once she got Beverly to stop fussing over her, Karen locked her door and wept, wishing she had never left her room, never grown up. Long after she felt the rest of the house go to sleep, she snapped on her bedside lamp and rummaged in the nightstand drawer for her box.

It was a wooden keepsake box of her grandmother's, old and scarred, but the intricate inlay was still visible. In it, Karen kept scraps of paper on which she wrote down whatever came into her head. She called them her thought pages.

She pulled out a clean sheet and began to write:

> They say a dog found me,
> torn and bleeding,
> more dead than alive,
> left there like discarded garbage.
> Perhaps I am.

They threw words around me,
like exposure,
massive trauma,
pneumonia.
But I wasn't there to hear them.

They say surgery lasted
six hours.
They removed
more than they left.
But I was already empty inside.

It was days before I opened my eyes.
Weeks before I spoke.
What could I say
after all their fine work –
they should have let me die … ?

Karen put the page into the box and put the box back in her drawer. Then she turned her head into the pillow and cried herself to sleep, her lamp still lit.

She spent many hours in her mother's treasured garden, sitting quietly in a lounge chair with her leg propped on a pillow, alternately reading, sipping iced tea, and staring into space, smelling the gentle fragrances of spring warming into summer. Before long, the hospital pallor began to fade and her cheeks grew pink in the sunshine.

Now that Karen was eating real food again, her mother had instructed Winola, the maid who had been with the family for as long as any of them could remember, to follow the girl around with tempting plates of goodies.

'If you keep this up, I'm going to be as fat as a pig,'

Karen complained, but not too loudly.

She had nothing to think about but getting well as she waited for Peter to come and rescue her – like the princess in the tower that her mother had read to her about as a child.

Twice each week, Beverly drove Karen back to Manhattan Hospital to continue her physical therapy. It would have been much easier to go to the local hospital for treatment but Beverly had waved the idea aside.

'I think it's best that we stay with the people we started with,' she said. 'They're most familiar with Karen's case and I don't mind the drive.'

Actually, Beverly hated driving into the city, fighting traffic in every direction. But this way, she reasoned, none of the personnel at the local hospital, including their long-time family physician, would need to know the truth.

Aside from those Tuesday and Thursday afternoons, Karen stayed at home, making one excuse after another not to leave the house.

'Come to town with me,' Beverly would suggest. 'We'll do a little shopping. It'll do you good to get out.'

'My knee hurts,' Karen would reply, even though her physical therapist repeatedly told her to use the leg as much as possible. But she was sure that all anyone would have to do was look at her to know immediately what had happened to her, despite her mother's fiction, and she wasn't prepared to cope with that just yet.

She tried, on a number of occasions, to talk about Bob and that night, but she was always cut off.

'You had a terrible accident,' Beverly would say.

'And we're not going to dwell on it anymore.'

'But I really need to talk about it,' Karen would press, wanting only the chance to explain her side of things so that her parents could forgive her for being so careless.

'What you need is to put it all behind you and forget it ever happened,' Beverly would declare firmly. 'Believe me, I know what's best.'

'Yes, Mother.'

Just before she left the hospital, Dr. Waschkowski had suggested she talk to a psychiatrist.

'We here are dealing with your physical healing,' he said, giving her a slip of paper with a name and telephone number on it. 'But that's only part of the problem.'

The idea of being able to ask a doctor why things in the park had gone so wrong seemed rather tempting to Karen, but when she mentioned it to her mother, the woman exploded.

'Only crazy people need psychiatrists,' Beverly fumed. 'You may have been careless, but that doesn't mean you're crazy. My God, that's all we need, on top of everything else – a psychiatrist messing around in this.' And she tore the piece of paper to shreds.

Two weeks after Karen's return home, Jill and the baby came to see her.

'Don't worry about the details of the accident, in case she's rude enough to ask,' Beverly counseled in advance. 'It's very normal to be fuzzy after such an ordeal.'

'Yes, Mother.'

It was eerie the way the woman actually seemed able to blot out reality and convince herself that her daughter was indeed the victim of some reckless automobile driver. Part of Karen wished she could do that, too.

Motherhood had transformed Jill. In addition to a healthy, happy glow, her figure, which had always been a bit too thin, had filled out in all the right places.

'It took having a baby to get boobs,' she said, laughing.

But it was the little pink bundle in the crib that most fascinated Karen – a perfect miniature person, with innocent blue eyes, the softest skin, and a fuzzy halo of honey-blond hair.

'She's so tiny. I never expected her to be so tiny.'

Jill grimaced. 'You wouldn't think that if you'd had to deliver her.'

'Do you think I could hold her?'

'Sure.' Jill swung the four-month-old baby out of her carrier and into Karen's waiting arms without hesitation.

Rebecca turned trusting eyes on the stranger who now cuddled her, and smiled.

'I think she likes me,' Karen cried.

'She likes anyone who'll hold her.'

Karen ran her fingers along a round pink cheek. 'If she were mine, I'd hold her all the time.'

'Tell me that after you have one of your own,' Jill retorted. 'When the house has to be cleaned and the diapers have to be washed and dinner hasn't even been started and your back is killing you.'

Karen bit down on her lower lip. Before she left the hospital, right before he gave her the name of the psychiatrist, Dr. Waschkowski had told her there would be no children. Of all the bad moments she had endured up to then, that was the worst – to hear her dreams and her future shatter against his words and know that she would pay for her carelessness for the rest of her life.

It was almost agony to hold Rebecca, to feel the warm little bundle snuggle up against her so trustingly, to smell the sweet scent of baby powder, to hear the contented little gurgles, to feel the tiny hand close itself around her finger and know that she would never experience this joy with a baby of her own.

Karen heaved a sigh of infinite sadness, and, despite her best efforts, a hot tear slipped out of the corner of her eye, rolled down her face, and dripped onto the baby's pink-and-white romper suit.

'Well, I think that's enough spoiling for a while,' Jill said, missing the tear and interpreting the sigh as a sign of weariness. She plucked Rebecca out of Karen's arms and turned to settle her back into her crib. Karen started to protest, but Beverly chose that moment to announce lunch.

'All right now,' Jill said later, after they had eaten Winola's tomato soup and tuna-fish salad and the baby had been nursed and changed and put down for a nap, when the two of them were in the garden with a tray of iced tea and cookies between them, 'enough about me and the baby. I want to know about you.'

'What about me?' Karen countered.

'Oh, come on, I've been waiting for months to find out what happened,' Jill exclaimed. 'The last time I looked, you're leaving my apartment with the hunk of the evening, and the next thing I know, you're in the hospital.'

'What did my mother say?'

'Your mother told us you were hit by a car, of course. But how on earth did it happen?'

Karen began to fix pleats in her cotton skirt. In

fifteen years of friendship, she had never deliberately lied to Jill. They had shared each other's triumphs as well as tragedies, had been each other's counsel as well as critic, and had never broken a promise or betrayed a confidence. She felt certain she could trust Jill with the truth, despite her mother's warning, and she so desperately needed someone to talk to, so desperately needed someone to understand. She opened her mouth but, just as it was all about to come pouring out, Jill began to giggle.

'When we first heard, you know, about you being hurt,' her friend confided, 'before we knew what had really happened and all, you understand, Andy said that maybe the hunk of the evening had been too hot for you to handle.'

Karen's mouth snapped shut and she stared at her friend. 'What would have made him think that?' she made herself ask.

'Oh, you know Andy,' Jill shrugged. 'His mind is always up somebody's skirt.'

'What did you say when he said that?'

'I told him it was ridiculous, naturally,' Jill replied. 'Anyone who knows you, knows that your heart is pure and your body belongs to Peter.'

'Now that you mention it, I think the hunk *was* pretty strong,' Karen said cautiously, testing the waters. 'I suppose it's not implausible for someone to think that he might have … overpowered me.'

'Don't be ridiculous,' Jill retorted. 'With those looks, why on earth would he need to overpower anyone? He must have women falling all over him at every turn.'

'Do you really think so?'

'Sure,' her friend asserted. 'And I set Andy straight

about it, too. Anyway, we all know that I'm the weak-willed one. I was destined to jump the gun. But you – you're the original iron maiden. You'll never be seriously swayed by anything short of a ring on your finger. So, come on, let's have all the details.'

Weak-willed or iron-tough, Karen digested silently. Were those the only acceptable options? She wondered how Jill could so arbitrarily reject any other possibilities, completely forgetting that, less than six months ago, she herself would have rejected them, too. It was the police and her parents all over again.

'It was a drunk driver,' she recited woodenly. 'A drunk driver hit me with his car. He came out of nowhere.'

'How awful,' Jill exclaimed, having already heard this from Beverly. 'But where were you when it happened? I mean, what were you doing?'

Karen's heart began to pound in her chest and a line of perspiration popped out across her forehead. She couldn't remember what her mother had told her to say.

'I don't really know that much about it.' She shrugged. 'It's mostly just a blur.'

'Oh, come on, you must remember something,' Jill urged. 'Like what street were you on? I mean, let's start with the hunk. You left the apartment with him. Was he involved in the accident?'

'Yes,' Karen began. 'I mean, no,' she hastily corrected herself. 'I mean, yes, I left the apartment with him, but no, he wasn't hit by a car.'

'Wasn't he going to get you a cab?'

'Yes, he was, but he didn't. I mean, we waited but – that is, yes, he did.'

Jill smiled encouragingly. 'Which is it – yes or no?'

'Well, you see, it was very late, and I – ' Karen was now so flustered she made the only excuse she could think of, rubbing at her eyes with feigned weariness. 'I'm exhausted,' she mumbled. 'I'd really like to talk some more, but I think I have to lie down for a while.'

'Absolutely,' Jill agreed with alacrity, noting her friend's sudden pallor. 'Your mother made me promise not to wear you out.'

'It was great seeing you,' Karen added. 'And thanks for bringing Rebecca. She's just adorable.'

'Of course I'd have brought her anyway,' Jill declared as she gathered up the baby's things, 'but I didn't have much choice. She and I are joined at the hip until solid food.'

Beverly met them in the foyer. 'You're not leaving, are you?' she asked.

'I promised Andy I'd be home early,' Jill replied, maneuvering the crib over the threshold, 'and if I don't hit the road pretty soon, I'm bound to get stuck on the Long Island Expressway until all hours. Besides, I don't think Karen's really up to lengthy visiting yet.'

'Well, you must come back when she's stronger. It's very important for her to have her friends around.'

'I will,' Jill promised.

'What happened?' Beverly asked the moment the front door closed. 'Why did she go running off like that?'

'She wanted details,' Karen replied, turning away.

ten

Peter Bauer steered the Pontiac off the Long Island Expressway onto Lakeville Road, heading north toward Great Neck. His back was stiff and his eyes burned in their sockets. He had planned on doing the journey from Bangor in something under twelve hours, but the closer he got, the heavier the traffic grew, and the slower he was able to travel. He had been driving now for almost fourteen hours.

A week ago, Peter had left Cornell with his degree in electrical engineering. It was his family's proudest moment, the first Bauer to graduate from college. He went home to Maine with his mother and father, his four brothers and his two sisters, to bask briefly in the glory of his achievement, and to attend the lavish party his parents had insisted on giving in his honor.

His whole exciting future was before him, and, as he lay in his lower bunk that first night, listening to the sound of his brother's breathing, he knew that everything was going just as he had envisioned on other nights in this same bed. He had gotten his education, his father was about to take him into the family business – a small company that designed and manufactured electrical components – and he had found the girl of his dreams.

Although he and Karen had not discussed it lately, he was confident that, despite her accident, they would get engaged as planned, and then go on to marry. Maybe not as originally scheduled, but as soon as Karen had recuperated enough to finish her degree at Cornell. He knew she would insist on that. Then they would settle down in Bangor and live happily ever after.

Peter pushed his sunglasses up onto his head and rubbed at his tired eyes as he waited for a traffic light. In the five months since the accident, he and Karen had spoken regularly on the telephone, lopsided conversations – at least until she got the hang of that tube in her throat – but he hadn't seen her since January. He had wanted to drive down from Ithaca on several occasions, but Beverly kept putting him off, suggesting that Karen wasn't up to company and it would be better if he waited until she was stronger.

'Her visitors are restricted to the immediate family,' she told him. 'But I can of course keep you posted on her condition.'

Peter didn't exactly feel like company anymore, but then, he supposed, he wasn't family yet, either, and Beverly was as good as her word, calling him weekly with comprehensive progress reports, more often if there were some sort of breakthrough, as when Karen drank her first liquid, said her first word, took her first steps.

It was Beverly, not the doctors, who had told him about Karen's injuries, when he arrived at the Kerns's doorstep at the end of December.

'We won't know what really happened,' she said, 'until Karen herself can tell us. But it appears to have been some sort of accident.'

She told him as much as she knew about the physical damages, except for the hysterectomy, of course. It would have been much too awkward trying to explain exactly why that had been necessary, and she decided there really wasn't any point in telling him something before he needed to know it. Again, it was Beverly who informed him, the day after she and Leo had had to hear the appalling account, that Karen's injuries were the result of an automobile accident.

'She doesn't remember much about it,' Beverly said. 'Which is just as well, all things considered. From what we've been able to piece together, she was crossing the street when a car went out of control and hit her. As simple as that. A hit-and-run. We assume the driver was drunk.'

'Was she thrown by the force of the impact, or did the car actually run over her?' Peter asked.

There was an abrupt pause on the other end of the phone. In the dozen or so times that Beverly had told this story, no one had thought to ask that question, and she found herself unprepared to answer it.

'I don't know,' she said lamely.

'The doctors should be able to tell,' Peter persisted, 'from the nature of the injuries.'

'I never asked them,' came the stiff reply. 'I mean, after all, what difference does it make?' What was this upstart from Maine trying to do? she wondered. Could he tell from her voice that she had fabricated the whole tale? 'The important thing is that she's going to get better, and that's what we should concentrate on.'

At his end of the line, Peter wondered why she sounded so defensive.

'Are the police investigating?' he asked.

'What is there to investigate?' Beverly retorted. 'No witnesses have come forward, and Karen certainly didn't get much of a look at whoever hit her.'

'Sometimes, people don't come forward because they don't realize they saw anything,' Peter suggested. 'But they might, if the circumstances were publicized widely enough.'

That was all they needed, Beverly thought in annoyance. She wanted to slam the receiver down in his impudent ear, but she resisted the urge. Although he intended to be some kind of engineer – an occupation that ranked barely above a garage mechanic by her standards – it was quite possible that this was the best match her daughter would be able to make, under the circumstances, and it would be foolish of her to do or say anything to jeopardize that.

'I think we would all just as soon forget about the past and focus our energies on the future,' she oozed. 'I'm afraid you'll only succeed in upsetting Karen enormously if you insist on pursuing such really unimportant issues.'

As he turned left into the residential village of Russell Gardens, Peter realized that it still rankled him to think that the person who had injured Karen so seriously, and then simply abandoned her there in the street, should be allowed to get away with it.

It was close to eight o'clock when he pulled into the Kerns's circular drive on Knightsbridge Road, and the sun was preparing to set. It danced off the colonial's brick walls, which now seemed more pink than red, set the white trim to shimmering, and glinted off the windows, turning them into solid gold. So it was that he didn't see Karen standing in the upstairs hall window, looking down at him with a mixture of anticipation and apprehension in her eyes.

She had been standing there, waiting, for more than an hour. She had been preparing herself for his visit for more than a week, ever since he had called to say when he would arrive.

'I'll be there the day after the party,' he told her. 'I'll leave early and drive straight through.'

'We'll have dinner waiting,' she promised.

For over two years now, whenever Karen had contemplated her future, it was at Peter's side – as his wife, as his helpmate, as the mother of the children they both wanted to have.

She had stolen many hours from her studies to scribble 'Karen Bauer' in the margins of her notebooks, and fashion elegant monograms out of two *K*s and a *B*. Peter was her biggest supporter, her best friend, her hero – the only man in the world who could make her heart turn over just by smiling. He was so much a part of her life that had she tried to picture it without him she would have come up blank.

Yet, at this moment, as she looked down on his sandy hair and lanky frame, he seemed a stranger to her, standing on the far side of a canyon of catastrophe, without a bridge.

It had been easy to maintain the link from opposite ends of a long-distance telephone line. There was safety in that. He had called twice a week, always with a joke or a story to make her laugh. Between the calls were the cards and the flowers. But now he was here, and Karen was suddenly sweating and shivering at the same time, wondering what he would think when he saw her. Would he be repulsed by the ugly scars, frightened by her frailty, shocked by her crutches? Would his love turn out to be trivial? She shut her mind against the thought, because he was the reason she was struggling so hard to become whole again, when so much of her had been lost. Turning awkwardly from the window, she maneuvered her crutches down the hall in the direction of the stairway.

She looked like a cadaver, Peter thought, as he stood in the foyer with Beverly and watched Karen, closely followed by Winola, negotiate the broad curving steps with infinite care, planting one crude wooden support firmly into the thick carpet, while holding on to the banister with the other hand, hopping off her good right leg, and then swinging the bad left one down under her. She was barely more than skin and bones beneath her cotton dress, her skin had a strange translucent quality to it, and there was something about her eyes, an expression in the blue-gray depths that he couldn't define and didn't remember ever having seen before.

'It takes me forever to get anywhere, but I have to be careful not to fall on this knee,' she said as she finally reached bottom, took her other crutch from Winola, and started toward him across the polished hardwood floor.

A fleeting frown puckered his narrow face and was gone. The Karen he knew would have said something like: 'I didn't want to fall at your feet and risk you getting all swelled in the head.'

'I thought you handled that rather masterfully,' he said with a smile, stepping forward to take her in his arms for the first time in so many months.

Karen stiffened. She had prepared herself for this moment, had even looked forward to the comfort of having him hold her. But, when he drew close, all of a sudden, it wasn't Peter reaching out to grasp her but Bob, and with a little cry she jerked backward, almost losing her balance.

'I'm sorry,' he exclaimed. 'I didn't realize a little hug would hurt.'

'She's still pretty sore,' Beverly said to cover the awkwardness.

'Well, would a kiss on the cheek be okay?'

'Sure,' Karen replied. But she had to steel herself against a shudder when she felt his warm breath on her cheek and his lips graze the corner of her mouth. One of the crutches slipped out from under her.

'Are you all right?' he cried, steadying her.

'These things have a mind of their own,' she said with a brittle smile as she slipped out of his grasp and planted the perverse pole more firmly on the slick floor. 'I figure by the time I get the hang of them, I won't need them anymore.'

'And that won't be much longer now, will it?' Beverly chimed in. 'Since you're making such excellent progress.'

Peter glanced from mother to daughter. 'I'm glad to hear it,' he said.

'Don't you agree our precious girl looks a whole lot better than the last time you saw her?' the mother coaxed.

'She certainly does,' he replied politely, thinking he had never seen her look worse.

'Never mind about me,' Karen said brightly. 'Tell us about graduation, Peter. Was it everything you hoped it would be? And the drive down – was it terribly long? Are you famished? You must be absolutely exhausted. Do you want a nap first? Or would you rather have dinner?'

'Dinner would be fine,' Peter replied. He had stopped outside Portsmouth for a quick lunch, but that was more than eight hours ago, with only a candy bar in between, and his stomach had begun to rumble. He could rest later.

'Wonderful,' Beverly said quickly, thinking if they waited much longer the roast would be ruined. 'Why don't you go wash up and then we'll eat.'

'Do you want me to see you to your room?' Karen offered, although the thought of having to navigate the stairs again, under his watchful eye, made her wince.

Peter grinned. 'That's all right. I know the way.'

This was his third visit to the Kern home, and on each occasion Beverly had put him in the big corner guest room with the damask curtains and antique-rose wallpaper. Peter took his suitcase and climbed the stairs. He had identified the strange expression in Karen's eyes. It was fear.

He took his time in the bathroom, letting the cool water run over his head and neck. Then he changed out of his jeans into slacks and a crisp sport shirt. By the time he entered the dining room, everyone was seated. He shook hands with Leo, who had come to the table in his suit and tie, winked at Laura, a teenager in ponytail and shorts who reminded him of his own sisters, and slipped into the chair beside Karen.

Dinner began. Salad followed the soup, a rib roast followed the salad, and peach pie followed the roast.

Coffee cups were filled, emptied and filled again. Second helpings made their way onto Peter's plate without his asking for them, and, all the while, the Kern family talked around one another, in a strange kind of play in which he was expected to take a part, except that he didn't know any of the lines.

'Spring is such a lovely time of year,' Beverly began.

'You can feel the energy in the air,' agreed Leo, blinking his myopic eyes.

'There's still two more weeks of school,' Laura fretted.

'It's the season when life begins anew,' Beverly continued. 'A fresh start, a clean slate. Isn't nature grand?'

'If you like spiders, mosquitoes and yellow jackets,' Laura parried. 'There's a hornet's nest behind the garage.'

'The garden has never looked so beautiful,' Beverly said proudly. 'Everything is in bloom. It's absolute perfection.'

'Perfection is in the eye of the beholder,' sniffed Laura.

'I thought that was beauty,' Karen put in.

Beverly pouted. 'They said it was going to rain today.'

'I took my umbrella,' Leo replied, 'but I didn't go out.'

'That's why it didn't rain.'

'Probably.'

'My arthritis flared up for nothing.' Beverly massaged her left thumb.

'Do you like the rain, Peter?' inquired Laura.

'Sometimes,' Peter answered, trying to keep up.

Four pairs of eyes turned to him.

'What does *that* mean?' the girl demanded.

'Why does it have to mean something?' her father asked.

'Because,' Laura told him, 'everything means something.'

'No,' Karen said, with an unfamiliar edge to her voice, 'not everything. There are some things that have no meaning at all.'

'We're not going to talk about that, are we?' Beverly exclaimed.

'We're not talking about anything,' Karen replied.

'There you are,' Beverly cried, flinging down her fork. 'A perfectly good pie, ruined.'

'A perfectly ruined pie,' chirped Laura.

'Don't be silly,' Leo argued. 'The pie is perfect.'

Laura giggled. 'There's that word again.'

'Very funny,' Karen said.

'Did someone make a joke?' Leo wanted to know.

'Go ahead,' said Beverly. 'Laugh all you want to.'

But no one was laughing.

'Is there more coffee?' Peter asked, feeling as though he had somehow stumbled into the Mad Hatter's tea party.

'Of course there is,' Beverly crowed, replenishing his cup with a flourish. 'There, you see, Peter understands.'

But Peter didn't understand at all.

'I like the rain when it's fine and misty and you can't hear it and you can barely see it,' he told Laura. 'Then it's fun to go out walking and feel the wet on your face.' It was called Ithaca rain, and he and Karen had often walked in it.

'Oooh, how romantic,' cooed the teenager.

Peter grinned, remembering. 'It can be.'

'We don't have rain like that,' Laura grumbled. 'Here it just pours down and drowns you.'

'It doesn't matter,' Karen replied.

'Romance doesn't matter?' Laura asked.

'I think romance matters,' Peter said.

'The rain doesn't matter,' Karen amended.

'Nothing matters to you anymore,' Laura said moodily.

Beverly dropped her coffee cup, the fine bone china shattering in the saucer. Leo almost choked on a piece of the perfect peach pie.

'Are you satisfied?' Karen glared at her sister.

'Don't take it out on me,' Laura retorted with a toss of her ponytail, her eyes flashing. 'It wasn't *my* fault.'

'Nobody said it was,' Karen hissed.

'No, indeed,' Beverly added.

'Of course not,' Leo soothed.

'*I* wasn't careless.'

There was a sharp intake of breath around the table.

'That's enough of that,' Beverly barked.

Leo sighed wistfully. 'It's been such a nice dinner.'

'I hate living like this,' Laura cried. 'Nobody can ever say anything.' She jumped from her seat and ran from the room. 'I hate it.'

'Teenagers,' Beverly sighed with a dismissive shrug. 'They can be so emotional.' She smiled benignly at Peter and then nodded at Karen. 'It's such a lovely night. Why don't you take Peter into the garden?'

'Yes, Mother,' Karen said obediently.

They went out onto the patio, seating themselves in separate lounge chairs, Karen's crutches drawn up on either side of her. The night air was warm and fragrant, and the lights from the house cast long shadows across their faces.

'What's going on around here?' Peter asked, as soon as they were settled.

'What do you mean?' Karen responded.

'I mean the tension at dinner,' Peter declared. 'It was like everyone was afraid to breathe.'

'Nothing's going on,' Karen told him.

'Is it something about me?' he pressed.

'Of course not,' she assured him. 'Everyone's been looking forward to your visit. I guess they must just have had a bad day, that's all.'

'And what about you?' he asked softly. 'Have you been looking forward to my visit?'

'Of course I have,' Karen replied in genuine surprise. 'How could you even ask that? Why, I was standing in the window for over an hour tonight, just waiting for the first glimpse of your car.'

'I'm sorry,' Peter said quickly.

'But I suppose I do owe you an apology,' she added because it was easier to talk in the dark. 'You know … for my knee being bad, and for you not being able to hug me.'

'You don't have to apologize,' he declared. 'I was just feeling a little sorry for myself. Look, maybe you shouldn't even be sitting out here like this. Maybe you should be in bed with a heating pad or something.'

Karen sighed into the shadows. He was such a good person, always so considerate, so caring, so willing to accept blame that wasn't his.

'We can sit a little longer,' she said.

He smiled broadly, although she could barely see it, and then leaned over to pick up her hand. 'It won't hurt to hold hands, will it?'

'No,' Karen assured him. 'It won't hurt a bit.'

'Is the arm all healed?'

'Pretty much.'

'Do you think you'll be ready for the fall semester?'

Karen looked off somewhere past his shoulder. 'I don't know,' she said. 'I haven't really thought about it.'

'You haven't?'

'No,' she said flatly.

A college degree, which had once been a primary goal, now seemed irrelevant to her, and the cloistered atmosphere of the Ithaca campus incredibly impractical. Nothing she had learned at Cornell had prepared her for, or protected her from, the nightmare of the real world.

'You've only lost one term,' he continued. 'That shouldn't be very hard for you to make up.'

'I don't want to think about it now,' she insisted, a bit more sharply than she had intended. 'I have a lot of other stuff to figure out first.'

'I wasn't trying to rush you,' he assured her. 'It's just that I know how important it is to you.'

Was, she thought sadly. It was strange how she had come to see many of the things that had mattered before December 22 as part of the past, not the future.

'I just need some time,' she said more reasonably.

'Of course you do,' he agreed, letting go of her hand.

'Time to get my priorities back in order.'

There was an awkward silence then, with each of them tense and unsure, trying to figure out what was really going on in the mind of the other.

'Does that mean maybe we should put our plans

on hold for the time being?' he asked tentatively, deciding to give her the option, but hoping she would reject it.

Karen's heart lurched painfully at his words. Her worst fear was about to be realized. Now that he was here, now that he had seen how awful she looked, he had decided he didn't really love her after all, and was trying to find a kind way out.

'If you think that would be best,' she said.

Peter sighed. 'I just want you to be sure.'

'I understand.'

There was another pause as the two of them sat there surrounded by the fragrant darkness, together but apart.

'You almost died in that accident,' he said after a while. 'I suppose an experience like that can have a profound effect. So I think you should take all the time you need to decide what it is you really want.'

'Thank you,' she murmured, wishing he wouldn't worry so much about letting her down easy and just say what he needed to say and get it over with.

That was it then, he thought. But he couldn't let her slip away from him without one last effort. He got out of his chair and stood beside hers, looking down at her through the shadows.

'Just do me a favor, while you're doing all that heavy thinking, okay?' he pleaded. 'Remember how much I love you.'

Karen gasped with relief. He wasn't trying to end their relationship. He still loved her, despite what she looked like, despite how she behaved. What had she been so worried about? She was so caught up in the moment that she didn't notice him bending down to brush his lips against hers.

It was so unexpected, his coming down at her out of the dark, that Karen couldn't help herself, she shuddered and cried out.

'What's the matter?' he asked, startled. 'Are you in pain?' He leaned toward her. 'Are you cold?'

The words came out of her nightmare.

Are you cold? he had asked. *Well, I can certainly take care of that.*

Without warning, she was fighting for air and pushing against him with all her might.

'What's the matter?' he cried.

'Get away!' she wheezed, trying to cover her face. 'Get away from me!'

He tried to grab at her flailing hands. 'Tell me what's wrong,' he shouted. 'Tell me what to do.'

At this angle, the lights from the house slanted across his face. Somehow, through her panic, she could see genuine concern in the brown eyes – *brown* eyes – and realized that it wasn't the demon from Central Park, it was Peter.

'I don't know what happened,' she gulped as her body, soaked with perspiration, went limp. 'I couldn't breathe there for a bit.'

'You scared me half to death,' he admitted, his own heart racing. 'I mean, you were staring at me like I was some kind of monster.'

'Was I?'

'Do you need some medicine or something?' he asked, peering at her, not only with concern in his eyes but with bewilderment.

She shook her head. 'No, no medicine. I'm fine now.'

'Are you sure?'

'Yes, I'm sure. It was nothing, really.'

'I wouldn't exactly call what just happened nothing.'

'I'm fine,' she insisted, feeling like a fool. 'I promise.'

'Well, even so,' he said, still a little unsteady, 'maybe we'd better call it a night.'

Karen let him lead her inside without resistance. She was more than ready to escape his scrutiny. They said their whispered good-nights in the upstairs hallway, just outside her room. Peter ran his index finger lightly down her cheek.

'I do love you,' he murmured.

'I love you, too,' she echoed.

He smiled, a happy smile that spread across his whole face. 'Then, as far as I'm concerned,' he breathed, 'that's all that really matters.'

Karen shut her door with a soft click and leaned against it, wondering if he were right.

Peter Bauer had never been her mother's choice of a suitable husband. Beverly had made no bones about that. He wasn't going to be a doctor or a dentist or a lawyer, he wasn't going to graduate from Harvard or Yale, and his family was not prominent in any way. That was three strikes against him, in her mother's book, which flatly eliminated him from any serious consideration.

He had, however, one thing in his favor, and if truth be told, it was the only reason Beverly had not insisted that Karen put a speedy end to the relationship the moment it became serious. Peter's father ran a very successful small business which, according to all indications, Peter would eventually own. So, although the boy might never set the world on fire, he would at least be able to provide well for his family, even as an engineer, and even if it meant that her daughter would have to live in the middle of absolutely nowhere.

Peter had told them that his father's manufacturing company would soon convert into producing parts for computers. Beverly knew nothing about computers, but Leo did and told her that they were going to be very important one day.

Although Beverly continued to encourage Karen to seek out what she called better options, she had resigned herself to Peter's presence in her daughter's life.

'After all,' she would say with a shrug, 'until you catch a bigger fish to fry, you don't want to let go of the one in the pan, or you may end up with no supper at all.'

Until the 'accident.'

Without bothering to wash her face or brush her teeth, Karen undressed and hoisted herself into bed, snuggling deep under the covers, despite the muggy night.

In the past five months, Beverly had not been able to say enough about Peter – about how thoughtful he was, how sincere, how loyal, and how much he obviously cared for Karen. Suddenly, all the doctors and dentists and lawyers that had been out there for the seeking were forgotten, there was no longer anything so terribly wrong with being an engineer, and she took every opportunity to tell Karen how fortunate she was to have found such an exceptional suitor.

The message was clear: a mere engineer should be grateful to have Beverly's daughter, even though she did come to him a little damaged. After all, he would be marrying up, as they said, and couldn't very well expect perfection. Karen didn't bother to protest the assumption. Peter was everything she had ever fantasized about in the dreamy nights of her girlhood, and she wanted nothing more than to marry him and live the fairy-tale life they had so often talked about.

Abso-u-lutely-topia, he had called it.

'We're going to have it all,' he would say. 'The beautiful wife, the hardworking husband, the cozy cottage, the white picket fence – and at least half a dozen cherubic children. Abso-u-lutely-topia!'

Karen frowned, remembering with a painful tightness in her chest that there weren't going to be any cherubic children, and that, in the detailed recounting of her injuries, it was the one thing her mother had somehow neglected to tell Peter.

'You can tell him yourself, when the time is right,' Beverly had said with a shrug. 'That, but nothing else.'

Karen squirmed at the directive. In her mind, she referred to it as selective honesty, which, as far as she was concerned, was the same as dishonesty. Not for the first time she wondered how she and Peter were going to share a life without truth.

But what was truth? she asked herself. Her mother, who had once preached the importance of total honesty between a husband and wife, now insisted that it wasn't necessary to disclose every sordid little secret. She was quick to point out that Peter had never considered it necessary to share the details of his previous exploits. Had he done so, Karen might have found cause not to marry him – just as he might find cause, were he ever to discover the truth about her 'accident.' It was infinitely better, Beverly concluded, that they both bury their pasts in the interests of building a wonderful future together.

Karen reached into her nightstand drawer for her

thought box and pulled out a blank piece of paper and a pen. In the gentle pool of lamplight, she wrote:

> Love is truth,
> the careful truth of time
> and constancy.
> Between eyes,
> between sighs.
> From girl to woman,
> from woman to wife.
> To life.

Without bothering to reread the words, she closed the box and tucked it safely away in the drawer, snapped off the light, and settled back against her pillows. Visions of white lace and rose petals began to dance before her eyes as she saw herself floating down the aisle, Peter standing there, waiting for her. He would smile and take her hand in his, and then he would take her away from all the pain and pity and reproach.

She closed her eyes with a contented yawn and pulled the covers up over her head, as though she were already nestling into that cozy little cottage with the white picket fence. She would find a way to tell Peter they would not be able to have children. He would be devastated, of course, but, as always, he would be loving and understanding, and perhaps, sometime in the future, they would think about adopting. There were bound to be some adorable little ones out there, with shiny faces and bright eyes, just waiting for a picture-perfect home.

At the other end of the hall, Peter lay in the guest bed

with his lamp still lit, listening to the subtle sounds of the Kern household as it settled itself down for the night, thinking how different it was from the rambling home in which he had grown up. The walls and floors back in Bangor creaked and groaned freely to accommodate the noisy brood who lived there. These walls and floors didn't seem to yield at all. Rather, it was the people who did the accommodating.

He laced his fingers under his head and stared up at the ceiling. His body was weary and sore from the long drive and yearned for sleep, but his mind would not cooperate. Not when there was so much to think about.

The change in Karen had almost overwhelmed him. The happy-go-lucky girl he remembered had become a frightened animal. While he could understand her reluctance to think about a future when her present was still somewhat in turmoil, her reaction to him had not been exactly normal.

He was now forced to concede that being run over and left for dead like a dog in the middle of the road had probably been much more traumatic than he had imagined and he could feel his anger rising, almost out of control, toward that nameless person who had stolen not only her health but her self-confidence as well. The quality that had always most charmed him about her was the funny little way she had of combining self-assurance with naïveté which always managed to make him feel just a bit more sophisticated than he actually was, and he loved her dearly for it.

Of course, it went without saying that sexually he was the more experienced. In fact, her innocence was one of the first things that had attracted him. Although he'd made a few half-drunken attempts at tempting her, in the back seat of his Pontiac, he was secretly pleased that she wanted to wait until marriage. He enjoyed the idea of being able to teach her, when the time came, and it meant a great deal to him to know that he would be her first.

Her accident was a setback, but he hoped it was only a temporary one. He wanted to believe that, as soon as she recovered physically, her confidence would return and her emotional distress would dissipate and she would be her old self again.

All she needed was enough love and encouragement to see her through, and that, he realized, was precisely where *he* came in. He could give her as much love and encouragement as she could handle. It was there, bubbling up inside him, in that part of his heart that had her name engraved on it. He would show her, in every way he could, that he was with her to the end. He would find a way to let her know that she could lean on him, depend on him, and share the bad as well as the good with him. A little smile began to play across his face, because he knew exactly how to accomplish that.

He reached over and picked up the small box he had placed on the nightstand beside the bed. Karen had said she needed time, but it was now perfectly clear to him that what she really needed was reassurance – reassurance that his feelings for her hadn't changed and weren't going to change, and that their life together was going to be exactly as they had planned it.

He flipped the box open. Inside, nestled against dark velvet, a diamond engagement ring sparkled in the lamplight.

eleven

The smell of coffee awakened him. For a moment, Peter thought he was at home in Maine, but it was much too quiet for the rambunctious bunch in Bangor. No floors complained, no walls grumbled. He opened his eyes. Sunlight flooded through the window between Beverly's damask draperies.

Peter glanced at his wristwatch, astounded to see that it was almost ten-thirty. He shook his head to clear away the cobwebs. It was practically the middle of the day, and he couldn't remember the last time he had slept so long.

Allowing himself one huge stretch, he jumped out of bed and padded into the bathroom, wondering if Karen was up yet. He had an idea that the two of them could go out for a while this afternoon, maybe even have a picnic somewhere. With the sun shining down on them, and the food between them, and her peculiar family nowhere in sight, they would be able to talk.

He dressed quickly after his shower, in clean khakis and a T-shirt, slipped the little velvet box into his pocket, and made his way downstairs.

'There you are,' Beverly accosted him before he had even crossed the foyer. 'My word, you must have been exhausted. We tried to be quiet. I hope we didn't disturb you.'

'I didn't hear a thing,' Peter said truthfully. ''I guess the drive down took more out of me than I realized.'

'Well, you look bright as a new penny now.'

'Where's Karen?' he asked.

'Oh, she'll be along soon, I'm sure,' Beverly told him airily. 'It takes her a while to get going in the morning, you know, ever since the accident. But there's coffee in the kitchen, and Winola will fix whatever you want for breakfast.'

'Hello there, Mr. Peter,' Winola cried when she saw him, displaying a big grin and a deep Mississippi drawl. 'My lands, how good you look. Miss Karen sure is a lucky girl.'

Peter chuckled. 'From your mouth to her ears, Winola.'

The maid began to laugh. 'Yessir, Mr. Peter, I'll tell her. You can be sure of that.'

'Do you think I could have a gulp of that coffee?' he asked, sniffing the aromatic air.

'Why, you surely can.' The maid snatched up a cup and filled it in a flash.

The coffee tasted as good as it smelled and Peter drank it down with relish.

'That's not enough,' Winola told him. 'You's a growing boy, you got to put something substantial under them ribs.'

'What do you suggest?' he asked with a grin.

The maid grinned back. 'How about some of my sour-cream eggs and a plateful of bacon?' she suggested.

'You remembered.'

It was what he had asked for every morning during his last visit, in January, when Karen was in the hospital and he was so worried, and Winola wouldn't let him out of the house without eating.

'Now you just set yourself down, Mr. Peter,' she instructed. 'Breakfast'll be ready in no time.'

'Winola,' he said as he watched her scramble up the eggs and sour cream and blend in her own combination of herbs and spices, 'I need your help.'

'Yes, Mr. Peter?'

'I want to take Karen out today, on a picnic, and I was thinking, if it was all prepared, she couldn't say no, could she?'

They had shared a number of picnics in the past – lazy spring afternoons on the banks of Cayuga Lake, and crisp colorful autumn days down at Cascadilla Park. All fun times, filled with laughter and warmth and closeness. He wanted to recapture that with her, if he could.

'Say no more, Mr. Peter,' Winola cried, her black eyes shining. 'The basket's in the closet, and I'll have it filled before you can finish your eggs. It'll do Miss Karen a world of good to get out of this house for a change.'

The eggs had been devoured and the picnic basket packed by the time Karen appeared, pushing open the kitchen door with the tip of her crutch.

'Good morning,' she said. 'Did you sleep well?'

'Like a log,' he told her.

She was wearing white slacks and a lemon-yellow blouse and her dark hair was tied up with a yellow ribbon. She had that fresh-scrubbed look he remembered so well, and he felt his heart do a cartwheel as she smiled at him.

'It looks like Winola's been taking good care of you.'

'You bet,' he confirmed.

'How about something for you, Miss Karen?' Winola asked.

'Just some juice, Winola, please,' Karen replied.

'That's not enough,' Winola complained.

Karen grimaced. 'If Winola had her way, I'd weigh four hundred pounds and be a circus freak,' she told Peter.

'You don't eat enough to keep a sparrow singing,' Winola muttered, wagging her head.

'Why eat if I'm not hungry?' Karen asked, earning only a scowl in response. 'Okay, I'll clean my plate at lunch.'

Winola grinned suddenly at Peter. 'Well now, I expect that'd be all right,' she conceded.

'What's going on?' Karen asked, looking suspiciously from one to the other. Winola never gave in so easily.

'A surprise,' Peter said.

'What surprise?'

'Winola has been kind enough to pack us a fantastic lunch, and I'd like to invite you on a picnic.'

'A picnic?' Karen echoed. 'What do you mean? You want to have lunch in the garden?'

'No,' Peter told her. 'I was thinking more of going out somewhere, maybe to a park.'

'Oh, I don't go out,' Karen declared.

Peter looked bewildered. 'What do you mean?'

'I mean, I don't go out,' Karen repeated.

'Why not?'

It wasn't an unreasonable question and perhaps she even should have expected it, under the circumstances. But it took her by surprise and left her momentarily flushed and flustered.

'I just don't,' she said lamely.

'Well, maybe you could make an exception,' he pressed. 'We used to have a lot of fun on picnics.'

'A picnic? What a wonderful idea,' Beverly cried, pushing through the door with an armful of fresh-cut roses and catching the end of the exchange. 'It's a gorgeous day outside and I can't think of a better thing for the two of you to do.'

'Mother,' Karen warned.

'Nonsense,' Beverly retorted. 'You've been cooped up in this house for weeks now. If you don't get out soon, you'll forget what the rest of the world looks like.'

'What a ridiculous thing to say,' Karen objected. 'I go to the city twice a week for my physical therapy, don't I?'

'And that's all you do, isn't it?' her mother countered. 'Go to the hospital and come right back home again. A change of scene would do you good.'

'I'll be right beside you,' Peter tried to reassure her. 'I won't let anything happen. If you're still nervous about cars, we won't walk in the street.'

Karen began to breathe hard and her hands, gripping her crutches, grew clammy. She was furious with her mother for interfering.

'I can't,' she whispered.

'Of course you can,' Peter urged.

'But I look so dreadful,' she cried. 'What if we run into someone I know?'

'What if you do?' Beverly countered. 'You smile very politely and tell whoever it is that you're recovering from an accident. What's so hard about that?'

Karen stared at her mother stubbornly. 'It's too soon,' she muttered.

'You'll be with me,' Peter said soothingly. 'You don't have to talk to anyone else if you don't want to. I can talk for you.'

'You can't spend the rest of your life hiding away in this house, you know,' her mother added.

'I'm not hiding,' Karen snapped irritably, because that was exactly what she was doing. It was humiliating to have to have this discussion in front of Peter, who couldn't possibly understand what was wrong, and watch him trying so hard to make it right. 'I'll go out when I'm ready,' she declared with as much dignity as she could muster.

'And when will that be?' her mother, as tenacious as any bulldog, inquired.

'When I'm ready,' came the reply.

Beverly threw up her hands in frustration. 'Take her on that picnic, Peter,' she instructed. 'Even if you have to carry her, kicking and screaming.'

Peter didn't have to carry her. He simply promised to bring her back home the moment she asked. They drove out to Steppingstone Park, a pretty little stretch of green lawn that rolled right down to the edge of Long Island Sound. Only a handful of people idled there on a Monday, mostly nannies with small children who paid no attention to the girl on crutches, and Karen recognized none of them.

There were several rough wood picnic tables scattered about, but Peter spread a blanket on the grass and he and Karen sat down on either side of Winola's basket.

'I'm starved,' Karen announced. 'Shall we see what Winola's packed for us?'

Without waiting for a reply, she dug into the big wicker hamper with all the fervor of a shipwreck survivor who hadn't eaten for a week.

'And to think,' Peter observed dryly, 'it was scarcely an hour ago that you weren't the least bit hungry.'

'It must be all this fresh air,' Karen retorted, a piece of cold chicken in one hand, a forkful of potato salad in the other. In fact, it *was* a beautiful day and she *was* hungry, and who could be serious over a drumstick and a dill pickle?

Peter couldn't help smiling. He had been right to bring her here. Already there was new color in her cheeks and a sparkle in her eye, and she seemed almost her old self again. He ached to be closer to her, the urge to reach out and take her in his arms was almost overwhelming, but something stopped him, a little voice that told him to tread slowly.

Between bites, Karen busied herself with the other goodies Winola had provided. She had laid out plates and napkins and forks and poured two cups of lemonade, like a little girl at a tea party, before she realized that Peter was just sitting there, watching her.

'What are you staring at?' she demanded.

'The most beautiful girl in the world,' he replied.

'Stuffing her face,' Karen added, knowing with a twinge of sadness that he wasn't really seeing her as she was now, but remembering her as she used to be. 'So, how come you're not eating?'

'Half a dozen sour-cream eggs,' he explained.

Karen chuckled. 'You know, one of the first things I wanted when they finally unwired my jaw was a plateful of Winola's eggs.'

'You'd better get her recipe,' Peter advised, 'before she takes it to the grave.'

Karen stopped with a blueberry muffin halfway to her mouth. 'It wouldn't do any good,' she said. 'I can't cook.'

'Surely, you jest,' he cried, clutching his chest. 'I thought acid indigestion was part of every bride's dowry.'

She chuckled. 'I can sew, I can knit, I can play the piano. But put me in the kitchen and I have two left hands.'

'But man cannot live by peanut butter and jelly alone,' he cried.

'Certainly not,' she agreed.

'Have you considered taking a culinary course?'

'Actually, I expect the man I marry to hire a chef,' she teased, as she so often had in other, happier moments.

'Not only the wench can't cook,' he huffed, 'she thinks I'm a Rockefeller. Well, my pride is clearly at stake here, not to mention my stomach. You leave me no choice but to call off the engagement.'

'Call it off?' Karen cried. 'How can it be off before it was even on?' She had almost forgotten how much fun it was to be with him.

'A mere oversight,' he said blithely.

He reached into his pocket and pulled out the velvet box, placing it gently on the blanket in front of her.

Karen stared at the small square shape. 'Is that what I think it is?' she asked, suddenly sober.

'Open it and see.'

One hand slid cautiously toward the box, then stopped. 'I thought you wanted to put things on hold for a while,' she whispered.

'Only because I thought *you* wanted to,' he replied.

She sat there, not moving, barely even breathing. It was about to come true, that one desperate dream she had clung to during all the bleak months of disillusion and despair. All she had to do was reach out and open the box.

'Before I look at this,' she said, 'we have to talk.'

'I'm not pressuring you,' he hastened to assure her. 'I know you need time. This is for when you're ready. It's just so you know that, as far as I'm concerned, nothing's changed.'

She looked at him with anxious eyes. 'Wait,' she warned. 'There's something I have to tell you first.'

'I love you, I want to marry you, and I'm all ears,' he said with a grin.

He wasn't making this very easy, Karen thought with a sigh.

'My mother should have told you months ago,' she began, 'but I guess she thought this was something best left between the two of us. The doctor didn't even tell *me* until just before I left the hospital. But it's something you have to know now because … well … it could make a difference.'

'Nothing's going to change my mind,' he asserted with a confident smile.

Karen remembered the way Dr. Waschkowski had explained about her lung, likening it to a balloon that deflated when it was punctured. She felt as though she were about to do some puncturing of her own.

'Peter, I won't be able to have children.'

It took him a moment to absorb her words, and he kept his face blank because he didn't want her to see how shocked he was, how disappointed.

'You mean, because of the accident?' he asked.

Karen nodded, her eyes sliding off his. 'I'm sorry.'

'Sweetheart, don't blame yourself,' he exclaimed. 'It's not your fault.'

'Maybe not,' she whispered, 'but I feel like it is.'

He didn't hold her responsible. How could he? It wasn't Karen who had so cruelly robbed him of the sons and daughters he had hoped to have, but some drunken driver who, in all likelihood, would never know and never care. Peter realized bitterly that the accident wasn't going to go away quite as simply as he had anticipated. Already, the shape of their lives was irrevocably altered.

'Did you really think that would make any difference between us?' he asked.

'Well, I wasn't sure,' she said honestly. 'I know how much you want children.'

'And you were afraid to tell me.'

'A little, I guess.'

'Sure I want children,' he told her honestly. 'But not having them isn't the worst thing I can think of. The worst thing is you being afraid to tell me about it. It makes me think you don't trust me.'

'Of course I do,' she cried. 'And I wanted to tell you, as soon as I found out.' I wanted to tell you everything, she thought, but my mother wouldn't let me. 'I just didn't think it was the kind of thing to discuss over the telephone.'

'I suppose I can understand that,' he conceded. 'But let's make a promise – one we'll never, ever break, okay?'

'What kind of promise?' she heard herself ask.

'Let's promise that we'll always be open and honest with each other. Completely honest. Let's not have any secrets between us. What do you say?'

But Karen couldn't say a word – there was something squeezing her throat.

'I want to know everything about you,' he went on. 'The bad as well as the good. Just as I want you to know everything about me. I mean, what kind of marriage would we have if we were afraid to talk to each other? Besides,' he added with a chuckle, 'secrets always have a nasty way of popping out when you least expect them to, so it's much better not to have any in the first place.'

She wanted to run then, but she could barely walk, and even were she able, there was no place for her to hide.

'What if – well, what if there was something that would maybe hurt the other person?' she asked in a small voice.

'Then you try to find a kind way of saying it,' he replied with a gentle smile.

Karen frowned, wondering if there were a kind way of telling him that she had let another man steal her most precious gift.

'Sweetheart,' he said earnestly, leaning forward, seeing her uncertainty. 'Surely you must know, after all this time, that there isn't anything you can't tell me.'

Her mother's voice went off in her head like an alarm bell. *Do you want to ruin your life?* it screeched. But Karen didn't know how she was going to be able to make the promise Peter was asking of her, when the very promise itself would be the biggest lie of all.

'Sometimes,' she suggested, gazing out across the

water, 'there are things that may be better left unsaid.'

'Between others, maybe,' he allowed, 'but not between us.'

Her blue-gray eyes turned toward him just long
enough for Peter to see the anguish in them. 'There's
so much you don't know.' She sighed. 'I wouldn't
know where to begin.'

Her words were so unexpected, they left him
speechless. He sat there staring at her, and despite the
warm afternoon sun, he felt cold. This delightful,
sincere young woman, who had always hung on his
every word – this innocent, guileless girl he had
thought he knew almost as well as he knew himself –
was now someone he wasn't sure he knew at all.

He didn't know how to respond, or whether he
should take her in his arms or turn away. What he did
know was that something had suddenly gone very
wrong with his master plan.

'So what is it I don't know about you?' he asked at
last, when the silence had become excruciating.

She shook her head. 'It doesn't matter,' she replied,
toying with a chocolate-chip cookie.

'Are you trying to say you don't want to marry me?'
he asked, holding his breath.

Karen dropped the cookie. 'Of course I want to
marry you,' she cried. Enough to think I could cheat
you and lie to you and steal your life from you, her
heart cried.

He let out an enormous sigh of relief. 'Then,
whatever it is, whatever's troubling you, we can work it
out, I know we can. You just have to trust me.'

She wondered if her mother could possibly be
wrong about Peter. She wondered if he loved her and
believed in her enough to understand. Karen wanted

so desperately to tell him the truth. She couldn't bear the thought of living with this horrible lie for the rest of her life.

Would you go into a store and pay top price for used merchandise? her mother's voice sounded in her ear.

Karen groaned inwardly, knowing she wouldn't, and knowing she had no right to expect that Peter would, either. But, by accident or design, she had already gone too far – as good as admitting she had secrets – and it was too late to retract her words and go on with the lie. She had no choice now but to trust him, and pray. She took a deep breath.

'I know what you want is for us to be the way we were,' she began cautiously. 'But that Karen is gone, Peter. She isn't coming back. Not ever. Whatever our future together might be, it's going to be different than we thought.'

'It doesn't have to be,' he argued, unable even to contemplate life without the sweet, innocent girl he loved so much.

'You don't understand.'

'I understand,' he said. 'I just don't accept it. I realize that not being able to have children of our own is a setback – maybe you could even consider it a serious one. But, what the hell, we'll have each other, and that's what counts. Besides, we can still be parents. There's always adoption, you know.'

Karen frowned, remembering that it was those very same thoughts that had carried her off to sleep last night. But she wasn't tucked up safely in her bed now.

'This isn't just about children,' she told him.

'I know – it's about the accident, too,' he conceded. 'You've had a ghastly experience and I can see that you've lost some of your confidence. But other people have been hit by cars and they get over it and go on with their lives. In time, so will you. I really believe that, and you just have to believe it, too.'

'I want you to look at me, Peter,' she said. 'Just for a moment, I want you to see me, not as you remember me from two years ago, or even six months ago, but as I am right now – as I was last night. Think about it. I cringe whenever anyone reaches for me. I hyperventilate at harmless shadows. I break into a cold sweat at the thought of leaving the house. Do you see me?'

'Yes,' he answered reluctantly.

'All right then, deep down inside, where all your good instincts live, do you honestly believe any of this is about an automobile accident?'

'I guess I don't understand,' he admitted.

'There was no car, Peter,' she said bitterly, 'no hit-and-run, no drunk driver. There was no accident at all.'

'But your mother said – '

'My mother lied. To you, to everyone.'

His eyebrows met over a puzzled frown. 'But then, what happened to you?'

Karen opened her mouth to speak, closed it, then opened it again. The end of the past and the shape of the future lay in her next words.

'I was … assaulted in Central Park,' she said.

'Assaulted?' Peter echoed.

'Yes,' she confirmed. 'The injuries my mother described to you … they weren't caused by a car. They were the result of a beating, a very vicious beating.'

It took him a moment to digest this. 'I don't get it,' he said. 'If you were assaulted by someone, then you were assaulted. Why lie about it?'

'Because that isn't all.' She took a tremulous breath. 'I wasn't just beaten up, you see. He, uh – well, he – he also … raped me.'

Peter stared at her in disbelief. 'Raped?' he finally managed to croak. 'What do you – ? Are you saying that someone – someone actually – ?'

'Yes,' she said.

He sat there, struggling to get his mind around her words. The whole thing was preposterous, way beyond the scope of his comprehension, and yet, with a sharp thrust of pain in his heart, he knew it made perfect sense. It explained Beverly's peculiar evasiveness and her efforts to keep him away from the hospital. It explained that craziness at the dinner table, too. And, of course, now he understood Karen's behavior since his arrival.

'I don't know what to say,' he said.

'I'm sorry,' she replied. 'I wanted to be … to be perfect for you.'

Perfect, he thought. There was that word again, and he almost groaned aloud. He wanted to put his arms around her and assure her it didn't matter, hold her close and promise to protect her for the rest of his life, beg her to believe that not all men treated women as she had been treated. He reached out and patted her hand.

'I never expected perfection,' he forced himself to say, because, of course, he had never expected anything else.

'I did,' she murmured.

'But why hush it up?' he exclaimed. 'It's a crime, for God's sake, and the person who committed it should be put in jail. What's the matter with the police down here? Didn't they investigate?'

Karen shrugged. 'They were looking into it, but my parents didn't want any publicity.'

Despite his turmoil of emotions, he could understand the practicality of that. After all, the world was not entitled to know everything – the right to privacy still existed. But the thought of someone else putting his hands all over her, putting his – and getting away with it! Peter felt as though he were about to throw up.

'Do they know who he is?' he gulped.

The easy part was over, Karen thought. Now came the hard part.

'They know,' she said.

'You mean, they showed you mug shots? You were able to identify him?'

'No … I told them who he was.'

'You *knew* him?'

'I met him at Jill's party. Remember, that's where I was that night. He was polite and attentive. When he offered to take me home, it never occurred to me that he had something else in mind.'

On a bright, sunny afternoon in Steppingstone Park, overlooking Long Island Sound, the bottom fell out of Peter Bauer's world. Of all the things he imagined happening to him in his life, he had never once considered that the woman he would choose to marry would go off with some other man and get herself violated.

He knew she was waiting for him to say something to her, something sympathetic and reassuring, as he always had, but no loving words formed behind his tongue. He felt betrayed.

'I don't understand,' he cried. 'I thought you loved me?'

'I do,' she assured him.

'We were practically engaged.'

'Yes.'

'Then how could you do such a thing to us? To me?'

Karen groaned. 'And you wanted me to trust you.'

'I didn't realize,' he began. 'I never expected – '

'The truth?' she asked softly. 'Peter, I made a mistake, and what happened, happened.'

'Why did you have to tell me?' he exclaimed.

'Would you have preferred to live with the lie?'

'Yes,' he agonized. 'No. I don't know. I just don't understand any of it. Why would you, how could you, let someone – ?'

'I didn't *let* him,' she whispered, tears flowing down her cheeks. 'I tried to stop him. I tried as hard as I could. That's why he beat me up. I never wanted anybody but you to be the first – the only – you have to believe that.'

Peter shut his eyes against her words. 'We don't have to discuss this anymore now,' he decided because his heart was hurting too much. 'We have lots of time. We can talk again tomorrow, or the next day, after we've both had a chance to, well, sort things out.'

Some things, he thought, were better left unsaid.

'If that's what you want,' she said dully.

'Yes,' he replied with a forced smile. 'I think that would be best.' He peered into Winola's basket. 'We came here for a picnic, didn't we? Well then, let's have one.'

Peter heaped his plate with chicken and potato salad and blueberry muffins, although he didn't know how he was going to get a single bite past the lump in his throat.

Karen stared into her lemonade as though it held some kind of answer.

The little velvet box lay forgotten on the blanket between them.

PART TWO
1964

It is said to begin with the father.

— *Maxine Kumin*

one

Amanda Willmont took the decanter from the table beside her chaise longue and poured another glass of sherry, carelessly spilling several drops on the polished mahogany surface.

The late-afternoon sunlight filtered through the windows of the elegant Jackson Street Victorian that crowned San Francisco's exclusive Pacific Heights, spreading a soft haze over the subtle grays and mauves of the large corner bedroom, just the way Amanda liked it. Life was easier when the edges were a bit blurred.

It was her favorite time of day, just before dusk, when her correspondence was finished, her charity work completed, and her household duties attended to, and she could slip into her favorite silk dressing gown and retire to the privacy of her room, knowing she would not be bothered until Robert came home for dinner – if he came home for dinner.

For the past two weeks, her husband had been noticeably absent three nights out of five, which usually signaled the onset of a new liaison. As was typical in such situations, this was Thursday, and Amanda hadn't seen him since Tuesday.

Not that she cared very much anymore. She had given up whatever romantic notions she might have had about her marriage shortly after the honeymoon, right after she had become pregnant with Bobby, as soon as her trust funds had legally been put into Robert's care.

'You are no longer to be pitied,' he had told her two months after the wedding. 'You now have a husband to parade around in public, a posh home in one of the best parts of town, and a secure place in San Francisco society. In exchange, you're going to let me do exactly as I please.'

What pleased him was to be successful in his own right, to live well, and to sample half the female population of the state of California. Before the Willmonts had reached their fifth wedding anniversary, he had achieved the first two and made a significant dent in the third. What he didn't have much interest in was a house filled with bothersome children. He moved out of his wife's bedroom on the day she announced her pregnancy, and never returned.

Amanda Willmont, who had been Amanda Drayton of the San Francisco Draytons before her marriage at the age of twenty-nine, was the only child of Horace Lowell Drayton, the financier and magnate, whose ancestors had been among the most influential in the city's development since the gold rush days. Her mother, a homely but refined woman, came from one of the oldest families on Philadelphia's Main Line.

Robert Willmont came from nowhere, but he had taken a modest law degree and, with the help of his wife's name and her father's backing, turned it into a partnership in one of the most prestigious law firms in San Francisco. Even Horace, who would never have considered the brash nobody as son-in-law material had his daughter not been descending rapidly into spinsterhood, was forced to concede that the man had made the most of his opportunities.

As public as his professional success was, Robert was careful to keep his personal successes private. It mattered little to him that his wife knew of his various escapades, but he didn't want to run the risk of his father-in-law's finding out and perhaps withdrawing his patronage. It didn't take any great insight to understand that, with her close-set eyes, thin mouth, beak nose and mousy hair, Robert hadn't chosen his wife for her looks.

Over the years, Amanda learned to shut her eyes to the realities of her marriage, and although it was painful, she eventually came to accept the arrangement. The sherry helped, and of course there was Bobby. The complaisant baby she held too briefly in her arms, the dutiful child who suffered her embraces with acute embarrassment, the fine young man who now smothered her with bear hugs whenever he was home – he had become her only reason for being.

Her heart would all but burst when she thought of him, so bright, so handsome, so well-behaved. And such a good boy, so kind and considerate, that he had never caused her a moment's anguish. He was consistently at the head of his class in school, appreciated by his teachers, admired by his opponents, and envied by his peers. In his entire life, whatever he had asked for, she never came upon a good-enough reason to deny him.

Amanda knew she had done herself proud in raising the boy. Going far beyond teaching him his letters and his manners, she had worked hard to instill in him a sense of responsibility for who he was and what was expected of him. He was no ordinary young man, after all, and she felt it was essential that he understand, at the earliest possible age, the tradition into which he had been born.

'Having wealth and influence means nothing in and of itself,' both her father and her grandfather had liked to say. 'True character is the ability to take whatever you are fortunate enough to be given and use it for the good of mankind.'

It was clear to everyone that, although his name was Willmont, Bobby was every inch a Drayton, and no one who had any contact with him doubted that he had an exceptional future awaiting him.

Indeed, Robert had had very little to do with his son's upbringing. On the rare occasion when he was home at all, he would closet himself in the richly paneled library with strict orders not to be disturbed. At the dinner table, he was usually too preoccupied with his own concerns to have much interest in a growing boy.

In just a few short weeks, that growing boy would be graduating, with honors, from Harvard Law School, as he had graduated from Stanford University three years earlier, and he had already been offered positions at no less than three of San Francisco's best firms, one of them being his father's.

'I didn't even know he interviewed with us,' Robert

said with an indifferent shrug when his wife attempted to express her appreciation.

The one and only time that Amanda could ever recall him involving himself in his son's affairs was in the middle of Bobby's third year at Stanford. It had something to do with a girl, and Amanda recalled that Robert had been furious. He ordered the boy home from school late one night. They met in the library, behind closed doors. But they spoke so loudly that Amanda, standing in the hallway, had no difficulty hearing at least part of the conversation.

'How dare you put me in this position?' Robert barked. 'I've worked my ass off for too many years to get myself accepted in this goddamn town to have you destroy it all with one of your stupid blunders.'

Bobby murmured something Amanda didn't catch.

'What did you think would happen, you fool? Did you think she'd say thank you and just walk away?'

Again, Amanda missed Bobby's response.

'He threatened me, that's what he did,' Robert shouted. 'Walked right into my office and threatened me – someone I wouldn't let shine my boots. "I don't really want to go to the police on your boy," he whines, "but my Polly's only seventeen, and someone has to look out for her." Of course he meant *me*. A hundred thousand dollars – that's what it's costing me to clean up your little mess. I ought to take it out of your hide.'

'Look, I'm sorry,' Bobby pleaded, his voice rising loud enough for his mother to hear. 'I didn't think he'd have the balls to go to you. Anyway, I never forced her to do anything. Believe me, she wanted exactly what she got.'

'It doesn't matter what she wanted or didn't want. Get it through your thick skull – she's only seventeen.

That's statutory rape in this state.'

Bobby laughed harshly. 'Let them prosecute. It's my word against hers, and I'll say I never even heard of her. Who do you think they'll believe? This town isn't going to convict me of anything. I'm a Drayton.'

There was the sharp sound of an open hand coming in direct contact with a soft cheek.

'You're a Willmont,' Robert roared. 'And don't you ever forget it. The Draytons are nothing but a bunch of lily-livered snobs, and there isn't a one of them who wouldn't disappear into the woodwork at the first hint of a scandal, including your dear sherry-nipping mother.'

'So what am I supposed to do?' Bobby asked with a mixture of petulance and belligerence in his voice.

'You're supposed to keep your mouth shut, that's what you do,' his father snapped. 'No bragging to your buddies, no boasting about your great conquest, and you make damn sure that you never come within a hundred yards of her again, understand?'

'How can I do that?' Bobby whined. 'She's all over the campus.'

'You see her, you walk in the other direction. Not a word, not a gesture, not so much as a look. Do you hear me?'

'I hear you.'

'I'll pay her medical bills. I'll pay the rest of her way through Stanford. Hell, with a hundred thousand bucks in the bank, she'll be set for life. But that's where it ends. Don't ever expect me to bail you out again.'

'No, sir,' Bobby murmured.

'You get in a mess, you get out of it. If you need to play that rough and tumble, figure out how to do it without having to pay the piper. It's time you learned. Because if you ever put me in a position like this again, I'll cut you off without so much as a cent. And make no mistake – I control all your mother's trust funds and I can do it. And I will.'

'You're not going to tell her about this, are you?' she heard Bobby ask anxiously.

'You mean, malign her sainted son?' Robert sighed. 'No, I'll let her keep her illusions. What else does she have? She probably wouldn't believe any of it anyway.'

The conversation continued, but Amanda had heard enough. Clearly, Robert had had a bad day at the office and was taking it out on the boy, misunderstanding some youthful prank or another. She was undressed and in bed, half an hour later, when Bobby came up to say good night.

He was still smarting from the humiliating encounter with his father. No one had ever spoken to him that way, and at that moment, he knew he would shed few tears if the man were to fall under a cable car. He sat beside his mother and held her hand. At least there was one parent he could always count on to see things his way.

The boy and his mother talked about his classes at Stanford and his position on the football team and his plans to go down to Mexico with friends during the Christmas holiday. Then he stood up and tucked the covers in around her and kissed her on the forehead.

'You're my best girl, you know,' he told her. 'You'll always be my best girl.'

A few minutes later, Amanda heard his sports car roaring out of the drive. Nobody ever referred to the incident again, and over the years, the conversation faded in her memory, until it were as though it had never taken place.

Amanda pulled the ruffles of her dressing gown around her and poured herself another glass of sherry. The amber aperitif had long since lost its taste, but she sipped at it anyway, slowly, hardly more than a drop at a time, as she had been taught to savor fine wines. It wasn't how it tasted that mattered, after all – it was how it made her feel.

Nothing had ever been said to any of the staff, but the large crystal decanter on the table beside the chaise longue was always kept filled. Most of the household help had come to Jackson Street from the Drayton mansion atop Nob Hill on the occasion of Amanda's marriage, and had known her since she was a girl. It didn't matter that they also knew her secret.

It didn't matter that her marriage was a sham, either. All that mattered was Bobby, and the important things he had been born to do. That would be her reward for all the lonely years, all the unfulfilled dreams.

There was a soft tap at her bedroom door. Amanda looked up in surprise. It was still way too early for dinner, and she couldn't think who might be rude enough to disturb her.

'Come in,' she snapped irritably.

The heavy door opened, and as the intruder entered, a big smile spread over Amanda's face.

'Bobby,' she cried in pure delight. 'What a wonderful surprise.' She frowned in sudden confusion. 'But aren't you supposed to be at school? Aren't we coming to Harvard next week to see you get your degree?' She started to whimper. 'Don't tell me I got the dates wrong. Don't tell me I missed your graduation.'

Robert Drayton Willmont bent over the chaise longue and wrapped his arms around his mother's frail frame.

'No, dear, you didn't get the dates wrong,' he soothed. 'I just wanted to see you.'

'Oh, Bobby, how nice,' she cooed. 'I'm so glad.' She smiled at him through blurry eyes. 'I do believe you've grown an inch or two just since Easter. Why, you must be taller than your father by now. Wait till he sees you. I do hope he doesn't have to work too late at the office tonight. He'll be so pleased.'

It was important to her that the boy think well of Robert, and she had played the game for so long that the lies rolled off her tongue like truth.

'How long can you stay?' she asked.

'Just a day or two.'

'You've made a very long trip for such a short visit. It isn't like you to be so frivolous.'

He knelt down in front of her and took both her hands in his, a thing Amanda could not remember him ever doing before, and she began to blink nervously.

'I have something to tell you, dear,' he said softly.

'Is it important?'

'Yes, it is.'

'Then why don't you wait until your father gets home?' she suggested. 'And then you can tell us both at the same time.'

'No, I can't wait for that,' he said with infinite patience. 'You see, there's been … an accident, and Father … well, he won't be coming home.'

'An accident? Did you say an accident?'

'Yes, dear.'

Harold Sutton, senior partner of Sutton, Wells, Willmont and Spaulding, had telephoned Cambridge at three o'clock in the morning.

'It's your father, Bob,' he said with no apology for the hour. 'He died of a heart attack an hour ago. I think you should get back here as fast as you can. It really would be best all around if you were the one to tell your mother.'

'She doesn't know yet?'

The older man cleared his throat. 'No,' he replied with obvious discomfort. 'Your father wasn't home at the time.'

The Harvard law student laughed aloud. He didn't need a road map to tell him where Robert Willmont had been found.

'Well, at least the old man went out with a bang,' he said. 'Good for him – he wouldn't have wanted it any other way.'

'Look,' Sutton entreated, 'your father's private life was just that, and we can't have any embarrassing publicity attaching itself to the firm.'

'Certainly not, sir,' the young man said, instantly somber.

'Yes, well, I'm glad you understand. I've talked it over with the other partners and we've decided to say that he was working late at the office when the, ah, unfortunate incident occurred.'

'Can you square that with the authorities?'

'I believe so. The police commissioner is a personal friend.'

'I'll catch the first plane out.'

'That'll be fine, Bob,' Sutton said. 'Just fine. And, by the way, don't think for a moment that this has any effect on our offer. We're still hoping you'll come with us after graduation.'

'One thing has nothing to do with the other, sir, I know that,' came the correct reply. 'As a matter of fact, after careful deliberation, I've decided to accept your offer.'

In truth, he had not made his decision until that very instant.

There was just the slightest hesitation at the San Francisco end of the line. 'Well, that's good news, indeed,' the senior partner said heartily. 'We'll be looking forward to it.'

'Thank you, sir.'

In Cambridge, a big grin spread across the young man's handsome features. Like father, like son, he could almost hear Sutton thinking.

'Now, you be just as gentle as you can with your mother. She's a bit fragile, you know.'

Amanda Willmont was indeed fragile, never more so than when she had consumed half a decanter of sherry.

'What kind of accident, Bobby?' she whimpered.

'It was a heart attack.'

'A heart attack?'

'Yes, dear.'

'Is he – was it – you mean, he's – ?' Somehow, she couldn't get the word out of her mouth.

'I'm afraid so.'

'When?'

'Last night. He was working late at the office.'

Amanda closed her eyes. Her husband had been dead for almost an entire day, and she hadn't even known it. A heart attack – an attack of the heart. The irony was obvious to her because she knew exactly where Robert had died, and it had nothing to do with the office. How kind it was of Bobby to want to protect her.

In spite of herself, she felt hot tears pressing against her eyelids. Robert had been an absentee husband for twenty-five years and she had learned to live with it. Now that he was dead, she missed him. She had played the part of a happy wife for more than a quarter of a century, and that had been a sham. Now she would play the part of a grieving widow, and that would be real.

'You're all I have now, Bobby,' she sobbed.

'Don't worry, dear,' he said. 'I'll take care of you.'

She smiled at him through her tears. 'You're such a good boy. You've always been such a good boy.'

'And you've always been my best girl,' he replied.

How like his father he was, Amanda thought, so tall and broad, with the same dark hair and beautiful face. In the dim light, it could almost have been Robert kneeling before her, looking up at her with such concern. Except, of course, for the one feature that Bobby had inherited from her side of the family, and which marked him as a Drayton above everything else – the extraordinary aquamarine eyes.

PART THREE
1969

Learn from the past, live for the present, look to the future.

– Anonymous

one

Karen Kern hurried up Fifth Avenue, as quickly as the slight stiffness in her reconstructed left knee would allow, and turned left on Twelfth Street. Both the temperature and the humidity registered in the upper nineties, and Karen was perspiring freely beneath her bulky black coat.

She had regained her health and most of her weight. Her skin glowed a rich bronze from weekends in the sun, setting her blue-gray eyes off dramatically. Her dark hair, which grew well below her shoulders, was pulled back at the nape of her neck. A pale touch of lipstick was her only makeup.

Shifting the sack of groceries she carried, she began to fumble for her door keys when she was still half a block from the solid concrete building where she shared an apartment with Arlene Minniken, her former roommate from Cornell.

'Good evening, Miss Kern,' Martin, the door-man, said as she approached.

Her parents had insisted on her living in a building that provided round-the-clock doormen for extra security.

'Hello, Martin,' she replied with the plastic smile she had perfected for almost every man with whom she came in contact, regardless of the circumstances.

The lobby of the ten-story apartment house was dim and functional, in contrast to the splendid opulence of Jill Hartman's building on West End Avenue, but Karen hardly noticed. She pulled an assortment of bills and advertising circulars from her mailbox and rode the tired, creaking elevator to the sixth floor.

Letting herself into her apartment, she dropped her coat on the floor, deposited the bag of groceries on the kitchen counter, and hurried over to flip the switch on the air conditioner. The unit was old and rattled so much that she and Arlene almost had to shout to hear each other above the racket, but it provided a mod-icum of relief that was better than nothing. Then she kicked off her shoes, fixed herself a vodka collins and collapsed on the living room sofa.

For the past six months, Karen had been working as the assistant manager of the Washington Square Book-ery, which wasn't exactly on Washington Square, but close enough for the owner to get away with the namesake.

Housed in the dim, quiet, faintly musty basement of an old brownstone, the Bookery specialized in pre-viously owned, rare, and hard-to-find books and peri-odicals. Peace posters hung everywhere, along with a sign that read, 'Make Love Not War,' and a cartoon of Lyndon Johnson riding the top of a bomb about to

plunge into a crying baby, which said, 'Bombs Hurt.'
Burning incense spread a pungent odor over everything.

A number of regulars, mainly friends and neighbors
from Greenwich Village, came in to browse and pass
the time of day with Demelza, the rather eccentric
proprietor, but the shop was not generally frequented
by uptown customers. Karen kept track of inventory,
placed orders, organized the woefully disorganized
owner, and made sure there was always a pot of herbal
tea brewing. The job was interesting and just a short
walk from the apartment, and the money didn't
matter because her parents footed the bill for her
major expenses.

When she wasn't at home or at the Bookery, Karen
could be found on a bench in Washington Square with
her nose deep in one of Demelza's treasures, or
wandering around the narrow streets of Greenwich
Village peering into secondhand shop windows, or
sitting by herself in one of the coffee houses that were
an integral part of the area's offbeat charm.

Nobody bothered her. Like marbles bouncing off
one another, people of the Village met, touched
briefly and then veered away, strumming their guitars,
selling their wares, keeping their distance and protect-
ing their own painful secrets behind hard, glossy
shells.

Had she had her own way, Karen would have chosen
one of the run-down walk-ups that passed for quaint
right in the heart of the unique little community, but
her parents had been adamant.

'It's bad enough you want to live in the city at all,'
her mother had said. 'But as long as you do, we're
going to make sure that it's someplace safe and

respectable, and not some bohemian enclave overrun by weirdos and freaks.'

There was no way Karen could explain to her parents what it was like when she crossed Washington Square South. More than merely entering another part of the city, it was like entering another life, a life she felt she belonged in – among the weirdos and the freaks.

They settled on the formerly deluxe apartment house on West Twelfth Street, a block off Fifth Avenue. It was quiet and well-maintained and offered enough security to satisfy the elder Kerns, and it suited Arlene, who split her time between Bellevue Hospital and NYU, where she was earning her master's degree in psychology.

Karen never went back to Cornell. Nor did she marry Peter Bauer. The two of them had spoken on the telephone several times after his return to Maine that dreadful spring, but their conversations were short and superficial. Peter spoke of the weather and told her about his job and his family, but he carefully avoided any mention of the future. Karen listened politely and didn't press him. There wasn't really any point. After a while, the phone calls stopped.

'What could you possibly have been thinking of, to tell him that ugly story?' her mother demanded once she had pried the circumstances of the picnic at Steppingstone Park out of her daughter.

'I couldn't marry him under false pretenses,' Karen replied defensively. 'I had to tell him the truth.'

'Truth, my dear girl, is what we want it to be,' Beverly retorted. 'Were you *trying* to push him away?'

'I was trying to find out if he really loved me – or just some fantasy he had of me.'

'Why? What's so wrong with fantasies?'

'Nothing,' Karen conceded. 'I just didn't want to build my marriage on one.'

'I daresay many a marriage has been,' Beverly declared. 'You have to understand – it isn't men who lead women down the garden path, but the other way around. It's all part of the game we play to get what we want. And there's no harm in it, because the men are getting what they want, too.'

'It just wouldn't have been fair to him,' Karen insisted stubbornly.

'Fair?' Beverly exploded. 'Has this whole awful thing been fair to any of us?'

'I don't want to talk about it anymore,' Karen snapped, her head beginning to throb.

Beverly threw up her hands in exasperation. 'Have it your way, then. Just remember that righteousness is a poor excuse for loneliness.'

Karen had hobbled away defiantly, but her mother's words stayed with her. She learned to accept the sympathy she received as the innocent victim of a terrible automobile accident. She never again spoke of what had really happened to her, but pushed it all down into a dark place within her, where no light could shine.

She discarded the crutches. The stiffness in her left knee grew less and less noticeable. The doctors assured her that, in time, it would disappear altogether. She took to wearing long skirts and high collars to hide the scars on her body, and perfected an attitude of polite disinterest to hide the scars on her soul. It was two years before she could bring herself to leave Knightsbridge Road for something other than a brief appointment. But when she did, in the summer of 1965, she left for good.

'Arlene Minniken wants me to share an apartment in the city with her,' Karen announced one evening at dinner. 'She thinks it would be fun for us to room together again.'

'You want to live in Manhattan?' Beverly asked, unsure she had heard correctly. It was her opinion that nice young ladies stayed at home until they married.

'Yes,' Karen replied. 'Lots of girls are doing it these days. Take Arlene, for example.'

'Arlene's home is in Tallahassee,' her mother declared. 'She couldn't very well commute to New York City. But you have a perfectly good home right here. If you want to get away so badly, you can always go back to college.'

'I don't want to go back to college,' Karen responded. 'I just want to live on my own for a while.'

'How will you support yourself?' her father asked.

'I'll get a job.'

'A job?' Beverly questioned. 'What kind of job?'

Karen shrugged. 'I don't know yet.'

'You know that isn't necessary,' her mother exclaimed. 'There *are* other options.'

'Mother, please, let's not start that again. I'm not going back to college, and I have no plans to marry.'

'I suppose we can help out with expenses' – Leo thought aloud – 'at least until you get on your feet.'

Karen beamed at him. With one sentence, he had not only resolved her financial qualms, he had silenced her mother in mid-argument, and that was not a frequent occurrence.

'Thanks, Daddy,' she said. 'That would be fantastic.'

'What with Laura starting at Mount Holyoke in the fall, and now you wanting to live in Manhattan,'

Beverly pouted, 'the house is going to be awfully empty.'

'I'll come back to visit as often as you like,' Karen assured her.

It was the end of summer before she found work. There were not many jobs available to someone without a college degree, certainly not ones her mother considered appropriate, which meant in the right part of town, in an acceptable industry, among respectable people. She took a position as a receptionist at Marilyn's Beauty Salon, where she was allowed to wear full skirts and high-collared blouses and oversized sweaters, and the patrons, mostly older women, patted her hand a lot. In addition to greeting customers and scheduling appointments, it was Karen's job to close the shop at night, making sure that curling irons and blow dryers were turned off. Hardly demanding work, but the pay was steady.

After that, she became a salesgirl at Lord & Taylor's. The department store stood solidly on Fifth Avenue, at what her father called the edge of the high-rent district. Everything about it was elegant – the architecture, the dramatic display windows, the merchandise, the personnel. After her training period, Karen was assigned to the lingerie department, where the senior saleswoman showed her how to recognize the buyers from the browsers and taught her how to clinch a sale to a wavering customer.

She soon discovered that it wasn't only women who bought lingerie. Men, sometimes awkward and embarrassed, came looking for finery for their wives or their mothers or their sweethearts or their mistresses. It didn't take Karen long to learn the difference.

One October afternoon, when she had been at Lord

& Taylor's for almost a year, a customer approached her, gray-haired, distinguished, and obviously wealthy, carrying a black satin negligee in his hands. It was the most expensive that the store offered and one of Karen's personal favorites.

'Excuse me, miss,' he said. 'I wonder if you can help me. I want to buy a birthday gift for my daughter, and I'm not at all sure what would be appropriate.'

Karen concealed a smile. She knew that men did not buy slinky black satin negligees for their daughters, but she had learned how to play the game.

'How old is she?' she asked politely.

'Well, I'd say she's about your age.' He held up his selection. 'Tell me, do you like this?'

'I like it very much,' Karen conceded. 'What size does she wear?'

He frowned at that. 'I don't know,' he admitted. 'But I think she's about your size. Maybe if you'd hold it up, I could get an idea of how it would look on her.'

Karen took the negligee from him and held it awkwardly against her body, fussing with the folds to get them just right. 'How's that?' she inquired.

He shook his head. 'I can't really tell for sure. I don't suppose you'd be willing to try it on for me?'

The hair began to rise on the back of Karen's neck. She had been trained to deal with difficult customers, but no one had told her what to do in this situation.

'I'm afraid not,' she murmured, thinking fast. 'As you can see, I'm alone in the department, and I'm not allowed to leave the floor.'

'Well, that's all right,' he said with an easy smile. 'Why don't I just take it anyway, and if my daughter doesn't like it, she can bring it back and pick out something else.'

Karen wrote up the sale as quickly as she could, the plastic smile fastened to her face, and breathed an enormous sigh of relief when he took his package and left.

The store closed at six. It was six-thirty when Karen slipped out the side door and hurried across Fifth Avenue to catch the downtown bus, joining a small knot of people who were already waiting.

'I think this was meant for you,' a voice directly behind her said. 'Even though you wouldn't try it on.'

Karen was so startled that she fell against an elderly woman standing in front of her.

'I beg your pardon,' she mumbled, as she bent down to retrieve the woman's fallen handbag. Straightening up, she glanced over her shoulder at the gray-haired man.

'I wanted to give it to you right there at the store, but I realized that might not be very appropriate, under the circumstances,' he said. 'So I waited for you. I thought we'd go somewhere for a drink, perhaps have dinner. Get to know each other.'

'I think you've made a mistake,' Karen said, her heart pounding.

'Really?' he asked with a smile. 'I thought you got my message very clearly. I certainly got yours.'

'What message?' she demanded. 'I gave you no message.'

'You knew perfectly well I wasn't buying a present for my daughter.' He chuckled. 'I don't even have a daughter.'

'I didn't know *who* you were buying it for,' she replied truthfully, praying the bus would come.

'I was buying it for you, of course.'

'Thank you very much, but no, thank you,' she said

as politely as she could because he might have been a good customer at Lord & Taylor's and she couldn't afford to offend him. 'That particular item isn't one I have any use for.'

'If you play your cards right,' he told her with a deep chuckle, 'an opportunity might present itself.'

Up the street, Karen could see the bus inching its way toward them, and in anticipation the knot of people began to surge forward. The gray-haired man pressed against her.

'I've been watching you,' he breathed into her ear, his hands, shielded by the press of people, beginning to roam over her. 'On the surface you're cool and proper, but I can tell that underneath the high collars and baggy sweaters you're hot.'

She pushed frantically against the people in front of her, trying to get away from him.

'Wait your turn,' someone snarled at her. 'We all want to get home, you know.'

'You'd better leave me alone,' she cried to her pursuer.

'You don't really mean that,' he cajoled.

'Yes, I do.'

'Your lips may be saying no,' he whispered, 'but your body is saying yes.'

'If you don't stop bothering me,' she shouted at the top of her voice, 'I'll call the police.'

The elderly woman whose purse she had retrieved turned around. 'Is that man annoying you, dearie?' she asked.

'Yes,' Karen half-sobbed.

'You leave this girl alone,' the woman advised tartly. 'She's obviously not buying whatever you're selling.' She shook her head. 'A man your age – you ought to be ashamed of yourself.'

The bus chose that moment to rumble up to the curb and open its doors. The elderly woman put her arm around Karen and guided her up the steps. The gray-haired man melted into the crowd.

After that, Karen stopped wearing makeup and added bulky coats to her shapeless clothing, regardless of the weather. The more unattractive she could make herself look, the safer she felt.

She quit her job at Lord & Taylor's. She answered phones for a Madison Avenue advertising agency, typed bills for a Park Avenue dermatologist, stuffed envelopes for a mail-order house, and stacked books at the public library. But nothing seemed to suit her for long. If the work didn't bore her, some man pursued her, pressing unwanted invitations on her until she sought other employment.

So it was that, in the winter of 1969, she came to the Washington Square Bookery, in answer to an ad for a clerk. The shop, housed in what the owner called a bunker, was long and narrow and crammed with shelves that boasted volumes on every obscure subject from the aalii shrub to zymurgy. In the back, tucked safely into barrister cases, was a treasure trove of first editions and out-of-print copies of works by such authors as Somerset Maugham, Emily Dickinson, Edith Wharton, Sinclair Lewis, Upton Sinclair, and Willa Cather.

The owner was a free-spirited woman in her forties with an ample figure, frizzy black hair that she wore in a thick braid down her back, and soft brown eyes that seemed to reflect the suffering of the whole word. The plight of Biafra was foremost in her mind when Karen first met her.

Her name was Doris Ulasewicz, from the Bronx, but there were very few who knew that. Everyone called her Demelza, after some obscure literary heroine she had unearthed.

'She was a woman with the soul of a saint and the heart of a prostitute,' Demelza explained. 'Something about that always appealed to me.'

'I guess it wouldn't have worked too well if it were the other way around,' Karen observed.

Demelza grinned appreciatively at the young woman. 'I think I'm going to like you,' she said.

'Thank you,' Karen murmured, unaccountably pleased.

'Now to business,' Demelza declared. 'I'm totally disorganized and brilliantly creative. I'm fine with anything under fifty dollars but absolutely frivolous with anything over that. I tend to fly off in too many directions at once, but I'm great at conceptualization. I'm insatiably curious but I never pry. I need someone to bring sanity to my life and work. Think you could put up with me?'

Karen looked around. The few customers that browsed in the aisles seemed harmless enough, the books seemed friendly and inviting, and the pungent smell of incense that tried valiantly to camouflage the basement's mustiness was not unpleasant.

'I could try,' she replied.

'That's all I can ask of anyone,' said Demelza. 'But before you get excited, I'd better tell you that I can't pay more than eighty dollars a week.'

That was ten dollars less than Karen had earned at the library, and she hesitated. With each job she had held, her salary had increased, if only slightly. Her goal was to be financially free of her parents as soon as possible. Yet here she was, actually contemplating taking a step in the opposite direction.

'Maybe I can give you a fancy title to make up for it,' Demelza offered, because she had already decided she liked this girl and had long ago learned to trust her instincts.

'What kind of title?' Karen asked, because she had a funny feeling about this no-nonsense woman with the bizarre name and the out-of-the-way little shop.

'Well, let's see,' Demelza thought aloud. 'Suppose we dub you – assistant manager?'

Karen laughed. 'My mother will love it,' she said.

'Is it a deal?'

'It's a deal.'

Karen practically skipped all the way back to West Twelfth Street, wondering why on earth she should be feeling so good about making less money.

'It wasn't just that I liked Demelza so much,' she explained to Arlene. 'It was something about the Bookery, too. I felt really comfortable there. This is going to sound crazy, I know, but it was almost as if the shop spoke to me and told me I'd be happy there.'

Arlene wasn't a psychology student for nothing. 'Then you made the right decision,' she agreed. 'As for the salary, well, as long as your parents don't mind, why should you?'

In fact, the Kerns were delighted.

'Assistant manager?' her mother exclaimed. 'That's just wonderful, darling. I can't tell you how proud we are.'

Which translated, Karen knew, into how impressed the neighbors were going to be once Beverly got through massaging the facts, and the two-woman operation had become a twenty-person staff on the scale of Barnes and Noble.

'And don't you worry about the money,' her father added from the extension phone. 'You'll get a check from us every month for as long as you need it.'

No one mentioned that this was her seventh job in three and a half years. No one suggested that it would be nice if she would stay in one place for a while. But the words hung in the air as though they had been said.

The focus of Karen's life had been on marriage and children. It never occurred to her that she would have to work for a living. The death of her dream left her aimless. The Bookery gave her purpose. She was not stepping into someone else's shoes that were either too big to fill or pinched her toes – she was creating a totally new position and she found, to her surprise, that she liked it. By the end of a year, Demelza had increased her salary twice.

'I didn't have any choice,' she freely admitted to her friends and customers. 'The girl's got me so well organized, I couldn't exist without her.'

Karen had indeed straightened out the accounts and put Demelza on a budget, and never complained about working long hours. She even developed a plan for increasing business that would draw uptown customers to the out-of-the-way shop.

But, more than that, the two women became friends. The refugee from Great Neck found a lot in common with the expatriate from the Bronx.

'When you're one of six kids and there's not enough food to go around,' Demelza said once, after snatching the last doughnut of the coffee break, 'you learn to be quick. Then, of course, you learn to get out.'

'When you're the older of two and getting so much attention you can't breathe' – Karen sighed – 'sooner or later, you have to get out, too.'

'My parents were delighted.'

'Mine were appalled.'

Karen was an avid reader of popular fiction, but now her employer opened her mind to the beauty of the classics that she had heretofore relegated to the category of required reading.

'You have to sample everything to evaluate anything,' Demelza instructed.

So, for a few precious hours each day, she would crawl into someone else's world and make it her own. Heathcliff haunted her, Becky delighted her, Inspector Jarret infuriated her, Madame Bovary made her blush, and Anna Karenina made her cry.

In addition to her new fictional friends, Karen got to know the scruffy lot who frequented the Bookery. The women wore long skirts and beaded headbands and attended an assortment of classes. The men wore beaded necklaces and hair below their shoulders. Many of the younger men were just hanging out, working temporary jobs until their draft numbers came up and it was time to head for Canada. Some of the others were career dropouts, searching for a reason to get up in the mornings. Several, with a foot in each camp, ran soup kitchens down on the Bowery or taught at places like NYU and Cooper Union. A few composed music or wrote poetry or tried to paint the shapes of their dreams.

Each had a story, and as Karen listened, the ragged clothes, unkempt hair, and shaggy beards disappeared, and she saw instead a group of lost souls, not unlike herself, struggling to find their way in a frequently hostile world.

In the backlash of Camelot, America had splintered into a dozen different subcultures, from the flower children of Haight-Ashbury to the civil-rights marchers of Selma to the drug addicts of Needle Park. Sentiment against the country's involvement in Vietnam was surging and Demelza defiantly displayed every antiwar poster and cartoon she could find.

The Kerns came to visit the Bookery one afternoon when Karen had been there for two months. It was a rainy Saturday in early April and Beverly, dressed in a bright splash of purple and fuchsia, gushed through the door with her umbrella dripping all over a 1923 issue of *Time*.

'My, what a day,' she exclaimed with a shiver. 'It's practically a gale out there.'

'Well, you blew into the right place,' Demelza said cordially, quickly whisking the vintage magazine out of harm's way. 'We have fresh tea waiting to warm you up.'

With cup in hand, Beverly looked around. 'Well, isn't this nice,' she said brightly. 'And so ... cozy.'

'Cramped, actually,' Demelza corrected her.

'Atmospheric,' Beverly suggested.

'Dark,' Demelza said.

'Don't your customers find it a little difficult reading in such light?' Beverly could no longer see her hand before her nose without her glasses.

'Heavens, we don't encourage our customers to read,' Demelza replied, a wicked little smile playing around the corners of her mouth.

'What about Karen? I don't want her to get eye-strain.'

'Demelza's teasing you, Mother,' Karen sighed.

'There are plenty of lights when we need them, but we think the shop has more ambience this way.'

'And it saves so much on electricity,' the newly budget-conscious proprietor put in.

'Ambience?' Beverly echoed with just the slightest hint of disdain.

'Well, we're trying for the archival look,' Demelza confided. 'You know – dusty, musty, hidden away. Isn't that where treasures are usually found?'

'Treasures?' Beverly openly sniffed at Demelza's array of peace and protest posters.

'Let me show you,' Karen beamed, leading her mother off to the special glass cases.

'I don't know about that woman,' Beverly remarked at dinner several hours later. 'She seems very peculiar to me. Don't you agree, Leo?'

'I didn't notice anything very peculiar,' Leo replied, attacking his Peking Duck as though it were a root canal.

'She's not peculiar,' Karen defended her friend and employer. 'She's just a little different, that's all.'

In the bright light of the Chinese restaurant, Karen wondered where the gray in her mother's hair had gone.

'Is she *on* something?' Beverly asked.

'What do you mean, *on* something?'

'You know – does she take drugs?'

Karen chuckled. 'What do you know about drugs?'

'Oh, I'm not as cloistered as you might think,' her mother retorted. 'I know what goes on in the world.'

'Well then, you know more than I do,' Karen replied.

'I smelled a very suspicious odor at that bookshop.'

'That was incense, Mother.'

'Are you sure? It was awfully sharp.'

'I lit it myself, just before you got there.'

'Well, nevertheless, I don't want you mixed up with anyone who takes drugs.'

'If Demelza takes drugs – and I certainly have no knowledge that she does,' Karen asserted, 'she's never done it at the Bookery. As long as she signs my paycheck each week, whatever she might or might not do someplace else is none of my business.'

Which was a neat way of sidestepping the issue, Karen thought to herself now, as the clanking air conditioner began to have some small effect on the stifling apartment. In the four months since that conversation with her mother, she had discovered that many of Demelza's friends did indeed smoke marijuana and she was pretty sure that her employer did, too.

Karen had to confess that the idea of being around people who used marijuana, or pot or grass or weed, as they called it, made her a little uneasy. She knew very little about drugs other than that they were addictive and illegal. Once in a while, someone wandered into the shop behaving a bit off-center, but Demelza usually laughed it off.

The first time, Karen was shocked. 'That guy over there looks weird,' she whispered with wide eyes.

'The word is *stoned*,' Demelza told her with a dry chuckle. 'Sorry, Peter Pan,' she called to the customer in question, 'but this isn't never-never land.'

Once, Karen watched as two young men at the back end of one of the aisles exchanged money for a small plastic packet containing something that looked like baby powder.

'There's someone over there selling talcum, I think,' she told Demelza.

This time, the Bookery owner didn't laugh. 'Where?' she demanded and, following Karen's finger, descended on the two men like a giant bat.

'You're history,' she cried, grabbing each by an arm and thrusting them in the direction of the door. 'We sell books and magazines in here – and that's all we sell.'

'What was that about?' Karen asked.

'There's dope and then there's dope,' Demelza replied. 'Some of it's easy and some of it's hard. No one deals hard stuff in my place.'

'Why do people use drugs in the first place?'

Demelza shrugged. 'Different people – different reasons,' she said. 'Some do it because it's fashionable, some because it's illegal, some because they've become dependent. Most of the people I know do it because, for a little while, at least, it makes the pain go away.'

The doctors had given Karen medicine in the hospital after her 'accident' and she could still remember how it made the pain of her broken body subside. She wondered if the drugs that Demelza was talking about worked the same way.

'What kind of pain do they have?' she asked.

'Not the kind I think you're thinking about,' the older woman replied. 'Street drugs aren't for toothaches and back strain. I was referring to the pain of living.'

'The pain of living.' Karen had never heard that before. She tucked the phrase into the back of her mind. Demelza never spoke of it again, but Karen never forgot.

* * *

Dinner was ready by the time Arlene arrived home from the university. Although no one would ever be likely to call Karen a gourmet cook, she had at least mastered the basics.

'Chef salad, iced tea, and French bread from the bakery,' she announced as her roommate passed the kitchen doorway. 'I couldn't bear the thought of turning on the oven.'

Arlene grunted her approval, dropped her books on the dining table, and was shedding her clothes before she even reached the bedroom.

'Look at me,' she cried fifteen minutes later, dripping from the shower, her long blond hair bound up in a towel. 'Soaking wet and sticky all over.'

'I'll call maintenance again,' Karen promised.

'If they can put a man on the moon,' Arlene fretted, referring to the incredible event they had recently watched on television, 'why can't they make an air conditioner work?'

Karen pushed her roommate's books to one side and set two places at the huge oak table with claw feet they had found at a secondhand store. In fact, the whole apartment was done in what Arlene dubbed Early Salvation Army. The overstuffed sofa and wing chairs were comfortable, if faded; the end tables were solid, if chipped; the bureaus were roomy, if warped; and the dining chairs were sturdy, if plain. But the two girls had had a lot of fun picking out each piece.

They were halfway through their salads when Karen said, as casually as she could, 'Have you ever taken drugs?'

Arlene bit into a crusty piece of bread. 'What kind of drugs?' she asked. 'Aspirin? Sleeping pills? Or the mind-control stuff we give the patients at Bellevue?'

'No, I mean street drugs. Like marijuana.'

'I tried pot once,' Arlene nodded. 'Years ago.'

'What was it like?'

Arlene shrugged. 'I guess it wasn't very special. I barely remember, and I've had no great urge to do it again.'

'The effect you got … was it like drinking alcohol?' Lately, and in private, Karen had been learning a great deal about the numbing effects of alcohol.

'No, it was nothing at all like that. Actually, it was nothing much of anything, as I recall. When you drink booze, you usually get fuzzy and your senses get dulled. When you do pot, you're supposed to get a real high. You don't lose awareness, so I'm told, you gain it. Why?'

'I've been invited to a party tomorrow night,' Karen informed her. 'And I think there'll be drugs there.'

'A party?' Arlene couldn't keep the surprise out of her voice because Karen rarely accepted invitations.

'Demelza's having a few people to her place for dinner and she invited me. We're even closing the Bookery early.'

'And she smokes pot?'

'I'm not really sure about that,' Karen replied, 'but I know her friends do and some of them are bound to be there.'

'Well, if you're asking for advice,' Arlene said, 'I'd say, don't do anything you don't want to do.'

'I *am* a little curious,' Karen admitted. 'You know, to find out what it's like.' *The pain of living*, she thought to herself.

Arlene picked up her glass of iced tea. 'Well then,' she said with a careless shrug, 'go for it.'

two

Long after Arlene had fallen asleep, Karen lay awake in the humid darkness, listening to the arrhythmic clanking of the air conditioner and thinking about dinner at Demelza's.

If she chose, she could count the number of parties she had attended in New York City over the past four years on one hand and have fingers left over. Her social life consisted mostly of a dinner out now and then, several movies, one or two Broadway shows, and an occasional concert at Lincoln Center, usually in the company of Jill or Arlene or Demelza.

She had a ready excuse for every man who tried to date her, and after a while even the most persistent stopped asking. If she occasionally caught herself yearning for male companionship, she had only to reflect that few men were interested in friendship at arm's length. With the advent of the contraceptive pill, 'free love' was the catchword on everyone's lips. Even casual dating meant obligatory sex – with all communication carried on between the sheets.

What a different world it was, she thought with a

sigh, and drifted off to sleep thinking about Peter Bauer.

A brief, apologetic note had arrived at the house on Knightsbridge Road a little over a year after the picnic at Steppingstone Park, wishing Karen well and telling her of his impending marriage.

'I wonder what took him so long,' Beverly sniffed.

The nightmare woke her just before dawn and she lay in her bed, sweat-soaked and shivering, until the familiar panic began to subside. It was always the same – something evil chasing her through a thick fog until she couldn't make her feet run anymore, and then the heavy hand reaching out to grasp her by the throat and cut off her life.

She took several deep breaths to settle her heart and thought about trying for another hour of sleep, but fantasies of Demelza's Greenwich Village loft kept her awake. Karen had never been inside a real Village apartment, and she couldn't wait to see what one was like.

Demelza had described her place as a cross between a church and a brothel. It was a fair assessment. The dirty brick building on Bleecker Street had once been a ribbon factory. Visitors reached the loft by means of a rickety self-service elevator with a heavy wooden gate that had to be raised and lowered manually. Karen arrived to find some two dozen of the Bookery regulars already there. She stepped out of the elevator and stood openmouthed at the edge of the single enormous room.

Exposed brick walls alternated with giant arched windows, and the vaulted ceiling was at least twenty feet high. One section of the loft was furnished with

Victorian velvet sofas and ornate side tables, another had two massive pews squaring off over a refectory table, and a third was strewn with half a dozen mattresses, heaped with colorful pillows. Each section was separated by a curtain of beads suspended by wires from the ceiling. Candles burned everywhere, and in the mixture of odors Karen detected the familiar scent of incense. It was different, bohemian, more than a little bizarre, and it suited Demelza perfectly.

'You made it,' the hefty hostess cried, descending on Karen with a highball in one hand and a plate of crudités in the other. 'Welcome to my heaven on earth.'

'This is fantastic,' Karen said, searching for the right adjective. 'It's so, well, it's so … eclectic.'

'Actually, I think you could call it MGM Extravagant,' Demelza replied. 'And it took years of careful planning.'

'It's definitely you.'

'Well, don't just stand there and gawk,' the Bookery owner urged, taking her guest's bulky coat. 'Take a deep breath and jump on in. You know everybody.'

Obediently, Karen took a few steps forward.

'Hey, Karen,' someone said immediately.

'Hey, Ethan.' She smiled at the slightly off-balanced skeleton beside her.

'You look different,' Ethan observed shyly. 'Not like you do at the shop.'

Karen glanced down at the simple blue cotton skirt and loose-fitting, high-collared blouse she had worn to work.

'It must be the clothes,' she teased.

'Exactly,' Ethan agreed. 'You know, your skirt

matches your eyes. And your eyes are the color of a cloudless sky.'

Her eyes were more the color of a stormy sky, but she smiled at him anyway. Ethan came from Nebraska, she knew, and was on his way to Canada. He was a regular at the Bookery and rather bashful, hovering as he did on the fringe of the group. But he managed to screw up enough courage to test her knowledge of the shop's inventory on a daily basis. Not more than eighteen, with straight straw-colored hair that he kept pushing out of green eyes, something about him always reminded her of a lost puppy.

'My momma's cornflowers are the same bright blue,' he told her, 'and they grow clean up to the sky.'

'Sounds lovely.'

He sighed wistfully. 'I sure hope I get to see them again someday.'

'I hope you do, too.'

'But it probably won't be till after my daddy dies.'

'Why not?' she asked.

'He threw me out – called me a coward and threw me out. He said he didn't have a son no more.'

'Because you didn't want to go to Vietnam?'

'Yeah.' Ethan shook his head sadly. 'He lost a leg on Guadalcanal. I just don't know how he's running the factory without me.'

She could see his pain and wondered how many families across the country were being destroyed by this war of somebody else's that so many young men didn't want to fight.

Ethan pulled out a ragged kind of cigarette and lit it. 'Wanna hit?' he offered after several deep puffs.

Karen knew what it was. She took a half step back.

'No,' she said firmly. 'No, thank you.'

Ethan grinned. 'Demelza said you were a virgin. I didn't believe her.'

'I beg your pardon?'

'She said you'd never used grass.'

'Why didn't you believe her?' Karen asked.

'I don't know,' he said thoughtfully. 'There's just something about you – a look in your eyes, maybe, that says you've been there and back.'

'You know, *you're* different here than at the Bookery, too,' she told him, neatly changing the subject. 'Much more open.' She nodded at the joint. 'Is it because of that?'

'I guess so,' he replied, taking another hit. 'It sort of smooths out the edges and makes everything mellow.'

Karen wondered how it would feel to be mellow. She tried to recall an occasion in the past, but more and more, her memory of that other life was fading into nothingness.

'What's it like,' she asked, 'to be mellow?'

'It's like wearing rose-colored glasses to a horror flick,' he replied.

'Marijuana makes you feel like that?'

He offered the joint. 'Don't take my word for it.'

This time she was tempted. 'Maybe later,' she said. 'Right now, I'm hungry.'

'The food's behind that screen,' Ethan directed. 'On the other side of the pew.'

Karen found the kitchen and soon had a plate heaped with salade niçoise and moussaka. A bottle of ouzo went with the meal. She filled a glass and wandered into the living room, sitting on one of the Victorian sofas. The party drifted around her – long gauzy skirts, flowing shirts, safari shorts, beads, sandals. People stopped to chat about the food or the heat wave or Demelza's outrageous home. Karen began to feel as relaxed here as she did at the Bookery.

A few of the guests were drinking ouzo, as she was, but most were passing pot around the way Karen and Jill used to pass photographs. Two of them were already sprawled on a mattress at the other end of the loft. It wasn't until she saw them shedding their clothes that Karen realized what they were doing and she blushed and turned away.

'Isn't this just the most fantastic party?' Ethan cried, plopping down beside her.

'You bet,' Karen agreed.

'For a small-town boy like me,' he said, taking a hit, 'New York is right out of Oz. I'm going to miss it when I go. I don't think they have anything like this in Canada.'

'Maybe you'll come back someday,' she suggested.

'Maybe I will, if you're still here,' he said, the weed making him bold. 'I guess you know I have this crush on you.'

'No, I didn't,' she replied with genuine surprise.

'Gosh, everybody else knows,' he asserted. 'I thought for sure you did, too. I mean, the way I'm always hanging around you at the shop and every-thing.'

'I thought you were interested in books.'

'I wouldn't know Henry James from James Mich-ener,' he confessed sheepishly. 'I just like talking to you.'

'I'm very flattered,' she said sincerely. Ethan had always behaved perfectly properly and she didn't feel the least bit threatened by his admission. He was still the lost puppy who waited hopefully for someone to toss him a bone.

'Don't you feel a little funny?' he asked her.

'About what?'

'Well, for one thing,' he said with a grin, 'you're the only one here tonight who's sober.'

Surprised, Karen looked at the other guests – except, of course, for the two on the mattress at the other end of the loft. She had consumed almost a whole glass of ouzo and hardly considered herself sober.

'I am?' she whispered. 'How can you tell?'

'Easy,' he giggled. 'We're all bent one way or another. If you were any straighter, you'd break.'

'Is "bent" another word for mellow?' she asked.

'Not exactly, but close,' he conceded.

More than once, Karen had taken a bottle to bed with her but she would not have described the experience as mellowing.

He held out his joint. 'See for yourself.'

Curiosity got the better of her. She took the butt and put it between her index and middle fingers as smokers did.

'What do I do?' she whispered.

'First of all, you gotta hold it right,' he instructed, repositioning the joint between her thumb and forefinger. 'Okay, now go ahead and pull on it, just like a Marlboro.'

'I've never smoked a regular cigarette,' she admitted.

'Oh,' he said, momentarily confounded. 'Well then, you close your mouth around one end and suck on it real hard and take a deep breath all at the same time.'

Karen did as she was told. Even before the smoke hit her lungs, her insides rebelled, her face turned beet-red, her eyes watered, and she barely avoided losing her dinner.

'I don't feel very mellow,' she gasped.

'It takes more than one hit.'

'What if I'd just as soon not do it again?'

He shrugged. 'How bad do you want to be mellow?'

Karen wrinkled up her nose, put the foul-smelling awful-tasting reefer to her lips and pulled on it. Again she gagged, her insides burned and her eyes watered, but not as much as the first time. By the fourth or fifth hit, she had the hang of it and suddenly began to giggle.

'If my mother could see me, she'd have an apoplectic fit.'

'Does your mother have apoplexy?' Ethan asked.

'No,' Karen replied, wondering why she had never noticed how intelligent he was. 'She has astigmatism.'

Ethan shook his head. 'You're not making any sense.'

'Nonsense,' she retorted. 'I'm making perfect sense.'

For some reason that seemed outrageously funny to her and the giggles began anew.

'I guess I don't have to ask how you feel,' he said.

'Very light,' Karen replied. 'Like I could tiptoe on air. I can't remember ever feeling quite this way before.'

'Maybe that's because you were never mellow before,' suggested Ethan.

Karen stretched up high above her head, wiggling her fingers in the air, and then dropped back against the velvet cushions. It looked as though she might close her eyes and drift right off to sleep, but in the next second she was alert again, every nerve, every muscle at attention.

'Just look at that, will you,' she urged, pointing to the bead curtain that divided the living area from the dining space. 'Look how beautiful those beads are.' She scrambled to her feet and made an unsteady beeline for the partition, motioning him to follow. 'You have to come, too,' she giggled. 'I need a hit.'

Ethan obeyed and passed her a fresh joint. She dragged deeply on it and turned to examine the intricacies of color and design that made up the small wooden balls that hung from high over her head.

'These are absolutely fascinating,' she breathed. As riveted on the beads as she was, something caught her eye and she glanced through the curtains.

'Look,' she cried in surprise. 'Someone's dancing. Oh, how lovely. What kind of dance is that?'

Ethan followed her gaze. Indeed, several couples now occupied the mattresses at the far end of the loft, going about their pleasures with complete abandon.

'I think it's called the mating dance,' he replied with a chuckle.

'I've never seen that before,' Karen said as her body began to undulate in imitation. 'Can we try it?'

Ethan stared at her. 'I guess so,' he gulped.

He seized the joint and took several quick hits, sensing that something far beyond his wildest expectations was about to happen. Trembling, he followed her across the loft. Although he would have sooner died than admit it, the young Nebraskan had never been with a woman.

Karen walked slowly around the mattresses, studying each oblivious couple.

'Aren't they magnificent?' she whispered. 'So graceful, so rhythmic.' She stopped in front of an unoccupied mattress and turned to him. 'What do we do first?' she asked.

'Uh, well, uh, I think we take off our clothes,' he stammered.

She giggled. 'I can't do that.'

'But that's how it goes,' he said. 'We take off our clothes and then we do the dance.'

'Let's do it with our clothes on.'

'Well, I suppose we could,' he ventured, not wanting to seem too anxious.

She stepped onto the mattress and began to twist her body in an awkward version of the mating dance, humming along with a tune only she could hear. Ethan licked his lips and moved toward her, figuring that, when the time came, the undressing part would take care of itself.

He felt her stiffen when he put his arms around her, but she didn't pull away. They swayed together for a few bliss-filled moments, sharing the end of his last joint. Her eyes were closed and her lips were turned up in a small smile. He couldn't resist. He leaned over and kissed her lightly.

Her head snapped back and her eyes flew open. 'That's not part of the dance,' she cried.

'Sure it is,' he said.

Karen squinted at him. 'I don't believe you.'

'Look around,' he invited.

She peered at the couples that surrounded them and, sure enough, she saw that lips were touching lips and hands were touching bodies and bodies were fused tightly together.

'They're so artistic,' she breathed. 'Look how that one's muscles ripple up and down, and how smooth this one's skin is – how it glows in the candlelight.'

Now she was fascinated by the candles, mesmerized by the gentle flickering.

'See how the flames reach for the sky? They look like the tongues of hell.'

One moment she was staring at the candles, the next she was sagging against him and he had to hold her to keep her from falling.

'What's the matter?' he asked.

The whole room had begun to spin out of control and a flurry of bright lights swirled before her eyes.

'Let's sit down,' she suggested.

'Okay.'

He let go of her and she dropped like a sack of flour.

'Plop!' she giggled. 'I need another hit.'

Ethan sat down beside her. 'I think you've had enough,' he told her. 'Besides, we're right in the middle of our dance.'

'So we are,' she agreed with an acquiescent yawn. 'I like the lights, though. Don't turn off the lights.'

He didn't know what lights she was talking about.

'The lights stay,' he said as he pushed her gently back against the mattress. She didn't resist. He slid his hand down her arm, brushing against her breast.

'The colors are so pretty,' she murmured. 'I can see them even with my eyes closed.'

He unbuttoned her blouse.

'They're red and blue and green and pink and purple and silver.'

He unzipped her skirt.

'See how they sparkle.'

He unhooked her bra.

'Look, now they're showering down on top of us.'

He slipped off her panties.

'Why, it's just like the fireworks on the Fourth of July.'

Even in the candlelight, he could see the scars, thin jagged welts from her neck to her knee. He wondered fleetingly what had happened to her as he pulled his T-shirt over his head and unzipped his jeans.

'I feel as though I'm going to break into a thousand pieces of light and float through the air,' she cried.

He had worshiped her from afar for so many months that he could barely contain himself as his hands moved over her body and his mouth found her nipples.

'There's that tune again,' she trilled. 'La-li-la-la, la-li-la-la. Everybody's dancing, the chandeliers are sparkling with a thousand pieces of light. La-li-la-la.'

Without any further ado, he rolled over on top of her and began to fumble between her legs.

Her scream split the loft, a scream not of pain but of terror as, through her daze, she understood what it was he had in mind.

'Stop it!' she shrieked, clawing at him like a cat, pushing against him with all her strength. 'Stop!'

Ethan blanched. 'What'd I do?' he implored. People were staring and he was mortified.

She was crying now. 'It was beautiful,' she sobbed. 'The music, the lights, the dancing, and you ruined it all.'

'I didn't mean to,' he pleaded.

Someone opened a window and Karen felt a sudden draft sweep across her. She shivered and, looking down, realized she had no clothes on. She froze. Images blurred. The music stopped. The lights vanished. The dance was over. Everything went black.

three

A bright shaft of sun was burning through her eyelids. Karen groaned, still half asleep, and pulled the sheet up over her head.

'Rise and shine, Sleeping Beauty,' Demelza chuckled from somewhere above her. 'There's no Prince Charming, but there is fresh coffee.'

Karen blinked several times and forced her eyes open, but everything was fuzzy and white. Then she remembered the sheet and pushed it down under her chin. High arched windows looked down on her. Karen glanced around. She was lying on a mattress in one part of a large room, it was definitely morning – and she didn't know what she was doing there.

'Where am I?' she asked.

Demelza loomed into view. 'In my loft, of course. You came to my party last night. You ate my moussaka, drank my ouzo, and then Ethan must have given you too much of the good stuff, because somewhere around midnight you passed out cold. You looked so comfortable, I decided not to wake you.'

'That's right,' Karen recalled. 'I got mellow, didn't I?'

'Quite,' Demelza chuckled.

'It felt wonderful. I was floating and I could hear this incredible music.' Karen frowned. 'Is that when I passed out?'

'Just about.' Demelza peered down at the girl for a moment and decided that, if she didn't remember anything else, there was nothing to be gained by reminding her.

'I'm so embarrassed,' Karen mumbled. 'Everyone must have thought me terribly rude.'

'I doubt anyone noticed,' Demelza said with a bright smile.

Actually, she had given everyone a terrible fright, screaming and clawing at Ethan like that, as though the devil himself were after her. Demelza didn't grasp the situation immediately, but in the flickering candle-light she saw the scars, and that was enough to make her push Ethan away, grab a sheet to pull over Karen's body, and persuade them all to go on about their business.

As soon as the party broke up, she fixed herself some tea and, bringing the thick mug with her, came back to stare thoughtfully down at Karen. After a while, she pushed the sheet aside and, with some effort, managed to put the girl's clothes back on. Then, tucking the sheet back in place, she sat down on a mattress, her back against the exposed brick wall.

Doris Ulasewicz was the oldest of six children. Her mother was an unstable woman, frequently unable to cope, and her father was a longshoreman who spent more days at the racetracks than he did on the docks. Doris always knew how the ponies had run by how he came home – singing or swinging.

From the time she was eight, she had protected her brothers and sisters from their father's ire and their mother's neglect. She cooked and cleaned, changed diapers, prepared formula and, when the ponies were running badly, she found a way to wheedle the grocer out of one more grapefruit, one more loaf of bread, one more quart of milk.

There was never enough of anything – never enough food, never enough warm clothes, never enough love. When she was thirteen, she slept with the butcher, on a rough wooden floor in a back room, for a pound of hamburger and a scrawny chicken. She stretched the meat into two meals and made soup from the chicken bones and a purloined onion. The following week, she got a pork roast.

At fifteen, she quit school and lied about her age to get a job behind the counter of a luncheonette. The wages were hardly worth her time, but the tips were occasionally good, she was fed a hot meal, and she was allowed to take home whatever scraps she could salvage. She saved every penny, and once a month she would go to the Salvation Army store and dig through piles of used clothing for pieces she could rework into outfits for the children.

Her only refuge was the public library. For a few precious hours each afternoon, she would escape to the musty stacks and lose herself in incredible worlds that were filled with beauty, mystery, and adventure. It was the beginning of a love affair with books that never ended.

On Pearl Harbor Day, she turned eighteen and

forever remembered the occasion, not as the beginning of a war for freedom, but as the beginning of her own freedom. Within a matter of weeks, her father was being called to work on the docks every day.

Doris got a job in a downtown Manhattan bookstore and never looked back. She moved into a cold-water flat on Houston Street, as far away from the Bronx as she could get, changed her name, and found a life. By the time she was thirty, she had gained forty pounds and saved enough money to start her own small business in the basement of a Washington Square tenement.

Her brothers and sisters had long since stopped relying on her, but she never quite got over the urge to nurture. Fortunately, there was always an abundance of needy souls and lost causes for her to champion. And as she sat there in her loft, sipping her tea and watching over Karen, Demelza felt that familiar tug at her heart.

The girl looked like an angel, so innocent and trusting, curled up in sleep, but Demelza had seen the scars and wondered what demons populated her dreams. The Bookery proprietor could not have said how she came to choose her needy souls and lost causes, or whether it was the other way around, but there was a real sense of tragedy about Karen that she had felt from the first day the young woman walked into her shop – and tragedy was definitely Demelza's thing.

Caretaker of the Down and Out, that's what the Village people called her. If there was a person with no place to stay, see Demelza. If there was someone who needed a handout, tap Demelza. If there was an outrage that needed exposing, tell Demelza. Any day of the week, she would gladly give her only warm coat to a freezing vagrant and her last dime to a starving child

Karen wasn't freezing or starving but she was certainly in need of something, if only Demelza could figure out what.

The candles had burned themselves down to nothing and dawn was painting the windows gray before Demelza's eyes closed. When she opened them again, it was past nine o'clock and they were late for work.

'I can't believe I fell asleep and stayed the whole night,' Karen was saying as she came out of the bathroom and helped herself to a cup of coffee.

'You look none the worse for the experience,' Demelza commented.

'I feel fine,' Karen said. 'In fact, I feel terrific. I can't remember the last time I had a better night's rest.'

'Pot has been known to have that effect on people.'

A shadow flickered across Karen's face. 'I didn't do anything to embarrass myself last night, did I?' she asked.

'Not that I saw,' Demelza replied glibly. 'Why?'

'Well, this is going to sound stupid, I know, but I've got this weird picture in my head – a dream, I guess, of me dancing without my clothes.'

Demelza shrugged casually. 'So what?' she said. 'You were among friends.'

Karen blanched. 'I took my clothes off?' she gasped. 'In front of everyone?'

'I don't think anybody was paying much attention,' Demelza reassured her. 'The candles were low, and besides, most of them had other things on their minds.'

Karen looked down at her crumpled blue skirt and

high-collared blouse. 'If I took them off,' she questioned, 'who put them back on again?'

'I did,' Demelza replied calmly.

'Then, you saw …?' Karen whispered.

'If you mean the scars, yes,' her hostess, her employer, her friend said gently. 'Whatever caused them, you must have had a rough time of it.'

Karen felt the prickle of tears behind her eyes, tears of embarrassment and anger that she was never going to live down her past, and tears of frustration that it could still hurt so much.

'It was a long time ago.' She sighed. 'I don't like to talk about it.'

'I didn't mean to pry.'

'You weren't – you never do,' Karen murmured. Demelza listened, Demelza sympathized, Demelza encouraged, but never probed, never criticized and never judged. In the six months that Karen had known her, she had learned to trust the older woman's advice, value her opinions and admire her discretion. In many ways, Demelza behaved the way Karen sometimes wished Beverly would behave.

'I had … an accident,' she said.

'I'm sorry,' Demelza replied with genuine concern.

'I was careless and I ended up in the wrong place at the wrong time. It wasn't exactly the high point of my life.'

Karen felt an unfamiliar flutter in the pit of her stomach. This was the most she had said about the night in Central Park in six years.

'But you're all right now.'

It was a statement, not a question, but it seemed to warrant some kind of answer.

'You probably noticed my left leg is a bit stiff,' Karen

said. 'The kneecap was smashed, but it's getting better.'

'I'm glad to hear it,' Demelza replied, her smile warm and real.

'I guess I'm self-conscious about the scars.'

'I can understand that,' Demelza told her. 'After all, they're a reminder of something you'd rather forget.'

'I can't ever have children,' Karen heard herself say. 'I always wanted to have children.'

'Because of the accident?'

Karen nodded. 'I expected to marry a wonderful man and raise a houseful of children. Now, I don't know what I'm supposed to do with my life.'

Sooner or later, Demelza thought, every riddle had an explanation, and every question had an answer.

'I generally think of life as a great big map,' she said. 'When I reach a dead end on one road, I simply look for another to follow.'

four

Karen crossed Washington Square South and hurried up Sullivan Street. The late-January wind whipped and roared around her, burning her eyes and ears, and pushing its icy way down her throat. She burrowed deep inside her coat, and bent her body into the swirling gale.

The coat was a Christmas gift from her parents. It was made of thick gray wool, and came down to her ankles, and weighed almost as much as Karen did. Her shoulders ached for hours after each wearing, but it kept her warm.

It had arrived in the nick of time. The winter had turned unbearably cold. Piles of dirty snow lined the streets, reducing traffic to single lanes. Sidewalks were salted, but it was too cold for the ice to melt. Vehicles crawled down the middle of roads, honking and skidding. Pedestrians sank into slush over their ankles, cursing.

Reaching the run-down building she sought, Karen scurried up icy steps and pushed through the door. It had once had a lock on it, but that was long before the present tenants.

The structure had four stories. The upper floors were subdivided into studios for artists who sought cheap living in a congenial environment, while the first floor contained four flats of three rooms each. It was toward one of these that Karen headed as she hastened down the narrow brown hall in the light of a single sixty-watt bulb. She stopped at a door on the left and rapped briskly. When her knock was answered, she crossed the threshold and the drab outside world disappeared. She stood in the middle of Paradise. Or, to be more precise, in the middle of the Garden of Eden as it was being painstakingly reproduced, in a Gauguin sort of style, on the walls and ceilings of the once dreary flat.

'Hey, girl, you're late,' cried a bear of a man in a paint-spattered shirt. 'We started without you.'

Mitchell Rankin wrapped her in a hug. He stood over six feet tall and weighed over two hundred pounds. Karen had no clear idea of his face, buried as it was beneath a woolly beard. He never asked to hug her, he just did it, and she had learned to accept it. In the four months she had been coming to Sullivan Street, there had never been anything in his embrace but the simple regard for one person by another.

'Hey, Karen,' a tomboy of a woman called from atop a crudely fashioned scaffold on the far side of the room. 'What do you think of my clouds?'

Karen glanced up at the globs of white pigment that were beginning to scud across one part of the ceiling. 'I think they look very … cloudlike,' she said.

There was a splash of white freckles across the woman's nose and cheeks. 'I could use an assistant Michelangelo,' she said with a deep stretch.

'Ione, be careful,' scolded Mitch. 'You're doing that balancing act for two, you know.'

'Never mind about us, you big gorilla,' retorted the woman called Ione, as tiny as he was big, as pale as he was dark. 'Just take the girl's coat so I can put her to work.'

Mitch helped Karen out of the gray maxicoat. Beneath it, she wore a long black skirt over black boots and a coarse muslin shirt, loosely bound at the waist with a rope belt. Her dark hair was tied off her face by a beaded headband and she had taken to outlining her eyes in heavy black pencil.

'You can't paint in that outfit,' Ione declared.

Karen shrugged. 'I didn't want to take time to change.'

'Mitch, get the girl my smock,' the tomboy instructed. 'It's hanging on the back of the closet door.'

As Mitch disappeared into the bedroom, a gaunt young man with thick glasses and a wispy reddish beard came out.

'Hey, Karen.' he said with a distracted smile.

'Hey, Kevin.'

'Ione, where's the dictionary?' he asked.

'On the back of the toilet.'

Kevin looked at her quizzically.

'I was doing a crossword puzzle,' she said with a toss of her short blond hair.

With a grunt, he turned back into the bedroom.

'He's got exams,' whispered Ione.

Kevin Munker was in his third or fourth year at NYU, Karen wasn't quite sure. He wasn't a student in the traditional sense, enrolling for four years to earn a degree. Instead, Kevin took the minimum three courses per semester and kept changing his major so that, each term, he would have a whole new list of requirements to complete. As long as he maintained a B average, he could keep his draft exemption.

Mitch reappeared with Ione's smock just as the front door blew open and two women came in. Jenna, barely out of her teens, with carrot-colored hair, deep blue eyes and traces of baby fat still clinging to her, studied fashion design at Cooper Union. Felicity, a stick of a woman at thirty, with high cheekbones and brown hair and eyes, was a dancer who made incredible pieces of jewelry whenever the spirit moved her, and sold them whenever hunger moved her.

'If you're not going to paint,' Mitch ordered, 'stay out until ten.'

Jenna and Felicity weighed the advantages of going back out into the cold. 'We'll paint,' they said together.

Karen couldn't imagine how all five of these people survived in one small apartment together, but they did. They called it communal living, the way of the future, and although unrelated, they considered themselves a family.

Ione Meecham came from the coal mines of Alliance, Ohio, arriving in New York with a fine-arts degree in her hand and stars in her eyes, hoping for a spot at the Metropolitan Museum. Two years later, funds depleted, she took a job teaching art history at NYU, which always amused Karen, since she looked far more like a student than a teacher.

Over the next dozen years, Ione earned a small measure of respect, rose from the rank of instructor to assistant professor, discovered that she really loved teaching, and met Mitchell Rankin, a starving artist with unbridled optimism.

Mitch was a farm boy from Montana who'd spent his young years surrounding himself with paints and canvas instead of comic books and baseball cards, translating the raw splendor of Big Sky country into impressionistic brilliance.

'Something's wrong with the boy,' his father had declared. 'He's not interested in things kids his age are interested in. And he doesn't give a damn about sugar beets.'

'There's nothing wrong with him,' his mother had protested. 'He's just different, sensitive. He sees beauty in the world where everybody else sees brutality.'

Mitch went from high school to Korea, where a mortar burst resulted in a patchwork of scars across his right cheek. He grew a beard to cover them. When he met Ione, he was painting buildings, not pictures, but he still had his dream. She said at least he hadn't been reduced to doing those awful portraits for the tourists who invaded Washington Square. She invited him into her home and her heart.

Next came Felicity Gravois. Mitch found her sitting on a curb, crying, beside a box holding all her worldly goods. She was six months behind in her rent and had been evicted.

'I'm a dancer,' she explained. 'A really good dancer. Only nobody seems to care about that.'

When she was eight years old, a society matron had taken her to see *The Red Shoes*. Felicity decided then and there that she would be a ballerina. She slept, ate, and breathed dancing, took any job to pay for lessons and, when all else failed, made up steps and danced them in her head.

'How long have you been in New York?'

'Three years,' she sniffled.

'Maybe you should think about going home,' he suggested gently. 'This can be a lousy city to be alone in.'

'The Saint Louis Institute for Orphans?' the twenty-three-year-old asked through her tears. 'I don't think so.'

'Come with me,' Mitch said.

'I never knew my parents,' Felicity told Ione. 'The orphanage called me Felicity for happiness and Gravois for the street where I was found. With that name, I figured I couldn't help but become famous.'

Jenna Bell had been sent after high school from Alliance, Ohio, with a letter from Ione's mother.

'This is the daughter of our new minister,' Mrs. Meecham had written. 'She wants to design clothes for a living, and has convinced her parents that she can only do this in New York. Everyone will feel so much better if you keep an eye on her, you being a teacher and all.'

'I'm free,' Jenna had cried her first night on Sullivan Street, whirling around, her carrot-colored curls sticking straight out. 'You have no idea what it's like to be a fourth-generation minister's daughter – with red hair.'

Ione helped the teenager find a job as a seamstress on Seventh Avenue and arranged for her to enroll at Cooper Union.

Kevin was next, and after that, the pattern was set. Sometimes the number taking refuge in the three-room flat swelled from five to as many as ten, depending on who needed a bed at the time. Karen met them in September, through Ethan, who lived there until just before Thanksgiving. When his number came up, they all went down to a street corner near Battery Park to see him off on the first leg of his underground journey to Canada.

There was something very comfortable about these people, and Karen soon found herself spending every possible moment with them. Their secret was that they genuinely cared about one another in a way Karen had never experienced before. There was no rivalry here, no petty jealousies among them. No one had anything another wanted because they shared everything they had – their money, their clothes, their abilities, even their bodies.

Karen knew that Mitch slept with Ione and sometimes with Felicity, and that Kevin slept with Felicity and occasionally with Jenna, and that Jenna spent several evenings a week with John, a sculptor who lived in a studio apartment upstairs. Like Demelza's loft, the bedroom floor was carpeted in wall-to-wall mattresses, and visitors were always welcome to join in.

Once, such an arrangement would have made Karen turn and run, but she had come a long way in a short time. Much of that, she realized, had to do with the matter-of-fact approach these people had to life and living, and the ease with which they accepted one another's boundaries. There was never any pressure. Certainly, no one ever pressured Karen. They took her into the fold and never challenged the limits she set. She was one of the family, on whatever terms she chose, and that was all they cared about. No one ever crossed the line.

Arlene was dating an orthopedist from Bellevue and

often did not come home, so Karen got into the habit of dropping by Sullivan Street several nights a week. The women cooked, the men rolled joints, and then they would meet to share the fruits of their labors. Sometimes, if it got late and Karen was feeling particularly mellow, she would grab a blanket and curl up, undisturbed, on one of the mattresses.

The Garden of Eden had actually been her idea, born while they were toasting in the New Year, having emptied the contribution can and splurged on a rather decent bottle of champagne. The wine bubbled right down to Karen's toes, and with the weed she had already smoked, heaven was a three-room apartment in the run-down heart of Greenwich Village.

'I love you all,' she said when the toast came around to her. 'You took me in and treated me like one of you, right from the start, and you never asked for anything in return. You nurtured me and encouraged me and gave me space, and then you waited to see if I would bloom. I want to thank you for that, and wish all of you as much happiness in 1970 as you gave me in 1969. If this place were a garden, you'd be the most magnificent flowers growing.'

It was the longest speech she had made in seven years.

'What a lovely thing to say,' Ione cried, rushing over to hug her.

'What a lovely idea,' Mitch said. He took a long look around the common room and a big smile slowly lit up his bearded face. 'I bet we could do it.'

'Do what?' asked Felicity.

'Why, turn this dump into a garden, of course … the Garden of Eden,' he replied. 'I could do the sketches right on the walls to get us started and I can get the paint cheap. All we need is enough manpower to bring it to life.'

'I don't remember the lease on this apartment saying anything about going Michelangelo,' Ione protested.

But the artist was in his element. 'The landlord'll love it once it's done. After all, we're going to provide him with something of inestimable value – an original Mitchell Rankin – free of charge.'

'What the hell,' Kevin said. 'The old place could use a face-lift.'

'I can make new curtains and pillows,' offered Jenna.

'I guess I can handle a brush,' Felicity allowed.

'Then it's settled,' exclaimed Mitch. 'I'll do some preliminary drawings in the morning.' He beamed at them. 'It will be my first masterpiece.'

And, as far as Karen could judge, it was.

Mitch had created a spectacularly lush version of Eden that was perhaps more Tahitian than biblical. A thick green carpet of grass populated by inquisitive little creatures and wildflowers crept up the common-room walls and was bordered by a colorful mass of bushes, out of which poked great stalks of hibiscus and birds-of-paradise.

In the bedroom, fish frolicked in a crystal-clear pool, and the kitchen flaunted a tangle of blooming vines, a preening parrot, and a wide-eyed owl peering through the branches of a jacaranda tree. The whole thing was tied together by fruit trees that dripped with peaches and pears and oranges. A smiling serpent hung down from a bough of apple blossoms. A big yellow sun occupied one whole corner of the ceiling, and in another, Ione's clouds dotted a brilliant blue sky. In addition to basic brushwork, Mitch was using his trademark serrated palette knife to create texture. As a result, the scenes had a three-dimensional look that made them come alive.

They would paint until ten o'clock, stopping only for supper. Then they would sit around, smoke a few joints and contemplate their handiwork. It was finished on the second Sunday in February, the same day Karen turned twenty-eight.

'So we have two things to celebrate,' Ione said, digging deep into the contribution can for enough money to buy a good steak and a bottle of Bordeaux.

Kevin brought some good pot. Felicity even baked a cake. Karen made an excuse not to go home to Great Neck. After the food and wine had been consumed and the best wishes offered, Kevin brought out his pipe and passed it around. Then they turned off the overhead lights and wandered from room to room, surveying their accomplishment by candlelight. Karen had never felt more at home, more at peace, more mellow.

'Would that reality could be like this,' Kevin sighed. He was a philosophy major this term.

'Life sure isn't the way I expected it would be when I started out,' Felicity mused. 'I expected to be dancing on Broadway by the time I was twenty. Then it was twenty-five. Then it was thirty. Now I wonder about thirty-five.'

Jenna giggled. 'I never expected I'd actually come to New York and study fashion design. But in five years, I want to have my own label and be sold in the most exclusive shops in town.'

Ione stretched like a cat. 'I'm going to have a healthy kid, and tenure.'

'In five years, I'm going to be hanging in the Museum of Modern Art,' Mitch proclaimed, 'Or, at the very least, the Guggenheim.'

'I just want to get my degree and get on with my life,' Kevin declared. 'So Nixon better keep his goddamn campaign promise and get us the hell out of Vietnam.'

Everyone turned to Karen, whose only plans were for a life that had nothing to do with her now.

'Where do you want to be in five years?' Ione asked.

Karen closed her eyes and looked into the future. But there was nothing to see because, she realized with dismay, she didn't have the faintest idea where she wanted to be in five *days*, much less five years.

PART FOUR
1971

Evil is easy, and has infinite forms.

– Blaise Pascal

one

May could be the most glorious month in San Francisco, once the winter rains had tapered off and before the summer fog rolled in, when the thermometer reached up into the seventies and the air smelled freshly scrubbed and the sun sparkled off the bay, and people went around with smiles on their faces. It was a month often overlooked by tourists, much to the delight of those who lived there and kept the splendor a closely guarded secret.

On one such perfect Tuesday in early May, Elizabeth Willmont was indulging in her favorite pastime – shopping. It was a rare occasion when a committee meeting was canceled at the last minute and Elizabeth found herself with a free day. She had promptly persuaded her husband to take her to lunch and then she made a beeline for Union Square.

It was no secret to anyone that Elizabeth loved to shop, and with her Modigliani-like figure and substantial bank account, that was understandable. The product of a Colorado millionaire and a French beauty, few things delighted the young socialite more than going from one store to the next, trying on item after item, selecting what pleased her and discarding what didn't.

By mid-afternoon, she had purchased three dresses, two suits, and a whole host of accessories. Ordinarily, this would have put an enormous smile on her face, but as she came out of Maison Mendessolle, the elite salon in the St. Francis Hotel, and turned onto Post Street, it was an uneasy frown that creased her lovely features.

Halfway down the block, Elizabeth stopped as though something in a display window had caught her eye and caught instead a glimpse of the reflection behind her. The girl in the red coat was still there.

Elizabeth sighed. She had first noticed the girl in the fine-china department at Macy's, just a slip of a thing with straggly hair and big brown eyes and blotches on her skin, who showed no interest whatever in Lenox or Minton and surely must have been roasting, all bundled up in that heavy coat.

Next, she turned up in the shoe department at Magnin's, when Elizabeth was buying the silk pumps. And then there she was in Maison Mendessolle, looking terribly out of place but standing her ground, while Elizabeth chose a gown for a charity ball she was helping to organize.

The girl never came close enough for conversation, although it was clear she had something on her mind. But she never let Elizabeth out of sight, either. And in that absurd red coat, she was anything but inconspicuous. Even the saleslady noticed.

'That person over there, Mrs. Willmont,' she whispered, 'do you know her?'

Elizabeth glanced casually over her shoulder. 'No, I'm afraid I don't.'

'Well, she certainly isn't one of our customers, and she's been staring at you for the longest time.'

Elizabeth shrugged it off. It didn't do to tell help any more than they needed to know. Gossip that was started by a careless remark could spread like a brushfire and devastate the select social circle in which the Willmonts traveled. But the girl was making her very uncomfortable. If she had something to say, Elizabeth wished she would say it and get it over with.

Not that she wasn't used to being stared at. As one of San Francisco's most beautiful and stylish young matrons, Elizabeth had been photographed, interviewed, emulated and envied from the moment Robert had brought her to California as his wife three and a half years ago.

Even before that, she had often found herself in the public eye. After all, she was the only daughter of Archer and Denise Avery of Denver, where her father owned Avery Industries, and where her family was every bit as influential as the Draytons were in San Francisco.

Having inherited her elegant French mother's flaming red hair, slanting green eyes, chiseled features and graceful ways, Elizabeth was indisputably the outstanding debutante of 1963, setting a standard for every Denver debutante to follow. By the time it was over, she had received no less than half a dozen marriage proposals. She declined them all, however, choosing instead four years at Vassar and then a handsome young attorney from

California whom she met at Aspen.

It was, as far as Elizabeth was concerned, love at first sight. She had lost one of her ski poles and was having considerable difficulty trying to negotiate the slope without it when he came to her rescue.

'I believe this belongs to you,' he said with a poker face, presenting her with the wayward bamboo stick.

'My goodness,' she exclaimed with a toss of her Raggedy Ann hair, 'I never even noticed it was gone.'

'Well done,' he declared with a hearty laugh and a broad wink of approval.

One look deep into his incredible aquamarine eyes was all it took. After returning to Vassar, she spent several anxious weeks – replaying every moment of their days together, recalling how well his ski outfit fit him, how wind-tanned he had been, what a decidedly sexy mouth he had, and how she had felt when he held her hand – until he finally telephoned.

Theirs was a long-distance romance that consisted of flowery letters and exorbitant telephone bills and three very closely chaperoned visits at the Averys' gingerbread mansion in the heart of old Denver.

'My family's horribly old-fashioned,' she had said, giggling on the occasion of Robert's third stay, during the spring break of her senior year at Vassar, when they were unable to escape from watchful eyes for so much as two minutes. 'I hope you don't mind.'

'Of course I mind,' he grumbled, unused to this cat-and-mouse game he was being forced to play. 'I suppose I'm going to have to marry you, just so I can get you alone.'

It was not exactly the proposal that Elizabeth had spent her girlhood dreaming of, but she hardly noticed. Her feet didn't quite touch the ground for the rest of his stay.

'I think I'd better know something about your prospects, young man,' Archer Avery declared, when his daughter came seeking his blessing.

Elizabeth would never forget it. Robert sat in her father's study, with just the right mixture of self-assurance and deference, and looked the intimidating patriarch directly in the eye, something that few of the boys who courted her had ever been brave enough, or foolish enough, to do.

'I'm a senior associate with Sutton, Wells, Willmont and Spaulding, sir,' he said with confidence. 'I believe that you're acquainted with Jonah Spaulding.'

The older man nodded.

'It was my father's firm, before he died,' Robert continued, 'and I have every reason to believe that I will be asked to join the partnership when the time comes.'

'I assume that means you plan on taking Elizabeth to San Francisco to live?'

'Yes, of course,' Robert replied. 'I'm sure she'll love it there. It's a lot like Denver. But we won't necessarily live there forever. You see, sir, once I've established my reputation at the bar, I'm planning on going into politics.'

Elizabeth's ears perked up. Robert had never said anything to her about having political aspirations.

'Politics?' Archer echoed, stiffening slightly.

'I'm a Drayton,' Robert explained. 'It's a matter of tradition that Draytons give something back. My ancestors have donated parks, established museums, and endowed schools. One set up the Drayton Foundation, which provides scholarships and does other philanthropic work. Several served as judges. Others built bridges and railroads. One even sponsored soup kitchens during the Depression. Each chooses his own way. I've chosen politics.'

Archer grunted and scowled and shifted uncomfortably in his chair. He was a bull of a man and not one who bothered to keep his feelings hidden, but then he had never been able to deny his daughter anything.

'Well, I just don't mind telling you, young man,' he rumbled, 'I don't like the sound of that. I don't like the sound of that at all.'

'I know that politics has always been a dirty word in some circles,' Robert said quickly. 'I can tell you that it certainly has been in mine. But times are changing, and I believe that government thinking has to change, too, if we expect to maintain the proper balance of interests in this country. And that means that some of us, no matter how reluctant we may be, have to do our bit.'

Archer clasped his fingers across his chest and squinted at the lawyer seated in front of him. 'Just how far do you intend to go with your bit, may I ask?'

For a moment, Robert allowed himself to look slightly surprised at the question. Then he grinned.

'Why, all the way to the White House, of course,' he replied.

Their engagement was announced the following week, and three months to the day after Elizabeth's graduation from Vassar, she and Robert were married at St. John's Cathedral, and then feted at a lavish reception for twelve hundred at the Denver Country Club, which the *Post* later described as one of the major social events of the decade.

The new Mr. and Mrs. Willmont honeymooned in

the south of France, at a villa that belonged to one of Elizabeth's French cousins. They spent some of their time swimming in the Mediterranean and browsing around the quaint little towns along the Côte d'Azur, but most of their time was spent between the sheets of the huge wrought-iron bed provided for their pleasure. The staff at the villa was kept busy changing the sheets several times each day.

Elizabeth delighted in every moment of it. Right from the start, Robert was able to generate such a feverish level of desire in her that their mutual climaxes left her laughing and crying and begging for more – far more than even her forthright French mother had led her to expect. She was prepared for an adjustment period, a time during which they would learn each other's bodies and each other's likes and dislikes, but there seemed to be no need for that. Somehow, he knew exactly how to please her.

'Now that you've had a chance to sample the goods, so to speak,' Elizabeth teased her husband one morning, 'I hope I was worth putting up with all that horrid chaperoning.'

But he only grunted and reached for her again. Robert was insatiable when it came to sex, openly fondling her at a restaurant, murmuring seductive suggestions in the middle of a concert, whisking her away from a cocktail party given in their honor by some distant relatives. He thought nothing of cutting short any activity in which they were engaged the moment the urge overcame him.

Elizabeth never objected. On the contrary, she found herself as eager as he. But Robert was a big man who could be somewhat rough in the throes of passion and she was unprepared for the intensity of it all. It wasn't long before she was black and blue on the outside and more than a little tender on the inside.

'Sweetheart, do you think we could maybe not do it for a day or so?' she asked one afternoon when Robert attempted to cut short a shopping expedition to Saint-Tropez.

'What do you mean?' he replied.

'Well, as you have reason to know, I'm not exactly used to all this … activity' – she giggled timidly – 'and I guess I must be extra-sensitive inside because, well, it's really kind of painful now, everytime we … well, you know.'

'Shit,' her husband exploded. 'We're on our honeymoon, for Christ's sake. And what the fuck is it that people are supposed to do on their honeymoon?'

'I'm sure it'll be all right again in a day or two,' she protested, wincing at his outburst.

He stamped his foot petulantly. 'And to think I got married just so I could have it whenever I wanted it.'

'Well, I certainly hope that wasn't the only reason,' she replied with a toss of her red hair.

'All those months I waited for you,' he grumbled. 'I never had to wait that long for anyone, but I waited for you. Now we're hardly married a week and already you're pulling the old headache routine.'

'It's not a headache and it's not forever,' she said. 'And the sooner we stop, the sooner we can start again.' She batted her eyelashes at him. 'In the meantime, maybe there's something I can do to make up for it.'

Robert looked at her in surprise. 'Now you're talking,' he said, taking her firmly by the arm. 'Let's go. I can't wait to see what you have in mind.'

What she had in mind – dinner on the terrace, a

bottle of champagne, a long leisurely bath and a back rub – didn't turn out to be exactly what he had in mind.

'That sounds awful,' she protested when he described what he wanted to do.

'I don't see how you can dismiss something until you try it,' he replied, nuzzling her. 'Most of the women I know really get off on it.'

Most of the women in Robert's circle were no doubt chic and sophisticated and older, and despite the fact that he had chosen her over the rest, Elizabeth didn't particularly care to come out on the wrong side of a comparison.

'All right,' she said with a reluctant sigh. After all, he was her husband now and anything between married people was supposed to be acceptable. Besides, she had promised to obey.

Elizabeth had to admit that what he proceeded to do to her was rather thrilling and she achieved three orgasms in rapid succession and was beginning to think she might agree with all those other women of his when he rolled over onto his back and pulled her down on top of him. The ecstasy quickly turned to revulsion.

'I don't know how to do it,' she mumbled, hoping he would suggest an alternative.

Instead, he gave her explicit instructions and held her head firmly so she couldn't pull away.

'I didn't hear you complaining when I brought you off three times,' he reminded her. 'Now let's see what you can do for me.'

Gagging and sputtering, she managed to make the best of it, but the experience was so distasteful to her that the very next morning she slipped down into town and bought some salve.

'That's too bad,' he murmured when she grit her teeth and told him she was no longer sore. 'I rather like it the other way.'

They came home after a month to the house on Jackson Street where Robert had been born. Amanda Willmont insisted that it was much too big a place for her now that she was alone.

'I rattle around in here and there's just no point to it,' she said. 'I want you and Elizabeth to have the house, and I can take a small apartment nearby.'

But Robert wouldn't hear of it.

'This house has been your home for more than thirty years,' he insisted, 'and no one's going to put you out of it. I think we should all live here together.'

'Don't you think you ought to consult with Elizabeth before you make a decision like that?' Amanda asked, trying not to look too pleased.

'Elizabeth will do what I say,' he replied. 'Besides, she's an old-fashioned girl and family means a lot to her. She'll love the idea.'

Elizabeth hated the idea.

'It's not that I'm not fond of your mother,' she said. 'It's just that I'd like us to have a place of our own.'

'But it'll be almost like having that,' he assured her. 'She's an old lady and she rarely comes out of her room. Besides, it really is a terrific house and I wouldn't be able to afford to give you anything nearly so grand.'

'I don't mind starting small,' his new wife replied.

'Well, sure,' he agreed with an irritable sigh. 'I wouldn't either, if we didn't have a choice. But we do, so why don't we take advantage of it?'

'I know I'm being foolish,' Elizabeth said stubbornly. 'But I think couples should be on their own when they get married.'

'Well, I wouldn't want this to be part of our decision,' he said, changing tactics, 'but the truth is, I'm worried about Mother. She's not well and she's getting weaker all the time. I don't think she's going to last much longer and I don't want her to be alone. I just wouldn't feel right if we were off having a grand time on our own and something awful happened to her and I wasn't there. I'm her only child, you know. I'm all she has in the world.'

Elizabeth's green eyes filled with sympathy and she covered his hand with her own.

'Of course you are,' she cried. 'And forgive me for being so selfish. I didn't realize she was that bad off. You certainly can't leave her alone, I understand that now, and I love you for being such a devoted son. Of course we'll move in with her. The most important thing is to help make her last days happy ones.'

Robert beamed. 'You'll see,' he promised. 'Everything is going to work out just fine.'

Within a month of taking up residence at her new home on the crown of Pacific Heights, Elizabeth learned two things. The first was that San Francisco was nothing at all like Denver. The second was that Amanda Drayton Willmont would probably outlive them all.

The city had taken a bit of getting used to. For someone who had grown up with crunchy white winters, rain was a poor substitute. For someone used to towering mountains, the endless stretch of the Pacific Ocean was disconcerting. For someone raised on the flat Denver plateau, the peaks and valleys of San Francisco's streets were a shock.

Once she had married a Drayton, her place in the city's inner social circle was ensured – but not her popularity. That she had to earn on her own. She was asked to join all the right clubs, serve on all the right committees, and sponsor all the right causes. It was an endless round of luncheons and parties and fund-raisers that left her head spinning and her calendar filled.

She said yes to everything, because she didn't realize she could have said no. Very soon, the Jackson Street parlor had been transformed into the principal gathering place for the 'planners of good deeds,' as Robert jokingly referred to them, and San Francisco's social matrons bustled in and out from morning to midnight.

Amanda was furious.

'Turning my house into a meeting hall,' she fussed on more than one occasion. 'That wasn't what I had in mind when I invited you to come and stay.'

'I'm very sorry they disturb you,' her daughter-in-law replied, biting her tongue. 'But the causes are so worthy.'

Perhaps because she was so young and so eager to please, Elizabeth soon became the darling of the elite crowd and, with her wild hair and classic beauty, the darling of the media, as well. Newspaper photographers fell all over themselves to capture her on film. Television cameras seemed to pick her out of a crowd. Although she rarely had anything earthshaking to say, reporters sought her out for comments on everything from haute couture to Haight-Ashbury.

She had inherited her mother's elegant Parisian style which, together with her father's generous allowance and her own boundless energy for shopping, resulted in an exquisite wardrobe that provided her with the perfect outfit for every occasion.

'Does your daddy own the majority stock in Magnin's?' Robert roared when he saw the bills.

'It's my money,' she reminded him. 'And I should think you would want me to look my best.'

'You're a Drayton now,' he snapped, 'and Draytons do not go around flaunting their wealth.'

Elizabeth smiled at him sweetly. 'The only thing I'm trying to flaunt is that I'm the wife of a very successful attorney who will one day be President of the United States. But if you think that's the wrong image, I'll gladly donate all my clothes to the charity of your choice and wear sackcloth to your firm's Christmas party next week.'

'Isn't there a compromise here somewhere?' he grumbled.

Always the politician, she thought with amusement. 'Sure,' she replied, looking pointedly at his six-hundred-dollar suit. '*You* can wear the sackcloth.'

Robert never mentioned her wardrobe again and Elizabeth continued to set fashion standards among her peers in the cosmopolitan city by the bay. Matrons of means tried to emulate her, less affluent ladies envied her, bachelors and husbands alike attempted, without success, to compromise her.

By the end of her first year as Mrs. Robert Drayton Willmont of Pacific Heights, Elizabeth Avery was a social triumph. She was one of the first to don a miniskirt, one of the last to abandon hats, one of the few to forgo the perils of platform shoes, and she stopped conversation dead when she wore a black satin pantsuit to the opening of the opera.

Early in their second year of marriage, Elizabeth

became pregnant, but lost the child in the tenth week. She was devastated, even though her doctors assured her that such occurrences were not uncommon and it in no way meant she couldn't have children in the future.

By the end of the summer, she had conceived for the second time. Fearful of another tragedy, Elizabeth cut her social obligations to a minimum and spent much of her time in bed. Her efforts were in vain. She miscarried again, this time during her fifth month, and along with the fetus she almost lost her life.

The doctors no longer made light of the situation. They suggested that it would be unwise for Elizabeth to risk a third pregnancy for at least a year. They recommended a long rest, perhaps even a change of scene. They advised the young couple to cease all sexual intercourse for at least three months and thereafter to exercise extreme caution.

If she had expected an explosion from her husband, she was surprised. He accepted the warning in stony silence.

'We can do that other thing you like so much,' she offered, because she felt so guilty.

'Sure,' he replied carelessly.

But she noticed that he began to stay up later at night, frequently not coming to bed until she was already asleep. Several times, when she went looking for him, she found him in the library, snoring over a briefcase full of work and a half-empty bottle of Scotch.

A despondent Elizabeth went home to Denver. Her mother and father and three brothers welcomed her back with loving concern and fussed over her as though she were a visiting head of state.

It was marvelous to be back in Denver, but she missed Robert more than she had ever believed possible, and cut her visit short after only three weeks. She returned home to find that he had moved into an adjoining bedroom.

'I just won't be able to sleep next to you and not want to – well, you know,' he said in explanation.

'I understand,' she said, although she didn't, not really.

'So I thought, until the doctors say it's okay again, this would be easier for both of us.'

The weeks slipped into months, the months moved toward a year. Once the doctors gave their permission, the Willmonts began to practice careful sex but Robert continued to sleep in the adjoining room. As time passed, husband and wife settled into a routine. Robert would stay with Elizabeth on Saturday nights, during which they would rekindle some of the hot flames of their honeymoon, and then they would share a long, leisurely breakfast in bed together on Sunday mornings.

But always, in the back of her mind, Elizabeth thought of it as temporary, and she lived for the day when the doctors would tell her it was all right to try again to have a child.

Shortly after Robert had informed Archer Avery of his intention to enter politics, he and Elizabeth had mapped out a strategy. The key, Robert told her, was to start small and build rapidly. He was sure that he could use his Drayton connections to capture a local election, and once he had proved himself a winner, he reasoned, the party bosses would fall all over themselves to promote him – all the way to the White House.

But first, Robert had to become a partner at Sutton, Wells, Willmont and Spaulding. This was essential, he explained, in establishing his credibility. Moreover, to maintain his timetable, he had to do it by the time he was thirty-two.

To keep the odds in his favor, he told Elizabeth upon her return from Denver, it would be necessary for him to maintain a higher visibility in the firm.

'For the past few years,' he said, 'I've been much more interested in my bride than in my business.'

Higher visibility, according to Robert, meant assuming a heavier workload that would involve stretching the limits of his specialization, accepting some of the cases that no one else wanted, and generally calling attention to himself through a clever combination of diligence and excellence.

'And the only way I'm going to be able to do that,' he said, 'is to work longer hours.'

'I hope you're not talking about weekends,' Elizabeth exclaimed. 'We can't possibly renege on any of our social obligations. Why, the telephone's been ringing off the hook ever since I got back, and now there's hardly a weekend right through Labor Day that we're not already committed.'

'Well, if weekends are out,' Robert said with a sigh of resignation, 'then I have no choice but to work late during the week.'

'How late?'

'That's hard to say,' he replied smoothly. 'Why don't we just play it by ear.'

Soon, Robert was staying on at the office one or two nights a week, sometimes not getting home until three o'clock in the morning. Occasionally, when Elizabeth awoke and went looking for him, she would find him sound asleep in his room with all his clothes still on.

'I worry about him,' she admitted to Amanda during one of the increasingly frequent occasions when the two women dined alone together. 'He's going to wear himself out. I'm not sure that becoming a partner one year sooner or later is worth ruining his health.'

But Amanda only shrugged. 'Men must do what men must do,' she said vaguely, leaving Elizabeth more confused than reassured.

'You're not getting enough sleep,' she said to Robert when six months had passed. 'If you keep up this kind of pace, you're going to make yourself sick. I think you ought to ease up a little.'

'I've never felt better,' he assured her. 'Besides, how do you think it would look to the partners if I were to tell them that my wife didn't think I was up to the job?'

'That's not what I said,' she protested.

'What if I did slack off?' he posed. 'You can bet the competition won't, and I can't afford to get left behind.' He winked at her. 'After all, I'm already thirty-one.'

'You know you're going to make partner someday. Does it really matter all that much when?'

'It matters to me,' he said flatly. 'And I thought it mattered to you, too.'

'You matter to me.'

'Then why don't you want me to have what I want?'

'I do want you to have it,' she protested. 'It's just that … I miss you.'

'I miss you, too,' he assured her. 'But we made a plan and we have to stick to it if we want to get where we're going. I intend for you to be the first First Lady of the twenty-first century. And, if accomplishing that means we have to make a few minor sacrifices now, I say it's worth it.'

'When you put it that way,' she conceded reluctantly, not bothering to tell him that being the First Lady was not really one of her greatest ambitions.

But then, for a month, he didn't work late at all.

'Things are a little slow right now,' he explained.

He showed up promptly for dinner at seven o'clock and even sat with her well into the evenings, as he used to, but he was preoccupied much of the time and seemed out of sorts.

Soon enough, the late hours began again. Only, instead of one or two nights a week, it was now three and even four. There was always an excuse, always a promise that it wouldn't be forever, and always a reminder of their ultimate aim.

But Elizabeth was lonely. While her days were filled with one charitable endeavor or another, her evenings were long and empty. Her mother-in-law was little comfort. Amanda retired to her room immediately after dinner and did not encourage company. To relieve the boredom, Elizabeth took to going out for walks after dinner, wandering up and down the steep streets, pausing sometimes to look in the windows of her neighbors, at families who had gathered to share the end of the day together. But then her heart would begin to ache for her two lost babies and she would turn away, searching for something to help her forget the tragedy.

So it was that she came to accept an invitation for dinner and the ballet one Tuesday evening shortly after the Willmonts had celebrated their third wedding anniversary.

It was an innocent-enough occasion, arranged by Marian Pinckton, one of San Francisco's formidable matriarchs, who worked with Elizabeth on a number of committees and who needed a partner for her visiting nephew.

'I apologize for this being such a last-minute thing,' Marian explained. 'But the lady who was supposed to join us came down with influenza this morning and I've been just beside myself trying to think what to do. Then I remembered you saying something about Robert occasionally working late during the week, and I was hoping that tonight might possibly be one of those nights.'

'As it happens, it is, Marian,' Elizabeth replied, barely able to contain her delight. 'And as I have nothing on my calendar for this evening, I'd be happy to fill in for you.'

The nephew turned out to be a fastidious gentleman in his early forties, with sparse hair and an Adolf Hitler mustache, who sat up very straight and didn't have two words to say to anyone around the dinner table, despite Elizabeth's best efforts. From the corner of her eye, she watched him separate his salad into little piles of tomato and cucumber and lettuce and onion, and then proceed to eat each ingredient in its turn. After that, he cut his filet mignon into minuscule pieces and then dabbed his napkin at the corner of his mouth with each tiny bite. Elizabeth half-expected to see him take his fork and spear one green pea at a time, and she had to try very hard not to giggle.

Everyone at the table seemed to talk around him, even his aunt, as though they didn't know how to include him in the topic of conversation and had decided not to bother.

How lucky I am to have Robert, Elizabeth thought to herself, making one of the unfailingly favorable comparisons she had become so fond of making since her marriage. He was so handsome, so winsome, so charming that people couldn't help but warm to him, and he quickly became the center of any group he entered.

Elizabeth felt very sorry for all the women in the world who were still out there looking, especially if her dinner partner were an example of what was available. Mrs. Robert Drayton Willmont smiled a private little smile. She knew she could afford to be just a tiny bit smug, because she already had a lock on the best man in the whole world.

The nephew took Elizabeth's elbow as they crossed the busy intersection at Van Ness and Grove on their way to the Opera House.

'I find that drivers at intersections can be exceedingly unpredictable,' he said. It was the longest sentence he had uttered all evening.

The San Francisco Opera House was an imposing building, with ornately gilded ceilings and crystal chandeliers. Naturally, the Pinckton box was in the center of the dress circle. The nephew sat primly beside her, his legs crossed, his hands folded neatly in his lap, his attention focused on the maroon curtain that would soon rise, making not the slightest attempt at any of the social graces. Elizabeth sighed and began to read her program.

From the second row of chairs, Marian Pinckton leaned forward and laid a hand on Elizabeth's shoulder.

'Don't be offended that he isn't taken with your charms, my dear,' she whispered in her young protégée's ear. 'He's one of *them*, you know.'

Fortunately, the lights dimmed at that moment, sparing Elizabeth the necessity of a reply. If she had understood Marian correctly – and how could she not have – it was the first time she had knowingly been this close to a homosexual person before, and the idea both enthralled and appalled her.

Elizabeth stole a sidelong look at the man next to her, seeing him now in a whole new light. She had a thousand questions, none of which she would ever dare ask. There were some things, she had been taught, that a lady just didn't discuss. Not that his sexual orientation made any difference to her in relation to this evening. She would gladly have part-nered King Kong if it meant one less night to spend at home alone.

The curtain went up and the ballet began and Elizabeth didn't think again about her escort until the first act was over and they filed out of the box for the intermission.

'Would you like champagne?' the nephew asked politely.

'Of course she would,' Marian answered for her guest. 'We all would.'

The nephew took Elizabeth's elbow again as the party of eight began to edge its way through the crowd toward the bar.

'I find that theatergoers at intermissions can be exceedingly unpredictable,' he said.

Elizabeth wasn't sure whether he had intended to be witty, but she burst out laughing – a delicious ripple that ran the length of the scale and back again. A nearby group glanced over in curiosity, among them a distinguished gray-haired gentleman.

'Elizabeth?' he inquired. 'Is that you?'

She turned at the mention of her name and looked up into the intelligent eyes of Stanton Wells, the managing partner of Robert's law firm.

'Hello, Stanton,' she said, offering her hand. 'How nice to see you.'

'How nice to see you, too,' Wells said and then glanced around. 'And where's that handsome husband of yours?'

Elizabeth chuckled. 'At the office, of course. You and your partners have him slaving away almost every night these days.'

'Really?' Wells asked in surprise. 'I wasn't aware of that. Well, I can see we'll have to do something to correct the situation.'

'No objection, your honor,' she quipped.

But Wells wasn't looking at her anymore, he was looking to her right. With some embarrassment, Elizabeth realized that the nephew still had hold of her elbow.

'I beg your pardon,' she said, hastily disengaging herself. 'May I introduce Mrs. Pinckton's nephew, who is visiting from Chicago.'

The two men shook hands stiffly.

'Are you enjoying the ballet, Stanton?' Elizabeth asked.

'Very much,' he replied. '*Giselle* has always been one of my favorites.'

'Mine, too,' Elizabeth agreed.

'We were on our way to get champagne,' the nephew said abruptly. 'Before the intermission is over.'

'By all means,' Wells murmured. Then he turned to Elizabeth. 'Enjoy the rest of your evening, my dear,' he said. 'And you can be sure I'll look into that little matter we discussed.'

While it was true that she would have preferred to have Robert at home with her in the evenings, Elizabeth was not the kind of woman to go behind her husband's back. She sat through the rest of the ballet wishing she had not been so flip with Stanton Wells. A complaining wife was not an attractive asset and the last thing she wanted was to damage Robert's chances of becoming a partner at the law firm.

She thought of seeking Stanton out at the end of the performance and asking him to forget their conversation, but she was afraid that would only make matters worse. It had been such a casual exchange, there was a chance he would forget all about it in the light of day. She fervently hoped so, but a nagging feeling told her that he wouldn't and that her flippant words would come back to haunt her.

She was right. The repercussions were almost immediate. Robert stormed into the house the next evening, well before the seven-o'clock dinner hour, the earliest he had been home on a weeknight in months.

'Just what the hell did you think you were doing?' he roared. 'Complaining to Wells about my hours and parading yourself around town on someone else's arm?'

'I wasn't parading myself,' she protested. 'I was doing Marian Pinckton a favor. And Stanton asked me where you were. What should I have said? Would it have been better if I'd told him a lie?'

'If you'd been at home where you belong,' he snapped, 'you wouldn't have had to tell him anything.'

'But it gets so tiresome being alone all week long.'

'Alone? You're not alone. My mother's here, and

you've got a houseful of servants at your beck and call.'

There was no point in telling him that Amanda was less than social, or that a servant turning down her bed or bringing her a glass of warm milk did not constitute company for an evening.

'I don't know why you're making such a fuss,' she said. 'What's wrong with Stanton knowing that you're in the office working? Isn't that what you wanted?'

'Forget about that,' he retorted. 'What's wrong is when one of my partners has to come and tell me that my wife is out cavorting with another man.'

'Stanton Wells didn't say anything of the kind,' she declared. 'And I wasn't cavorting.'

'Then why did this guy have his hands all over you?'

'He had his hand on my elbow, for pity's sake. He was guiding me through the crowd.'

'I don't want any man putting his hands anywhere on you for any reason. I refuse to be humiliated by gossips wagging their tongues behind my back. Besides, you know perfectly well if you give a man a hand, he'll try to take an arm.'

A vision of the nephew behaving as Robert suggested suddenly popped into Elizabeth's head and she began to laugh.

'I don't see anything funny about this,' he growled.

'You would, if you knew,' she gasped.

'Knew what?'

'The other man you're so concerned about – well, he's Marian Pinckton's nephew, on his obligatory annual visit. He separates his salad and he cuts his meat into pieces the size of a crouton – and he's a homosexual.'

'You're kidding,' Robert scoffed.

'Honest Injun,' she assured him.

'How do you know?'

'Marian told me herself.'

'Well, I'll be damned.'

'I tried to wait up for you last night. I wanted to tell you all about it, but I fell asleep. Too much wine, I guess.'

'Nevertheless,' he said, somewhat mollified, 'it doesn't look right for you to go out without me like that. After all, you're my wife, and as such you have your reputation to protect, not to mention the Drayton name. I feel I must insist that you don't do it again.'

Elizabeth sighed heavily. She supposed there might be some truth in what he said. 'I'm sorry if I disappointed you,' she said. 'I won't do it again.'

'Do I have your promise?'

'You have my promise.'

'There's my good girl,' he said, kissing her lightly on the cheek. 'Besides, you're always so busy with all your charity work, I should think a few quiet evenings at home would be good for you.'

'Yes, Robert.'

Elizabeth had been as good as her word, thereafter politely declining all invitations that did not include her husband and even curtailing her nocturnal walks. She had a television set installed in her sitting room and spent the better part of her evenings involved in the triumphs and tragedies of the Partridge Family, who were always able to sing their way out of trouble, or Marcus Welby, who reminded Elizabeth of her family doctor back in Denver, or Ironside, who solved his San Francisco cases from a wheelchair.

* * *

It was eerie, she thought as she left Post Street for the interior of Gump's Department Store, but in some ways the fictional characters that now kept her company had become more compelling than many of the real people she knew.

Except for the girl in the red coat, that is – the one who had been following her all afternoon. She was certainly compelling enough. Elizabeth glanced over her shoulder, and like the proverbial itch she couldn't scratch, the girl was still there.

Gump's of San Francisco was a store unlike any other on earth. A playground for the rich, it boasted an eclectic collection of trinkets from every corner of the world and came within an inch of being a museum – a museum where the entire collection just happened to be for sale. Elizabeth often thought how much fun it would be to work for a while as a Gump's buyer.

She had nothing particular in mind to purchase on this day, but she walked purposefully to the stairs and started up. It was the red coat that finally got to her. Not so much that it was ridiculously out of season as that it was a color she dearly loved but could never wear because of her hair.

The furniture galleries on the third floor were not usually very busy, but there must have been a sale in progress this day. Elizabeth passed quickly through room after room until she finally found one, featuring an elegant dining suite, that was out of the way and empty. Then she stopped and whirled around, catching the girl completely off-guard.

'If there's something you want to say to me, please go ahead and say it,' she suggested kindly enough. 'We're alone here.'

'You're his wife, aren't you?' the girl said, after

taking a moment to recover her composure.

'I beg your pardon?'

'I said, you're Bobby's wife.'

Elizabeth winced. She detested the nickname that Amanda had bestowed upon her son during his infancy, and she had always refused to use it herself. How disconcerting it was now to hear it come rolling off the tongue of this unlikely stranger.

'If you mean Robert Willmont,' she said, 'yes, I'm his wife.'

'I know,' the girl confirmed. 'I've seen your picture in the paper lots of times, and Bobby would kill me if he knew but sometimes I take myself up to Pacific Heights and watch you coming and going.'

Up close, it was clear that the girl was younger than Elizabeth had first thought, probably not even out of her teens, and if it weren't for the blotches and the unkempt hair, she would have been quite pretty.

'You called my husband Bobby,' she said. 'Does that mean you know him well?'

The girl snorted. 'You could say that. Three or four nights a week for almost eight months now.'

Elizabeth felt as though someone had punched her in the stomach.

'Why would you say a thing like that?' she asked with difficulty.

'Because it's true,' the girl declared.

What Elizabeth wanted was to spit in the girl's face, scratch her eyes out, scream obscenities at her. Only, of course, she couldn't do any of those things.

'What do you want?' she asked rigidly.

'I want you to let him go.'

Try as she might, Elizabeth was unable to conceal her dismay. 'Are you talking about divorce?'

The girl nodded eagerly.

'But that's absurd.'

'Why?' the girl demanded. 'What's the point of holding on, now that you know?'

'I'm afraid I don't know anything,' Elizabeth corrected her.

The girl sighed. 'Bobby said you wouldn't understand. He said you'd fight the divorce. He said you don't care anything about his happiness, you just married him because he's a Drayton. I know you don't sleep in the same room together anymore, and you can't even give him children.'

It was like a knife thrust into Elizabeth's heart.

'My husband told you all that?'

'Sure,' the girl replied easily. 'Bobby tells me everything. Sometimes, that's all we do – just talk, for hours and hours. You see, we love each other.'

'He said that?' Elizabeth murmured.

'I know he wanted to tell you himself,' the girl assured her, 'but sometimes men are so slow about things. So I thought if I explained it to you – you know, woman to woman, then you'd see that we were really sincere and that it wasn't just some casual fling. Please, you'll let him go now, won't you – now that you see how it is? We're just meant to be together. I may not be so smart or so beautiful as you, but I guess I know how to make him happy better than you, and I can give him all the children he wants.'

With that, the girl opened her coat to reveal a swollen belly.

The knife twisted agonizingly. 'Are you saying that's my husband's child?'

'Well, of course,' the girl said. 'What'd you think?'

But Elizabeth didn't know what to think. Of all the

demons that had populated her worst nightmares, the demon of duplicity had never been among them. Was it possible that for these three and a half years she had been married to a man she didn't even know?

She looked back on all those evenings she had sat alone, waiting for Robert to come home from work. She remembered how sweet and sympathetic he had been after the miscarriages. She considered how much their Saturday nights and Sunday mornings meant to her. She thought about all their plans for the future. None of it made sense. She wondered if someone were playing a very cruel joke on her, but she couldn't imagine that anyone would hate her that much.

'Did my husband send you to speak to me?'

'Gosh, no!' the girl exclaimed. 'Jeepers, he'd split my lip or worse if he knew I was here.' Seeing Elizabeth's startled look, she shrugged. 'He did that once, when I made him mad. Sometimes, he hits me around when he's had too much to drink. Some men are like that, I guess, but I don't care, because he always comes back. I don't have anyone else.'

Elizabeth stared at the girl, overwhelmed with elation, because she now knew for certain that this was nothing but a horrible mistake.

'Now I know there's been a misunderstanding.' She breathed in relief. 'You see, my husband doesn't drink at all the way you describe. More important than that, he's a gentleman. He would never lay a hand on a woman. So it's obvious you must be talking about someone else.'

The girl reached up and pushed the hair back off her face, revealing a jagged scar down her cheek.

'It took eleven stitches,' she said, 'because he hit me

with the back of his right hand, the one he wears that big Harvard ring on.'

The elation, all too fragile, collapsed like a balloon. Elizabeth felt her knees beginning to buckle and then the room started to spin, and she reached out and grabbed hold of the back of a chair to steady herself.

She tried to think what she could possibly say next, but everything was so jumbled up in her brain that the only thing that came to mind was the hope that this whole confrontation wasn't real, after all, just a horrible scene from one of her television shows, and Marcus Welby was waiting in the wings with a miraculous cure.

Archer Avery had never taken a serious look at anyone other than Elizabeth's vivacious French mother in their entire thirty years together, and it was that kind of loyalty and devotion that Elizabeth had been raised to expect from her own marriage, which now made Robert's betrayal just that much harder to bear.

She wanted to hate the girl as she stood there, blooming with life. She wanted to make her the villain of the piece and blame her for everything. But for some reason, Elizabeth found herself feeling sorry for her instead. Perhaps it was because the girl was so young and vulnerable and because, sooner or later, Elizabeth realized dully, Robert was going to betray her, too.

'I hope you have a healthy baby,' she said in a toneless voice, and then she turned and walked away.

The girl stood stock-still, confusion and uncertainty written all over her face. She knew the interview was over, but she had not gotten what she had come for and time was running short.

Over the past eight months, Bobby had painted a very vivid picture of his wife, describing her as aloof and unemotional and far more interested in embellishing her wardrobe than in pleasing her husband. He claimed that she had lost all interest in sex once the doctors told her she couldn't get pregnant, and that she even went so far as to turn him out of her bedroom without a second thought. He confessed that it was her continuing coldness that forced him, in desperation, to look elsewhere for fulfillment.

But the woman who had faced her here today had been anything but cold. In fact, although the girl had prepared herself for icy indifference and brittle rejection, Elizabeth Willmont, had, under the circumstances, been kind and even compassionate. Still, Bobby insisted that the marriage was a sham, and the only thing the girl cared about was making sure that her baby had a name and a father. After all, however he had been conceived, this child was a Drayton and deserving of his birthright.

She wrapped her coat tightly about her and made her way out of Gump's. If she hurried, she would get home in time to have dinner on the table when Bobby arrived. That and a bottle of wine would put him in a good mood, and one of her special back rubs would make him amorous, and she would do that thing she knew he liked best.

Then they would talk.

two

Elizabeth scrambled out of the taxi that brought her home to Jackson Street and hurried inside. She brushed past Preston, the butler, who was waiting with her mail and her messages, and went directly upstairs to her room, avoiding Amanda, declining dinner, refusing to take telephone calls.

She couldn't bear the thought of having to speak to anyone, and she couldn't wait to get her clothes off. Her fingers clawed at the buttons and yanked at the zippers and ripped at the hooks in her haste. Her teeth were chattering, she was shivering all over and she felt so horribly dirty and defiled. But when her clothes lay in tatters at her feet, she realized that simply undressing wasn't enough, so she ran a hot bath and scrubbed at herself with a stiff brush until her skin was as red as her hair.

Then she put on a fresh nightgown and crawled into bed, pulling the crisp clean sheets right up to her chin

– sheets that Robert hadn't yet had a chance to sully. The steaming bath had soothed her only momentarily. As reality slowly crowded in, the shivering resumed, her head began to throb, and it became increasingly painful for her to breathe. She felt like crying but her eyes remained dry.

Outside her windows, daylight was fading. Elizabeth lay in the half-dark and listened to the sounds of the house. A closing door, a creaking floorboard, a muffled voice – proof of life going on around her. She had never really cared much for this house of her husband's, but now she found a peculiar comfort in its endurance.

Sometime around eight o'clock, she rang for a pot of tea and some aspirin and waved aside the concerned inquiries of the maid who brought up the tray. She quickly washed down two of the aspirin with the hot liquid and then, on second thought, another two. But she knew she would need something much stronger than Bayer to get her through this crisis.

Despite her cosseted upbringing, Archer and Denise Avery's daughter was a realist. She understood that there were things to be done and decisions to be made, but not tonight, not when her emotions were so hopelessly muddled. Tomorrow would be time enough to sort it all out. Elizabeth shut her eyes and prayed for the numbing, healing, dreamless sleep that could always make intolerable burdens seem lighter in the morning.

It was not quite ten o'clock when she heard Robert come in. It was the earliest he had arrived home on a Tuesday night in six months. He slammed the front door and barked something at one of the servants, and then he was charging up the stairs and down the hallway.

Elizabeth sighed deeply and reached over to snap on her bedside lamp. She had hoped that he would spend the entire evening out so she would not have to face him so soon. But in a matter of seconds he would be at her door and that meant she had to decide right now how she was going to treat his treachery.

She examined her options. While it would certainly be cathartic to lash out with the full force of her outrage, it might perhaps be more prudent to hide the hurt and preserve what was left of her dignity. She didn't want to give him the satisfaction of knowing how devastated she was, but neither did she wish to leave him with even the slightest impression that she condoned any part of his behavior. Above all, she had to steel herself against any attempt he might make to sweet-talk her into forgiveness. She was still weighing her options when he entered the bedroom.

'Preston said you weren't feeling well,' he said with genuine concern in his voice.

The shivers had subsided beneath the covers and the aspirin had eased the throbbing, but the pain inside was as sharp as ever.

'It's just a headache,' she answered.

He came close and bent down to kiss her, but at the last moment she turned to plump her pillow and his lips brushed her ear. His hair was mussed, his face was flushed, and his clothes were all askew as though they had been put on in a hurry. A spot of red wine marred the front of his shirt. Elizabeth felt her stomach grind.

'Is there something I can do for you?' he asked. 'Rub your head, perhaps?'

Elizabeth could think of a number of succinct

responses to that particular question, but none of them were appropriate for a young lady of her upbringing.

'No, there's nothing you can do,' she replied in a flat voice. 'Nothing at all.'

Robert shifted from one foot to the other. Despite her anguish, Elizabeth had to suppress a smile. She could not recall ever having seen him quite so ill at ease before, and she took a perverse pleasure in that.

'Okay, I think I know what this is about,' he said with a harsh chuckle, realizing this was not a matter that she was going to shrug off. 'But believe me, the whole thing is utter nonsense.'

'There's a spot of wine on your shirt.'

Robert glanced hastily down at his front. 'I didn't notice,' he said. 'It must have happened at lunch.'

'No,' she reminded him. 'We didn't have red wine with lunch.'

'Look, I don't know what she told you,' he blurted, 'but I think you owe it to me to hear the truth.'

Elizabeth's eyes widened slightly. 'The truth?' she echoed. 'Do you mean the girl lied to me?'

'Of course she lied to you,' he asserted. 'All women like that lie.'

'By "like that," do you mean young, vulnerable – or pregnant?'

'Desperate,' he corrected. 'So desperate she'd make up just about any story.'

'Did she make up the pregnancy?'

'So she's pregnant,' he said harshly. 'What does that prove? It doesn't prove I had anything to do with it. All I did was be nice to her a couple of times. She worked in the building and I'd see her in the elevator. So maybe I said she looked good once or twice. Maybe I bought her a drink one night, I don't remember, and now she's in trouble and she sees "meal ticket" written across my forehead.'

'It's late and I'm very tired,' Elizabeth said.

'Look, it's blackmail, I tell you,' he insisted. 'Plain and simple. She probably got knocked up by some nobody or other and grabbed at a chance to make it into the big time.'

'Just picked you out of the elevator, did she?'

'More likely the social register.'

Elizabeth gave her husband a loathsome look. 'She knows about my miscarriages, she knows we don't sleep in the same bedroom, she calls you *Bobby*, for God's sake – and all you did was buy her a drink?'

Robert glared at his wife, wondering why she couldn't be as dim and manageable as his mother. Then, with an exaggerated shrug, he tried a new tack.

'So maybe I saw her a few times. Maybe I told her my troubles. Do you think you're the only one who has troubles? Those were *my* babies you lost, too, you know, but did I ever get any sympathy? No, everyone was always hovering around *you*, consoling *you*, comforting *you*, being strong for *you*. "Poor Elizabeth." "How tragic for Elizabeth." Well, maybe I needed someone to comfort me, and had to find it where I could. But that doesn't mean I slept with her.'

'And the moon is made of green cheese and there really is a tooth fairy,' his wife snapped. 'What if that girl is carrying the only child you'll ever have in this life? Think about that and then ask yourself if you really want to be so cavalier about it.'

Robert sank down on the end of the bed with a groan, because that was the very thought that had been torturing him for months, ever since the girl, grinning with unabashed pride and devotion, had told him the news.

'Okay, so I made a mistake,' he admitted, his head in his hands, his fingers sunk into the thick dark hair that curled fashionably around his ears. 'I'm human. But you know me, you know my ... appetites, and I was afraid to touch you, afraid if you got pregnant again too soon, I might lose you, like I almost lost you the last time. So I took up with someone who didn't matter, someone I could use and forget. I never intended it to be anything more than that.'

'Well, it is now,' Elizabeth reminded him.

'Yes, I guess it is,' he sighed.

'All those nights,' she said bitterly. 'All those nights that I sat home alone, while you were supposed to be working harder to advance sooner. I feel like such a fool.'

'You weren't supposed to find out.'

'And that would have made it all right?' Elizabeth shot back. 'What I didn't know couldn't hurt you?' She shook her head sadly. 'And to think I actually felt guilty for going to the ballet with Marian Pinckton's homosexual nephew.'

'That was different,' he protested. 'You were out in public. Whatever I did, I was discreet about it.'

She turned on him sharply. 'You bastard – do you really think you can compare the two?'

'I told you it didn't mean anything.'

Elizabeth glared at him. 'She followed me around all afternoon, in and out of every store on Union Square, to beg me to let you go so you two could live happily ever after.'

'Whatever she may have told you,' he declared, 'I never once said I'd marry her.'

'Whether you did or didn't doesn't seem very important now. In any case, I wouldn't dream of standing in the way.'

Robert looked up sharply. 'What are you talking about?'

'I'm talking about a divorce, of course.'

She had not intended to say that, but the moment the words were out in the open, she felt an enormous burden lift from her shoulders.

'Don't be ridiculous,' he snapped. 'There's never been a divorce in the Drayton family.'

If he had intended to intimidate her by his declaration, he had miscalculated.

'There's never been one in the Avery family, either,' she retorted, 'but that doesn't mean there never will be.'

'You mean you'd really be willing to give up everything we have because of some … some nobody from North Dakota?'

'Is that where she's from?'

He sprang off the bed. 'Who the devil cares where she's from?'

'I guess it's not important.'

'Then tell me you're not going to throw away our lives because of her.'

'If I decide to divorce you, it won't be because of the girl,' Elizabeth declared. 'It will be because I don't want to be married to you anymore.'

'Why not? You wanted to be married to me yesterday, and I'm the same person today that I was then.'

'You really don't understand, do you?' she charged. 'Yesterday I didn't know who you really were. Today I do, and I'm not at all sure I want to stay with someone I can't trust.'

'Well, that's a hell of a thing to say to me.'

Elizabeth shrugged. 'It was a hell of a thing you did to me.'

The starch seemed to melt right out of him.

'Please,' he implored, 'you're my wife. I love you. I picked you over a thousand others I could have married. I've never loved anyone but you and I never will. I need you. God, I never realized how much until this moment. You're my strength, my center. I'm nothing without you. Think of the future, think of all our plans to make this a better country. None of it would mean a damn to me if you weren't there to share it. If you leave me, I'm finished.'

Elizabeth stared at her husband in surprise. Of all the words spoken between them over the years, he had never come close to saying anything like this. There had even been a catch in his voice, and in the dim light of the lamp, she could see tears glistening in his magnificent black-fringed eyes. It was a vulnerable side of him that he had never shown before, and – she couldn't help it – her heart turned over.

'I never realized,' she whispered.

'It's hard for a man to admit he's not as confident as everyone expects him to be,' Robert said. 'It's like admitting he's scared.'

Elizabeth shook her head slowly, more confused than she had ever been in her life. She had been raised with simple values and a very clear understanding of right and wrong. Robert had betrayed her, that was certainly true, but she wondered if perhaps she did bear part of the blame. She had been so consumed with her own grief over the miscarriages that she had failed to consider his feelings. Not only had she accepted all the attention as her due, she had run off to Denver and abandoned him. Had she helped to push him into someone else's arms when he wasn't strong enough to resist?

The threat of divorce had been intended to hurt Robert as he had hurt her. But Elizabeth now realized that, regardless of the anguish he had caused her, she was still hopelessly in love with her husband, and try as she would, she could not conceive of spending the rest of her life without him. Despite her earlier determination, she felt the anger that had been coiled so tightly inside of her beginning to loosen.

'I suppose there might have been fault on both sides,' she conceded. 'Maybe I could have been more sensitive to your needs. But what you did ... I mean, there just isn't anything worse that could happen between a husband and wife.'

'If I could undo it, I would,' he cried, covering his face with his hands. 'I'd make it all go away.'

'It's a little late for that,' she observed.

'Please, give me another chance,' he urged. 'Give *us* another chance. I'll make it up to you, I promise. I'll do penance, I'll toe the line, whatever you want. I swear I'll never let you down again. Just give me one more chance.'

'Even if I would be willing,' Elizabeth sighed, 'there's still the other problem.'

'I'll take care of it,' he said flatly.

'You can't abandon her, Robert, if that's what you're thinking. She's your responsibility. Besides, we aren't just talking about her, we're also talking about a child – *your* child. There has to be some kind of acknowledgment, arrangements made, an understanding.'

'I said I'd take care of it.'

Elizabeth's eyes widened at a sudden thought. 'But it's even worse than that, isn't it? We'll never be able to keep this a secret. Sooner or later, it'll get out – this kind of thing always does. And then your political career will be ruined. I can't imagine this country electing a President with an illegitimate child.'

'Perhaps not,' Robert allowed.

Elizabeth brightened for a moment. 'I don't suppose she would let us adopt, let us give the child a name and a good home, and go back to North Dakota?' she wondered aloud. Then she shook her head. 'No … if it were me, I'd never give up my baby. I'd sooner die.'

'Don't worry,' Robert assured her. 'I'll handle it.' He leaned down and kissed her lightly on the forehead. 'You get some rest now,' he said gently. 'Just put it all out of your head and leave everything to me. There's a solution out there – it's just a matter of finding it.'

He snapped off the lamp and left the room with a self-satisfied smile that his wife missed. Women had been put on this earth to be manipulated, he knew. It was all in knowing the right approach.

Elizabeth snuggled under the covers. It had been a ghastly day, but now it was over. The crisis was past, the healing could begin. Robert would take care of the girl and the child somehow, and even if they never got to the White House, life would go on. In time, the whole episode would be nothing more than an unpleasant aftertaste. Her eyes closed and she slept.

A week later, the body of a young girl washed up on Baker Beach. An autopsy confirmed that she had drowned, and a coroner's inquest, finding no evidence to the contrary, ruled the death a suicide, citing the fact that she was pregnant and unmarried as the probable reason. No one came forth to claim her.

On the sixth of August, Robert was invited to join the partnership of Sutton, Wells, Willmont and Spaulding.

PART FIVE
1979

There is always one moment …
when the door opens and lets
the future in.

— *Graham Greene*

one

Autumn was a fleeting, frosty breath that swept across Manhattan Island, chasing off the last remnants of summer before vanishing into winter. Snow followed quickly on the heels of Thanksgiving, but didn't stick around for Christmas. Icy air was all that was on hand to welcome in the New Year.

Karen locked the front doors of Demion Five, double-checking to make sure they were secure before she crossed to the curb to hail a taxi.

Burglaries riddled this exclusive section of Madison Avenue, and shop owners had resorted to installing security barriers and sophisticated alarm systems. Pretty soon, she thought with a sigh, New York was going to resemble an armed fortress. In its two years of operation, Demion Five had been burgled three times. The first time, a week after the opening, vandals had destroyed half the inventory. When Karen arrived, she found priceless books soaked with water, canvases slashed, clothing shredded.

'Vindictive bastards,' Demelza exclaimed, surveying the devastation. 'They did this because there wasn't any money.'

'Why would anyone think we'd be stupid enough to leave money lying around?' Karen demanded.

The co-owner of the eclectic uptown establishment threw up her hands in disgust. 'Let's just call it another form of insurance we have to pay. From now on, we make sure that a hundred bucks stays in the register overnight.'

A cab pulled up to the curb to discharge a passenger and Karen grabbed it right out from under the noses of a timid Oriental couple. She pulled the door shut, gave the driver the address of her Sixty-third Street town house, and fell back against the seat. It was one of the less than chivalrous things New Yorkers did to get from one place to another, and doing it always made Karen feel a little mean inside.

The modest girl from the suburbs had been transformed into a cosmopolitan city-dweller. The long hair she had worn through much of the decade had been discarded in favor of a soft curly crop, Elizabeth Arden had taught her the artistry of makeup, and Saks Fifth Avenue had reshaped her style of dress. Slim suits and tailored blouses now occupied her closet. As the Washington Square Bookery once accommodated one kind of clothing, uptown now required quite another.

Demion Five was Ione's brainchild. The art history professor had conceived the idea primarily to help promote her husband's work, but it was also a unique concept in shopping. When her father died, leaving her a bit of money, she decided to act. The first thing she did was approach Demelza.

'I know art, but I don't know anything about running a business,' she confessed. 'I want to open a shop that's not like anything I've ever seen, with rare books and magazines like you have at the Bookery, but also with quality art and fashions and jewelry and things. I don't want a department store – I want this to be like an elegant home where the customers feel comfortable, as though they were calling on old friends. I see a setting with lots of sofas and chairs and carpets and morning coffee and afternoon tea.'

'I always thought the Bookery was like that homey part without the elegant,' Demelza observed.

'Exactly,' Ione agreed. 'I guess what I want to do is add a little something to your act, and take it uptown.'

Karen practically wriggled with excitement. 'I think it's a marvelous idea,' she cried. 'And of course this kind of thing has to be uptown. It would never fly down here.'

Demelza gazed thoughtfully past Ione's shoulder. For the past thirty years, she had intended to live and die in her beloved Greenwich Village, but times had changed. Starving artists were no longer in fashion, and 'bohemian' had become a derogatory term. The war in Vietnam was over and the country was trying to heal itself. Long hair and love beads were out, the Establishment was in. Different was tiresome, causes were boring. It was everyone for himself.

Thanks to Karen, the Washington Square Bookery was doing a brisk business dealing in titles that were unavailable anywhere else, but the customers were now largely citywide and the locals who used to drop by for tea and sympathy had grown fewer and farther between.

The Village was metamorphosing. Most of the innocents who wanted to change the world were gone, replaced by drug addicts and chronic malcontents. The coffeehouses, those bright spots of sawdust and magic where gentle visionaries sang their songs of protest, had become dark corners where sinister shadows dealt their deadly panaceas. Hope had become despair, protesters had become terrorists, love had become sex, music had become noise, 'us' had become 'me,' and the quaint little community was rapidly becoming passé.

So Demelza did the only reasonable thing – she went uptown. She sold the Bookery and added her money to Ione's. The two women knew exactly what they wanted. It took five months before they finally found the right rental on Madison Avenue, and after that, they never looked back.

The result was part gallery, part boutique, part café and part drawing room, concocted of velvet and lace and ribbon, rich woods and lemon oil. It was bright and spacious and cozy and charming and chic all at the same time.

Mitch's paintings adorned the walls as they would in any fine home. Jenna's fashions peeked out of armoires in the upstairs boudoir. Rare books and periodicals filled the shelves in the paneled library. Felicity's one-of-a-kind jewelry creations sparkled from a circular showcase in the foyer. And a selection of superb sculptures done by Jenna's live-in, John Micheloni, were judiciously placed throughout.

Armchairs and sofas that Demelza had procured and Jenna had recovered were scattered everywhere. Small tables and chairs graced the balcony, where coffee and tea and baked goods were served. And wafting into every corner were the gentle strains of Bach or Mozart.

Stepping through the front doors was like stepping into another time, a bit of Victoriana that they had managed to create in the middle of a city that couldn't seem to wait to tear down its past in favor of its future.

It was fresh and fun and trendy, and it caught on. A month after the shop opened, there was a small write-up in the *Times*. After that, people wanted to be seen at Demion Five. Slowly, Mitch's paintings began to sell. Several of Jenna's creations made their way to fashionable Manhattan events. A few of John's sculptures found niches in discriminating homes. And Felicity was accepting commissions that would keep her too busy to pine for Broadway. The partners of Demion Five and their little consortium were becoming successful and embarrassed.

'I've compromised every principle I ever had,' Mitch declared when he agreed to do a painting for Gracie Mansion, the mayor's residence. 'I took a wife, I quit drugs, I pay taxes, I wear suits, I grovel before idiots incapable of understanding my work, and worst of all, I'm getting rich.'

He and Ione had married shortly after the birth of their daughter Tanya. The Rankins still lived on Sullivan Street, because it was so near NYU where, along with tenure, Ione had an associate professorship. But they now owned the run-down tenement and were in the midst of a total renovation.

The rest of the family had moved on. Jenna and John shared a loft in Soho. As soon as the Vietnam war was over, Kevin Munker completed his bachelor's degree. Shortly thereafter, to everyone's amusement, he applied to graduate school and went off to Boston.

Felicity took a flat in Chelsea. Demelza traded Bleecker Street for West End Avenue. Ethan never came back.

'I never had any principles to compromise,' Felicity said with a sigh. 'But it is a little awkward having so much money.'

Jenna giggled. 'I opened a savings account. I think it was maybe the third time I've ever been inside a bank.'

'I made more money in 1978 than my daddy made in any ten years of his life on the docks,' said Demelza. 'I keep thinking there must be something immoral about that.'

The taxi slid up in front of the dun-colored house on Sixty-third Street, between Lexington and Third, which Karen had called home ever since she had become the assistant manager for Demion Five. Her parents had been so thrilled by her decision to move uptown that, although she no longer needed their assistance, they had underwritten the rent for two years.

Karen tipped the cab driver extravagantly, emptied her mailbox, and let herself into the first-floor apartment, turning on the lights and the stereo on her way to hang up her fur-lined coat. WQXR was featuring a Brahms symphony during this hour and the flowing melody suited her mood.

The apartment was a study in browns and whites. White walls, white window treatments, white area rugs, brown velvet sofas and chairs, warm wood accents, polished parquet floors, a few lithographs displayed here and there for a dash of color, and the soft glow of lamplight throughout.

There was a wonderful painting of Mitch's at

Demion Five, done in his inimitable serrated palette knife style, that would have been perfect over the fireplace. On the surface, it was a simple clearing in a wood, yet the longer one looked, the more complex it became, until the outwardly deserted space was seen to be inhabited by hundreds of creatures. It was a riveting canvas, but even with her acceptable salary, beyond her reach.

Karen dropped the mail on the entry table and clacked down the hall into the bedroom, where she kicked off her pumps, shrugged out of her navy gabardine suit and silk blouse, and slipped into fuzzy gray slippers and a shapeless robe. Padding into the kitchen, she tossed some ice cubes into a glass and poured herself a Scotch. Then she headed for the living room, pausing on the way to pick up her mail.

She was completely alone, to do whatever she wished whenever she wished. Even after five years, she hadn't quite gotten used to the idea. Part of her still listened for Arlene's key in the door. More than once she caught herself setting two places at the table. Then she chuckled because all that was behind her.

This place was hers alone. At least, the first floor of the town house was hers. There was a gay man in the basement apartment who taught English literature at Hunter College, and an elderly couple, German refugees who wore long sleeves to cover the tattooed numbers on their forearms, who lived upstairs. But each had their own space, as she had hers. And each had their own secrets, as she had hers.

Once the door was shut, Karen was surrounded by her own choice of furnishings. She knew exactly where things were, she could eat as she pleased, mess around with her thought pages without fear of prying eyes, watch the television programs she preferred, and she didn't have to see or talk to anyone unless she wanted to. There were even times when she would let the telephone ring unanswered.

'I called you last night, but you weren't home,' her mother would say on those occasions. 'Where were you?'

'Out to dinner,' Karen would reply glibly, because she knew her mother would prefer the lie to the truth.

'With anyone special?'

'Just friends.'

Beverly sighed. 'Not those peculiar people you're in business with?'

'Formerly peculiar,' Karen corrected her. 'Now they're all fine upstanding members of the Establishment.'

'I'm glad they're so successful,' her mother said with a sniff.

'But they're still not good enough,' Karen remarked. 'No doctors, no lawyers, not a dentist in the bunch – and none of them even came close to going to Harvard or Yale.'

'Well, really,' Beverly protested, 'you make me sound like such a snob. I thought, once you moved out of that degenerate neighborhood into a decent part of town, you'd be in a position to find more, shall we say … suitable companionship. You're not getting any younger, you know.'

Karen had stayed on at West Twelfth Street after Arlene got her Ph.D., married her orthopedist and moved to Scarsdale, because it was familiar and convenient and close to her friends. She originally intended to find another roommate, if only to ease the financial burden on her father. But, as the months and then the years passed, she came to understand that she didn't really want anyone moving in on her. By the time she was ready to move uptown, it never occurred to her to seek a roommate.

It was her sister Laura who told her about the apartment on Sixty-third Street. An ex-roommate from Mount Holyoke and her husband were being transferred to Chicago. It was a real find and Karen should rush right over to see it. She did and it took her all of a minute and a half to make up her mind.

Now, as she sat on a brown love seat that faced its mate across a walnut coffee table and sorted through the mail, she wondered about the vagaries of life that could put one in the right place at the right time just as easily as they could put one in the wrong place at the wrong time.

Although she never spoke about that night, now almost half her life ago, the memory dogged her like a relentless shadow. The few men who were persistent enough to get her to agree to a date were soon put off by her aloofness and her insistence that they meet and part in very public places. She didn't mind. Somewhere along the way, she stopped mourning for the life she had lost and learned to live with the life she had, and quite happily spent her time with what she had come to think of as the Sullivan Street set.

Occasionally she saw Jill Hartman. Not unexpectedly, the Hartmans had divorced soon after Andy finished law school. Their daughter was now a delightful teenager.

A lot of things had changed since she and Jill had been girls together. Divorce, for one thing, which had been such an anathema a generation ago, was now an acceptable solution to marital problems. Legalized abortion had removed the necessity for shotgun weddings. And, perhaps most ironic of all, careers were now something that women were looking forward to rather than falling back on. Whereas, twenty years ago, girls had dreamed of marrying doctors and dentists and lawyers, today they dreamed of *being* doctors and dentists and lawyers.

'God,' Jill liked to say, 'were we ever raised in the Dark Ages.'

The Dark Ages, indeed, Karen thought now as she sipped her Scotch. Just the other week, she had read about a man who was actually on trial for raping a woman he had taken on a date. They even called it that – date rape. The prosecution argued that a woman who accepted a date with a man was not automatically agreeing to have sex with him, that she had the right to say no, and he was obliged to believe she meant it. The pendulum had swung. Karen didn't know whether to laugh or cry.

She turned resolutely to the mail, separating the thick stack into four piles: advertising circulars to be tossed away unopened, magazines to be read at a later time, bills to be paid on the tenth of the month, and, finally, the cards – more than two dozen of them, to be opened and read right now.

Today was February 8, 1979, and Karen was thirty-seven years old. Tomorrow, after work, she would make a trip out to Great Neck to be fussed over by her family. Laura had dutifully landed her lawyer and now had two adorable babies, whom Karen took enormous pleasure in spoiling. Winola would make one of her special double-chocolate birthday cakes and her mother would fudge the number of candles on top and no one would dare breathe a word about spinsters or maiden aunts or unmarried women.

But tonight was hers, to scrutinize herself in the bathroom mirror and pluck out the stray gray strands that had mistakenly wandered into her dark hair, open a can of soup instead of taking the time to prepare a proper dinner, contemplate the inexorable passing of time, and wonder how the next year of her life would differ from the last.

The Brahms symphony concluded and she was on her way to the kitchen for another Scotch when the intercom buzzed.

'It's Ione,' the art history teacher replied to Karen's query. 'Can I come in and talk?'

'Sure,' Karen replied.

'Mitch and I had a fight,' Ione groused, following Karen into the living room and dropping into the nearest chair. 'I had to get out of Eden for a while.'

Of all of them, Ione had changed the least. With her short blond hair, big gray eyes and tomboy body, she still looked more like a schoolgirl than a forty-five-year-old wife, mother, professor and business mogul.

'I'm having Scotch,' Karen offered.

'Make it a double,' said Ione.

When Karen returned with the drinks, Ione was gazing balefully at the stack of cards.

'It's your birthday,' she moaned. 'I forgot it was your birthday.'

'No you didn't,' Karen reminded her. 'You sent an adorable card.'

'I mean I forgot right now. You probably have big plans for tonight and I just barged right in.'

Karen shrugged. 'I didn't have anything important

on. Actually, I'm going out to my folks over the weekend and I was just planning to wash my hair tonight.'

'Well, the least I can do to make up for spoiling your evening is to take you out to dinner.'

'Nonsense,' Karen declared. 'I can whip up something right here and you can stay and share it with me.'

'I'm too restless to hang out,' Ione replied. 'I feel like kicking up my heels, going to an extravagant restaurant and raising a little hell. Come on, say you'll go with me.'

'Well, I don't know . . .' Karen began.

'Please,' Ione urged. 'I don't want to go alone.'

'Okay,' Karen gave in.

'Great!' Ione cried, pushing her in the direction of the bedroom. 'I'll give you ten minutes to get dressed. And you can choose the restaurant.'

Karen wore the only one of Jenna's originals she could afford to own, a flowing patchwork dress made of colorful bits of silk and velvet and brocade with a high lace collar, and chose the Sign of the Dove, a nearby French restaurant that featured the most charming garden room. It had been the group's favorite since they had come uptown.

It was eight o' clock when they arrived at the bright yellow building on Third Avenue. The restaurant was packed, there was a long line, and people were being turned away.

'I'm surprised,' Ione admitted. 'I didn't really think the place would be so crowded tonight.'

'I think it's crowded every night,' Karen told her with a disappointed sigh.

'Well, let's just see if they've got some little spot

they're overlooking,' Ione said encouragingly. 'You keep our place in line.'

Before Karen could stop her, Ione pushed her way to the front of the crowd and Karen saw her whisper a few words into the maître d's ear. The man smiled broadly and nodded. Ione turned and motioned Karen forward.

'What on earth did you say to him?' Karen asked, feeling the irate stares of people who had been in line in front of her.

Ione shrugged. 'I told him you were a famous European gourmand.'

Karen was trying to decide how to respond to that when she caught sight of a familiar bulk up ahead.

'Look,' she exclaimed. 'There's Demelza!'

'Really?' Ione grinned. 'Look again.'

Karen looked again and there, too, were Jenna and John and Felicity and even Mitch, along with eight-and-a-half-year-old Tanya, who came bounding over to throw her little arms around her best grown-up friend. Then there were hugs and kisses all around, as if they hadn't seen each other for months.

'Aren't birthdays wonderful?' Tanya cried happily.

'Surprise!' Demelza shouted. At fifty-six, her dark hair was turning white, but she still wore it in a thick braid down her back.

Karen turned to Ione. 'Big fight with Mitch, huh?' she accused with a smile.

It was a wonderful party. They laughed and ate and drank and ate and laughed and drank some more. For a while, it almost seemed that they were just as they used to be. Except, of course, Karen knew with a small pang of sadness, they weren't. Success, and the times, had changed them all. Going uptown had been much more than a geographical move – it had been a psychological one as well. Not so long ago, they had ridiculed people who went to restaurants like this. Now they thought nothing of dropping six or seven hundred dollars for someone else to do the cooking and the dishes.

Karen could remember when having a little money in the contribution can meant they could splurge on a good bottle of wine. Now they were hiring financial advisers and buying real estate and investing in high tech companies. They had traded the *Village Voice* for the *Wall Street Journal* and the mellow edges of marijuana for the numbness of Scotch. They no longer spoke of the future and what they hoped to accomplish, only of the present and what they had already accomplished. Dreams had become responsibilities. They had joined the Establishment.

The little family that had been her anchor for so long was gone. Like a rough diamond that had been cleaved into brilliant but separate gems, they would never be one again.

'I really miss you guys,' Karen heard herself saying.

'Yeah,' Mitch agreed. 'We should do this more often.' He was trimmer than he had been in their lean days, and his woolly beard had been reduced to a neat graying fringe.

'At least once a month,' Felicity said. Now almost forty, her wafer-thin body looked more anorexic than stylish.

'Or even once a week,' John added.

Karen had always thought of the sculptor as an awkward Ichabod Crane, but with the onset of affluence, he had developed a distinct resemblance to Sherlock Holmes. He admitted to being from New

Jersey where, it was rumored, his people had more than a nodding acquaintance with organized crime. To his credit, even in his leanest years – and there had been many – he had never taken a dime from any of them.

'Then it wouldn't be special,' Jenna reminded him. The carrot-topped, rosy-cheeked former teen had matured into a Rubenesque delight.

At that, a busboy wheeled up a cake, the top aflame with exactly the right number of candles. As the waiter popped the cork on a bottle of champagne and began to pour, Karen caught a glimpse of the label. Dom Perignon. She smiled softly to herself. They had indeed come a long way.

When the glasses were filled, Demelza rose to her feet.

'I know it's Karen's birthday,' she said, 'which is lovely and all that, but not really why we're gathered here tonight.'

Tanya held up her glass with the two drops of precious bubbling wine her mother had allowed her to have.

'Do we drink now?' she whispered.

'Not yet,' Demelza told her. 'After my speech.'

'Will you tell me when?'

'Yes.'

'Do you promise?' the little girl insisted. This was going to be her first taste of champagne and she didn't want to miss the moment.

'I promise,' Demelza said. 'As you all know, I've been the manager of Demion Five for the two years of its existence,' she continued. 'Two embarrassingly successful years, I might add. God help me, I have entered the top tax bracket.'

'Who'da thunk it,' Mitch muttered.

'Of course, there's a perfectly good reason for all of this. Demion Five has become a bigger winner than we ever thought it would. Let's face it, it's one thing to fantasize about something and quite another to turn it into reality. It took nothing less than a superhuman effort to put five such distinct specialties into one house and make it work so well, as though they were joined at the hip from birth and always intended to enhance one another. Ione dreamed it, I designed it, but the truth is, ladies and gentlemen, and little lady,' she said with a wink at Tanya, 'Karen made it happen.'

Everyone turned and applauded Karen.

'The only reason I was able to sell the Bookery for enough money to join up with Ione in the first place was because Karen turned it into a decent business. In her quiet way, she sees what needs to be done and does it.'

'Hear, hear,' everyone saluted. Karen blushed.

'Now?' Tanya asked.

'Not yet,' Demelza murmured. 'So, as the manager of Demion Five,' she continued, 'I wanted you all to be the first to hear that I am no longer the manager of Demion Five. Say hello to your new manager. To Karen.'

'To Karen,' everyone echoed, raising their glasses.

Demelza turned to Tanya. 'Now,' she prompted and they all drank.

'Speech!' everyone cried.

Karen looked around the table, stunned. 'I – I don't know what to say,' she stammered. She turned to Demelza. 'If you make me manager, what will *you* do?'

'Same thing I already do. Get in everyone's way, make a general nuisance of myself. Nothing's going to change. You've been doing the work from the beginning, you deserve to have the title. Besides, I miss my books. Now that I'm a woman of means, I want to spend more time poking through them and maybe even travel around in search of new treasures.'

'I still don't know what to say,' Karen admitted.

'Demelza didn't mention it,' Ione put in, 'but there's a significant raise that goes along with the promotion.'

At that, a happy grin spread across Karen's face. 'Now I know what to say,' she said. 'I can buy Mitch's painting.'

two

The woman appeared to be about Karen's age, short and round with asymmetric blue eyes and dark-blond hair worn in a ponytail with straight-cut bangs, and this was the third time in less than two weeks that she had braved the blustery winds of March to come and look at the Micheloni sculpture.

It was one of John's best creations, a representation of Paul Revere on his midnight ride, a rough black mass that vaguely resembled a horse, topped by a sweep of translucent alabaster that suggested a cape. It stood barely a foot high, but it had enormous impact. And a five-figure price tag.

Karen had placed it on a marble pedestal in a lighted niche at the back of the oval foyer, a position she set aside for only the most spectacular pieces. Like Mitch's painting of the clearing in the wood that now hung over the fireplace in her apartment, it was a work of art she truly appreciated. But her admiration was reserved for working hours because not even her significant boost in salary was enough to cover the cost.

The woman circled the pedestal slowly, considering the sculpture from every angle, with an expression of adoration mixed with indecision.

'Excuse me,' she said finally, taking a deep breath and walking over to Karen. 'Would it be possible for me to see the manager?'

'I'm the manager,' Karen replied, smiling politely and introducing herself. 'How may I help you?'

'Well, it's come down to a choice,' the woman announced. 'Either I take that exquisite thing home with me, or I move into your shop.'

Karen chuckled. 'I know exactly how you feel. If I had the money, it would have gone home with me a long time ago.'

'That's just it,' the woman acknowledged. 'I can't afford to buy it, but I can't resist. You see, my husband just got a big promotion at work, and he's a Revolutionary War buff, and I thought this would be a really special way to celebrate.'

'This is certainly special,' agreed Karen.

'But he'd kill me if he knew how much it cost. So I was wondering if maybe we could work something out.'

It wasn't the first time a customer had inquired about the possibility of financing a purchase. Demion Five's usual policy was to refuse courteously and suggest a lower-priced item. But Karen found herself hesitating because there was something engaging about the woman, and a candidness that showed clearly in her delightfully asymmetrical face – one blue eye being noticeably larger than the other.

'Would you care for a cup of tea?' she asked. 'I always deliberate better over a cup of tea.'

'I'd love one,' the woman replied.

'Okay, now, what did you have in mind?' Karen asked when they were settled at a table on the balcony with a pot of Earl Grey and a plate of Ione's fresh apple-berry muffins between them.

'My name is Nancy Yanow and I'm a photographer,' the woman began. 'At least, I used to be before I became a mom. I worked for the *Philadelphia Inquirer* one summer and the *Reading Times* for several years, and I had a pretty good reputation. I won an award for my series on Kent State in 1970. Anyway, I got to cover some pretty exciting stuff. The *New York Times* bought one of my pictures once. My name was still Nancy Doniger back then.'

'That sounds exciting,' Karen offered.

'It was,' Nancy replied wistfully. 'Anyway, my kids are both in school, and that leaves me with lots of free time. Newspaper work wouldn't fit my life now, but I was thinking about maybe going out on my own, you know, into artistic photography. I've kept up with my camera and I know quality work is selling these days and I thought that, if you liked the kind of thing I'm doing, we might arrange a trade where I could pay for, say, half of the sculpture and then give you enough of my stuff to cover the other half.'

It was an intriguing idea, Karen thought. Not that Demion Five wasn't doing just fine as it was, but adding a new dimension could have benefits.

'We've never had an arrangement like that,' she said slowly, although she knew the idea of bartering would appeal to both Demelza and Ione.

'Oh,' Nancy sighed.

'But that doesn't mean we couldn't.'

'Oh?'

'Of course, I'd have to see your photographs – that is, before I could commit to anything, and I'd have to discuss it with the owners, too.'

'Of course,' Nancy concurred, her whole face lighting up. 'I could bring in some samples tomorrow or the next day if you're available, or, better yet, you could come up to my place and see just about everything.'

'Let me check my schedule,' Karen suggested.

The two women went into the back, where Karen had her tiny cluttered office.

'If you're the least bit claustrophobic,' she warned, 'I don't recommend that you come any further.'

'I'm more curious than claustrophobic,' Nancy said, following her inside. 'Besides, this is at least twice as big as my darkroom.'

Karen flipped through the pages of her appointment book. 'The only day I have available this week would be Thursday.'

'Thursday's fine,' Nancy replied.

'It probably makes more sense for me to see everything you have, and I can't really concentrate that well here, so why don't I come to you?'

'Wonderful,' said Nancy. 'Come at noon and I'll make lunch.'

'You don't have to do that,' Karen assured her.

'I know,' Nancy declared. 'Here, let me give you the address.'

The brownstone in which the Yanows lived was on West Seventy-eighth, in a quiet little block tucked behind the Museum of Natural History. Nancy was waiting at

the front door, opening it against the gusty wind
before Karen even had a chance to push the buzzer.

'Hi,' she said. 'Come on in. I've got a good fire
going and some hot cider to warm you up.'

'Sounds great,' Karen replied.

Nancy led the way up a flight of stairs. 'We have the
top two floors,' she explained gratuitously. 'My brother's got the bottom two.'

'Did you flip a coin?'

'No,' Nancy chuckled. 'It's my brother's house. We
rent from him.'

The upper duplex was spectacular, with heavy
beamed ceilings and hardwood floors and window
walls overlooking a garden in back. The top floor was
divided into thirds, with two bedrooms at one end, a
master suite at the other, and a large playroom in
between. Downstairs, each room opened naturally into
the next – kitchen into dining room into living room
into study. The darkroom was a closet off the kitchen
that had most likely started out as a pantry.

The furniture was a hodgepodge of styles and
periods. Oriental carpets were scattered throughout
and Navajo throws were draped over the sofas. Most of
the exposed brick walls were lined with shelves that
were in turn crammed with books, but several framed
photographs were hung here and there for dramatic
effect. One was a portrait of an ancient woman with a
youthful twinkle in her eye. Another highlighted a
solemn little boy with a big tear on his cheek. A third
captured a boy and a girl sharing an apple.

'Did you do these?' Karen asked.

'Uh-huh,' came the reply.

'They're great.'

Nancy beamed. 'I did them when I was in my people

phase. Now I'm in my place phase.'

'I can't wait to see more.'

'I thought we'd eat first, if that's all right,' Nancy suggested. She ushered Karen into the kitchen, where wood blended into tile and the tile gave way to wood again.

'I thought my apartment was impressive,' Karen observed. 'But what you've done here is … well, it's incredible.'

'I wish I could take the credit,' Nancy said.

'Your brother did all this?'

'We knew from the time he was six that he was meant to be an architect. He could do the most fantastic things with Lincoln Logs.'

'From the looks of it, you were right.'

'He lost his wife to cancer three years ago,' Nancy confided. 'He got through it by taking on this place. He gutted the building practically to the foundation and rebuilt from there.'

The lunch, which more closely resembled a banquet, was delicious. The two women chatted throughout the meal like old friends rather than potential business colleagues. Somewhere between the crab bisque and the baked salmon, Karen learned that Nancy's husband Joe was the sales manager for a large industrial products firm and that her son Roger was in the second grade and her daughter Emily in the first.

'It sounds like you have a great family,' Karen said.

'Are *you* married?' Nancy asked.

'No,' came the reply.

'Are you interested?'

'I was once,' Karen replied, and for an instant the mask slipped. 'But it didn't work out, and I don't really think about it much anymore.'

A little smile fluttered around Nancy's mouth. 'Well, you just never know when you might stumble over the right opportunity again, now do you?' she murmured.

She led Karen into the study and sat her down on an overstuffed sofa. Then she hefted a large black portfolio onto an oak coffee table and flipped it open. Faces of every age and emotion stared up at Karen, each with a tale to tell, speaking silent volumes, even in black and white. Karen picked one up. In it, an old man sat on a bench staring into space with an expression of such emptiness that Karen felt her eyes moisten.

'He looks like he's waiting to die,' she whispered.

'He was,' Nancy said. 'His wife had just died. They'd been married for sixty-three years. They used to go to the park every afternoon so she could feed the pigeons. Hundreds of pigeons would wait for them at that bench. He told me that the day after she died he went to the park because he knew the pigeons would be waiting, but when he got there, they were gone. It was as if they knew.'

Karen looked into the old man's face, into his eyes. Even if Nancy hadn't told her the story, she felt she would have known it.

In the next picture, a little boy had slipped on a jungle gym at a playground and was dangling precariously. Above him, a teenage boy reached out a helping hand. The teenager was black. Karen saw both fear and relief in the little boy's eyes as he grasped for the helping hand. She needed no explanation for that story.

'Hollywood may think it invented talking pictures,' she murmured, 'but these are the real thing.'

'Now for talking places,' Nancy said, lifting another portfolio onto the table. Inside, Karen saw New York

City as she had never seen it before – a block of empty shops on the Upper West Side with boarded-up windows that even the rats had abandoned, an elite block of Park Avenue on garbage day, the Queensboro Bridge coming out of the dawn, Broadway during a blackout, the Empire State Building in a snowstorm, a Lower East Side tenement house burning out of control, a foggy shadow of the Staten Island Ferry.

'Look,' Karen said when she had seen everything, 'I don't claim to be an art critic, or know anything at all about design or composition, but if these are half as good as my instincts tell me they are, you and your husband are going to own a John Micheloni sculpture that I would give my eyeteeth for.'

'You really like them?' Nancy breathed.

'Not only do I like them, I think they're going to raise the level of Demion Five at least one notch.'

'You know, you're the first outside person I've actually shown any of these to. Joe kept telling me they were good, but of course he's not exactly what you'd call objective.'

'Nancy, they are good,' Karen asserted. 'Really good – and not even your delicious lunch would make me say that if I didn't mean it.'

The photographer grinned. 'I was so nervous the other day when I approached you. At first, I was just going to ask if you would do some sort of payment schedule for me. But once we started talking, well, you were so nice, and I just had this feeling that you'd understand what I was trying to do here.'

'I want you to bring both portfolios into the shop first thing Monday morning,' Karen instructed. 'Can you do that?'

'Of course I can.'

'I'll have the owners there and maybe a couple of
other people and we'll see what the reaction is.'

'I'll be there,' promised Nancy. 'And if this deal
works out, if I get Paul Revere, I promise you can have
all the visiting rights you want.'

three

By the time the bitter winds of March had given way to the gentle rains of April, limited-edition photographs were a fixture at Demion Five. By the time spring flowers had begun to blossom beneath the May sun, Paul Revere had become the focal point of the Yanow living room, and Nancy was as good as her word – Karen had become a regular visitor at Seventy-eighth Street.

The two women spoke daily on the telephone, met for lunch, and spent Saturday afternoons together. Karen had to go all the way back to her girlhood, to the lazy weekends she had spent with Jill, to find a time when she had enjoyed as close a friend.

On the first Saturday in August, Nancy arrived at the town house on Sixty-third Street at ten o'clock in the morning.

'You're two hours early,' Karen protested when she opened the door wrapped in her terry-cloth bathrobe, her hair soaking wet. 'I just got out of the shower.'

'Joe's taking the kids to the beach,' said Nancy by way of apology. 'He dropped me off on the way.'

'Well, have a seat,' Karen told her. 'There's fresh coffee. I'll be ready in half an hour.'

Nancy poured herself a cup and took it into the living room. She loved the serenity of Karen's apartment, the muted browns and stark whites, the brief flashes of color, the simplicity of the furniture, the quiet. It was easy to relax here, where there was never a need to worry about tripping over toys or sitting on something sticky. Fastidious Karen, Nancy thought with a smile. You could eat off her floor, you could see your reflection in the polished surfaces of her wood, and there was never a thing out of place.

Except, this morning, there was a scarred wooden box that had been left open on top of the desk. Nancy was not by nature a snoopy person. It was the incongruity of the box that drew her attention. She peeked inside. On top was a page covered with Karen's neat, precise handwriting. Nancy couldn't resist – she picked it up and started to read.

> The death of a dream
> is surrounded by pain,
> emptiness,
> regret,
> guilt.

> The tragedy of life
> is filled with opportunity,
> unrecognized,
> ignored,
> lost.

* * *

Fascinated, Nancy picked up the next page.

Half an hour later, Karen appeared in navy-blue slacks and a flowing white blouse, her hair smartly fluffed.

'As long as we have some extra time,' she was saying, 'I thought we could – '

The words died in her throat as she saw Nancy with the wooden box on her lap and the thought pages beside her.

'Stop!' she cried instinctively. 'Those are private.'

'I'm dreadfully sorry!' Nancy was both startled and embarrassed. 'I didn't realize … I saw the box sitting there, and my curiosity just got the best of me. I didn't think.'

Karen gathered up the papers and stuffed them back in the box and then shoved the box into one of the desk drawers.

'They're nothing important,' she said woodenly. 'Just a bunch of silly doodlings.'

'They *are* important,' Nancy contradicted her. 'And I had no right to read them without your permission.'

There was a long and distinctly awkward pause.

'I suppose you're wondering what that stuff was all about,' Karen said finally.

Nancy's uneven blue eyes reflected nothing but genuine caring. 'Not if you don't want to tell me,' she said.

'It was a long time ago,' Karen murmured, looking down the tunnel of years. 'I was very naive and I made a terrible mistake, and I had to pay the price.' She let out a shaky breath. 'Some mistakes you can simply shrug off because you know you won't ever make them again, but there are others that … well, I've had to learn to live with what happened. I don't talk about it very much. The notes and things – nobody was ever supposed to see them – they help.'

Nancy heard the sigh and felt the pain. 'I'm so sorry,' she apologized. 'I never meant to intrude.'

Karen shrugged. 'Well, it's over and done.'

'But since I did,' Nancy continued, 'I want to tell you something. The things I read – they were very good.'

'Don't be silly.' Karen shrugged. 'They're nothing.'

'You're wrong – and you ought to do something with them.'

'Perhaps I should wallpaper my bathroom.'

'Perhaps you should publish them.'

Karen laughed outright. 'Who'd publish my nonsense?'

'Literary publications take poetry all the time, and most of it is written by people who are working through problems, just like you. I've read stuff in periodicals that isn't half as good as yours. You had one poem in there about winter that actually gave me chills on an eighty-degree day in August.'

'Look, I appreciate the compliment, but my stuff is just for me,' Karen said with finality, now mortified that she had made such an issue of it. 'So let's pretend you never saw any of it and we can forget it and be on our way, okay? As long as we have time, I want to stop at the cleaner's.'

Only Nancy did not forget. In fact, an idea that had been lurking around the edges of her mind for some time began to come into full focus.

'I want to say something,' she said two weeks later, when they were enjoying a late lunch, 'and I don't want you to say a word until you've heard me out.'

'Okay,' came the casual reply.

'I'm doing well, right? I mean, my photographs are selling, right?'

'Right,' Karen said.

'Well, I was thinking, if my prints are popular – how about a book?'

'A book of photographs?'

'Exactly. You see, I've had this idea for a while now, and it's something I can't really do with a single print. I want to do a whole year in Manhattan, all four seasons, and how the city changes with each one. Different perspectives, all tied into the calendar. The man who sits on a bench three hundred and sixty-five afternoons a year – how do the seasons affect him? The mother who pushes a baby carriage around every morning – what difference do the seasons make to her? How is a river affected, or a park, or a schoolyard? What do you think?'

'I think it's good,' Karen replied, the wheels beginning to turn. 'A book, if it's priced right, could be a real hit. We could sell it right out of the shop.'

'There's just one hitch,' Nancy said.

'What?'

'Well, the book I'm imagining needs to have more than just photographs in it. It needs to have words. Words that will tie everything together, you know, the way illustrations enhance stories. I want to "illustrate" my photographs with words. But I don't want to use any stuff that's already been written. I want ideas that are just as fresh and original as my pictures. Only I wouldn't know how to do that myself.'

'Then find someone,' Karen responded without hesitation. 'It's such a good idea, I don't know how anyone could turn you down.'

'That's what I hoped,' Nancy said with a Cheshire cat grin that spread all over her face.

Karen choked. 'Don't be silly. You can't mean me. I'm not a writer.'

'As it happens,' contradicted Nancy, 'I'm in a position to know better.'

'Well, I'm certainly not a professional writer,' Karen pointed out.

'So what? You're as good as many professionals I know. I want you to illustrate my book with poetry.'

Karen frowned. 'My things aren't the kind of things you could use for something like this,' she argued.

'I'm not talking about what you've got in your box at home,' Nancy assured her. 'That's private and it should stay that way. I'm talking about you and me going out and creating something brand new and exciting together.'

There was a long pause.

'You really think I could do it?' Karen asked finally.

'Absolutely,' Nancy confirmed. 'Look, five months ago, you took a chance on a nobody photographer just because your instincts told you that you were right. Well, don't insult me by assuming that my instincts aren't every bit as good as yours. I say you can do it. I *know* you can do it.'

Karen didn't believe it for a moment. She had done enough reading in her lifetime to know that the pages in her box were little more than sophomoric jottings. That anyone might want to buy them was ludicrous. And yet, the idea was tempting. To create a work that would live and breathe all on its own would, in some ways, be like creating a new life, something she was so often reminded she could not do.

She took a deep breath. 'When do we start?'

four

Karen added a final coat of lip gloss, fluffed out her hair, and stood back to consider herself in the mirror.

Labor Day had come and gone, taking with it the pastel clothes and white shoes of summer. Although the midday temperature had climbed well above seventy, it was October, officially autumn, and time for more sober attire.

It had taken two hours of trying first one thing and then another before Karen settled on a simple taupe dress that had hung in her closet since being purchased, patiently waiting for an occasion to be taken out and worn. Matching pumps and a thick gold bracelet created by Felicity completed the outfit.

She turned, checking from every angle, looking for anything that might be amiss. But everything was just as it should be. With a satisfied sigh, she picked up her purse, let herself out of the apartment and walked over to Lexington Avenue in search of a taxi that would take her to the West Side.

'It's just a small get-together for my brother's fortieth birthday,' Nancy had explained in early September. 'He's been an absolute recluse since his wife died and I want to do something special for him. Joe's sister and brother will be there with their spouses and offspring.'

'But it's a family gathering,' Karen objected. 'I don't belong there.'

'Of course you do,' Nancy insisted and would hear no argument.

In truth, the Yanows were almost like family. In the past six months, Karen had been in and out of their house as if it were her second home. Although she'd never met the guest of honor, she probably knew Nancy's husband and their children better than she knew her own niece and nephew and brother-in-law, now that Laura had moved to Boston.

'Can I help with anything?' she asked.

'Yes,' Nancy replied. 'I have my eye on that new Rankin, the little one with the clown. I think my brother would love it. If I give you a deposit, do you think you could put it away for me?'

The painting was a whimsical Rankin, with the subject balancing nonchalantly on a unicycle while the rest of the circus whirled all around him with dizzying speed. 'Sanity-in-sanity,' Mitch called it, and it always made Karen smile.

'Done,' she said. 'But I won't put it away. I'll just mark it 'sold' and leave it hanging. Better for business.'

Now the painting was wrapped and waiting in

Nancy's study and all there was for Karen to do was get herself crosstown.

Joe Yanow answered her ring. A jovial man, even rounder than his wife and almost as short, with crinkly laugh lines and thinning hair, he gave her a broad smile and a big hug. It was a Mitch Rankin kind of hug and Karen had become used to it.

'Nancy's in the kitchen, the kids are up in the playroom, and everyone else is in the study watching the Orioles cream the Pirates.'

'I'll try the kitchen,' Karen decided as a huge groan escaped from the study, 'in case the hostess needs a hand.' She had never been able to muster much enthusiasm for baseball, not even the World Series.

The kitchen was in turmoil, which meant that Nancy had everything under control. After the barest of greetings, the hostess shoved a platter of canapés into Karen's hands.

'With all the complaining going on in there, a diversion is surely in order,' she suggested.

Karen carried the assortment of ham rolls, stuffed celery and deviled eggs into the study.

Up close, there was a good deal of resemblance between Ted Doniger and his sister except that Nancy was short while Ted stood at almost six feet. They shared the same sharp nose, easy smile, square jaw and blond hair, but Nancy's eyes were a cool blue, while Ted's were a rich hazel with warm gold flecks in them.

He was wearing gray slacks and a pale-yellow turtle-neck sweater that looked like cashmere, and he was smoking a pipe that smelled delicious. He might not have been what some considered handsome, but Karen thought he had a nice face, a comfortable face.

'I'm not sure what all the excitement is about,' he

whispered as he helped himself to a ham roll and a deviled egg from the plate of canapés. 'We hated the Pirates when we were kids growing up in Reading.'

'That's okay,' Karen whispered back. 'To me, a strike is when workers want more wages, a batter is what I whip up to make pancakes, and a run is something I'm always getting in my stockings.'

The gold flecks began to dance in his eyes. 'That's pretty good,' he said appreciatively. 'Of course, some of the others might consider it heresy.'

'Then I won't repeat it,' Karen told him as she moved on with her platter.

As if by design, the children clambered downstairs the moment the final pitch was thrown. Roger and Emily rushed to give Karen a hug, but the others hung back.

'The snot-nosed monsters are mine,' Joe's sister announced, nodding to two scruffy little boys.

The three Doniger girls peered out from behind their father.

'I don't think she bites,' Karen heard Ted whisper.

The oldest, blond like her father, round and blue-eyed like her aunt, took half a step forward.

'I'm Gwen,' she said. 'I'm twelve.'

'Hello, Gwen,' Karen answered with a smile. 'I'm Karen. I'm thirty-seven.'

Gwen gasped and the others giggled.

'That's pretty old, isn't it?'

'It depends on the day,' she was told.

'I'm Jessica,' the middle girl ventured. She had straight brown hair and her solemn brown eyes were fixed warily on the strange woman. 'I'm almost nine.'

'When I was nine,' Karen responded, 'I was in the fourth grade.'

'I'm in the fourth grade,' Jessica said.

'I'm Amy,' the youngest piped up. 'I'm five and my mommy's in heaven.'

Karen smiled at the towhead with her father's golden eyes. 'You're very grown up for five,' she said, 'and I'll bet your mommy is looking down at you right this minute and feeling very proud of you.'

'Do you think she can see me right through the roof?' the little girl asked, searching the heavy beamed ceiling.

'I think she can see you anywhere,' Karen declared. 'That's what's special about being in heaven.'

'Do you think Herman can see me, too?'

'Oh, Amy,' Gwen exclaimed.

'Who's Herman?' Karen asked.

'He's our hamster,' Jessica explained. 'He died last week and we buried him in the yard.'

'I think all those we love find a way to stay with us,' Karen said, 'even after they're gone.'

The five-year-old tucked her hand inside Karen's and leaned close. 'I kept his little red ball,' she whispered. 'It was his favorite toy. I sleep with it under my pillow.'

'When I was your age, I had a kitty,' Karen whispered back. 'When he died, I did the same thing.'

Nancy had stretched her classic Sheraton dining room table to its limit to accommodate the eight adults and seven children who crowded around it. She had planned to seat Karen between Joe and Ted, but Amy insisted on sitting beside her new friend and Gwen slipped quickly into the seat on Karen's other side.

'Well,' Nancy said and smiled, 'so much for my place cards.'

The dinner was sumptuous. Mrs. Peagram, the stout

matron who kept house for Ted and the girls, did the serving and clearing, which allowed Nancy to stay with her guests.

The company made its way through lemon consommé and butter-lettuce salad to individual Rock Cornish hens stuffed with wild-rice pilaf and served with tiny glazed carrots and onions and tender tips of asparagus. Karen wondered where Nancy had found fresh asparagus this time of year.

'Shouldn't they have let this poor chicken grow up first?' Gwen murmured.

'It's not a chicken – it's a special kind of hen that doesn't get any bigger,' Karen just had time to reply before she felt a tug at her sleeve.

'Would you cut my meat for me, please?' Amy asked. 'I'm too little to do it by myself.'

Karen smiled. 'One meat-cutter coming right up.' She started to slide the child's plate over and then changed her mind. 'If I put my hands on top of yours,' she suggested, 'we can do it together. Then, when you're old enough, you'll know how.'

'Oh, let's do it that way!'

Karen placed Amy's small hands in the correct position on the knife and fork, then covered them with her own hands and carefully guided the utensils until they had reduced the hen to bite-sized pieces.

'Oooh, that was fun,' the little girl exclaimed. 'Can we do it again next time?'

'Only if you promise to eat every morsel.'

Amy's eyes widened in dismay. 'But I'm a picky eater,' she exclaimed.

'Who told you that?'

'Mrs. Peagram,' came the solemn reply. 'She says it all the time.'

'Well, I used to be a picky eater, too,' Karen confided. 'Then one day, I ate everything on my plate. That plate was so clean it didn't even have to be washed, and everyone was so surprised that their mouths hung open. After that, they called me a piggy eater.'

Amy giggled and then frowned. 'But I don't like to eat what's good for me.'

'Oh, but that's not how it works,' Karen told her. 'You don't eat because you have to – you eat because it's so much fun. Corner that onion, crunch that carrot, down that rice, chomp that hen. The carrot says, "If she thinks I'm good for her, she won't eat me and I'll escape." The onion says, "If I make myself slippery, she won't like me and I'll escape." It's all a big game, you see – you against the food. Now, the question is, who's going to win, you or the food?'

Amy turned immediately to her plate and speared a piece of carrot with her fork. At the foot of the table, Nancy grinned. Across the table, Ted Doniger watched.

five

I don't know,' Mitch said, cocking his head to one side. 'It still looks crooked to me.'

Karen leaned as far back off the ladder as she dared and squinted up at the painting.

'We've almost got it,' she insisted.

'A little more on the left,' Mitch directed.

'My eye tells me more on the right,' she replied.

'Look, I'm the artist,' Mitch insisted. 'I tell the manager. I say, on the left.'

'I'm the manager,' Karen declared. 'I *sell* the artist. I say on the right.'

'Get the spirit level,' Mitch demanded.

'What spirit level?' Karen retorted. 'I've never needed a spirit level. I've got a perfect eye.'

'Then get another opinion.'

'A little more on the right,' a voice behind them said.

Karen turned so abruptly that she almost fell off the

ladder and Mitch had to grab hold of her to make sure she didn't. Ted Doniger was standing there with his feet apart and his hands in his pockets.

'That's what I said,' she affirmed.

'How can you say that?' Mitch argued.

Ted shrugged. 'I've got a perfect eye,' he replied with a smile.

'You'd better believe him,' Karen told Mitch. 'He's an architect. He also owns one of your paintings.'

'And if you stop fussing over this one long enough for me to get a good look at it,' Ted said, 'I may own two.'

Mitch looked at Karen. 'A little more on the right,' he grumbled.

Karen pushed the right corner up a fraction of an inch and climbed down off the ladder.

'There,' she said to Ted. 'Now you can look all you want.'

Mitch had taken to the sea this time to create a violent storm that threatened to topple a solitary sailboat into the teeming, roiling depths.

'The movement is great,' Ted observed. 'The urgency, the recklessness, the precariousness – all balance so well. It's got very much the same feeling as my clown, and yet it's totally different.'

Karen smiled. 'I wasn't sure at first, but Nancy really did choose the right gift.'

'Nancy spent too much money,' he replied.

'So, what brings you here?' Karen asked.

In the month since the birthday party, she had seen him several times – at a Sunday brunch, once or twice in passing on the weeknight evenings when she and Nancy worked on their book, on the Saturday afternoon when they had all gone to the Hayden

Planetarium – and a friendship had begun to grow between them in the nice slow way that lasting friendships always grew, like her friendship with Mitch and John and Joe Yanow had grown.

They found they had a lot in common and that it was easy for them to talk to each other. They made each other laugh.

'I come bearing an invitation,' Ted announced.

'Sounds promising so far,' Karen said with a warm smile. 'Speak more.'

'Mrs. Peagram is making the turkey, Nancy is making everything else, and the girls and I would very much like you to come to our place for Thanksgiving.'

The smile dimmed. Thanksgiving was the one traditional holiday that Beverly Kern took very seriously. Friends and relatives were culled from as far away as Palm Beach and Grosse Pointe. Laura and family were coming down from Boston, of course, and Karen's appearance at Knightsbridge Road was mandatory.

'I wish I could,' she sighed, 'but that's the one day of the year, above all others, that I'm obligated to spend with my parents.'

The disappointment showed clearly in his eyes. 'That's too bad,' he said. 'We'll miss you. You've sort of become part of the family.'

It was true. As the Sullivan Street set had once accepted her into the fold, so now did the Doniger/ Yanow clan, going out of their way to include her in many of their activities.

'That's because you've made me feel so welcome,' Karen responded. 'It's been a little like discovering a whole new brother and sister I never knew about.'

'I'm very glad you feel that way,' he said. 'I mean, you know, comfortable with us.'

Karen grinned. 'So comfortable I don't even mind you seeing me in my sweats.'

He had caught her one Sunday morning, dropping off a book Joe had ordered from Demelza, when she was in a hurry and hadn't bothered to dress.

'But I like your sweats,' Ted protested. 'They look very … comfortable.'

The two of them laughed.

'Someday,' she said, 'you wait and see, sweats are going to become haute couture.'

'Are you going to be spending the whole Thanksgiving weekend with your family?' he asked.

'Not a chance. I have to work on Friday. It's always one of our busiest days.'

'Well then,' he declared, 'all is not lost. You can come for leftovers.'

'I thought you'd never ask.'

'One condition, though – you have to promise to wear your sweats.'

Karen poked him in the ribs. 'Very funny.'

Ted turned back to Mitch's oil. 'How much?' he asked.

'Forty-five hundred,' Karen told him.

'Why not bring it with you when you come and we'll see how it looks.'

It was the first time Karen had been invited into the downstairs half of the house on West Seventy-eighth Street, and it was every bit as dramatic as the upstairs, with the same high beamed ceilings, exposed brick walls, and polished floors. But the resemblance ended there.

While Nancy's taste ran to the eclectic, Ted's was strictly modern. Leather, chrome, and glass dominated the furnishings, with only a few touches of warmth. A bentwood rocker had found its way into the study, Breuer chairs surrounded the thick glass slab that served as the dining table, and the sleek desk in the study was made of black walnut. Neutral-colored rugs had been used sparingly. The whole effect came amazingly close to Karen's own concept of interior decoration, and she was enchanted.

'This is exactly the effect I tried to achieve in my apartment,' she exclaimed. 'Clean, airy, elegant.'

'Then you should feel right at home,' he said with a smile.

The Doniger girls declared the leftover party to be even better than the holiday, and to be honest, Karen thought so, too. After dinner, they tried Mitch's painting everywhere, except in the study, where Ted had already hung the clown. They would even have considered the kitchen, but Mrs. Peagram shooed them out. They settled finally on the living room, over the mantel.

'That's it,' Ted declared, as Karen and Nancy held it in place. 'Perfect.'

'Quick! Get the hammer and hooks,' Nancy directed her husband, 'before he changes his mind.'

The Rankin really did look wonderful there, against the dark-red brick, above the rough stone fireplace. Ted had it fixed in place in no time.

'What do you think?' he asked with a mischievous wink. 'A little more on the right?'

Karen hooted.

'What's so funny?' Nancy inquired, looking from one to the other.

Ted winked at Karen. 'You had to be there,' he said.

* * *

The week before Christmas, Karen mailed her presents home to Great Neck – a brocade-covered photograph album for Beverly, a cashmere scarf for Leo.

'I'm going to stay in town on Tuesday,' she told her mother.

'Why?' Beverly wanted to know.

'Because we're open until nine on Monday, and we open again at nine on Wednesday, and to try to do Great Neck in between would be too much of a hassle. But I won't be alone. I've been invited over to Nancy's.'

'It seems to me you're spending a great deal of time with that family,' Beverly observed. 'Just like you used to with those Village people.'

Even after the enormous success of Demion Five, there was still a note of disdain in her mother's voice when she spoke of the Sullivan Street set.

'They're nice people,' Karen said mildly, 'and I like them.'

'Who are they, exactly?'

Karen sighed. 'You know perfectly well who they are. Nancy is a friend I met at the gallery.' She had not yet told her parents about the book. 'And Nancy's husband, Joe, and their two children, and also her brother and his three children, who share the same house.'

'What about the brother's wife?'

'She died a few years ago.'

'Oh?' There was a note of sudden interest in Beverly's voice. 'What does he do?'

Karen sighed in exasperation. She wanted desperately to tell her mother that Ted was a garbage collector, just for the effect she knew it would have.

'He's an architect,' she said flatly. 'And a friend.'

'An architect?' Beverly echoed. 'Is he starving, that

he has to live with his sister?'

'Hardly.'

'What has he built?'

'I haven't the faintest idea.'

Her mother sighed. 'Well, I suppose it could be worse. Anyway, we'll miss you. Everyone will be here. I'll tell them that an indigent architect was more important.'

Architects, Karen was well aware, ranked even lower than engineers in that outmoded pecking order Beverly Kern still clung to, despite the fact that her daughter was in her late thirties and still unmarried.

'We're friends, Mother,' Karen repeated.

'Yes, dear.'

It was the best Christmas Karen could remember, from the moment she arrived, barely past dawn, to participate in the official present-opening, to the moment she departed, near midnight, with Ted insisting on seeing her safely to her front door.

Gwen had asked her aunt to take a photograph of herself and her two sisters, and her father had helped her frame it. 'So you won't forget what we look like when you're not here,' she said when she gave it to Karen.

'I'm going to put it on my desk at work,' Karen told her. 'Since that's where I spend most of my time.'

Jessica had made a small ceramic box in school. 'For your most precious things,' she whispered.

'I'll keep it right next to my bed,' Karen promised, 'so it'll be the last thing I see at night, and the first thing I see in the morning.'

Amy had drawn a picture of a little blond girl with a big shaggy dog.

'Who's that?' Karen asked her.

'Me, of course,' she said.

'No – that person next to you?' Karen said, pointing to the dog.

Amy giggled. 'That's not a person. That's Duster.'

'Who's Duster?'

'He's the dog I'm going to have one day.'

'I think I'll put this on the door of my refrigerator,' Karen decided. 'That way, every time I go into the kitchen I can wave to the two of you.'

Ted laid a package gently in her lap.

'Let's see,' she said, weighing it. 'This feels heavier than a feather, but lighter than a bread box.'

The girls giggled. 'Open it! Open it!' they cried.

It was a book on modern interior design, with hundreds of color photographs of the most exquisite rooms, done by some of the foremost decorators in the world.

Karen's mouth hung open as she turned the pages. 'It's fantastic,' she said. 'One room's more magnificent than the next. I intend to spend months going through this.' Her eyes shone up at Ted. 'You couldn't have picked anything better.'

He smiled. 'I'm glad you like it.'

'I love it,' she assured him. 'I really do.' Then she jumped up. 'Now it's my turn.'

Karen had worked with Jenna for weeks. Together, they had created a sweat suit for each of the girls, as well as one for Ted. Gwen's was red with patchwork appliqués of plaids and prints, Jessica's was pale blue with diagonal paisley insets, and Amy's was bright pink and decorated with pastel circles, squares and triangles. Their father's was done in navy and featured bold stripes in red and green and yellow.

Ted laughed until there were real tears in his eyes,

and the four of them had to go and try on their new outfits before they would touch another present.

'You look fabulous,' Nancy said, searching for the camera when they paraded back in.

'They did turn out rather well, didn't they?' Karen was immensely pleased with herself.

'You couldn't have picked anything better,' Ted said, the gold flecks twinkling in his eyes.

After the presents, it was time for a hearty breakfast.

'Opening all those presents really works up the appetite,' Joe insisted as he helped himself to a third stack of pancakes.

When the last biscuit, the last egg, the last drop of maple syrup had disappeared, the two men bundled the children into their snowsuits and took off for a romp in the park. Karen and Nancy tackled the kitchen, but no sooner had they gotten the breakfast things cleared away than it was time to start on dinner.

'Now I know what they mean when they say a woman's work is never done,' Karen groaned with a grin.

Nancy chuckled. 'I can't tell you how much it's meant to have you with us,' she said as they began to soak bread crumbs and chop up the celery and onions. 'I don't just mean today, I mean the whole past ten months.'

'Well, you make me feel like one of the family,' Karen told her.

'You make it easy,' Nancy said. 'You might not see it, of course, because you didn't know them before, but your being around has really made a big difference in Ted and the girls. It's put the light back in their eyes.'

'You give me too much credit,' Karen murmured. 'I think it's probably more a case of grief just running its course.'

Nancy gave her a sidelong look. 'Well, whatever,' she murmured.

It was much later, after the trip to the park, after dinner, when everyone was stuffed to the limit and sprawled in front of a crackling fire, listening to the last of the Christmas music on the stereo, that Gwen and Jessica crept up on either side of Karen.

'Will you come spend New Year's Eve with us?' Jessica asked, her solemn brown eyes now full of trust. 'Daddy says if you come we can have real champagne at midnight instead of apple cider.'

'Daddy says the sad times are over,' Gwen added. 'And he says if you come it means that 1980 will be an extra special happy year.'

Karen looked over at Ted. He was sitting on the floor, with his back up against Nancy's chair, cradling a sleeping Amy in his arms. Karen couldn't remember ever seeing Laura's husband do anything like that with her niece and nephew, and she couldn't help but envy Nancy enormously.

If God had told her to go out into the world and pick herself a brother, she knew she wouldn't be able to find a better choice than Ted Doniger.

'I guess we've been monopolizing quite a lot of your time,' Ted said afterward as he left the car motor running and walked Karen up the steps of her town house. 'We really would love to have you join us on New Year's, but of course we'll understand if you have other plans.'

'Well, as a matter of fact, I *am* expected some-where else,' Karen admitted, handing him her cache of gifts as she fished for her keys.

The Sullivan Street set's New Year's party had long since gained the status of an annual event, and this year's celebration was doubly special. The Rankins had finished their renovation, having divided the old tenement building into four truly elegant duplex suites, each five times the size of the flat they once rented.

'I see,' Ted said.

'It's an annual thing, with a group of friends. It all started when we were very young and very poor and needed one good meal a year to keep us going.'

He smiled. 'It goes that far back, does it?'

'Little did we realize what success would do to us,' Karen said, only half in jest. 'But I'm pleased to say that I'm not totally spoiled. I would be willing to share the evening.'

'You would?' he said, brightening.

'What if I went off to my party for a while and then came around to your place?' she offered. 'In time for the champagne, of course.'

'That would work,' he replied with a nod. 'Is the party nearby?'

'It's in the Village.'

Ted frowned. 'You're not going down there by yourself, are you?'

Karen chuckled. 'If you're asking whether I have a date, the answer is no. But I always take a taxi, so it's quite safe.'

'Still, it's no night for you to be chasing all over the city on your own.' He scraped his toe against the top step. 'Look, maybe this is out of line, and you can tell me if it is, but I'd feel a whole lot better if you'd let me take you down there and then bring you back.'

Karen couldn't help staring at him. It had been a very long time since anyone had been that concerned about her welfare. She decided he really was the big brother she had never had.

'I love it that you're so concerned about me,' she said, 'but I wouldn't dream of letting you do that. However, I am willing to negotiate.'

'Oh?'

'How about you coming along to my party with me? I'm sure the Rankins would be delighted to have you, at the very least because you're the proud owner of two of Mitch's best paintings. Besides, they've just finished renovating their building and they kept a very special room in it that you might get a kick out of seeing.'

A broad grin spread quickly across Ted's face. 'You've got a deal,' he declared.

With that, he handed her back her packages, brushed his lips against her cheek and was gone, bounding down the steps two at a time.

To anyone observing from a distance, he looked far more like a carefree teenager than the middle-aged, widowed father of three.

SIX

Ted Doniger married his high school sweetheart two weeks after he received his license to practice architecture, and expected to spend the rest of his life with her.

They met when Ted was a junior and Barbara a freshman. What began as an intense adolescent infatuation eventually evolved into committed adult love.

'You're too young to tie yourself down to one girl,' his mother argued when Ted was saving up for a ring. 'You haven't experienced anything of life yet.'

'Your mother's right, son,' his father felt compelled to agree. 'What happens when you go off to college and meet somebody else?'

'I'll probably meet hundreds of girls,' Ted replied, thinking only of the young woman with the straight brown hair and solemn brown eyes. 'But none of them will be Barbara.'

With his dream and her determination, his good humor and her good sense, his energy and her serenity, they were two sides of the same coin – opposite and inseparable. There was never anyone else for either of them. From the very beginning, they knew that one day they would be husband and wife. But that day would not come until Ted could properly afford to support her and the family they would have. He was adamant about that.

'You're not going to scrub, you're not going to scrimp, you're not going to do without,' he said the afternoon she saw him off to Yale. 'We're going to have a decent place to live and a car and enough extra money for movies and ice cream and vacations every summer.'

It took eight years.

His first job was with a small firm on the outskirts of Philadelphia, which was barely close enough to Reading for him to commute every day from the little cottage behind her parents' house, but not close enough to allow him very much time with his new bride.

'We can afford to live closer, if you like,' he told her. 'But if your parents are really willing to let us have this place, just for the cost of fixing it up, maybe we should grab it.'

Barbara Doniger was not only in love, she was very wise. If she could wait patiently for him to finish four years of college, two years in the army and two years of graduate school, she could wait for him to come home for dinner.

'We'll start a savings account,' she said. 'And every month we'll make a deposit, just as if we were paying rent, and before you know it, we'll have enough to build our own dream house.'

'A dream house, eh?' He smiled. 'Is that the plan, Mrs. Doniger?'

'That's the plan,' she told him firmly. 'And it isn't going to cost so very much, either, because I happen to know an exceptional young architect who'll design exactly what we want for free.'

Five mornings a week, Ted got up before dawn, leaving the house at six to drive to Philadelphia, some sixty miles away. Barbara got up with him so they could share breakfast together, packed him a lunch so they could save money, and got into the habit of fixing a peanut-butter-and-jelly sandwich for herself around three in the afternoon so she could wait to have supper with him when he came home at night, which could be anywhere between eight and ten o'clock, depending on his workload.

One day in April of 1967, he made the usual two-hour trip home in eighty-six minutes, reaching the hospital in Reading just seconds after his first daughter was born.

'I guess I didn't plan very well,' Barbara yawned as she drifted off to sleep. 'I thought it would take much longer.'

Jessica was born in Hartford, Connecticut, a year after Ted took a job with a medium-sized firm that specialized in the kind of steel-and-glass office buildings that had begun to pop up all over the northeast. Amy was born in New York, six months after Ted accepted a junior partnership in a large and prestigious firm known for its distinctive hotels and unique office complexes.

Each time, in each place, he and Barbara resolved to build their dream house, and each time they were thwarted by a better offer in another city. But this time Barbara would not be denied. They rented an apartment on the west side of Manhattan for convenience, and spent their weekends driving from one suburb to another, from New Jersey to Long Island to Westchester County, hunting for just the right place. One crisp September afternoon they drove into Hastings-on-Hudson and knew their search was over.

'Here,' Barbara said.

'Here,' Ted agreed.

The very next week, they placed a deposit on a beautiful two-acre site that sloped down toward the river and began to design their house.

'I want large rooms, high ceilings, and lots of windows,' Barbara declared. 'And a big pantry in the kitchen. And closets – endless closets.'

'Every room will have a river view,' Ted decided. 'The house will have two arms that extend out, sort of like a V with a flat bottom, and the girls will have one wing and we'll have another.'

'Can we have a garden?' she asked.

'Of course,' he told her. 'And we'll have a play area for the girls, and a patio with a barbecue, and a front porch where we can sit in the evenings and watch the sun go down.'

'I can't wait,' she breathed.

But Barbara was already sick. Every specialist Ted consulted told him the same thing – a year, perhaps two, no more than that.

They kept the seriousness of it from the children and from each other and even from themselves as long as they could. Every night, Ted would snuggle close beside her, willing his strength into her body and praying for a miracle even as he watched her slowly fading away.

'She's always been there,' he told his sister wretchedly one drab day in May when the ambulance had been summoned to rush Barbara to the hospital for the last time. 'She's not just my wife, you know, not just my friend – she's the best part of me. She's my strength, my purpose. Whatever dreams have come true, whatever plans have worked out, whatever I've accomplished – all of it – it's only because she was there, backing me up. What will I ever do without her?'

'What you have to do,' Nancy told him, holding tight to his hand. 'You'll go on.'

The doctor, a well-meaning but taciturn man, came out of Barbara's room just then and tapped Ted on the shoulder.

'She wants to see you,' he said.

Ted started to stand up but his knees buckled under him.

'Get hold of yourself,' Nancy hissed. 'You have to be strong now, for her.'

He nodded numbly and struggled to his feet. It was only a few steps across the corridor, but it took an eternity for him to reach her door and all his effort to push it open. She looked so small lying in the hospital bed, so helpless, her brown eyes too big in her pale face. What was left of her glossy brown hair barely grazed the pillow. The tubes were gone, the masks, the wires, the machines – symbols of modern medicine that had not been able to heal. Had they been there, he might have smashed them with his fists.

She tried to smile at him as he came toward her and

that pitiful attempt alone was enough to fill his eyes and pinch his throat.

'Hi,' she whispered.

He sat down on the bed beside her and held her shoulders and kissed her lightly.

'I love you,' he said in an unsteady voice. 'I've always loved you. I guess I haven't said it anywhere near as often as I should, but that doesn't mean I don't feel it.'

'I know,' she murmured.

'I've never loved anyone but you – not anyone. Not from the moment I first saw you in that ridiculous pom-pom skirt.'

'No sillier,' she breathed, 'than you in your Bermuda shorts.'

'We made quite a pair, didn't we?' he said with a painful chuckle.

Her eyes flickered closed for a moment and he thought she might be slipping away, but then they opened again.

'The children . . .' she sighed, her voice weaker, her effort stronger.

'What?' he asked. 'What about them?'

'Love them . . .'

'Always,' he told her.

'Find someone . . .' she managed, and he had to bend close now to hear her. 'Make a family ... build ... build that house . . .'

'No!' he cried.

'Promise . . .'

'No,' he sobbed, burying his head against her. 'You can't ask me to do that. I could never love anyone but you. Never! I'll take good care of the girls. I'll be the best father to them that I know how to be, but I don't want anyone else. Please, don't make me promise.'

But Barbara could no longer hear him.

Ted took her home to Reading to be buried. Nancy stayed behind with the girls. For two days he allowed himself to be surrounded by people who knew and loved him and who had known and loved Barbara.

'I'm sorry,' he kept saying to her parents. 'I'm so sorry.'

'It wasn't your fault, son,' they told him. 'It was nobody's fault. Don't blame yourself.'

But he did. He blamed himself for all those years he had made her wait, all those lost years they could have had together.

When he returned to New York, he and Nancy and the girls had a quiet ceremony of their own. It was a godsend having Nancy there to take care of everything, but eventually she had to go back to Reading. Joe needed her and she did have two little ones of her own.

'Why don't you take a couple of weeks off?' she urged her brother. 'Go away somewhere, get some rest.'

'It's better if I work,' he told her.

'Well then, why don't I take the girls home with me? Mom's already said that she and Dad would love to have them for a while.'

'Gwen and Jessica have school,' Ted said. 'I don't want to disrupt their routine any more than necessary.'

'Will you be all right?'

'Sure.'

'How will you manage, I mean, with everything?'

'I don't know,' he said. 'I suppose I'll have to hire a housekeeper. Someone to cook and be here with the girls when I'm not home. I think that would be the best solution.'

Nancy hired Mrs. Peagram before she left. The plump little widow, with the knot of gray hair on top of her head, had lost her husband in the Korean War, before there were any children, and had never re-married. She was fair, if strict, and believed in reward-ing success more than punishing failure. The girls never entirely warmed up to her, but she had the household running smoothly in no time.

Ted went ahead and purchased the property in Hastings-on-Hudson but he never built the house. The idea of living there without Barbara was much too painful. Occasionally, he would drive up on a Sunday and walk the boundaries of the site or sit on the slope and look out over the steady river while the children played catch or tag or munched on a lunch that Mrs. Peagram had prepared.

He bought the house on West Seventy-eighth Street instead, and not only did he design the new interior, he did much of the actual renovation work himself. It was hard, mindless labor and exactly what he needed. While he and Barbara had dreamed of getting out of the city as soon as possible, his decision to stay was based on practicality. The fifteen-minute commute to and from his office, even at the height of the rush hour, gave him more time to spend with the girls.

When the Yanows moved to New York a year later, Ted offered them the upstairs apartment. The ar-rangement suited everyone. Nancy slipped into the role of surrogate mother that Mrs. Peagram had never quite filled and Ted soon settled into a comfortable routine – with his work to sustain him, his children to fulfill him, and his sister to support him.

He had no interest in meeting women. The very idea of dating seemed a betrayal. For the most part, he was quite content with his neat, safe life. If he sometimes missed the kind of intimacy that could be found only with a woman, it was a momentary distraction. For him, the act of love was as emotional as it was physical. On the few occasions when he even bothered to look at the women who continually circled around him, there wasn't one among them with whom he felt the slightest desire to share anything intimate.

Until now.

Now, as he puttered in his little patch of garden under a thin April sun and watched Gwen pulling weeds and Jessica teaching Amy to do a cartwheel, it occurred to him that, as usual, Barbara had been much wiser than he. She had tried to tell him not to bury himself beside her and shut his heart to the idea of being whole again. He had never dreamed that someone would come along to fill even a portion of that aching void inside him. But someone had – when he wasn't looking, when his guard was down, when he least expected it.

It was Nancy's fault, of course, for bringing her into the house, first as a business associate, then as a friend, and finally blending her into the very fabric of the family.

'She's nothing to do with you,' his sister had insisted the day before his fortieth birthday party. 'She's my friend. We're working on a book together, Joe and the kids adore her, and I thought it would be nice to include her. But if the idea really bothers you that much, I'll just tell her not to come.'

'You can't very well do that once you've invited her,' Ted grumbled.

'Then grin and bear it.'

From Nancy's careless account of her career-oriented friend, he expected something of a barracuda to show up – insecure, power-hungry, and typically overdressed, overconfident, and overanxious. He was totally unprepared for the gentle, amiable, utterly delightful woman who had captivated his daughters in less than thirty seconds.

'You've very good with children,' he told her on that first evening. 'The girls are usually quite shy with strangers.'

'I love kids,' she said simply.

He couldn't understand why she wasn't married, with a houseful of her own to nurture, but as winter slipped and skidded its way into spring, he realized how very glad he was that she wasn't.

It began on his birthday with just a vague recognition of someone new entering his space. By Christmas, he had become comfortable with her. By Easter, he thought of her as a good friend. By Labor Day, he found himself inventing opportunities to see her. And by the time 1981 rolled around, he was ready to put aside his guilt and acknowledge that he wanted her to be a lot more than a friend.

She was bright and amusing and self-reliant, and still there was something terribly vulnerable about her – a way she had of holding back sometimes, to observe rather than to participate, or an expression in her eyes when she didn't know he was watching.

On New Year's Day, he invited her up to Hastings-on-Hudson. A foot of snow lay on the ground and chunks of ice floated slowly down the river. The girls immediately set to building a snowman and Ted and Karen began to walk.

'It's magnificent up here,' she breathed when they had tramped the length of the property. 'I'm so sorry you and Barbara didn't get to build your dream house.'

'I think you would have liked her,' he heard himself say. 'I know she would have liked you.'

'Knowing you, knowing the girls,' Karen replied, 'it's obvious she must have been very special.'

He was well aware that she saw him as a sort of surrogate brother, and was quite comfortable with him on that basis. He had no inkling of how she would view a change in that status. In the eighteen months they had known each other, she had not once indicated, by a single word or deed, that she desired anything else. All by itself, that set her apart from almost every other woman he had met in the five years since Barbara's death.

It occurred to him that he really knew very little about her. She rarely spoke of herself, except to provide brief answers to direct questions. Their conversations were mostly about him or the girls or the Yanows or Demion Five. She had walked into the middle of his life, but as of yet, he had not been invited into hers.

'I suppose you're one of those feminists,' he suggested once when she teased him about his tendency to cling to traditional gender roles. 'An emancipated woman who chose career over family.'

'Sometimes,' she replied enigmatically, 'life has very little to do with choice.'

'What does it have to do with, then?' he probed.

For a moment, Karen's face clouded over and a haunted expression filled her eyes.

'Survival,' she said. Then her face cleared and she was smiling and teasing him once again.

It was the first time he had seen beneath her sunny, serene surface, the first glimpse he had of a darker side. He wondered what misfortune shrouded her past, but he didn't press her. He didn't want to appear to be prying and run the risk of pushing her away. Besides, it didn't really matter. In the silence of the night, and the emptiness of his bed, he couldn't stop thinking about her.

Two or three evenings a week, when he knew she was upstairs working on the book with Nancy, Ted would invent a reason to come knocking on the door. After a while, the frequency of his visits prompted Nancy to observe, privately, that she had seen more of him in the past several months than in the past several years.

'Is that a complaint?' he asked.

'Nope,' she said with an impish grin. 'In fact, let me know when you run out of excuses. I'm sure there are a few I can suggest.'

At Ted's instigation, Sunday evenings became family occasions. Either upstairs or downstairs, the Yanows and the Donigers would gather together for dinner, a few games, a little conversation and a lot of fun. Karen was always included.

Late one summer Sunday, when the children were asleep and the adults were lingering in the garden, Amy woke up screaming from a nightmare and neither Ted nor Mrs. Peagram could manage to calm her.

'Let me try,' Karen offered.

She sat down on Amy's pink-and-white canopy bed in the little girl's candy-cane room, and calmly took the child into her arms. Her voice was too low for Ted to catch the words, but it didn't matter. In less than ten minutes, his youngest daughter was sound asleep again.

'What did you say to her?' he whispered.

'I told her that her mother had sent me to chase away the hobgoblins and keep her safe while she slept.' He caught a sudden mischievous glint in her blue-gray eyes. 'Then I bribed her.'

'With what?'

'I promised that, whenever I'm here, I'll come and tell her a story before she goes to sleep so that her dreams will be filled with beautiful things – and there won't be any room left for scary monsters.'

It became a ritual. Three, sometimes four nights a week, Karen would sit on the edge of Amy's bed and spin magical tales of little girls and little boys in a faraway world where the sun always shone and birds always sang and flowers always bloomed, and there was no such thing as sadness.

'Is there such a place?' Amy asked her.

'Oh yes,' Karen told her. 'If you believe.'

Before long, Jessica and Gwen, too, were sidling into Amy's room, climbing up on the end of the bed to listen, and from the doorway, Ted watched and realized how much his daughters needed a mother. Mrs. Peagram kept the house spotlessly clean and the girls properly fed and clothed and supervised their homework, but she wasn't very good at nurturing. She just didn't have the knack.

Karen had the knack. She wasn't Barbara, of course – no one would ever be Barbara. Yet, in some ways, she was a lot like Barbara. She seemed to know many of the same things Barbara had known and she did many of the same things Barbara had done, and more and more, he couldn't seem to keep himself from smiling whenever she was around.

She was interested in his work, genuinely fond of the children, and perfectly at ease in his environment. Without even being aware of it, he began to picture her running the house, raising the girls, and growing old beside him.

'Is Karen coming tonight?' Jessica asked, interrupting his thoughts, and yet not really interrupting them at all.

'Is today Sunday?'

'Sure.'

'Then Karen's coming.'

'I want to show her my science project before I turn it in.'

'Good,' Ted replied. 'As I recall, she was the one who gave you the idea.'

'Yeah.' Jessica grinned. 'She did, didn't she?'

'Watch me, Daddy!' Amy cried suddenly. 'I'm going to do a cartwheel!'

'I'm watching, sweetheart,' he called.

The effort was a bit lopsided but the chubby youngster managed to pull it around.

'Did you see?' she chortled, jumping up and down. 'Did you see?'

'I saw, and it was wonderful.'

'Will Karen be here before it gets dark? I want to show her, too.'

'I think so.'

'Make sure, Daddy, will you? I want her to see me.'

'You know, Dad,' Gwen observed idly, 'if you

married Karen, we wouldn't have to keep asking when she's coming all the time. She'd already be here.'

'You mean every night?' Amy asked, overhearing.

'Sure,' Gwen told her, 'and mornings and afternoons, too.'

'Would she be here to tie my shoes for school?' the first-grader pressed.

'Of course,' Jessica put in. 'She'd be here just like Mommy used to be.'

Amy's eyes widened. 'Just like Mommy?' she gasped, although she was too young to have a very clear image of Barbara.

'Well, not exactly like her,' modified Gwen, the only one of the three of them who could really remember. 'But almost.'

The little girl turned to her father. 'Are we going to marry Karen, Daddy? Is she going to be almost like Mommy?'

'Would you like that?' he asked, amazed at how simple the most complex things could become when seen through the eyes of a child.

'Oh yes,' Amy breathed.

'Sure,' Jessica said.

'Why not?' Gwen shrugged and then lowered her voice to a whisper. 'She's a lot nicer than Mrs. Pea, anyway.'

As if on cue, Mrs. Peagram came to the back door. 'It's time for lunch,' she announced in her high-pitched Boston twang. 'Come on in now, girls, and let's get those little hands washed.'

Ted thrust his trowel into the soft dirt of the flower bed and stood up with purpose.

'You go on in with Mrs. Peagram and have your lunch,' he directed his daughters.

'What about you, Daddy?' Jessica wanted to know. 'What are you going to do?'

'I'm going to go clean myself up a little,' he told her, looking down at his soiled jeans, 'and then I have an errand to run, across town.'

seven

Karen sat cross-legged in the middle of her living room floor, in a baggy red sweat suit, surrounded by black-and-white photographs. A yellow pad lay beside her, a ballpoint pen was clamped between her teeth. There was a smudge of ink on her chin.

The book that she and Nancy had envisioned nearly two years ago was almost finished. They had made the final photo selections, from among the thousand images captured on film, just last week. All that was wanting now were the words.

'No pressure,' Nancy had assured her, handing over a thick stack of prints. 'Just take these home with you, live with them for a while, and see what comes.'

At first, nothing had come. Karen spent hours staring at a blank pad, chewing on the end of her pen, trying to think like a poet. Finally, she tossed the pad and pen aside, stopped thinking, and began to stare instead at the images themselves, spreading the prints out around her, concentrating on their stories.

Eventually, she found words to describe the children of Harlem as they stood in the path of a gushing fire hydrant on a suffocating summer day, and the cold breath of death that reached into a Bowery doorway in the middle of winter to claim a man beneath a blanket of newspapers, and the rebirth of the earth as the first spring crocus pushed its head through the hard crust of clay along Riverside Drive.

But autumn had totally frustrated her. With a sigh, and time running out, Karen reached for the twelve visions of that enigmatic season for perhaps the hundredth time. This time, one of them caught her attention and she reached out and pulled it toward her. It was a bleak illustration, in which Nancy had caught the last leaf falling from the only tree in an otherwise treeless section of Morningside Park. She yanked the pen out of her mouth, grabbed her pad, and began to write.

> The last tear of autumn
> falls unnoticed.
> A silent cry,
> frozen on the cheek of winter.

Now, at least, she had a beginning, a direction.

An hour later, she had covered half a dozen pages. So engrossed was she that the unexpected sound of her door buzzer severed her concentration like a chain saw.

'Hi,' Ted said when she opened the door.

'Hi,' she replied, wondering why he was standing on her doorstep, looking so freshly scrubbed, in the middle of the day. 'Don't tell me I forgot something,' she gasped. 'Did we have plans?'

'No, no,' he assured her hastily. 'I just happened to be in the neighborhood, so I thought I'd stop by. But if you're busy, I can be on my way.'

'Don't be silly,' she told him, because the mood was broken now and the words were gone. 'Come on in.'

'I thought maybe you'd be out on a day like this.'

Karen was quickly gathering up her papers, stacking them neatly on the desk. 'I've been trying to work.'

'And I interrupted you, didn't I?'

He sounded so genuinely distressed that she felt her irritation at the intrusion melt away.

'It's all right, really,' she assured him. 'I wasn't having much success, anyway.'

Ted had been to her apartment on a number of occasions over the past year and a half, and each time he entered he was surprised by how familiar it felt. When he sat down on one of the love seats, it was just like slipping into a comfortable old sweater.

'I think this book is a wonderful idea,' he said, glancing down at the photographs on the floor. 'I know it's going to be a success.'

'Providing I hold up my end of the bargain.' Karen sighed. 'I don't know why I let Nancy talk me into this.'

'Someday you'll be glad she did,' he said with such genuine conviction that Karen smiled.

From the very beginning, he had put her at ease, teasing her like a kid sister, treating her like a valued friend, until it was hard to remember that they hadn't known each other all their lives. In large part, she supposed, the instant comfort came from his being Nancy's brother. But Karen knew it was also because he had never attempted anything more than a quick peck on the cheek or a hand on an elbow to guide her across a street that she felt as close to him as if there were actually a flesh-and-blood connection between them.

Like his sister, Ted was bright and clever, and Karen looked forward to the now frequent occasions when she saw him. But even more important to her than the time spent with him was the time she spent with Gwen and Jessica and Amy.

In many ways, the three girls had come to symbolize the innocence Karen had lost, the daughters she would never raise, the children she would never bear. She answered their questions, cheered their successes, and basked in every smile and every giggle they chose to share with her. And always behind them stood their father, steady, sober and safe.

Still, she hadn't realized how deeply entwined she had become in the lives of the Donigers until this very moment – because this was the first time Ted had ever appeared on her doorstep unannounced.

'Can I get you something to drink?' she asked, suddenly remembering her manners.

'A glass of water would be fine,' he replied.

'How about some iced tea?'

'Only if you'll have some, too.'

She returned from the kitchen with two frosty glasses and a plate of cookies.

'Looks good,' he said.

They sipped in silence until Ted set his glass down on the coffee table and stood up, walking to the fireplace and pretending to study the Rankin oil that hung above the mantel.

'Amy would like you to come before dark tonight,'

he said. 'Jessica's taught her how to do a cartwheel, and she wants you to see.'

'Of course I will,' Karen replied warmly.

'And Jessica wants to show you her science project.'

Karen nodded. 'Oh, good. I've been anxious to see how it turned out.'

Their words sounded strangely formal and stilted to them both. Karen shifted uncomfortably in her seat, wondering what had happened to their usual light banter. Ted ran a finger along the edge of the mantel.

'Uh, Gwen thinks we ought to get married,' he said, trying to make his tone light, 'so we wouldn't always have to schedule appointments to see you.'

'Oh, she does, does she?' Karen replied with a smile, relieved to have the conversation back on track.

'Actually, all three girls would like that,' he added.

'Those little devils.' She chuckled. 'You never know what they'll come up with next.'

Ted turned around to face her then. 'As a matter of fact,' he said softly, 'all four of us would like that ... very much.'

Karen opened her mouth to say something clever and then closed it again when she realized he was serious. But it didn't make any sense, because they didn't have that kind of relationship. They were just – friends.

'I don't understand,' she stammered finally. 'I mean, you never – that is, I didn't – I mean, you and I aren't – well, you know – like that.'

'Just because we haven't been doesn't mean we couldn't be,' he observed.

'But we're friends,' she protested. 'Good friends. I count on your friendship. I don't want that to change.'

He shrugged. 'I happen to think that friendship is a pretty solid foundation to build on.'

Just like an architect, Karen thought wryly, beginning to squirm anew in her seat. She valued the relationship they had forged more than she could ever say, and she wondered whether it would survive her turning him down.

'I'm really very flattered,' she began gently, 'but the idea of marrying you – well, it just never entered my head.'

'I know I'm not exactly the knight in shining armor you probably expected to come riding over the hill,' he conceded. 'I've had some of the stuffing knocked out of me, I admit it. I'm too much of a workaholic and not enough of a romantic. I like theater and the symphony, but I don't go very often. I'm not much of a party animal. I guess you could say I'm a real stick-in-the-mud. I'm not well-traveled or well-read. On top of that, I'm middle-aged, I've buried a wife, and I've got three kids to raise – altogether, nobody's idea of a prize package. But I'm faithful and honest and a good provider, I think, and the thing is, I care for you in a very special way, and I think we could make a good life together.'

He stopped talking suddenly, surprised that he had actually managed to make that whole speech without stumbling.

'How can you say all those awful things about yourself?' Karen demanded. 'You're certainly no more middle-aged than I am, and you're terrific at parties. You may not say much, but you're a great listener. I don't go to the symphony all that often myself, and the bookshelves always seem to be filled at your place. I'm not so well-traveled, either, I'll have you know. I've never even been to Europe. And there are a whole lot more important things for a person to be in life than romantic – like sensible and stable and sincere, and your children are absolutely terrific. How can you say you're not a knight in shining armor? I can't imagine any woman who wouldn't be proud to ride off with you.'

'Is that a yes?' he asked.

Karen stopped short. She had been so eager to come to his defense that she hadn't really given much thought to the effect her words might have on him.

He was so terribly nice and the last thing in the world she wanted to do was hurt him. But she had long ago resigned herself to the idea of being unmarried, choosing instead to devote herself to a career, whatever it turned out to be, and she was not uncomfortable with that decision. Now all she had to do was find a way to let him down gently.

'I think maybe you should give me a little time,' she heard herself say. 'You know, to kind of sort things out.'

'Of course,' he exclaimed. 'Take all the time you need. I know this is a pretty big decision for you to make.'

The biggest, she thought. 'Thank you,' she murmured.

Ted reached for his iced tea and politely drained the glass. 'Why don't I let you get back to work,' he said. 'I mean, it's not as though I''m not going to see you again in a few hours, right?'

'Right,' she agreed.

The moment the door closed behind him, Karen made for the kitchen, filling her tea glass with Scotch and drinking it down in one long swallow.

The plastic composure she had cultivated for the past eighteen years, that singular ability to draw a curtain across her emotions, crumbled as she giggled and cried and shivered all together. She refilled her glass and went back to the living room, where she collapsed in a heap. Halfway through the second Scotch, she began to feel very foolish.

'Why didn't you just come right out and say no?' she reproached herself aloud. 'Why did you have to leave him dangling as though there were some hope?'

The day Peter Bauer walked out of her life, Karen had been devastated. Although, clearly, she had been the one to betray him, she had been unable to shake the feeling that, in some indefinable way, he had betrayed her as well. She determined that she would never again put herself in that position. The yardstick of the 1960s still hung over her in the 1980s. In her heart, she knew that no man would ever be able to forgive her for what she had let happen on that cold December night, as Peter had not, and would shrink from her at the first mention of it – at the first sight of the result. Of course, she had to admit, she had never been willing to let anyone close enough to test her theory.

Instead, she had come to terms with being single. In many ways, she found she was well-suited to the solitude, and the consequent peace and privacy it afforded. Then, too, the state of spinsterhood no longer carried the stigma it once had. Karen knew women who were enjoying a whole new kind of life-style. They were out in the business world, being successful and single. Some lived intimately and openly with men to whom they were not married. A few were even choosing to have babies without having husbands.

Downing the last of her Scotch, Karen sighed a sigh of defeat, knowing in her heart of hearts that, even though she had truly made peace with the way her life had turned out, she would gladly have given up Demion Five and her posh East Side apartment and her Rankin oil for just one day of being elbow-deep in diapers and dirty dishes and Tinker Toys. That was the irony of what Ted had come across town to suggest. Had he offered her Mrs. Peagram's position instead of a marriage proposal, she might have been tempted to accept.

Karen laughed outright. Nothing less than two stiff drinks could have brought her to admit anything like that. But it was true. In just a few short months, she had become so involved in the lives of Gwen and Jessica and Amy that she couldn't imagine a more rewarding assignment than to spend every single day with them, helping them to learn and grow and blossom into beautiful young women. It would go a long way toward making up for the children she could never have.

Sometimes she liked to imagine, when she sat on Amy's bed in the evenings and spun out her stories, that these three little girls were indeed her very own. She couldn't have loved them more. But to marry a man just so she could stay close to his children? There seemed something not quite honest about that.

It wasn't that she didn't like Ted. On the contrary, she liked him enormously and probably even loved him, as a sister would love a brother. But the thought of having to share a bed with him, or let him see the ugly scars that screamed the truth of her youthful indiscretion, made her shiver all over again.

No, she would have to tell him again how flattered she was by his proposal, and then decline – even knowing it would mean she would lose the girls, because things would be too awkward after that. How many men who had been rejected would still want the woman who rejected them underfoot all the time?

Karen bit her lower lip and felt tears stinging her eyes. She was going to miss the children terribly, she knew. Not only that, she was truthful enough to admit that she was going to miss Ted terribly, too.

eight

The photographic essay was finished and scheduled for production the second week in May.

'Jesus,' Demelza breathed when she saw it. 'I knew Nancy could take pictures, but I never dreamed Karen could write this kind of poetry. This is dynamite. We'll order five thousand copies.'

'Do you think you can sell that many?' Nancy gasped.

'At least,' the co-owner of Demion Five told her. 'What are you going to call it?'

After considerable debate, the two women had named the book *Four Seasons* because, after all, that was exactly what it was.

'Not to be confused with Vivaldi,' Nancy said.

'Or the restaurant,' Karen added.

Demelza priced the book at $49.95.

'My goodness,' the photographer exclaimed. 'Isn't that a bit steep?' Actually, she considered it outrageous.

'It's a bargain,' Demelza told her. 'Fifty Yanows for a dollar apiece? Fabulous presentation? Even without the poetry – which could be a lovely little book in its own right – it's an absolute bargain.'

'I had no idea,' Nancy conceded, even though her single prints, which were limited to a run of fifty, sold for as much as two hundred and fifty dollars each. But then, they were individually signed and numbered.

'You have to remember,' Demelza continued as though she had read the photographer's mind, 'it's not so very different from marketing your prints. We're still talking limited edition.'

'Five thousand doesn't sound so limited to me,' Nancy observed.

'If we start promoting by the middle of July,' Demelza said, 'we should be sold out by Christmas.'

'Sold out?' Nancy exclaimed. 'Are you serious?'

Demelza smiled. 'I suggest you start planning your next book.'

Nancy's head was spinning and Karen was feeling as giddy as a newborn colt as the two women made their way over to Ninth Avenue and a new, highly touted Italian restaurant. They had promised themselves a night on the town when *Four Seasons* was finished.

'Why do I feel as though I'm in a leaky rowboat about to plunge over Niagara Falls?' the photographer wondered as they were shown to their table.

The poet chuckled. 'Well, look at it this way,' she suggested. 'It's not your life you're in danger of losing, just your credibility.'

'Thanks,' Nancy replied dryly. 'That makes me feel lots better.'

It was a prix-fixe restaurant without a menu. The fare was whatever the chef felt like preparing that particular evening. Reservations were required, and the place, which could accommodate only forty diners at a time, was booked at least two months in advance.

They discussed different ways of promoting the book through the minestrone, the in-store fanfare that Demion Five would be likely to launch over the hot and cold antipasto, and the incredible idea that their work could become a coffee-table necessity between bites of cheese ravioli.

It wasn't until they had begun to dig into their veal scallopini that Karen casually dropped her bombshell.

'Ted asked me to marry him.'

The fork fell from Nancy's hand and her uneven blue eyes almost popped from her head.

'And you waited through three courses to tell me?' she cried indignantly.

'Well, actually, it's been a bit longer than that.'

'How long?'

Karen shrugged. 'About a month.'

'A month?' Nancy squealed. 'A whole month and you never breathed a word of it?'

'Well, I wasn't sure how you'd take it.'

'How I'd take it? I've been hoping and praying for this for a year and a half now.'

Karen picked at her three-star food.

'The thing is, you see, I've never really thought of Ted in that way,' she mused.

'Oh?' Nancy said, and the word hung there between them.

'Don't misunderstand. It's not that I don't care about him,' Karen insisted. 'I do, a great deal, and you know how much I adore the girls. But, well, I wasn't planning on getting married.'

'Why not?' was all Nancy could think of to ask.

'It's just a choice I made, a long time ago,' Karen replied, gulping her Chianti.

Nancy had decided that Karen was ideal for her brother the first day the two women met at Demion Five, over tea and muffins and Paul Revere. She wasn't sure what it was about the stylish boutique manager, among all the other women she had considered and rejected, that made her so positive so immediately, but the idea had caught on something inside her head and refused to be dislodged.

'Why would you make such a ridiculous choice as that?' she asked, as Karen toyed with her veal.

'I've been alone so long,' came the reply. 'I'm set in my ways. I need my space.'

'It's about a long time ago, isn't it?' Nancy asked softly, shrewdly. 'About what happened to you – what you wrote about?'

Karen looked away. 'It's about a lot of things,' she murmured.

'But things can change,' Nancy insisted. 'If we want them to.'

There was a pause then, neither of them knowing quite where to go next.

'I believe that everyone has two selves,' Karen said finally. 'The public self that they show to the world and the private one that sustains them. For some people, the public self is merely an extension of the private self. For others, though, the public self is a mask for the private self, and without it they wouldn't survive.'

Karen stopped there, and Nancy considered her words. This woman had been her closest friend for two years, in great part because they shared so many common interests, common values and common instincts, and Nancy had long ago seen beneath the self-assured facade.

'Sometimes sharing can be a means of survival,' she suggested.

'Not in this case,' Karen asserted. 'You'll just have to take my word for that.'

'I think you're selling yourself short,' Nancy declared. 'And Ted, too.'

'Perhaps I just have a different perspective.'

'Then why say anything at all?'

'Because you and Ted are so close and I don't want this to come between you. And because you and I are close and I don't want it to come between us, either.'

'He might not come to me.'

Karen thought about that for a moment. 'Then go to him. There are so many good women out there. Don't let him shut the door because one failed him.'

'He really cares about you, you know.'

A shadow flickered across Karen's face. 'He deserves better.'

The next evening, she dropped by for a bedtime story unannounced, choosing the tale of the princess and the pea. As soon as she finished, she tucked the covers around Amy, kissed Jessica and Gwen good night, and went in search of Ted, finding him in the study, of course, hunched over his drafting table, the light from the lamp glinting off his golden hair.

'Are you busy?' she asked hesitantly.

His face lit up when he saw her.

'Never too busy for you,' he replied, snapping off the lamp and standing up to stretch his back muscles.

Then he moved over to sit on the sofa. 'Are the girls in bed?'

'One is, another is on her way and the third is probably on the telephone.'

'Come sit down,' he invited, patting the sofa.

Karen chose the chair across from him.

'You must have thought I was ignoring you,' she began.

'Nonsense,' he told her. 'I know how hard you and Nancy have been working to finish the book.'

It would have been so much easier, she thought, if he weren't always so nice and so understanding about everything.

'Well, I didn't want you to think that I'd forgotten your ... your kind offer.'

He grinned at her, the gold flecks in his eyes dancing. 'You make it sound like we're talking about a job.'

'Oh, I didn't mean to,' she apologized. 'It's just that I ...'

Karen faltered. She had simply meant to thank him, decline his proposal, and then leave, as quickly as possible.

'It's been such a short time,' she heard herself saying instead. 'We barely know each other. I mean, we're friends, and I really do like you, but ...'

'... you don't love me,' he finished for her.

She looked down at her hands twisted in her lap. 'It's not that so much,' she whispered, wishing she didn't have to do this. 'But there are things about me, things you couldn't possibly understand that – well, it isn't you, you see, it's that – well, I can't marry anybody.'

He looked at her thoughtfully for a moment, while

she struggled with her hands.

'For a long time after my wife died,' he said finally, 'I was convinced that I never wanted to get close to anyone again. Losing her had hurt too much, and I knew I couldn't risk going through anything like that a second time. So I built an invisible wall around myself, a bomb shelter, if you will, and I locked myself into it so I could be safe. I had my work, I had the girls, and I figured that was enough. But I was wrong, because all of life is a risk – and safe is as good as already dead.'

Karen pried her eyes away from her hands to glance up at him. He was sensitive and he was caring and he was trying so hard, but he just didn't understand.

'And for me, it's the other way around,' she told him. 'Safe is the only way I can live.'

'Does that leave any room for negotiation?'

Her glance slid past his shoulder. 'I do like you, in a very special way,' she said. 'I trust you more than any man I know. I feel good when I'm with you. I look forward to the time I spend with you and the girls, and all that means more to me than I can say.'

'That's a start.'

'But it's not enough.'

'Why not?'

Her eyes fastened on her hands once again. 'Because I can't ... I can't be a wife to you.' She sighed. She had come to think of other women as being lush and green inside, where she saw herself to be brown and shriveled.

A pensive frown creased his forehead. 'I'm not going to pry,' he said. 'I don't need to know any more than you want to tell me.'

'I had ... an accident,' she heard herself say, when

she hadn't intended to say anything at all. 'It was a long time ago, but because of it, there are – things that don't work like they should.'

'I'm not looking for grand passion at my stage of life,' he replied sincerely. 'I don't really expect to have again what I had with Barbara. But the feelings I have for you are warm and comfortable and constant, and that's enough for me. I'd just like you to be a part of my life, to share all the laughter that's ahead, and the tears, too.'

'You make it sound so simple,' she responded. 'Only it isn't that simple.'

Ted took a deep breath. 'It can be,' he assured her. 'It can be as simple as taking on three little girls who adore you, and their father who thinks the world is an okay place again because you're in it. And it wouldn't ever have to be anything more than that, unless, of course, you wanted it to be.'

'I do believe you *are* offering me a job,' she said with a sudden grin. 'Mrs. Peagram's job.'

'Well, that may not be exactly what I had in mind,' he returned with a grin of his own. 'But I'll take what I can get.'

Karen sighed again. He made it sound almost idyllic, as in the fairy tales she told the girls, where the prince and the princess, no matter what problems stood in their way, always rode off into the sunset together to live happily ever after. But fantasy was one thing and reality was quite another.

'I wish – ' she began.

'Look,' he interrupted. 'I have to run up to New Haven tomorrow. I'll be gone two, maybe three days. Why don't you think about it some more, until I get back. Then we can sit down and talk again.'

'Well, if you insist,' she conceded, although the last thing she wanted was to have another conversation like this.

'Let's put it this way,' he said. 'I know you came here tonight to turn me down. That's pretty obvious. So I have very little to lose by postponing the moment – and maybe a great deal to gain.'

Karen couldn't help chuckling. 'This would be a whole lot easier if I didn't like you so much.'

'I'm counting on that,' he replied.

'What's happening in New Haven?' she asked.

'Something of an honor, actually,' he told her. 'My alma mater has invited me to participate in a symposium on changing trends in architecture and then I've been asked to submit a proposal for a new computer complex.'

'Yale is in New Haven,' she said.

'Indeed it is,' he agreed.

Karen began to laugh as she hadn't laughed in years because there were some things that had no rhyme or reason, they just happened, at a time and a place of their own choosing, and there was no point in trying to figure out how or why.

'You went to Yale?' she sputtered.

'Twice,' he confirmed. 'Both undergraduate and graduate school. Why? Does that make a difference?'

'Not to me,' she giggled. 'But my mother is going to love you.'

nine

Four Seasons, by Yanow and Kern, was presented to the public on the thirteenth of August. Its appearance at Demion Five was preceded by a solid month of promotion, designed to whet the appetite of every status-conscious patron of the arts within a hundred-mile radius of Manhattan.

'By the time this little item hits the shelves,' Demelza predicted, 'there won't be a self-proclaimed connoisseur anywhere within hailing distance of this city who'd let himself be caught dead without a copy on his coffee table.'

Karen and Nancy were on the scene that Thursday from two until six, seated behind a table, as the stack of books in front of them slowly dwindled, autographing every first-day purchase with a flourish. Trays of canapés were passed about, champagne bubbled, and the shop was jammed.

'I told you they'd come,' Demelza murmured,

breezing by with a platter of rumaki.

Finally, it was closing time. The last canapé had been eaten, the last drop of champagne drunk, and the last paying customer politely ushered out the door.

'My right hand will never be the same,' Nancy complained as she flexed her fingers in agony.

'Oh, the price of fame and fortune,' Demelza declared.

'That remains to be seen,' Karen remarked. 'Two hundred copies sold does not five thousand make.'

'After twelve years in my employ,' Demelza chided, 'I can't believe you haven't learned how to recognize a winner. Hasn't any of my clairvoyance rubbed off?'

Karen shrugged. 'I guess in this case, I'm not exactly what you'd call objective.'

By the end of October, two-thirds of the limited edition of *Four Seasons* had been spoken for.

'Trust me, the rest will be gone before Christmas,' Demelza proclaimed.

'I don't believe it,' Nancy gasped when Karen handed her a five-figure check for her share of the profits.

'I know,' Karen agreed, having banked a similar check earlier in the afternoon. 'Too bad we didn't print ten thousand copies.'

'That's okay,' Nancy told her. 'I've got a great idea for our second effort.'

Karen laughed. 'I was afraid you'd say that.'

Nancy shrugged. 'Well, at least you didn't say no.'

They began work on *Mirror Images*, a contrasting study of the people of New York, two days later, finishing the layout at three o'clock on the afternoon of November 14.

Four hours later, Karen and Ted were married in a simple ceremony in a judge's chamber, after which they celebrated with close friends and family at the elegant Four Seasons Restaurant.

'How appropriate,' gushed Beverly Kern. She smiled benignly at her new son-in-law. 'Was this your idea?'

'Actually, it was Karen's,' he told her.

'How very clever of you, darling,' she trilled at her daughter.

'Thank you, Mother,' Karen responded graciously.

'He's one of the most successful architects in the country,' Beverly had informed her sister-in-law Edna shortly after the engagement was announced.

'I'm so happy for Karen,' Edna replied. 'For a while, there, it didn't seem that she was ever going to settle down.'

'Well, I suppose it did take her longer than it might have,' Beverly sniffed. 'But then, she wasn't about to marry just anybody. He had to be suitable. Ted's a Yale man, you know.'

'No, I didn't know.'

'I suppose an architect is better than no one,' she said to her husband with a heavy sigh. 'But a widower with three small children? What can Karen be thinking of?'

'What's wrong with that?' Leo inquired. 'Seems like a pretty good fit to me, all things considered.'

'To have someone else's children foisted on her? How can that turn out to be anything but disastrous?'

'You worry too much,' Leo told his wife.

* * *

'We're so happy for Karen,' Beverly told Ted's mother during the reception. 'Your son is such a lovely man and so successful, too. And those adorable little girls of his – why, they're just an extra added bonus, aren't they?'

'We think so,' Ted's mother replied.

Karen never discussed what finally tipped the scales in Ted's favor. Not with Nancy or Jill and especially not with her mother. She told everyone it was because he had made it very easy for her to say yes and impossible for her to say no. But of course there was more to it than that.

There was knowing that a career, while not a totally unsatisfactory substitute for marriage and mother-hood, was still just that – a substitute. There was, in the final analysis, the desire to be connected to another human being, not to be alone any longer. And there was curiosity. Or perhaps it was that, in the secret place where her best instincts dwelled, Karen believed she had come upon a man who might care more about who she was than about what she had done.

It had always been her fantasy that a knight in shining armor would simply appear one day, like a sunburst, to claim her. He would ignore her imperfec-tions, look deep into her eyes and take her breath away.

Ted Doniger had sneaked up on her. There was no sunburst, no breathless moment of awareness. In the guise of a friend, he gained her confidence. In the guise of a surrogate brother, he gained her affection. Before she quite realized how it happened, she began to trust him with her laughter, her hopes, and her fears. From that grew the fervent faith that he would not turn away from her defiled body, and the belief that he would protect her from the harsh glare of an indifferent world. Further, she knew this was likely her last chance to have the life she had been raised to want – the children, the home, the status, the security, and he had offered it to her on whatever terms she chose to name.

'A good marriage is your only chance for happiness,' she could still hear Beverly saying. Although her values were no longer her mother's, she knew she would be a fool to turn Ted down.

'I know what a private person you are,' he had said, 'and how much you value your own space. I wish the apartment was big enough for separate rooms, but we can at least have separate beds, if that would make you more comfortable.'

Ted Doniger was a man of infinite patience. He intended to spend the rest of his life with this woman, and he was prepared to wait as long as necessary for the intimacy that so obviously troubled her. Just having her in the house all the time, where he could look at her and talk to her and watch her with the girls, would be enough.

'Do you want to go on a honeymoon?' he asked.

'I hadn't thought,' Karen murmured, uncomfortable with the implication of the question. 'Is it … obligatory?'

'I think it's up to the two people involved,' he replied casually. 'But since I'm still in the middle of the Yale project and you and Nancy are just starting a new book, it might work out better if we didn't plan anything right away.'

'That sounds reasonable,' she agreed with relief.

A honeymoon, with all that the word implied, would have been too much for her to handle, and she silently thanked him for his understanding. It was going to be difficult enough to change her whole life, not to mention her home, and she was counting on having the children around to help smooth the transition between dropping by and moving in.

They asked Felicity to create their wedding rings and she produced complementing free-form chunks of gold, Ted's plain, Karen's set off by a thin row of diamonds. Karen asked Jenna to design her wedding dress, requesting something simple, without a veil or a train, and not white – she would not have been able to deal with the deceit of wearing white. Jenna created a short swirl of pale-peach satin that suited Karen's coloring and figure perfectly and complemented Ted's dark-blue suit and tie.

The ceremony was brief but dignified and the reception was later described as elegant. Afterward, however, Karen could remember very little of either, except that she had been surrounded by all the important people in her life. What she did remember vividly was going home to West Seventy-eighth Street.

With the best of intentions, Nancy had whisked the girls upstairs following the festivities, bundling them into bed beside her own Roger and Emily. Mrs. Peagram had been given the weekend off.

The downstairs apartment was dark when Ted unlocked the door, and ominously quiet. For a moment, Karen had the foolish thought that they had come to the wrong address. She walked behind him into the kitchen, her high heels tapping smartly against the hardwood floor, echoing her heartbeat.

'It's so different here without the girls,' she murmured.

Ted snapped on the kitchen light. There was a bottle of champagne in a bucket of ice on the counter, with two long-stemmed glasses standing beside it. A card was propped against the bucket. It read: 'To a long and happy life together' in Nancy's distinct, slanted handwriting.

'My sister the romantic,' Ted chuckled. 'She must have sneaked down here just ahead of us.'

He reached for the bottle and extracted the cork with a resounding pop.

'Leave it to Nancy.' Karen smiled, wishing fervently that she was back in her own town house, standing in her own kitchen, about to down a shot of brandy before going to sleep in her own bed.

Ted poured just enough champagne into each goblet so it would not overflow. Then he handed one to her.

'I may not have much control over how long a life we'll have,' he said, smiling at her and touching his glass to hers, 'but I promise that I'll do everything I know how to make it a happy one.'

He was unfailingly nice and he was trying so hard to put her at ease. Karen was glad they still had on their coats so he couldn't see how hard her knees were knocking. Except she could see that her hand, holding the champagne, was trembling.

'Shall we light a fire?' he asked, noticing. 'We can sit and enjoy our champagne while we warm up.'

It sounded exactly like the kind of thing her knight in shining armor would have suggested.

'It's really late,' Karen heard herself reply. 'And I'm exhausted. Would it be all right if I just went on to bed?'

'Sure,' Ted said easily. 'You go ahead.' He leaned over and kissed her lightly on the cheek, the way he always did. 'I think I'll stay up for a while and unwind. Just holler if you need anything.'

Karen went quickly down the stairs, intending to be fast asleep by the time he finished unwinding. During the past week, she had moved her clothes and personal items over from East Sixty-third Street. She knew which bed was hers, which bureau, which closet, which shelves in the medicine cabinet, where the towels were kept, and how the light switches worked. She would not need any help.

It took her less than five minutes to undress, wash off her makeup and brush her teeth, pull a nightgown over her head and slip between the sheets, leaving only the lamp on Ted's side of the room lit. In addition to trading the double bed he had shared with Barbara for twins, Ted had fashioned a kind of partition out of draperies which had the effect of splitting the space in half.

Karen lay stiffly in the unfamiliar bed, staring at the unfamiliar half-room, and wondered what on earth she was doing there. This house, which had always echoed with light and laughter, now seemed like a silent tomb, with menace lurking in every corner.

'Please, let me go to sleep,' she whispered into the shadows. 'Let the morning come quickly. Let the girls come back early.'

The mist became fog, collecting at her feet, stealing up her legs, swirling about her body, engulfing her. Soon, she could see less than a yard ahead through the thick gray soup. She looked frantically around, searching for the path that had been there just seconds before –

but it was gone, gone in the fog, and she was lost and alone. With him.

She knew she couldn't stand still, she had to keep going. She plunged ahead blindly, running as fast as she could, knowing that outrunning him was the only thing that would save her. Her breath was coming in short, hard gasps now, and a sharp pain began to knife its way through her chest, but there was no stopping. Above the pounding of her heart, she could hear him behind her, getting ever closer.

She summoned one final burst of speed to push herself forward and fell head over heels into a thicket of bushes. Familiar bushes, with brambles that scratched her skin and snared her hair. She knew she had been there before. With every last ounce of energy she possessed, she tried to scramble free, but it was too late. He was already there.

The flames licked around the logs in the fireplace, radiating a comforting warmth. Ted sipped at his champagne and thought about what he had done. He had married a woman who didn't love him because he didn't want to be alone any longer. Yet he felt more alone now than he had before.

He couldn't fault Karen, he knew. She had been totally honest with him. He was the one who had insisted it didn't matter, that he could live with it. But had he been honest with her, or with himself?

It was their wedding night, the only one they would ever share, and all he had wanted was to sit quietly with her for a while and perhaps talk a bit, not about anything terribly important, just to know that she was warm and alive and really there with him. Only she had fled instead, and he didn't know how he was supposed to interpret that.

They had always been so easy with one another, so companionable, that her abrupt departure had thrown him off-balance. He thought back over the past several weeks, in search of any clue that might help him understand, but he could find none. She had been her warm, beguiling self right through all the wedding preparations, arranging the details of the reception, moving her things into place, putting most of her furniture into storage, subletting her apartment. They had seen each other almost every day, discussing at length every decision that needed to be made. And through it all she had been so positive, seemed so happy.

During the ceremony, she looked beautiful in the dress that Jenna had designed, and her eyes sparkled. Her hand even quivered engagingly when he slipped the ring onto her finger. And then, at the Four Seasons, she was absolutely radiant, smiling and laughing a lot, standing beside him with her arm tucked in his.

No, it was only after they left the restaurant that her mood changed, once they were alone with each other. He wondered if the one thing neither of them had wanted to happen had happened, after all – that, in getting married, they had indeed spoiled their friendship.

The fire so lulled him and his thoughts so absorbed him that he didn't know how long the sound had been pushing against the edges of his awareness before it forced its way in. It was an eerie sound, part moan, part sob, part shriek, more like a wounded animal than anything human, and it took him several seconds to realize that it was coming from inside the house. He was on his feet in an instant, crossing the living room in three strides and charging down the stairs.

Karen appeared to be in the throes of a nightmare. She had obviously been thrashing around the bed because she was all tangled up in the sheets. The harder she struggled, the more ensnared she became, and the more ensnared she was, the more desperate her cries became.

Ted touched her shoulder, shaking it gently to awaken her. 'Karen,' he whispered. 'Karen, wake up.'

But she only gasped and shuddered and pulled away.

He shook her a bit harder. 'Karen, it's all right,' he told her. 'I'm here, you're safe. It's only a bad dream.'

The bedding was soaked with perspiration, and her nightgown was slippery as she resisted him, so that he had difficulty getting a firm grip on her. He sat down on the side of the bed and, reaching over, tried to pull her into his arms, to hold her to him and rock her back and forth as he had done so often with one or another of his daughters during the first years without Barbara. But she wouldn't let him. While his daughters would wake up and calm down as soon as they realized where they were, Karen flailed at him, her sobs and screams growing louder and more urgent.

With one hand, Ted snapped on her bedside lamp, hoping that the sudden light might awaken her and she would see that he was with her and there was nothing to fear. But when he looked, he saw that she was already wide awake.

'It was just a bad dream, that's all,' he soothed, still trying to catch hold of her and remembering how she had been the one to get Amy past her bout with nightmares. 'Just a bad dream. It's all over now, see?

You're in your new home and I'm right here and you're perfectly safe.'

But his words didn't seem to make any difference. Her fists continued to lash out against his chest as though her life depended on fighting him off, and she was staring at him as though he were a monster from hell.

PART SIX
1981

Who shall fill up his cup, for he
has drink enough to spare.

– *Theocritus*

one

The Boeing 727 slid smoothly up to the gate at San Francisco Airport, the door opened, and the United States congressman from California, followed by his wife and their two-year-old son Adam, stepped out and started the long walk toward the terminal.

At forty-three, his handsome face was beginning to show the wear that was often called 'aging' in a woman and 'character' in a man. A light frosting of gray dusted his dark hair.

'Congressman Willmont,' called a pretty young reporter, detaching herself from a loose knot of newspeople on the other side of the security barricade and brandishing a microphone in his face. 'Rumor has it that you've come home early to announce for the Senate. Do you have any comment on that?'

The congressman flashed a dazzling smile and allowed his aquamarine eyes to twinkle ever so briefly.

'Miss Evans, isn't it?' he asked the attractive blonde.

'Yes, sir. Janice Evans, Channel Seven.'

'Well, Miss Evans,' he said, scooping a half-asleep Adam up into his arms as the cameras began to click, 'you know I never comment on rumors.'

'Make an exception,' the brown-eyed blonde urged.

'Come on, Congressman, give us a break,' another of the journalists complained. 'It's been a slow news day.'

Robert Willmont chuckled. 'I wondered what you were all doing out here in the middle of the afternoon.'

'Help us out.'

'I'd like to, but the simple truth is, my family and I have come home for the holidays, just as we do every year.'

'But why two weeks early?' someone asked.

'If you must know,' the congressman replied pleasantly, 'my mother hasn't been very well, and it's important to me to spend as much time with her as I can.'

This was not news. Amanda Drayton Willmont's health had been precarious for as long as any of them could remember.

'Perhaps your wife would tell us,' the persistent Janice Evans pursued. 'Mrs. Willmont, how would you like to be the wife of a United States senator?'

Elizabeth Willmont smiled, the way she had been taught from early childhood to smile at prying strangers.

'I'm very proud of my husband in whatever capacity he chooses to serve,' she replied.

'Come on, Bob,' a veteran from the *Chronicle* urged. 'You *do* want a shot at that Senate seat, don't you?'

'Someday, perhaps,' Robert agreed. 'But right now, I'm perfectly comfortable in the seat I have.'

'Someday's awfully indefinite,' someone objected.

'I'll make you all a promise,' Robert said. 'When I decide to run for higher office, you'll be among the first to know.'

'Thanks for nothing,' someone else muttered.

'Would you rather be among the last?'

Most of the group shrugged good-naturedly.

'Whenever you're ready,' a KRON mainstay drawled, 'all you have to do is whistle, and we'll come running. You do know how to whistle, don't you, Bob?'

Everyone hooted, including the congressman, but his smile was turning brittle around the edges by the time Randy Neuburg pushed his way through the crowd.

'Where the shit have you been?' Robert snarled as his aide quickly ushered the Willmonts toward the exit.

'Caught in a traffic jam,' came the reply.

'This wasn't supposed to be a media event, goddamn it. No one was even supposed to know we were coming in today. Now I'm standing here with egg all over my face – will I run, won't I run?'

'Sorry, boss,' Randy apologized. 'There must have been a leak.'

'Well, see how fast you can get us out of here.'

'The limo's right out front. I'll send it back for the luggage.'

Randy Neuburg had served as Robert's aide since the charismatic partner of Sutton, Wells, Willmont and Spaulding had been elected to Congress three years earlier. He was unusually bright and intuitive for one so young, and totally committed to the causes Robert espoused, and Robert had very wisely plucked him from the associate ranks of the law firm and taken him to Washington.

Like the man he worked for, Randy was a product of Harvard Law School, but unlike Robert, he was West Virginia born and bred and had completed his undergraduate work on scholarship at Princeton. It was a sense of adventure that prompted him to accept the offer that the San Francisco firm tendered him in the spring of 1977. He had never been to the sand-and-surf nirvana called California. It was a sense of destiny that persuaded him to sign on with Robert. Two summers clerking for a West Virginia state senator had left him with a lingering taste for politics.

Randy was a skinny youth who developed into a slight man, with large ears, an unruly shock of red hair almost as bright as Elizabeth Willmont's, a face full of freckles, and clear blue eyes behind horn-rimmed glasses that never lost sight of an objective. Some of his less charitable schoolmates at Princeton used to liken him to Alfred E. Newman, the character from *MAD* comics, but Randy shrugged the epithet off. Let them say what they would, he knew he was smarter than the whole lot of them put together.

To underscore that, he went back to Princeton for his fifth reunion, counselor to a United States congressman – and a congressman who was enjoying a growing reputation as a real up-and-comer at that.

It was the Ridenbaugh case that first catapulted Robert's name onto the front pages and evening newscasts around the state. Joseph Ridenbaugh was accused of swindling some three hundred people out of almost $15 million dollars by selling home sites for the Happy Sands Retirement Community in a part of the California desert that had no water and no hope of getting any for less than $250,000 per house. When the whole scheme began to unravel, Joseph liquidated what he could, transferred the balance of his assets into his mother's name, and took off for Trinidad.

Robert accepted the case on behalf of one Samuel Pappas and the 302 other persons who had been defrauded. He launched an intensive investigation that some felt more closely resembled a witch hunt. Together, he and a new associate assigned to him – one Randy Neuburg, fresh out of Harvard – spent three months digging into every corner of Joseph Ridenbaugh's life, hunting for any legal lapse that would give them what they needed. Just when they were gray with exhaustion and about to concede defeat, Randy unearthed an ancient partnership agreement between Joseph and his mother, Alice, with no recorded dissolution, that had somehow slipped through the cracks.

Applying a liberal interpretation to the agreement, Robert argued that its existence made the mother as liable as the son. He attached every piece of real property he could find in Alice Ridenbaugh's name and sued the partnership. The defense attorney hoped the jury would feel sorry for the gray-haired lady who claimed to have no head for business and no idea about her son's activities.

They didn't.

When the dust finally settled, the duped investors got at least some of their money back and Alice Ridenbaugh was facing criminal prosecution as an accomplice to fraud. Joseph, having set up house with a native girl on Trinidad, showed no inclination for returning to the United States, at least not as long as his Cayman Islands bank account held out.

Robert was heralded as a crusader, a champion of the little man, a benefactor of senior citizens. Two months after the verdict, he was approached by a certain group of people who suggested he might consider running for the United States Congress.

Robert was nothing if not quick to take advantage of an opportunity. With a prayer of thanks to *Pappas* v. *Ridenbaugh*, and with the full weight of the old Drayton name and his law firm's connections behind him, he jumped feet first into the political whirlpool. Even in the affluent district where he campaigned, he was able to defeat the conservative incumbent by a comfortable margin.

'It played almost like the war-hero scenario,' Randy, a student of history, observed on the day after the election.

'Stick with me, kid,' said the congressman-elect, who had been a child during World War II, an adolescent during Korea, and too well-connected to get within a continent of Vietnam. 'There's no telling how far we can go.'

But James Randall Neuburg knew exactly how far they were going to go, and he had already reserved his ticket for the full ride.

Capitol Hill was a prestigious plateau, and over the years many had carved out a piece for themselves and settled into it with considerable complaisance and limited vision. But in Randy's clear blue eyes, the House of Representatives was nothing more than a brief resting place on the journey up Pennsylvania Avenue.

The West Virginia lawyer had no great desire to

reign over the Oval Office himself, understanding clearly that the qualities one needed to be elected President of the United States had nothing to do with the qualities one needed to run the government. But he knew at first glance that Robert Willmont, with his looks and charm and his utopian philosophy of making America strong again, would make an excellent leader. And Randy Neuburg, standing in the shadow of power and quietly wielding a substantial share of it, would be the one to transform his mentor's ideals into a practical road map for steering the nation into the twenty-first century.

It was pretty heady stuff for the twenty-six-year-old son of a West Virginia steelworker and a seamstress.

'You got brains, Randy, and determination, and they got you a scholarship to Princeton,' his father told him. 'Make the most of it.'

Randy intended to.

'There's only one thing that really means a damn,' he once overheard the state senator say, 'An' it ain't money, and it ain't sex, and it ain't no sheepskin from some snot-nosed Ivy League college, either. It's power. That's what it is – power, pure and simple. Gettin' it, holdin' on to it, knowin' how to use it.'

It was a message the young law student never forgot. Now, halfway through Robert Willmont's second congressional term, Randy was seeing it in action.

'So, what's the word from upstairs?' Robert asked once they were safely settled in the limousine. 'Go or no-go?'

'Upstairs' was a euphemism for the particular machine that controlled party politics in California. They were no longer the cigar-smoking back-room boys of old, they were now chief executive officers, bankers, financiers and image makers who met in fortieth-floor penthouse suites and were a hundredfold more powerful than their predecessors had been.

No candidate was elected to public office in the state without their endorsement, and few who had it were defeated. They saw something in Robert Willmont that greatly appealed to them – an attractive, intelligent man who successfully straddled the fence between conservative and liberal interests, who carried the weighty Drayton mantle with polished assurance, and who was a proven vote-getter.

They saw him as a man who believed in a strong America but an America that was generous, a man who believed that the balance of trade meant exactly that, and that free enterprise was not in conflict with a worker's right to earn a fair wage. They noted that he was not above deploring the quality of education in California – once in frustration he had even suggested that the best solution might be to bus every school child into Oregon.

He campaigned in one of the wealthiest sections of San Francisco, where he himself had been born and raised, on a platform that said: 'If we can't get past the philosophy of *me first* in this country, we're going to wake up one day and find *us last*.'

His sincerity couldn't be questioned – the Draytons were too well known for their generations of philanthropy. And it soon became clear that he could stir a crowd in the same youthful, energetic way that John F. Kennedy could in the days of Camelot. In the rarefied air where the power brokers met and considered and orchestrated, he got the nod.

'It's a go,' Randy said.

A broad grin spread across the congressman's face

and he reached across and slapped his aide on the knee.

'Well, all right!' he exclaimed.

Randy had been sent back to San Francisco a week earlier to open a dialogue with the nameless, faceless upstairs people. He had prepared his speech carefully, with exactly the right mixture of confidence and humility.

The House of Representatives was an excellent training ground, but the congressman was a quick learner and easily bored. He was eager to take the next step up, into the Senate. Everyone knew the doddering incumbent standing for reelection was vulnerable.

Randy's mission was to feel the upstairs people out and, if possible, get the green light. The time was right. Robert knew it, Randy could feel it. Upstairs agreed. The young congressman's record in the House, while perhaps not dramatically distinguished, was certainly consistent. In his one-and-a-half terms, he had accomplished exactly what he had set out to accomplish. He had learned the ropes, played the game, and earned the respect of his colleagues. He had made his deals and kept his promises, and had won the devotion of his constituents as a sincere representative of his district who, although born to wealth, possessed genuine compassion for those less fortunate.

Furthermore, *Pappas* v. *Ridenbaugh* still lingered in the minds of a substantial number of Californians. It was a significant issue that they felt went right to the heart of Robert's character. Randy knew they would be able to capitalize on that during their campaign against the grandfatherly incumbent. He also knew that, if they were forced to wait until the next Senate seat was contested, *Pappas* v. *Ridenbaugh* would be past history, and useless to them.

'Get Mary Catherine out here – tomorrow, if possible,' Robert was saying, 'and let's start the wheels in motion.'

'Yes, sir,' Randy replied, jotting the congressman's trusted administrative assistant's name down in his notebook.

Robert turned to the woman sitting beside him, holding the sleeping child. 'So tell us, Mrs. Willmont,' he mimicked the pretty young reporter, 'how would you like to be the wife of a United States senator?'

Elizabeth had been paying only marginal attention to the conversation, yet she forced a weary smile.

'Step two,' she murmured obediently, but her words lacked enthusiasm.

As far as she was concerned, the birth of her son was the crowning achievement of her life, and it had taken a great deal out of her. It was her fourth pregnancy, the other three having ended in miscarriages. The doctors had warned her that not only were the chances of her being able to carry a baby to term slim to none, but the risk to her health was considerable, and they had embellished their dire predictions with a lot of multi-syllabic words she couldn't pronounce and didn't understand. Elizabeth thanked them politely, paid their exorbitant fees, and proceeded to ignore their advice.

Robert was then in his first term in the United States House of Representatives. He was busy and excited and each moment brought him new challenges. Elizabeth was able to share in his glory, but not in his day-to-day involvement. Once the fervor of the campaign and the election were over, her life seemed to lose its focus.

'I know something you can do,' Robert told her when he came home one night a week after the election. 'You can find us the right place to live.'

'To rent or to buy?' she asked.

'To buy,' he replied with a confident grin. 'I think you can count on us being in Washington for a while.'

Elizabeth spent a month searching for the perfect house, finding it finally on a graceful wooded acre in Rock Creek Park, and she spent another three months having it redone. At last, this was the home that would truly be just hers and Robert's. She put all her energy into the redecorating, supervising the entire project herself, thinking and then rethinking even the smallest detail, personally selecting each fabric, approving every paint sample, shopping endlessly for exactly the right pieces of furniture.

The result was gracious and comfortable and spoke softly of good taste and breeding. Those who were fortunate enough to be invited into it were charmed.

It took no time at all for the nation's capital to be as enchanted with the lovely Mrs. Willmont as San Fransicso had been a decade earlier. Soon her style was being imitated by other Washington wives, and her advice on fashion, always a step ahead of vogue, was being sought by women from Capitol Hill to Embassy Row.

'They know class when they see it,' Robert observed to Randy when, only a few months into his first term of office, Elizabeth was asked to join the planning committee of one of the capital's most prestigious annual balls.

But once the Rock Creek Park house was completed, Elizabeth again found herself without focus. Her charity work, while certainly worthy, no longer gave her the satisfaction it once had, and the various luncheons and teas she chose to attend each week filled time but not the growing emptiness inside. She knew only one solution to that particular problem. So, at the ripe old age of thirty-four, she made one last stab at motherhood.

'Why would you want to go and do that?' Robert asked in dismay when she told him she was pregnant.

'Because I heard my biological clock ticking,' she replied. 'Very loudly.'

'Do you think it was wise, under the circumstances?'

'I guess I wasn't thinking wise, I was thinking baby.'

'Sweetheart, you don't have to do this, you know,' he assured her. 'Not for me.'

'I'm not doing it for you,' she replied.

'But children aren't essential for us anymore. I mean, we're doing fine just the way we are.'

'No, you're doing fine, Robert,' she told him. 'I'm doing carpeting and fund-raising.'

'What about the doctors – did they say it was all right to try again? I mean, the risk?'

'I don't care about the doctors,' she declared. 'I want to have a baby.'

'Don't you think maybe we're a little old to be starting a family now?' he persisted.

Elizabeth shrugged. 'Apparently not.'

'But won't it look, well, a little strange to people? I mean, at our age?'

'If you mean people here in Washington, who cares?' she retorted. 'If you mean people back home, I rather think that voters like having a family man in office – young or old.'

'Really?'

'Really,' she confirmed. '*I* certainly do, at any rate. I

automatically assume that politicians with children are … well … more stable than ones without.'

'I'd have to see some polls on that,' he retorted.

But by the time Adam Drayton Willmont was born, ten days before 1980, Robert no longer cared about polls. His wife had made it through the delivery, and he had an heir.

Almost from the start, Elizabeth had problems with the pregnancy, but she was determined not to lose this baby. She curtailed her charitable activities, accepted very few social invitations, and managed to keep up a brave front for her husband, which wasn't too difficult because he was so preoccupied with his work that he often left for Capitol Hill well before she awoke in the morning and came home long after she was asleep.

But she couldn't hide from her doctors. They saw her weekly, changed her diet, pumped her full of vitamins, and performed endless tests to monitor fetal progress. Her first miscarriage had occurred early in the pregnancy, her second in the fifth month, her third in the fourth. The day she entered her sixth month and felt the baby kick for the first time, Elizabeth cried with relief.

'Don't get your hopes up yet,' the doctors cautioned, knowing that a sixth-month abort or even a still birth, with her history, was a very real possibility. 'You have a long way to go.'

'I'm going to make it,' she told them fiercely. 'We're both going to make it.'

She began to bleed two days later.

'What do I do?' she begged the doctors. 'Tell me what to do.'

'Nothing,' they replied. 'Absolutely nothing.'

They meant exactly that. Elizabeth spent the last

four months of her pregnancy in bed, and she almost didn't survive the eighteen-hour labor, but Adam was perfect.

The doctors called it a miracle.

Even after two years, Elizabeth was still struggling to regain her strength, and the long flight from Washington had taken its toll. She yearned for her bed, although it was barely the middle of the afternoon. It wasn't that she was no longer interested in her husband's political ambitions, it was more that she had just so much energy to expend, and she chose to expend it on her son.

Adam was her life now. Her charitable activities, her social commitments and her congressional obligations became peripheral. When Robert was at home, he was included in what she thought of as her heart circle. When he was not, she rarely thought about him at all. Her days were full of Adam – his first words, first steps, first lessons. Her nights were filled with planning – for his education, his future, his happiness.

Robert wanted to employ a nanny. Elizabeth refused.

'I have no intention of letting a stranger raise my son,' she declared.

'You're the wife of a congressman,' he retorted, 'and a Drayton. You have obligations.'

'I'll maintain an association with one or two worthy charities and I'll attend every social and political function that you feel is necessary to your advancement,' she said firmly. 'But my only obligation is to Adam.'

Although it was often beyond her endurance, she forced herself to accompany Robert to as many as three social events a week without complaint, charming even the crustiest of statesmen with her sweet smile and well-bred manners.

It was the little pink pills that got her through. Her doctors prescribed them when she complained of lethargy. One per day, they said, would fix her right up. By the end of six months, she was taking as many as three a day, sometimes four if she were facing an especially late evening.

Elizabeth had been looking forward to the Christmas break, and was delighted when Robert told her they would have an extra two weeks away from Washington. Even the thought of Amanda's grousing hadn't dimmed her anticipation of the quiet month ahead. But what she had just half-heard had.

If Robert intended to announce his candidacy for the Senate during the holiday, there would be no rest. Instead, there would be a nonstop round of press conferences, photo sessions, and interviews, with people underfoot every moment, and she would be expected to participate. She sighed deeply and made a mental note to have her prescription refilled.

Robert settled back against the leather cushions. It was going to happen just as he had dreamed it, and one day very soon he would have it all. The endless schooling, the long apprenticeship at Sutton Wells, the confining proper marriage, the petty congressional duties he performed, the tiresome committees on which he was obliged to serve – each was merely a rung up his ladder to the White House. When he looked at it like that, he knew it was worth it.

The limousine pulled up in front of the house on Jackson Street. Robert took Adam, Randy helped Elizabeth, and the four of them went up the steps.

'I want to spend a few minutes with Mother,' Robert

told his wife, handing the boy over. 'And then Randy and I have some people to see.'

Elizabeth hardly heard him.

'Where are we headed?' Randy asked half an hour later as the two men climbed back into the limousine.

'I don't know where *you're* headed, old man,' replied the congressman with a sly wink. 'But I'm on my way to give an interview.'

Randy grinned on the outside but cringed on the inside. It wasn't that he was a prude. In fact, he wasn't in the least. But, after three years, he knew that Robert's sexual appetites sometimes got the better of his good sense – and boffing a news reporter on the eve of announcing for the United States Senate was certainly not what Randy considered using good sense.

two

The jumbo jet sped steadily toward the sunset. Mary Catherine O'Malley sipped her champagne, nibbled at her smoked-salmon appetizer, and contemplated the strategy session that would begin almost the moment the plane touched down – the announcement that would result from that session, and the impact it would have on the rest of her life.

She had been working for Robert Willmont for a scant three years now and he was considered damn lucky to have her, because Mary Catherine was regarded by many to be the best administrative assistant on Capitol Hill. She had earned that reputation over almost thirty years of shepherding congressmen through the political quagmire.

For a girl from the wrong side of the Winston-Salem railroad tracks, with only a high school education to her name, who had started her career as a temporary filing clerk, that wasn't half bad.

She did her share of stumbling in the beginning, but she was a quick learner and it took her hardly any time at all to realize that she was smarter than most of the duly elected world-beaters with their multiple degrees who moved in and out for a few years at a time.

By the time Mary Catherine attended her sixth congressional swearing-in ceremony and her third Presidential inaugural, she was on a first-name basis with just about everyone in Washington who counted. She was invited to most of the parties that mattered, the press courted her, insiders sought her advice, and politicians trusted her. Over the years she discovered where all the bodies were buried, where all the skeletons lurked, and which pairs of shoes hid Achilles' heels, and she accomplished it all without ever having to take off her clothes.

Mary Catherine was barely five feet tall, but people rarely realized that. They noticed instead that, at the age of forty-eight, she still displayed a classic hourglass figure, an abundance of glossy brown hair, and brown eyes that were faintly reminiscent of Bambi.

She managed her staff with the patience of Penelope and the determination of a drill sergeant, she managed the public with humor and impartiality, and she managed her congressmen with the utmost tact and discretion.

Robert had inherited her from his predecessor, and two months into his first term, he had actually written that conservative gentleman a note of appreciation.

'If you don't know what to do or how to do it,' he was soon telling everyone, 'ask Mary Catherine.'

Born seventh in a family of nine to a schoolteacher mother and an alcoholic father, Mary Catherine had learned the wisdom of knowing the right answers and keeping a low profile by the age of six. Her gentle North Carolina drawl camouflaged an exceptional mind and her soft Southern ways managed to convince many a man that he was really the one in charge.

When she was twenty-nine years old, a White House aide asked her to marry him. He was reasonably handsome and fun and even quite bright, and by that time, they had been enjoying each other's close company for some months.

'What will you do after your Administration is out of office?' she asked him.

'Oh, we have five years before we have to worry about that,' he said and laughed.

'But then what?' she persisted.

'Go back to Boston, I guess,' he replied. 'It's too hard to tell your friends from your enemies in this town.'

But after all it had taken to get herself established, Mary Catherine had no intention of leaving Washington, in five years or ever. She refused his proposal with sincere regret. While the two of them vowed to remain intimate friends, less than a year later, when the Administration he worked for ended so abruptly, so tragically, the aide said good-bye and faded into memory.

Robert Willmont was Mary Catherine's third congressman from California. With her ability and experience, she could easily have had her pick of the biennial crop, but she liked Californians. They had a style that other members of the House often lacked. Women seemed to sit up straighter in their presence, men tended to order wine instead of bourbon.

This one, however, had a lot more than style. He had looks and he had brains and he had an ambition that wasn't going to quit with a third-floor office on the House side of the Capitol Building. This one was on his way up, as they said, and he was the one Mary Catherine had been waiting for.

Like almost everyone else who came with purpose to the nation's capital, the soft-spoken North Carolinian dreamed of ending her career in the White House. For decades, she had studied the mostly indistinguishable features of those who took up residence in the Senate and the House, looking for just the right combination of qualities that she could help hone into a presidential great. In the part of her gut where her most trusted instincts lay, Mary Catherine knew that Robert Drayton Willmont was the one.

The prestigious law firm of Sutton, Wells, Willmont and Spaulding, while officially neutral when it came to politics, was nonetheless pleased to provide the congressman, and former partner, with a suite of offices on the twelfth floor of its Front Street building.

Five days after Mary Catherine hit San Francisco, she had leased an apartment on Telegraph Hill for herself and anyone else from out of town who might need it, outfitted the Front Street headquarters, hired two secretaries and a clerk from a local temporary agency, and called in two assistants from Washington to help set up operations.

At two o'clock in the afternoon of Thursday, December 17, perfectly timed to take advantage of the evening newscasts, she stood beside Randy Neuburg, just outside the glare of the television lights, as Robert Willmont announced to the press and the people of California his intention to be a candidate for the United States Senate.

Mary Catherine approved of Randy. He was smart and realistic, and under her tutelage was developing into one of the most savvy aides in Washington. To the congressman's right was his lovely wife, holding their cherubic little boy Adam in her arms. A nice touch, the shrewd administrative assistant conceded. Mary Catherine approved of Elizabeth Willmont, too. Not only was she beautiful and fashionable, she had the kind of grace and charm that was considered an enormous asset in Washington and which would play very well in the media.

From the corner of her eye, the assistant scanned the local newspeople she would get to know again in the eleven months to come. In the front row sat a pretty young blonde with brown eyes, a short tight skirt, one leg thrown ever so casually over the other, and an insolent little smile on her face. She was the only member of the group who wasn't taking notes. Mary Catherine frowned. She had seen that same smile on a number of other pretty young faces over the past three years and it always triggered an alarm bell in her head. A slight sigh beside her told her that Randy was noticing, too.

'I think it went well,' Robert observed once the lights had been turned off and the reporters had rushed away with their stories.

'It'll play in Pasadena,' Randy agreed.

'So long as the conservative voters of our good state continue to focus on my sound fiscal policies and the liberal voters concentrate on my progressive social programs,' the candidate summed up, 'I think we've got it made.'

He stretched broadly and made a point of glancing at his wristwatch. 'See that Elizabeth and the boy get back to Jackson Street, will you?' he directed his aide. 'I'm late for an appointment.'

Randy and Mary Catherine exchanged glances.

'I don't have anything down in the book for you this evening, Congressman,' the administrative assistant noted.

Robert grinned. 'It's just a quick stop.'

Quick, as in before she has to do the six-o'clock news, Mary Catherine interpreted.

Quick, as in quickie, thought Randy.

'Do you think that's really such a good idea?' the aide wondered aloud. 'I mean, the media is bound to be all over you every minute from now on.'

The congressman chuckled. 'Oh, I've become an expert at dodging those snoops.'

'Still, you know, all it takes is one slip,' Randy persisted.

'Well, if I do slip,' came the reckless reply, 'I know you'll be there to pick me up.'

'It's the blonde in the first row,' Randy said as soon as Robert had departed.

Mary Catherine nodded. 'Janice Evans, from Channel Seven. Another reporter! You'd think he'd learn, wouldn't you?'

'All I can say is that he'd better make damn sure there are no hidden cameras around this time.' Randy sighed. 'I've done my last second-story work.'

Shortly before the congressman's reelection to the House, Randy had actually been induced to commit burglary to clean up a particularly messy liaison. The wide-eyed young woman in question had claimed to be a graduate student in political science from some Midwestern university, spending the summer soaking up the Washington scene. But she was actually a scandal-sheet stringer hoping to make it big on a major-city newspaper.

Only after Randy had broken into her apartment and retrieved some incriminating photographs and negatives was the congressman able to dump her. Then, in case she might have had in mind to spread any unfortunate publicity, he arranged, with the help of a small-time lowlife who owed him a favor, to have the stringer implicated in a prostitution and drug deal, thereby destroying her credibility. He never even blinked when she was arrested, convicted, and sentenced to nine months in prison.

Mary Catherine sighed. If Robert Drayton Willmont had one fault, one weakness that could cost them all everything were he not very careful – were she and Randy not constantly vigilant – it was that he didn't know how to keep his zipper zipped.

PART SEVEN
1991

It is circumstances and timing
that give an action its character,
and make it either good or bad.

– Agesilaus

one

Karen emptied the last of the wardrobe containers and heaved a sigh of relief. It was the thing she hated most about moving, trying to find places in a new home for all the things they had so easily accumulated in the old, and this was the fourth occasion in ten years she had had to do it.

It was especially difficult this time because the house here in San Francisco was smaller than the one in Tucson had been. When they had made the first move, from New York to Atlanta, they had gone from the compact brownstone apartment on West Seventy-eighth Street into a stately six-bedroom colonial. Again, when they went from Atlanta to Houston, it was into a sprawling hacienda that had taken Karen almost an hour to walk from end to end. And when they had to make the hop from Houston to Tucson, they had found an equally spacious adobe. But now, with Gwen grown and Jessica almost finished with college, they had no need for all that acreage.

Karen secretly thought Atlanta and the colonial too pretentious, Houston and the hacienda too hot, and Tucson and the adobe too dry. But she liked this house, set on a hill overlooking the Pacific Ocean, at the southern edge of San Francisco, in a section of the city known as St. Francis Wood.

It was quasi-Mediterranean in style, with stucco walls and a red tile roof, inlaid wood floors, high arched windows, and a stunning art deco skylight. There was a delightful solarium off the kitchen that they turned into a breakfast room, and a sunporch off the master bedroom that they glassed in.

'Quintessential 1920s,' Ted said when he saw it.

'We don't really need more than three bedrooms,' Karen told Gwen over the telephone, 'now that Amy is the only one at home full-time.'

'But what if Larry and the twins and I want to come out when Jessica's there?' her oldest stepdaughter had protested from her home outside Philadelphia. Brightest of the three girls, she was the image of her father except for her blue eyes.

'Your dad has already thought of that,' Karen assured her, thinking of the sunporch.

'How come you picked San Francisco?' Jessica asked from her dormitory at the University of Colorado. The middle girl was the tallest of the three and the only one with her mother's brown hair and eyes and quiet determination.

'As usual, it picked us,' Karen replied. 'Your father's been commissioned to design a megacomplex in China Basin.'

'Why do we have to move again?' Amy complained. She had grown into a lively teenager, combining her father's coloring with her mother's serenity. 'I only have one more year of high school. It'll be absolutely awful to have to go to a new school for just one year. I won't know anyone, I won't have any friends, I'll be miserable.'

'I know the timing isn't very good,' Karen conceded with a sigh. 'But we didn't have much choice. It's an important project and your father couldn't turn it down.'

'It's not fair!' the teenager exclaimed.

Karen had to agree it wasn't.

There were more than enough hotels and shopping malls and office complexes being built on the East Coast to have kept Ted busy for two lifetimes. But his eyes had always been fixed on some distant horizon.

If Karen had thought that, by wrapping herself up in Ted's ready-made family, she would automatically have the idyllic life she had dreamed of having, she soon learned otherwise. Trying to meet her personal needs for privacy and orderliness and fulfillment in the midst of four other people who had long since resolved those issues among themselves required constant compromise and difficult periods of adjustment. With every assignment Ted was unable to resist in yet another new city, she was forced to abandon whatever nest she had painstakingly constructed and begin building again, compounding the problems.

She felt isolated by the southern hypocrisy of Georgia, awed by the sheer size of Texas, and haunted by the eerie desert winds of Arizona, but she eventually grew accustomed to each – just in time to leave. She made very few friends along the way, and those she did make were superficial.

Karen missed Demion Five more than she had ever

expected she would, not to mention the Yanows, Demelza, and the Sullivan Street set. She saw her life now as quite dull compared to the excitement she had left behind. She turned inward to her family, only to find her family striking outward. Ted was absorbed in his work and the girls were involved with their schools and activities. The more they blossomed, the less they seemed to need her. That left only her partnership with Nancy.

In ten years, the two women had collaborated on seven books. Their second effort, *Mirror Images*, completed just after the Donigers moved to Atlanta, sold well enough at Demion Five for a major New York publisher to approach them with a proposal for future endeavors.

'We'll get a lot more exposure working with a publisher than we do printing our own books and selling them through Demion Five,' Nancy had told her. 'Besides, we've just about exhausted the New York market anyway.'

What Spectrum Publishing had in mind was to take the same format they had used in their first two books and go national with it.

'You mean, take a good cow and milk it until it's dry?' Karen had observed. But she had to admit the idea appealed to her and would go a long way toward easing her loneliness. Within a few weeks, Nancy was on a plane to Atlanta.

'As long as you were already here,' she said, 'Spectrum figured this was as good a market as any.'

The team of photographer and poet spent three weeks exploring the city as Karen never would have on her own. They titled the book *Phoenix Risen*, choosing to concentrate on the triumph over devastation that truly set the Georgia city apart from much of the Civil War South.

They did Washington, D.C., next, focusing on the two separate cities that shared the same space, and produced a black-and-white indictment they called *Dichotomy*. It soon became mandatory for anyone who aspired to be someone in the political sphere to claim it in his library.

Then came Houston. The two women called that effort *Southern Comfort*. They took a detour through the antebellum elegance of New Orleans to do *Amazing Grace*. And then, in Arizona, they broke tradition and did their first book in color.

'This can't be done in black and white,' Nancy declared emphatically at the end of her first visit to the Southwest. 'Look at all the colors – they're just bursting to be told.'

They decided not to focus on any one city, either, as they had before. Instead, they wove the peoples and places of the whole state together, and named the result *Tapestry*.

The endeavor brought Nancy out west six times and took almost two years to put together, a luxury they hadn't enjoyed since their first book, but it was worth it. They were rewarded with a product that reviewers declared embodied a great deal more than a photographic journey through the Southwest, and an extraordinary initial printing of twenty thousand copies.

The cover featured a Hopi youth, standing on the boundary of his reservation, staring out toward the mountains. About him, Karen had written:

The color of pain
is purple

for distant peaks
never to be reached,
and green
for the land
never to be roamed.

The color of pain
is brown
for the blood
of countless ancestors,
and red
for the pride
that still burns within.

The color of pain
is gold
for the hope
that rises with the sun
and sets with the moon.

The color of pain
is gray
for the apathy
of yesterday
and the indifference
of tomorrow.

As far as Karen was concerned, the best part of *Tapestry* was the four months that she and Nancy spent together, crisscrossing the state in a four-wheel drive, from the Grand Canyon to Chiricahua and from Yuma to Mexican Water. Each time they set out on one of their forays, she had the strange sensation that she was escaping.

The girls were growing up so fast. First it was Gwen, graduating from high school with honors, going back east to the University of Pennsylvania, and then on to business school and a nice young man from Wharton. Then Jessica, surviving her sister's limelight and departing for the University of Colorado, with ideas about medical school after that. And before long, it would be Amy's turn to find her niche in the world – such a different world than it was when Karen was her age. The concept of home, which used to be a noisy, crowded place, in whatever city they happened to be, was too rapidly becoming a silent, empty place.

Over the years, Karen's relationship with Ted had settled into one of uneasy intimacy. The nightmares grew less frequent, until their occurence was rare, and the strangeness of blending two adult lives into one slowly dissipated; but the carefree camaraderie they had shared before their wedding night never fully returned.

The energy that Ted hoped to put into his marriage and family he put into his profession instead, working long hours, six and sometimes seven days a week. The drapery wall he had erected between them back in New York came down, but not the invisible one that neither seemed able to penetrate. The twin beds were pushed together to look like a king-sized one, but it was illusion rather than reality.

What passed for lovemaking between them began a few weeks after the wedding, with Ted admitting to himself that being able to look at Karen and talk to her was not going to be enough, after all. It started with casual gestures of affection – a kiss, a hug, a touch, and slowly progressed to acts of consummation that mostly occurred when, for whatever reason, Karen had consumed more alcohol than usual.

The first time they attempted actual intercourse, she bit down so hard on her lip that it bled, and clutched the sheets so tightly that they tore. Neither of them ever mentioned it. Eventually, she learned how to separate Ted from her nightmare and was able to meet his needs with a modicum of liquor and a minimum of panic. There was no thought of her own satisfaction. Too many layers of guilt and shame and humiliation were in the way.

To the rest of the world, however, theirs looked like the perfect marriage, the embodiment of the American Dream. The girls were bright and attractive. The parents were well-dressed and soft-spoken. They had a sheepdog named Duster and a tabby named Cat, and an unnamed station wagon. And there was enough money. But the things they once believed they had in common were not strong enough to bind them together, so they grew apart.

They never discussed what was happening – or not happening – between them. They discussed the children, the house, their work, but never the serious issues that, board by invisible board, were pushing the wall between them higher and higher. It was almost as though they were fearful of saying or doing anything that might spoil the illusion, so they surrounded themselves with the girls for as long as they could and, when they were obliged to be alone with each other, they were considerate but not close.

'I sometimes think we should never have married,' Karen said on one of those occasions.

'Probably not,' Ted agreed.

'I would understand if you wanted a divorce.'

'I don't … Do you?'

'No.'

So they went on the way they were, because something was better than nothing and the illusion seemed more important than the reality. Until one hot Thursday in the spring of 1990, when Amy's tenth-grade class took a field trip out into the Arizona desert and her horse, spooked by a rattlesnake, set off at a dead run.

Amy was a good rider but the bolt was so unexpected that she lost her balance and was thrown from the saddle almost immediately, which would not have been so bad except that her right foot caught in the stirrup and she was dragged a hundred yards or more before two of her classmates were able to head her off and stop her horse.

At the hospital, the doctors found multiple contusions and abrasions, two broken legs, a dislocated right hip, and a skull fractured in three places.

Karen and Ted paced the hospital corridors until well after midnight, the scene in different ways all too familiar to both of them, but the doctors couldn't say anything except that surgery had gone as well as expected and that the next forty-eight hours would tell.

They dragged themselves home in a daze, Karen helping an exhausted Ted to undress and get into bed. Then she went into the kitchen and downed two stiff shots of brandy before returning with one for him.

'This will help you sleep,' she said, sitting down on the side of the bed and holding out the glass.

'I don't want to sleep,' he cried, although he was shivering with fatigue. 'I want to be awake in case she needs me. I should have stayed there with her.'

'The doctor said he would call if there was any change,' she reminded him. 'The hospital is only ten minutes away.'

'It's all my fault,' he sobbed suddenly.

'What is?' she asked.

'I've been so wrapped up in my work I haven't had time for her. I know so little about what she's doing, what she likes, what she thinks. We hardly see each other anymore. I can't even remember the last weekend we spent together.'

'All the weekends in a lifetime wouldn't have prevented this accident,' Karen said. 'You're a wonderful father, and if you could ask her, she'd tell you she couldn't have wished for a better one.'

'It all goes so fast,' he mumbled. 'One day, they're babies, the next, they're teenagers, and the day after that, they're grown up and gone, having babies of their own.'

'That's what it's all about,' Karen observed.

'But are they ready?' he asked. 'Are they strong enough? Are they wise enough? Did we do a good enough job? That's what I don't know.'

'We did the best we could.'

The platitude seemed to work for a moment. He swallowed some of his brandy and looked as though he would calm down, but then his tears broke out afresh.

'I'm so lonely,' he cried from the very center of his soul. 'I don't want to be lonely anymore.'

Before she quite realized what was happening, he had his arms around her and she was holding him, as she had so often held the girls when they were frightened or unhappy.

'I'm here,' she murmured. 'Don't worry. I'm here.'

The first night they spent in the house in Atlanta,

Amy had awakened screaming. When Karen reached her room, she found the eight-year-old cringing on the floor.

'This is a scary place,' the child sobbed over and over. 'This isn't my room – it's a scary place. I'm all alone here. I want to go home.'

'It's not your *old* room,' Karen told her, sitting down on the bed. 'It's your *new* room.'

'I want my old room,' Amy cried.

'Tell you what,' Karen said. 'Why don't you come up here with me so the two of us can take a good look at this room, and then maybe it won't be so scary.'

Uncertain, Amy crawled up next to her stepmother.

'You know, a room just doesn't get to be your very own room until you've looked at it from your very own bed,' Karen told her. 'Wait a minute now – this *is* your very own bed, isn't it?'

Amy nodded. It was her familiar pink-and-white canopy bed from home.

'Well, then, are these your very own sheets?'

The bedding was white with pink ribbons and brown teddy bears frolicking across it.

Amy nodded again.

'So far, so good,' Karen declared. She glanced around the generous L-shaped space that they had hung with pink-and-white festooned wallpaper. 'Now let's see – is that your very own toy chest against the wall?'

A third nod came in reply as the child eyed the gaily decorated trunk that housed her favorite things.

'Is Snoopy sound asleep inside?'

'Yes,' Amy admitted. 'Unless I woke him up.'

Karen listened. 'I don't hear a single peep, do you?'

The little girl shook her head.

'Well, I guess that means he's just as snug as that old bug in a rug,' Karen declared. 'But I think we should whisper anyway, just in case.' She lowered her voice. 'Is that your very own dresser and desk and chair over there?'

Amy looked at the pink-painted furniture that had been brought from her room in New York. 'Uh-huh.'

'Now peek inside that closet – are those your very own clothes hanging up?'

'And that's my bathrobe on the bedpost, and my slippers on the floor, and my Raggedy Ann and my panda and my picture of all of us at the wedding.'

By this time, Karen was leaning against the headboard and Amy was nestled in her arms.

'Well then, you'd better tell me: What are all these things doing here if this isn't your very own new room?'

The little girl shrugged. 'It's bigger than my old room, and it's shaped funny, but I guess it isn't so scary after all.'

'In that case,' her stepmother suggested, 'suppose you snuggle down under the covers and close your eyes and think about how special this room is going to be, just because it's yours, and about all the new friends you're going to make who'll want to come here to play.'

'Are there any little girls my age nearby?'

'I have it on good authority that there's one right next door.'

'Maybe I can meet her tomorrow,' Amy ventured, stifling a yawn. 'I can't wait till tomorrow.'

'In that case, the sooner you go to sleep, the sooner tomorrow will come.'

'Don't go yet.'

'Don't worry. I'm right here.'

'Are you going to turn off the light right away?'

Karen smiled. 'Not until you're in dreamland.'

'Promise?'

'Promise.'

Ted found them both there the next morning.

As she had once held her daughter, so now Karen held her husband on the night of Amy's accident and the unexpected honesty held them both. He thought he had married a woman, but she knew he had married a shell. She thought she had married a shell, only to discover that she had married a man. With a silent splinter, the first crack appeared in the invisible wall.

'It's going to be all right,' she murmured. 'You'll see, everything's going to be all right. Amy will be fine. We'll all be fine.'

Somehow, she thought.

Amy recovered. She missed the last month of school but had no trouble making up the work. She spent the summer in a wheelchair, but by the fall she was back in class, first on crutches, then with a cane, and finally on her own two feet again. The skull fractures healed, having done no serious damage. Her hair grew a little funny around the scars, and she fretted until it was long enough to cover them, but that was the worst of it.

The best of it was that Karen and Ted began to talk to each other, first during the long nights of Amy's stay in the hospital, then during the months of her convalescence.

'I married you for the wrong reasons,' he acknowledged. 'I didn't realize it then, but I do now. You see, you were like Barbara in so many ways, and I missed her so much, and I thought I could make her come alive again through you. But of course I couldn't, and I blamed you when I shouldn't have.'

'I married you for the wrong reasons, too,' she conceded. 'I thought I could get back some of the things I felt I'd been cheated out of, without having to pay the price. But I ended up cheating you instead.'

'What sort of things?' he asked.

'The chance to know what being married was like,' she replied. 'The chance to have children to raise. The chance to have the kind of life I was brought up to believe I was supposed to have.'

'The accident you had – it prevented all that?'

'Yes,' she said truthfully. But she didn't elaborate.

Of course, he had seen the scars and wondered about them. But he would never ask.

'I didn't realize it was that bad,' he mused.

'The doctors had to remove my uterus,' she explained. 'My college sweetheart couldn't handle it. I guess he wanted children more than he wanted me. After that, I guess I just withdrew. I was afraid of being hurt again.'

'I can understand that,' he said. 'I suppose men can be very selfish and insensitive sometimes.'

'Well, it might not have been all his fault,' she heard herself say.

'Marrying me wasn't what you expected, was it?' he observed. 'I turned out to be selfish and insensitive, too.'

'No,' she said quickly. 'Don't blame yourself.'

'Well, where do we go from here?' he asked, holding his breath. 'Do you want a divorce?'

'Do you?' she countered, not daring to breathe.

His response was rapid and sincere. 'No, I don't.'

Karen sighed with relief. 'Neither do I.'

'All right then,' he declared, 'as far as I'm concerned, we start our marriage over again – from right this minute – and not only do I promise to love and honor you and keep you in sickness and in health, but I promise to keep you safe from harm for as long as we both shall live.'

Less than a year later, they moved to San Francisco.

Karen took her mid-morning cup of tea into the living room. The three Rankin oils she and Ted owned between them were stacked against one wall, waiting to be uncrated. The clown would go in the office, they had already decided on that, but it was up to Karen to choose where to hang the other two. She was about to begin ripping the first crate apart when the front doorbell rang.

A large woman in her late fifties, with full lips, a broad nose, narrow brown eyes, and frizzy salt-and-pepper hair pulled back into an unfashionable bun, stood across the threshold with a casserole in her hands. There was something about her that reminded Karen of Demelza.

'Hi,' she said, when the door was opened. 'I wanted to bring this to you yesterday, because I know how horrific moving-in day can be, but I had an emergency at the office and just didn't get home in time to get it done. So I took this morning off, and here it is. I hope you can use it.'

'Thank you,' Karen replied. 'That's very kind.'

'I'm Natalie Shaffer and I live across the street,' the woman continued, nodding in the direction of a stately Tudor two houses down. 'Welcome to The Wood and to San Francisco and even to California, come to that.'

Karen introduced herself. 'I guess I have to admit to

all three,' she said with a chuckle. 'We came from Tucson.'

'Never been there,' Natalie announced. 'But if you have time to come over for a cup of coffee, you can tell me all about it.'

'I've just made a pot of tea,' Karen ventured. 'Why don't you come in and join me?'

'Tea?' Natalie echoed, stepping into the foyer. 'My goodness, you're civilized. I thought Arizona was still one of those wild and woolly places.'

Karen laughed. 'In many ways it is, but I'm originally from New York.'

'Are you?' pounced Natalie. 'How delightful – we're twice neighbors. I'm from Pennsylvania.'

'My husband comes from Pennsylvania,' Karen exclaimed. 'From Reading.'

'Well then, we're practically family,' Natalie assured her. 'I'm from Scranton.'

Karen poured another cup of tea and found a box of cookies in the cupboard, and the two women sat down at the breakfast-room table.

'I'm amazed you can find anything, a day after moving in,' Natalie marveled, biting into a cookie.

Karen shrugged. 'I used to be the manager of a shop that depended on my being able to unpack and organize in record time. My employer used to call me the Unbearable Neatnik. I guess some habits are hard to break.'

'I wanted to be a flower child,' Natalie said with a chuckle. 'My husband used to call me the Unbearable Beatnik.'

Karen sipped her tea with a soft smile. After ten years and four moves, she knew she was about to make a real friend.

'What do you do that you have emergencies and you get to take mornings off?' she asked.

'I'm a psychiatrist,' replied Natalie and immediately burst out laughing. 'I'll wager no one's ever accused you of having a poker face,' she cried. 'It froze like a sphinx the minute that word came out of my mouth.'

'Did it?' Karen managed to say. 'I can't imagine why.'

The neighbor grinned. 'It gets worse, I'm afraid – my husband's one also.'

'Really? Both of you?' Karen blurted in her discomfort. 'I guess psychiatry must be … profitable.'

Natalie chuckled. 'Shrinks are in, shame is out. With ninety-eight percent of the population among the walking dsyfunctional these days, there's no longer anything wrong with an otherwise perfectly sane person seeking help.'

'I didn't mean to offend you,' Karen said hastily.

'I'm not offended,' Natalie replied. 'On the contrary, I think this is the beginning of a great friendship.'

By the end of three weeks, Karen no longer thought about Natalie in terms of her profession. They were having too much fun together. Soon, the Shaffers were coming to dinner every other Friday night, and the Donigers were going across the street for brunch on alternate Sundays.

The Shaffer home was a collector's bad dream, crammed with antiques representing every period from Elizabethan to Bauhaus. Threadbare Orientals that rightfully belonged in a museum covered the floors, original Tiffany lamps lit the rooms, a real

Fabergé egg kept the papers on a side table from scattering, and Karen found a cabinet of first editions tucked into a corner that would have had Demelza drooling. Mostly, however, there was clutter – papers, books, magazines and dust.

'Neither of us is particularly good at housekeeping.' Natalie shrugged without guilt.

Herbert Shaffer was a jolly man of sixty, with bushy eyebrows and a funny little mustache. It seemed to be a race whether he would go bald before he went gray. He had a surprising interest in architecture, and he and Ted hit it off immediately.

The first Friday the Shaffers came to dinner, they sat in the green-and-cream living room afterward, drinking brandy from crystal snifters and carrying on an animated discussion about everything from movies to music to food to California wines, and eventually to the five-year-old drought.

'Isn't that the most beautiful book?' Natalie exclaimed during a break in the conversation, nodding toward a copy of *Tapestry* that Ted insisted be kept on the coffee table. 'I saw it down at B. Dalton's and – I don't know – there was just something about it. I had to have it. I guess that's where I got my wild and woolly notions about Arizona.'

'Yes,' Karen murmured noncommittally.

'I understand the authors travel around the country in a jeep. A couple of free spirits, I guess.'

Amy giggled.

'What's so funny?' Natalie inquired.

'That you call my mother and my aunt free spirits,' she replied.

'Your ... what?'

'Nancy Yanow is my aunt,' Amy explained. 'She

takes the pictures. And Mom writes the words. But she uses her maiden name so no one will know it's her.'

'That's not why at all,' Karen objected. 'It's just the way we started.'

Natalie gaped at Karen with a mixture of astonishment and admiration.

'You never said,' she complained.

Karen shrugged. 'It never came up.'

'I asked you what you did,' the psychiatrist insisted. 'You said you were a housewife.'

'I am.'

'And a mom,' Amy put in.

'That's right,' Karen said, giving her stepdaughter a hug. 'The other is just a hobby.'

'You've done a first-rate job with your Amy,' Natalie remarked one day during a shopping excursion. 'I'm looking forward to meeting Gwen and Jessica.'

'I'm afraid I can't take much of the credit.' Karen sighed. 'The girls aren't mine. I only wish they were. Their real mother died when they were young.'

'You look pretty real to me,' Natalie observed.

'That's not what I meant.'

'I know what you meant, but you don't know what you're talking about,' the psychiatrist said bluntly. 'Amy is the way she is as much because of you as anyone else.'

'Well, perhaps.'

'How come you never had any of your own?'

'I had … an accident some years ago,' Karen confided reluctantly. 'I wasn't able, after that.'

'Not something you care to discuss,' the psychiatrist suggested. 'Me and my big mouth.'

'It doesn't matter anymore,' Karen replied with a shrug.

'One of the by-products of being a shrink,' Natalie said casually, appraising her friend through the professional corner of her eye, 'is that you get in the habit of asking too many questions. Of course you also get to be one hell of a listener. So, if you ever feel like talking, you know, about anything at all, I'm just across the street.'

Karen smiled politely, a bit of the old plastic smile, but said nothing. Years ago, she had told Nancy all she intended to tell anyone about the assault in Central Park. Since then, she had managed to put the past behind her and now she wanted only to leave it there. Despite their new understanding, she had not even told Ted. Several times, she thought she might, but the fear stopped her – the same fear that the truth would disgust him and he would turn away from her as Peter had.

She sometimes wished there had been someone to tell who might have listened without condemning, who might have understood, who might have been able to help her deal with the anger and frustration. But there hadn't been anyone there for her.

Now it was a different world. Rape was a topic that was being discussed openly, and rape-counseling centers were springing up all across the country. Along with date rape, acquaintance rape was beginning to gain acceptance. More and more, women were coming forward to say: 'Yes, I went with him, but I did not want to have sex with him. I said *no*.'

How desperately Karen had longed to say those very words to the New York police, to her mother, to Peter, to the whole world, and have someone stand up beside her and agree. But no one had, and after almost thirty years, she had pretty much convinced herself that she had been the villain of the piece instead of the victim.

* * *

The balmy days of September stretched into October and the Bay Area held its collective breath, hoping for rain. The drought had brought severe water rationing.

'We had enough water when we were in the middle of the desert,' Karen observed wryly. 'Now here we are, surrounded by water, and the reservoirs are dry.'

'It's not the weather, it's the politicians,' Natalie told her. 'Down in southern California, they're swimming in their pools and watering their lawns just like they always did, while up here we're recycling every possible drop and taking communal showers.'

Karen had never had much interest in the workings of government, at any level. Although she dutifully voted in every election, she paid scant attention to the players. She had the general impression that politics had degenerated to a fairly dismal level, that corruption was everywhere, and behavior once considered abhorrent was now being condoned.

Over the last decade, a growing distrust and disgust with the business of politics had culminated in total disinterest. Karen stopped reading newsmagazines altogether, began to skip the front sections of the paper, and paid no attention to the evening news. She made an effort to watch some of the Thomas-Hill hearings, but the entire spectacle appalled her.

'It's progress,' the psychiatrist told her. 'A generation ago, a woman would never have been allowed to confront such a man about his behavior. Anita Hill may not have stopped the Thomas confirmation, but she accomplished something just as important. She opened a door that won't be easily shut again.'

Karen pondered that for a while. 'I suppose you have a point,' she conceded, 'but I'm suffering from an incurable case of apathy. I don't even know – or care – who's going to run for President next year.'

Natalie nodded. 'I understand how you feel. But it happens that we have someone right here in California that I wish would take a stab at it.'

'Why?'

'Because I think he's a good man. It's clear he really cares about the state and I think he cares just as much about the country, too. I heard him speak at an AMA luncheon last month, and he was honest enough to tell us what a mess we're in, and smart enough to show us exactly how he'd fix it.'

'What's his name?' Karen asked. 'If he runs, maybe I'll vote for him.'

'Willmont,' Natalie replied. 'Robert Drayton Willmont.'

two

On Thursday, October 24, Randy Neuburg squeezed his way past a throng of media representatives into Robert Willmont's private office in the Old Senate Office Building, shutting it firmly behind him.

'It's a zoo out there,' he exclaimed. 'I've never seen so many reporters stuffed into one place before. How do you think they all knew it was today?'

Robert leaned back in his chair and grinned. 'Mary Catherine told them.'

It was still the same boyish grin, but now it spread across a face that showed the erosion of middle age and the pressures of responsibility. 'Handsome' had described him in his youth. At fifty-three, the more appropriate word was 'distinguished.'

'Well, every single paper in the country must have sent someone hightailing it over here, not to mention all three networks and CNN,' Randy informed him.

'They've just about finished with the lights. Are you ready?'

'As ready as I'll ever be, I guess.'

They were brave words and bravely spoken, but Randy hadn't served this man for thirteen years and learned nothing about him. He knew that, behind the cool facade, the senator had to be as nervous as he had ever been. Only halfway into his second six-year term, he was about to take the biggest gamble of his life.

As though he had read his aide's mind, Robert sighed. Like a runaway horse on a slippery hill, he felt out of control. The slow, careful journey to the White House that he had plotted so many years ago had turned into a reckless dash. Somebody else was holding the reins – a group of somebody elses, actually, and he was helpless to do anything but hurtle and leap in whichever direction they chose.

'It's too soon,' he had argued when the upstairs people approached him in the middle of summer. 'My game plan was to finish up this term and then be in position for 1996.'

'Fuck your game plan,' they replied. 'Now's the time.'

'What if we can't take him? I'm finished.'

'You can take him,' they said with easy assurance.

'But I promised my wife she'd be the first First Lady of the twenty-first century.'

'She'll get over it.'

In fact, Elizabeth Willmont didn't even seem to remember the promise. But then, with the little pink pills never far from reach, she sometimes didn't seem to remember very much of anything. She regarded her husband's consuming desire for the White House as the fulfillment of his dream, and focused all her attention on the fulfillment of her own.

Adam was eleven years old now, smart as a whip and as striking as his parents, with the flaming Avery hair and the extraordinary Drayton eyes.

'He has your cunning and my curiosity,' Elizabeth told her husband once, because she knew he was too busy to notice.

Mother and son went everywhere together – the zoo, the ballet, the Smithsonian. They hiked in Rock Creek Park and in Muir Woods, graced the Drayton box at the San Francisco Opera, sailed Chesapeake Bay, and watched hang gliders swoop across the cliffs at Fort Funston.

'Would you like to try that?' she asked him once.

Adam, nine at the time, considered the kitelike figures and then shook his head. 'It looks like fun,' he said, 'but a kid could get killed doing that sort of thing.'

'What are you going to be when you grow up, young man?' his paternal grandmother asked him. The dowager socialite was past eighty and still hanging on.

'Useful,' the boy answered.

Elizabeth delighted in him. He entranced her as Robert once had and more than made up for his father's frequent absences – absences she had long since ceased to care about.

'What would you say to closing out this century in the White House instead of starting the new one?' Robert asked her one late-August evening over dinner in Rock Creek Park.

'Whatever you think best,' she replied absently.

'God,' he exclaimed in disgust. 'You'd think I was talking about buying a new car.'

Elizabeth glanced up. 'Do we need one?'

Robert looked at the still beautiful but now indifferent woman across the table from him and wondered where the naive, adoring girl he had married had gone.

'Tell them it's a go,' he instructed Randy the next day. 'And let's start testing the waters.'

Randy cleared his throat. 'Uh, there's something maybe we should talk about first.'

'Sure,' the senator replied. 'Shoot.'

'Gary Hart,' the aide said.

'What about him? He was a damn fool who had a shot at the White House and shot himself in the foot instead.'

Randy leveled a look at his boss that said it all and the expression on Robert's face suddenly darkened.

'You're way out of line,' he snapped. 'What I do on my own time is my own goddamn business.'

'In California, where you can do no wrong, maybe. But once you become a national candidate, what you do becomes everyone's business,' Randy insisted. 'And since you pay me a lot of money to give you advice, maybe you ought to listen to some of it.'

The senator sighed. 'All right, say it.'

The aide knew he would have to phrase his next words very carefully. 'There are people out there who don't know a thing about your extracurricular activities, and wouldn't care if they did,' he said. 'And there are people who do know but believe the things you stand for are more important than a minor transgression here and there.'

'I should hope so,' Robert interjected.

'But also out there are the Moral Righteous, who believe they were appointed by God to tell everyone else how to live. And sharing the ears of these paragons of virtue is the media, who don't give a damn what you stand for or what you could do for the country or for the world. The polite days are gone, Senator. All that counts now is the story – the front-page, three-inch-head, above-the-fold story.'

Unexpectedly, the senator chuckled. 'And you want me to promise that I won't give them the one they're looking for?'

'A sizable group of folks have worked long and hard to get you to this point,' Randy replied bluntly. 'You owe it to them – to us – and, yes, to the country – not to blow it.'

'Hart should have had you in his corner.'

The aide shrugged. 'He misjudged both the press and the people. It was a blunder that no one, with the exception of the incumbent, of course, wants to see you make.'

'None of that nonsense made any difference back in JFK's time,' the senator said with a sigh. 'Back then, people were able to separate what was important from what wasn't.'

'That was thirty years ago,' Randy observed. 'Things have changed since then, and you have to accept that.'

Robert was not stupid. He knew his dalliances were potentially dangerous for a politician, but he was still a man – a man with substantial needs and a wife who had lost all interest in satisfying them. It was a pity that the media were no longer as well-bred or as tolerant of the human condition as they had once been. It was going to make the next year very tedious.

'Okay, I hear you,' he said. 'But there's one thing I'm going to insist on, and I won't compromise.'

'What's that?' Randy asked, not sure he wanted to hear the answer.

'No Secret Service. I won't have any official watch-dogs monitoring my life – knowing what I eat for breakfast every morning, where I keep my socks, when I take a crap.'

'What about protection?' his aide protested in panic. 'You know what kind of nuts there are out there.'

'If you feel it's necessary, we'll hire a private firm, a discreet firm. One that will answer only to me, not to Washington. I promise you I'll be as good a boy as I can, but I'll do it on my own terms.'

Randy sighed, knowing it was pointless to argue and reasoning that half a bargain was better than none. 'All right. When it comes to it, we'll decline the Secret Service. And I'll have Mary Catherine start scouting around for the right private group.'

The senator smiled benignly. 'Anything else?'

In answer, Randy placed a folder on the desk. 'These are some of the areas the upstairs people have tar-geted,' he said. 'I recommend we start testing the ones on the top page.'

Robert scanned the sheet. Locations in a dozen major political markets across the country jumped up at him.

'Looks good,' he remarked. As always, his aide was two steps ahead of him.

'I also recommend we hire a public relations firm to handle you.'

'Handle me?' Robert inquired, raising an eyebrow.

'You know, image builders,' explained Randy. 'They do media strategies for politicians, all based on num-bers and high-tech prestidigitation. They analyze a candidate and they figure out the best way to present him to the public.'

'I haven't had any trouble with my image up to now,' Robert objected.

'Not in California, no,' Randy agreed. 'But you've kept a low profile in Congress – making allies instead of enemies – building your political base. That's left you basically unknown across the country. So now we're going to push your national awareness up as high as we can, make you a household name.'

'I see your drift,' murmured the senator.

'I've done some research,' Randy continued, 'and I think that Smoeller and Dobbs is our best bet. It's a small firm, but dedicated, with impeccable credentials.'

'They're not the ones remaking Willie Smith, are they?'

'No,' Randy said emphatically. 'We certainly don't want any connection whatsoever with that debacle.'

'And I don't want to be associated with those people who went around promoting the Kuwaiti incubator scam, either.'

'Absolutely not. Smoeller and Dobbs is a firm with a spotless reputation.'

The senator appraised his aide. 'One of the smartest things I ever did was to take you on, wasn't it?'

'The true test of any leader' – Randy grinned – 'is whether he's wise enough to surround himself with his equals. Speaking of which, Ms. Dobbs will be here at three o'clock.'

Mariah Dobbs was a no-nonsense lady who looked more like a *Playboy* centerfold than the successful businesswoman she was. She displayed a short skirt over long legs, a generous curve beneath her suit jacket, intelligent gray eyes behind oversize designer glasses, and a radiant mane of gold hair.

'Given enough access, enough money, and the right buttons to push,' she said at the start of their first meeting, 'I can sell anything – or anyone – to anybody.'

'That sounds encouraging,' Robert replied, flashing his dazzling smile and feeling a familiar rise in his groin.

'If I agree to take you on, Senator, we'll naturally be spending a considerable amount of time together,' Mariah said pleasantly. 'So I think we should have a clear understanding of our relationship right from the start.'

'Certainly,' Robert murmured, shifting ever so slightly in his seat.

'I keep my professional life totally separate and apart from my personal life,' the public relations expert declared. 'Which means that the only portion of our anatomies that will interact will be our minds.'

'I wouldn't have it any other way,' Robert demurred.

'On that basis,' she went on as though he hadn't spoken, 'I plan to study your persona, in depth, over the next few weeks, familiarize myself with your political philosophy as well as your particular strengths and weaknesses, so that we'll be better able to promote you. Off the top of my head, however, I'd say that since a significant part of your message appears to be quite liberal, it might be prudent if the rest of you came across as being fairly conservative. I recommend white shirts, dark suits, traditional ties, keep your hair cut short, and skip the beach this summer.'

'I can handle that,' he said. I can handle you, too, he thought. There wasn't a woman in the world he couldn't have, if he wanted her. Some took a bit more persuasion than others, perhaps, but it was all part of the game. It would be no different with this one.

'People are going to know that you're a rich boy,' the public relations executive continued, 'but I want them to see that you're *using* your wealth, not just enjoying it.'

'I hear you, Mariah.' He caressed the name.

'Dobbs,' she corrected. 'Professionally, I prefer to be known as Dobbs.'

'All right, Dobbs,' Robert corrected himself.

'Also,' she added, refusing to be sidetracked, 'trade the Lamborghini in for something more conservative. A Mercedes is okay, if you're fixated on European cars, but make it black. Red is fine for a playboy, but I don't think that's the image you really want to promote in Peoria.'

'Okay, the Countach goes,' Robert agreed, thinking she had certainly done her homework. The Italian sports car was kept at home, in the garage at Jackson Street, where he drove it infrequently but flamboyantly, at a hundred and ten miles an hour down the treacherous Coast Highway.

'And whenever you go out socially, I recommend that you go with your wife, or with your wife and son. We want people to see you as a dedicated family man.'

The senator shot a look at his aide. 'I *am* a dedicated family man,' he asserted.

'Yes, well, that's all I'm prepared to say for now,' Mariah concluded. 'I'll go through the background material your staff has put together and touch base with you in a week or so with a more complete proposal.'

She slipped the thick folder Randy had provided

into her briefcase, coolly shook Robert's hand, and turned to leave. But at the last moment she turned around and, removing her glasses, produced the definitive *Playboy* smile.

'Well, gentlemen, will I do?'

The senator laughed outright. 'You'll do,' he said, adding to himself – you'll do just fine.

'Good,' she replied with a toss of her gold mane. 'Because I plan to retire on what you're going to pay me.'

Randy produced a broad grin the moment the door had closed behind her. 'With that little ace up our sleeve, how can we lose?'

'Let's not get too cocky,' Robert suggested. 'By Labor Day, we should have a clear picture of where we stand.'

By Labor Day, the picture was indeed clear. According to every major newspaper, poll, and political pundit in the target areas who could squeeze himself onto the Willmont bandwagon, the senator from California was someone with a legitimate chance of unseating the incumbent.

No one close to the senator was very surprised by his swift climb up the political ladder. He was that rarity of rarities – a man of both image and substance. He had the dashing looks, the persuasive charm, the keen intelligence – and the right message at the right time.

'I believe in a balance of trade with Japan or no trade with Japan,' he assured the auto industry in Detroit.

'Hear, hear,' his audience applauded.

'But I won't force Japan to buy American automobiles. Hell, *I* won't even buy American automobiles.'

'So what are you telling us?' bristled a CEO into sudden silence.

'Learn how to make a Toyota.'

'Half of every federal tax dollar is used just to keep up with interest payments on the national debt,' he told a caucus of housewives in Cleveland. 'Isn't it time Washington learned what all of you have known for years – that you can't spend what you don't have?'

'I'm four-square behind foreign aid,' he assured a contingent of Third World diplomats in New York, 'as long as it comes after American aid.'

'It's time to take responsibility for your own actions,' he suggested to the NRA. 'Either you find a way to get guns out of the hands of children, or I promise you – I will.'

'Contrary to popular doctrine, the meek are not going to inherit the earth,' he assured a group of industrialists in Dallas. 'By the time we get through with this planet, not even the cockroaches will survive.'

He became the king of the sound bite, but even the media sensed there was more to him than one-liners. He made some of the people angry and he made some of the people laugh, but he made enough of the people go home and take a good long look in the mirror. By the end of October, all that was left was the announcement.

Mary Catherine poked her head in the door. She was wearing a new red wool dress, she had a fresh perm in her gray hair and her Bambi eyes sparkled.

'We're all set,' she said.

'Is Elizabeth here?' Randy asked.

'She and Adam just came in.'

Robert pulled himself out of his chair, reached up to straighten his tie, and stepped out from behind the desk.

'How do I look?' he asked.

'Like a man about to step off a cliff,' replied Randy with a grin.

'Like the next President of the United States,' Mary Catherine told him.

'Okay,' he said. 'Then let's go do it.'

three

'I don't think we should do a book on San Francisco,' Karen told Nancy on October 24.

'Why not?' Nancy queried. 'It's one of the most popular cities in the country.'

'That's why,' Karen explained. 'As far as I can tell, it's been photographed, lithographed, silk-screened, etched, sketched and painted to death. It's already so overexposed that I'm not sure we could find anything new to say.'

'Spectrum's not going to want to hear that.'

'Well, I have an alternative.'

'I'm all ears,' declared Nancy.

'I'd like to do a book on water.'

'Water?' came the blank response.

'Water. When we lived in Tucson, there was always plenty of it. We were in the middle of the desert and we took it for granted. But here in San Francisco we're surrounded by water and we literally have to count drops. There's the ocean and the bay and the delta and rivers and streams and lakes and ponds and, if someone's been careless, even a puddle. And, all the while, people are taking family showers and trying not to flush their toilets.'

'I didn't realize it was that bad,' Nancy murmured.

'It's just the irony of it,' Karen told her. 'Besides, it may be the only story left to tell about this place.'

'Water, huh?'

'Well, why don't you think about it,' Karen suggested, 'and run it past Spectrum.'

'Don't have to,' Nancy said. 'I think it's a terrific idea. Let's do it.'

'Really?' asked Karen.

'Really.'

'My sister-in-law is coming out in the beginning of December,' Karen told Natalie. 'We're starting another book.'

'About San Francisco?' the psychiatrist asked.

'About water.'

Natalie threw back her head and roared.

'I'll want an autographed copy of that one,' she said.

'I'd like you to meet Nancy, if you have time.'

'I'll make time,' Natalie asserted with more than a hint of sarcasm. 'That is, if I can tear myself away from the Willie Smith rape trial.'

'Oh … that.' Karen stiffened imperceptibly, but good psychiatrists were trained to see imperceptibles, and Natalie Shaffer was very good.

'Not planning to watch, eh?' she said.

'No,' came the short reply. Then a shrug. 'He'll be acquitted.'

'Why do you say that? Do you think he's innocent?'

'I think he's guilty,' Karen replied. 'But he'll be acquitted anyway. The jury will say it was her fault because it was three o'clock in the morning and she went with him.'

'Come on,' Natalie argued. 'This is the 1990s and rapists are getting convicted every day.'

'Acquaintance-rapists?'

'All kinds, although admittedly acquaintance rape is a lot harder to prove.'

'He'll be acquitted,' repeated Karen.

'Nancy's coming out in December,' Karen told Ted when he came home that evening.

Her husband grinned. 'The new book?'

'She liked my idea about water.'

'So do I.'

'Would you like a glass of wine?' she asked.

'Sure,' he replied, heading toward the study.

Since coming to California, the Donigers had been making a conscientious effort to switch from Scotch to wine. On evenings when Amy was in her room doing her homework, Ted would drink a glass with the national news, and Karen would sip at hers as she fixed dinner.

It was just past seven and the newscast was in full swing. As usual, Karen was not paying attention. She inserted a corkscrew into a chilled bottle of chardonnay.

'. . . *surprise move, an unexpected hat has been thrown into the Presidential race,*' the anchor was saying.

With a practiced jerk, Karen pulled the cork free.

'*Robert Drayton Willmont, the charismatic senator from California, made his announcement at a press conference held in Washington late this afternoon.'*

She half-filled two glasses.

'*Ladies and gentlemen,'* another voice said. '*My wife Elizabeth and my son Adam have set their hearts on being the next residents of sixteen hundred Pennsylvania Avenue.'*

The voice paused for a titter of appreciative laughter. Karen took Ted's glass and started down the hallway that ran from the kitchen to the study.

'*Since I have always made every effort to give these two very special people in my life everything they ask for, I am today declaring my candidacy for President of the United States.'*

She reached the door of the study and, for some reason, an icy shiver slid down her spine.

'*It should come as no surprise to anyone that this country is in very serious trouble,'* the candidate continued. '*To be more specific, we are standing on the brink of moral, intellectual, and economic bankruptcy. I believe that America deserves a leader who will first recognize that, second, admit to it, and third, do something about it.'*

It was something about the voice, something familiar. She was sure she had heard it before, and the memory pushing its way into her consciousness was not a pleasant one.

'*I saw a bumper sticker the other day,'* the voice went on. '*It read: 'New World Order – Same Old Lies.' Now if that's what you want for four more years, then turn off your television sets and put aside your newspapers for the next twelve months, because I'm not interested in anyone's megalomaniacal new world order at the cost of those who are suffering in America now.'*

She took three steps into the study and stopped. The television set was behind her, so that the voice seemed to come through her rather than toward her.

'*I say you've been lied to enough. I say you've been deceived enough. I say you have the right to know what's going on. After all, it's your country. And it's in trouble. But I think we can keep it viable. Yes, even after twelve long years of trickle-down leadership, even after decades of neglect, I'm not ready to give up on America yet. But I can't do it without you. So I'm going to take advantage of every opportunity the media will give me to tell you the very unpleasant but necessary truth about what has been done to you and what is still being done to you, and exactly what we have to do to fix it.'*

'That would be different,' drawled Ted.

As though the whole world were now running in slow motion, Karen turned to face the face on the television screen. The once-dark hair was almost buried in silver, and the crevices of middle age etched his face. After twenty-nine years, she might not have remembered the set of the jaw or the shape of the mouth or the angle of the nose or even the little black mole on his right cheek – but she would never ever forget those eyes.

The wineglass shattered against the hardwood floor.

It was ten o'clock the following evening when Karen crossed the street and pressed the Shaffers' door-bell. It was the dream that drove her there – the dream about being chased through the fog that she hadn't had in years, but which had come back last night.

She had stayed indoors all day, drinking cup after cup of tea laced with brandy, not even bothering to dress until just before Amy came home from school. Dinner was a scramble of leftovers.

It was the unbelievability of it that she couldn't seem to grasp, that after all these years she should have to come across him again – and the unfairness that he had not only escaped retribution of any kind but had become so successful.

'I'm sorry to bother you so late,' she apologized when Natalie answered the door in her bathrobe, 'but you said – if I ever needed to talk . . .'

'Come on inside,' the psychiatrist replied instantly, leading Karen to the back of the house and the room they had turned into a cozy office.

'I don't know what to do,' Karen whispered. 'I thought it was all over and done with long ago, part of the past – and now it's all back, just like before, and I don't know what to do.'

Natalie closed the door behind them. 'Sit down,' she invited and watched Karen squirrel into a deep leather chair. 'Now, what don't you know what to do about?'

Shadowed eyes peered out of the chair. 'I want to kill him,' Karen said.

'Kill who?'

'I didn't want to tell Ted. I thought *he* might kill him and I couldn't let him do that. I couldn't let him ruin his life. But my life is already ruined – he ruined it, so what difference would it make if *I* did it ... if I killed him?'

'Ruined what?' Natalie asked. 'Kill who?'

Karen suddenly giggled, a high, shrill, scary sound.

'Here he is, after all this time, and he's running for President, can you believe that? He's running for President! I could have gone the rest of my life never having to see him again, and what happens? I end up in California, and he's running for President.' The giggle turned to a groan and she began to shiver. When she spoke again, her words stumbled over chattering teeth. 'He doesn't deserve to be President.

He doesn't even deserve to be alive.'

Natalie hustled over to a tray on a sideboard and poured a glass of brandy.

'Here,' the psychiatrist ordered. 'Drink this down.' She had to hold the glass herself to keep it from spilling.

'I never thought I'd see him again,' Karen went on. 'I thought I was done with it all. The nightmares had gone away. Ted and I were starting to put our marriage together. Sometimes, days went by and I didn't even think about it. And then there he was, big as life, coming right through the television screen, talking about truth, for God's sake – truth!'

With a gasp, Natalie sank into the opposite chair. 'Are you talking about Robert Willmont?' she asked in disbelief. 'You want to kill Robert Wilmont?'

'Why not?' Karen flared. 'He almost killed *me*.'

The words hung in the air for a moment, until Natalie was able to absorb them.

'Why don't you tell me about it,' she suggested calmly, although she felt anything but calm.

'I never knew who he was – that is, his whole name,' Karen began. 'No one had a last name back then. So he was just Bob when I met him. Bob from Harvard Law School.'

Natalie knew the California senator had gone to Harvard Law School.

'Do you remember,' Karen asked, 'when I told you I'd had an accident and because of it I could never have any children of my own?'

'I remember.'

'Well, *he* was the accident.'

The psychiatrist listened in silence to the story that Karen had to tell, and Karen told it all, beginning with the party at Jill Hartman's, describing the assault in Central Park, detailing her months in the hospital and the biased police investigation, moving on to her parents and their incredible reaction, and ending with Peter Bauer.

She told it as she had never been allowed to tell it, not just chronicling the bare facts, but clothing them in her deepest-buried feelings, exposing her fears, revealing her humiliation and degradation. Even though she was recounting something that had taken place more than half her life ago, she could recall every detail as vividly as though it had happened yesterday.

From a quarter of a century of professional practice, Natalie Shaffer had learned the art of detached listening, a method of filtering information without betraying anything other than objective interest. But the technique failed her now. Robert Drayton Willmont, the man she had voted for in two senatorial contests, the man she intended to support vigorously in the upcoming presidential campaign, the man she looked upon as the one real hope for the country, was turning into a monster before her very eyes.

'He told the police that you initiated the sex and then refused to leave the park with him?' she asked when the story was finished.

'That's what the investigator said.'

'And you're positive this is the same man? You couldn't be mistaken? After all, it was such a long time ago.'

'There are some things you never forget,' Karen said stonily. 'Maybe I could have mistaken the face, or even the voice, but as long as I live, I'll never forget those eyes.'

Natalie got up from her chair and went to pour a brandy for herself. 'I think *I* need one of these now.'

'I didn't mean to burden you,' Karen apologized, 'but I just needed to talk to someone. You know, someone who would maybe understand my side of it.'

'What's not to understand?' Natalie shrugged. 'It's the old guilt-by-association ploy. You were there – ergo, what happened must have been your fault.'

'In all this time,' Karen confessed, 'you're the first person I've ever told.'

'Besides Ted, of course.'

Karen shook her head. 'I couldn't tell him. I was too afraid he wouldn't want me if he knew, that he'd run away, like Peter.'

Natalie sighed. She desperately wanted Karen to be mistaken, to find some loophole in her story that would show that the man responsible for the terrible things she had described was someone other than the charismatic senator from California who had come forward to lead the nation back from the brink of disaster. But the psychiatrist had been trained to detect even the hint of duplicity, and Karen's years-old recollections were far too clear, far too detailed to leave much room for doubt.

'In December,' she mused aloud, 'voters in Louisiana will go to the polls to choose between a crook and a racist. If what you say is true, next year this country may be asked to choose between an incompetent and a rapist. I'm not sure I know what's to become of us.'

Karen's eyes widened. 'You called him a rapist,' she whispered.

'Of course I did,' Natalie replied. 'What else would I call him?'

Karen began to laugh and cry at the same time. 'Are you saying you don't think it was my fault?'

'Not from what you've told me,' Natalie declared, and then turned a thoughtful glance on her visitor. 'Why? Do *you* think it was your fault?'

'Everyone seemed to think it was,' sobbed Karen. 'They said I went with him and so I must have been looking for trouble. I must have teased him and led him on. They said he was a fine upstanding citizen, so why would he have done such an awful thing unless I had provoked him. The police, my parents – they told me what was past was past and to forget about it and get on with my life. But I guess I never did.'

'Of course not,' said Natalie. 'You're still struggling with what happened to you because no one ever let you deal with it.'

'What do you mean?'

'I mean, when a person is assaulted, as you were, it isn't just the body that needs to heal. The mind also has to heal. The doctors mended your body, but no one understood how important it was for you to mend your soul as well.'

'I never thought of it that way,' Karen marveled.

'You were never allowed to talk about it, you were never allowed to confront your attacker, you were never allowed to work through your fear and anger. Instead, you were made to feel guilt and shame, because that's what the people around you were feeling.'

Tears ran down Karen's cheeks. 'I always felt exactly that way,' she whispered, 'even though I never really thought I did anything wrong.'

'What was that?' Natalie asked.

'I said I felt that way even though I didn't think I did anything wrong.'

'I'm sorry, I didn't catch that last part.'

'I said I didn't think I did anything wrong.'

'Once more,' the psychiatrist urged.

Karen took a deep breath. '*I didn't do anything wrong,*' she almost shouted.

Natalie sat back in her chair. 'You've just taken the first step toward healing.'

'But how can I heal when he's still out there, walking around as free as the wind? When there are still people – my own family – who think that what he did was my fault?'

'As long as *you* know it wasn't,' the psychiatrist said, 'does it really matter what anyone else thinks?'

'It matters,' Karen said bitterly. 'Because it isn't fair. My whole life, ever since that night, I've felt so unworthy, so dirty. All my parents wanted to do was sweep it under the rug – sweep *me* under the rug. They couldn't even call it what it was, you know – they always referred to it as my "accident."'

'You can blame them, if you need to,' the psychiatrist replied. 'But the truth is, they probably didn't know how to deal with it any more than you did.'

'Maybe not,' Karen conceded. 'But that's no excuse for them not believing me, is it – my own parents? All these years, I doubted myself because of them. I had no confidence in my own judgment. I could hardly bear to look at myself in the mirror. I was never able to have a decent relationship with a man. I believed the most important thing was that no one ever find out, that as long as no one knew, everything would be all right. But all the time I thought I was coping, I wasn't coping at all. Everything is still churning around inside of me, like a volcano waiting to erupt.'

'Let it,' Natalie advised.

'You don't mean I really should go out and kill him, do you?'

'Is that your only solution?'

'I can't deny the idea has real appeal,' Karen declared.

'I don't doubt that,' Natalie replied reasonably. 'But, on the other hand, what will killing him accomplish? Will it give you back what he took from you? Will it justify all your years of torment? Will it restore your self-respect?'

'Well, I won't really know until after I do it, will I?'

Natalie stared at her visitor for a minute before she began to chuckle. 'Well, at least you still have your sense of humor.'

Karen shrugged. 'I feel like I have to do something.'

'I agree,' Natalie assured her. 'But now that capital punishment is back on the books, killing Robert Willmont will only succeed in ending what's left of *your* life, too, and where's the justice in that?'

'Maybe I don't care,' Karen said. 'Can you honestly tell me he deserves to live?'

'Perhaps not, but *you* do,' the psychiatrist observed. 'Despite the years of pain and anguish and betrayal you've suffered, look what you managed to create. You have a marriage with real potential, you've raised three beautiful girls, you're producing a series of wonderful books. Now, I'm certainly not saying that you wouldn't have had a happy life if you'd never met up with Robert Willmont. I'm only saying that, on balance, you've done very well for yourself, and I'd think long and hard before I decided to throw all that away on a momentary act of revenge.'

'Tell me the truth,' Karen urged. 'Do you think the man who did those things to me deserves to be in the White House?'

There was a long pause.

'I'd like to think that people can change,' Natalie said slowly. 'That a man who raped you and beat you half to death at twenty-three could have learned how to build rather than destroy at fifty-three. But to be honest with you, even though I sometimes think the White House has become little better than a whore-house, no, I guess I have to say I don't think Robert Willmont belongs in it.'

Karen smiled an almost luminous smile. 'I can't believe how good it feels to finally tell someone, to say all the words right out loud, for God and the whole world to hear.'

'Don't stop there,' Natalie suggested.

'What do you mean?'

'I mean, go home. Talk to Ted. It's time, and if I'm any judge of character, you may be in for a very pleasant surprise.'

The idea of telling her husband dredged up all the painful memories of Peter in Karen's mind. But she knew Natalie was right. Ted was a good man – understanding, compassionate, supportive, and they had lived with the lie between them long enough.

'In spite of myself, I guess I'm a lot stronger now than I was then,' she said, knowing it was true. 'If Ted turns away from me – like Peter did – it'll hurt, but I can handle it.'

'I do believe you can,' declared the psychiatrist.

With a little nod, Karen stood up. 'Thank you for

listening,' she said sincerely. 'I can't tell you how much it's helped.'

And it had. By sharing her pain, she had lightened its load. By letting the ugliness out of the dark, she knew she could begin to put the excruciating episode into some sort of perspective.

'What will you do?' Natalie asked.

'I'm going to take your advice,' Karen replied. 'I'm going to tell Ted.'

'And then what?'

Karen shrugged. 'We'll see,' she said.

It was after midnight when Karen let herself back into the house, but Ted was still awake, sitting patiently at the breakfast-room table with a fresh pot of tea ready.

'I waited up,' he said simply, 'in case you wanted to talk.'

'I do,' Karen responded, sitting down across from him.

He poured tea for both of them, adding the dollop of honey he knew she liked in hers. Then he wrapped his hands around his cup and waited for whatever was to come.

Half an hour later, they were both drained.

'I should have told you long ago,' she said, 'and I've felt guilty all these years for deceiving you. But I knew you'd never have married me if you'd known. So I let myself behave very selfishly and kept it from you.' She stared at the bottom of her teacup. 'If you want that divorce now, I won't blame you.'

Instead, he came around to sit beside her.

'I guess I can't honestly say how I would have felt back then,' he said slowly. 'But I don't think it would have been much different than I feel right now, which is appalled and devastated and outraged – but not at you. Never at you.'

'Really?' she breathed.

'Despite what the police or your parents or Peter might have thought, I know you well enough to know that you could never have been to blame for what that man did to you.'

She blinked as though she hadn't heard properly. 'You honestly mean that?'

He put his arm around her and drew her against him. 'Of course I do. I guess, on some level, I always knew there was more to it than an automobile accident, because the scars on the inside always seemed so much deeper than the ones on the outside.'

'You could see that?'

He nodded. 'You shouldn't have had to live with this all alone for so long,' he said. 'But at least you won't have to anymore. You've got Natalie to help you now, and I trust her. And you've got me to support you in any way I can. If you want, I'll even go out and kill the bastard for you.'

'No,' she murmured with a little smile. 'I don't want that.'

'Whatever it takes for you to work through all this, just know that I'm right here with a shoulder to lean on or cry on, or anything else you need or want.'

They made their way upstairs, into the peach-and-aqua master suite, where they undressed in the dark and got into Karen's bed and held each other as tight as they could.

'You're safe now,' he murmured into her sweet-smelling hair. 'I'll never let anyone hurt you again.'

four

Janice Evans hurried down Front Street in the November sunshine, on her way to the Willmont campaign headquarters.

The newly announced presidential candidate and his entourage had been in town for little more than a week and already they had everything organized. Mary Catherine had telephoned her at eight-thirty.

'The senator has agreed to an interview,' she said. 'But he wants to make it very clear that he intends to choose the topics.'

'Agreed,' Janice replied. 'I can be there in an hour.'

'The senator can see you at eleven,' Mary Catherine informed her.

The pretty blond reporter had come a long way since the day when, as a fledgling staff member of a local television station, she had stuck her microphone in the face of a congressman at San Francisco Airport, and much of her success was directly attributable to the exposure she had received from covering his subsequent campaign.

During his numerous forays up and down the state, Robert had used her as his official press-pool representative – and his unofficial bed companion. He would feed her information that she would then dutifully share with the rest of the media.

The networks got to see a lot of the attractive, well-spoken, well-informed journalist, and liked what they saw. When the campaign ended, Janice was brought to New York as a background reporter for one of the major television news-talk programs. Today, she was one of a quartet of rotating hosts on the show and had earned the respect of her colleagues.

She had kept her figure, but her blond hair now received a lemon rinse every month to hold its highlights. The laugh lines around her mouth and eyes, which used to come and go, now came and stayed, and she found herself using heavier makeup to keep her complexion looking fresh and clean. She was thirty-six years old.

'When I'm elected President,' the newly elected senator promised, 'the job of press secretary is yours, if you want it.'

'I want it,' she said.

Janice Evans had developed into more than just a pretty, if somewhat hardened, face. She was also articulate and single-mindedly dedicated. She would eventually have risen to the top of her profession even had she not gone to bed with Robert Willmont, but the shortcut certainly hadn't hurt. They were two of a kind, the journalist and the politician, and they used each other, with total understanding, at every opportunity.

'Janice Evans to see the senator,' she said when she reached the twelfth floor.

'Is he expecting you, Miss Evans?' a striking African-American receptionist asked with a polite smile.

'I believe he is.'

'Just a moment, please,' the woman said, reaching for the telephone.

The one thing they had each insisted on was discretion. Public knowledge of their relationship would have ruined them both. Janice suspected that Randy Neuburg and Mary Catherine O'Malley knew what was going on, but if they did, it went no further than that. As far as the rest of the world was concerned, she was just another newswoman covering a story.

'I have an idea I'd like to pursue,' she said to her producer on the fifteenth of October. 'I think Robert Willmont is going to be our next President, and I'd like to do an in-depth segment on him. You know, give the public an advance peek inside the man.'

'What makes you think he's even going to run?'

'Come on,' she admonished. 'I've been on his trail for ten years. I know his organization. They're gearing up.'

'Well,' the producer said, unconvinced, 'we'll see.'

On October 25, he stopped by her office. 'That idea you had about Robert Willmont,' he said. 'It's a go.'

Janice hid a smug grin. 'Do I get a free hand?'

'If it's quality.'

'Have I ever given you anything but?'

'No,' the producer had to admit. 'You haven't.'

It was true. Janice had an uncanny nose for news and a discriminating eye. Her results were frequently fascinating, occasionally explosive, but always in good taste.

'The senator will see you now, Miss Evans,' the receptionist said cordially, turning from the telephone.

'Hi there, beautiful,' Robert beamed as soon as they were alone. 'How's New York?'

'Getting chilly.'

'Well, if you lock that door, I'll do what I can to warm you up. God, I've missed you. Randy's had me living like a monk for months.'

Janice chuckled. 'If the press could hear you now.'

Robert sighed. 'I liked it better when the press knew its place. Or at least when reporters recognized that a man's sex life has nothing to do with his ability to run the country.'

Sex for Robert, while admittedly more pleasurable, was as fundamental as feeding or relieving himself. When he was hungry, he ate, and he wasn't particular what food was put before him. When his bladder was full, he emptied it, and it didn't matter whose bathroom he used. And when his libido swelled, he thought nothing of turning to whatever acolyte was at hand. And there were always many. Even the reality of AIDS failed to curtail Robert's appetite. The past few months under Randy's watchful eye had been pure hell.

'Well, if you're in real need,' Janice said, 'I'll be home later on tonight.'

She had kept her Cow Hollow flat, well aware that, in the media business, nothing was permanent.

'Unfortunately,' the senator replied with a grimace, 'so will I.'

'In that case . . .' Janice reached back and snapped the lock on the office door.

* * *

Randy perched on the corner of Mary Catherine's desk and glanced at his wristwatch. 'What time did she come in?'

'About eleven,' the administrative assistant replied. 'They skipped lunch.'

'Jeez, it's two-thirty,' Randy groaned. 'You'd think he'd have more sense. Going at it in his office, for God's sake, where anyone can breeze right in.'

'They locked the door.'

'Doesn't he have an appointment or something this afternoon?'

Mary Catherine shook her head. '*Time* was supposed to be here at three, but the photographer got stuck in Chicago, so they rescheduled for tomorrow.'

'How much longer, do you think? The *Chronicle* wants a comment on the Yugoslavia sanctions, and ABC wants a statement on the bombing in Beirut.'

'Considering how long you've had him on the straight and narrow' – Mary Catherine shrugged – 'another hour or two.'

'And it's only November,' sighed Randy.

five

Karen stepped out of the Jacuzzi that Ted had installed in the master bath as part of remodeling the St. Francis Wood house and began to towel herself dry. She normally used the tub in the evenings, to relax before going to bed, but had chosen to take advantage of it this morning.

On Natalie's advice, she had thought long and hard about the unique opportunity that fate had given her. Once she calmed down, she could see that the psychiatrist was right – murdering Robert Willmont might provide a momentary pleasure, even a genuine sense of satisfaction, but not much else, and she had no intention of settling for that.

'What will you do?' Ted asked.

'I don't know,' she replied honestly. 'I don't know what I *can* do.'

But she knew she would do something. The feelings she had buried for so long could no longer be denied.

It was ironic to think she might have heard or read his name many times, might even have seen a newspaper photograph of him, and it would have meant nothing to her. It wasn't so unreasonable – she hadn't been looking for him. Rather, she had stuffed the image of him down inside of her where, over time, he became less and less of a man and more and more of a monster. It was one of the techniques she had developed to cope with the guilt and the shame and the loss.

As much as she had hoped, during the long years of recuperating, reevaluating and refocusing, that he would come to some agonizing end, as all monsters should, she now came to realize that what she really wanted, even more than his destruction, was vindication for herself. She wanted the whole world to know exactly what he was – underneath the slick facade, behind the dazzling aquamarine eyes – and she knew that nothing less than exposing him in some horribly humiliating way would satisfy her.

Her plan was ridiculously simple. She would seek him out, in a public forum, where there were bound to be members of the media interested in a juicy story. They would be able to tell, the moment they saw the shock on his face when she confronted him, that she was speaking the truth. He might live, but he would be politically ruined. And he would never be President of the United States.

The forum she picked was an early-December ceremony in Golden Gate Park where the senator was scheduled to preside at the groundbreaking for the Natural History Museum's new Drayton Pavilion. In addition to social and political VIPs, the press would be there in full force, hoping to persuade the candidate to make a few off-the-cuff comments that would play well on the evening news. It was a perfect setting.

Karen tucked her towel around her and leaned over the sink to brush her teeth, but the terry cloth slipped and dropped to the floor. She stared at herself in the mirror. In two months, she would be fifty years old, half a century, and she was pleased to note that she had not yet succumbed to middle-age sag. Her figure had retained its slenderness and regular exercise kept her muscles toned. Once clothed, the disfiguring scars could not be seen. Her skin was still good and a trip to the beauty salon every six weeks removed the gray in her dark hair. With just a modicum of makeup, she knew she could pass for thirty-five.

She slipped into a winter-white turtleneck, matching stirrup pants, and a red-white-and-black tweed raw silk jacket. Winter-white pumps and a pair of Felicity's chunky gold earrings and matching bracelet finished the outfit. She brushed her hair off her face, catching the shoulder-length curls with a black velvet bow at the nape of her neck.

The ceremony was scheduled for two o'clock. Just after noon, Karen drove her Volvo wagon into Golden Gate Park and down John F. Kennedy Drive, stopping a block and a half from the museum. Traffic-control barricades had already been put in place, personnel in mobile television vans were setting up their equipment, and the area was beginning to fill with curious onlookers who sensed the makings of a media event.

It was one of those magnificent winter days for which San Francisco had long been famous – sunny, windless, and sixty-five degrees. Karen melted into the crowd that milled around the area and waited.

At five minutes before two, a pair of motorcycles

with lights flashing led a convoy of limousines into the parking lot that flanked the main concourse and fronted the five museums that shared this section of the park.

The crowd, which had swelled to over a thousand, pushed forward, taking Karen along with it. She was perhaps twenty feet away when he stepped out of the second limousine, and in the first instant of actually seeing him, she thought she might faint. It was only the people pressing against her for a glimpse of the candidate that kept her upright.

The other limousines were emptying now and the party of some thirty dignitaries, surrounded by reporters, television cameramen and still photographers, was making its way to the bandstand at the far end of the concourse.

The new mayor was there, along with several members of the board of supervisors and a fair selection of the city's most prominent personalities, but Karen didn't recognize anyone. She barely even looked at them, so focused was she on the self-assured man with the memorable eyes.

She paid no attention to the overblown speeches that honored the Drayton dynasty. She simply waited for the right moment, the brief lull that was bound to come, when she would step forward and face him. She had it all very carefully rehearsed – every word, every move.

'Hello, Bob,' she would say, planting herself in his path. 'You remember me, don't you – and what you did to me? Of course you do. I can see it in your eyes, and now so will the rest of the world. They're known as the Drayton eyes, aren't they? Well, the Draytons should have gouged them out the day you were born.

You raped me, you beat me, and you left me for dead all those years ago, without so much as a second thought. And now you think the people of this country should elect you President of the United States?'

The moment came and almost went before she recognized it. The speeches were over, the group of dignitaries was moving away from the bandstand toward the museum for the symbolic shovel of dirt. As expected, reporters were shouting out their questions.

'What do you think about the Sununu resignation?' one called.

'Come now, Dave,' the senator admonished the newsman. 'We're here today for something that has nothing to do with politics.'

'Everything you do between now and next November has to do with politics, Senator,' the newsman replied.

The candidate grinned. 'In that case, Mr. Sununu was merely the first of the rats to desert a sinking ship.'

'How about the Keating verdict?' another asked.

'If they put him in jail and destroyed the key, it wouldn't make up for what he's done,' Robert replied.

'And the Kennedy Smith trial?'

'No comment.'

'Thank you, ladies and gentlemen,' a redheaded man who looked like a dwarf beside the candidate said smoothly. 'The senator would now like to get back to the purpose at hand, the groundbreaking for the Drayton Pavilion.'

He put his hand on Robert Willmont's arm to guide him through the crowd. But Karen Doniger stood in the way. She stared up at the monster who had invaded her dreams for so many years and opened her mouth to say the words that would damn him to eternity. But he looked right at her, from less than two feet away, with a polite smile that held not so much as a flicker of recognition.

She had taken him by surprise, leaving him no time to prepare. He could not possibly have been that good an actor – he didn't know who she was.

In the seconds it took for that to register on her, he moved on past, the crowd surging after him. Stunned, she dug her heels into the grass and stayed where she was. The moment was gone, she would have to find another.

Karen turned and hurried away, not looking back and not pausing until she reached her car. With shaking hands, she unlocked the door and scrambled behind the wheel, started up the engine and sped off, coming out of the park onto the Great Highway, which ran along the Pacific Ocean.

She parked the car and, kicking off her shoes, walked along the beach. It was low tide and the soggy sand curled beneath her weight. She went down to the water's edge and stood there, staring out into the depths, as the frigid foam lapped around her feet and sucked the coarse brown granules from beneath her stockinged toes.

Finally, she went back up the beach and dropped down on the dry sand. Her head was spinning. It was inconceivable to her that the horror which had etched itself like acid into her very core meant so little to him that he wouldn't even remember her – that the most catastrophic episode of her life was nothing more than a minor encounter he had long since forgotten. Of all the scenarios she had conceived, this had not been among them.

She didn't know how long she sat there, watching the gentle waves flow and ebb, letting the sea spray drizzle over her, before she began to laugh. Hugging her knees to her chest, she threw back her head and laughed, peal after peal swallowed up by the pounding surf.

A whole new perspective engulfed her, and with it came the realization that, to a large extent, she had created her own hell. She had allowed the monster to torment and terrify her for almost thirty years. But today, she had stood two feet away from that monster – and seen that he was in fact nothing more and nothing less than a man. She had looked into the aquamarine eyes of a *man*, a man she knew she would never again have cause to fear.

Slipping her shoes back on, Karen got up and walked slowly back to the Volvo. There would be another opportunity for her to expose Robert Willmont for what he was, of that she was sure. She would just have to think of a different approach, now that it was clear he did not remember her.

There was no hurry. There was still plenty of time.

SIX

'No one's going to stop us now,' Randy exclaimed the morning after Super Tuesday. The Willmont candidacy had taken half of the dozen primaries with at least fifty-three percent of the vote.

Robert grinned. 'We're looking good, my boy. We're definitely looking good.'

'Jeez, we even took forty-two percent of Texas.'

'It's all in the message,' the candidate said smoothly.

'I know you weren't keen on hiring her, but you've got to admit that Dobbs is worth twice what we're paying her.'

The public relations expert had deftly created an image of the California senator that was all but irresistible. Men responded intellectually to Robert's no-nonsense manifesto. Women reacted emotionally to his carefully groomed good looks and boyish charm. Senior citizens viewed his conservative appearance as sincere and approved of his obvious devotion to his mother as well as his wife and son. People everywhere found themselves listening to what he was saying.

The issue was clear – if America was going to be saved, everyone had to do his share. No one would be exempt and no one would profit at the expense of others. 'Save America!' the banners read, and in a few brief months those two words had become synonymous with Robert Drayton Willmont.

Mariah Dobbs had indeed done her job, and the only negative ever expressed by the senator was that ice water ran in her veins. In the four months that she had been on his team, traveling with him, sitting beside him on airplanes, in limousines and at endless strategy meetings, sharing early-morning breakfasts and late-night dinners, sometimes even sharing hotel suites, she had never thawed. The end of an evening was always followed by a polite good-night and the firm snap of a lock on a bedroom door.

For a sexually active man being kept in rigid check, it was agonizing. He began to dream about her, waking before dawn with thoughts about the things he wanted to do to her and the things he wanted her to do to him. More and more, as time went by, hotel maids found his sheets wet and sticky.

'Are you a lesbian?' he asked her once in frustration.

Cool green eyes appraised him. 'No, Senator,' she replied.

'Then why the deep-freeze act all the time?'

'I believe I made it clear at the beginning that I don't mix pleasure with business.'

'We could put it on a business basis, if you prefer.'

'I can leave, if you prefer,' she retorted.

It was exasperating. He rarely had a problem getting a woman into bed. On the contrary, he was usually fighting them off. But this one didn't seem the least bit inclined. Several times he had come very close to forcing the issue, but then backed off, knowing he could not risk alienating her. But he wasn't used to a woman being in control of him, and the more unattainable she was, the more he wanted her.

'I'm sorry if my presence bothers you,' Mariah remarked with a frosty edge in her voice. 'I'm sorry if your marriage isn't everything you need it to be. But, as it happens, mine is.'

'I didn't know,' he muttered, taken by surprise. No one had told him the bitch was married. Not that it made any difference to him, but it did help to explain her lack of interest.

'It wasn't necessary for you to know,' she told him. 'All that's necessary is for you to convince the voters that you are first and last a devoted family man.'

She was the only woman he had ever met, he confessed to Mary Catherine, who flat out intimidated him.

'Dobbs is okay,' he said now, with a shrug. 'But she didn't go out and win those primaries. I did.'

Randy smothered a grin. There weren't many women who failed to fall under Robert's spell. In fact, he could remember only one, a staff secretary during their first term in the Senate. She was right out of Brigham Young University – fresh, eager, lovely, and clearly not buying what Robert was selling. She was also smart, and solved the problem of unwanted attention by not staying around very long.

But this time, the senator had met his match.

Whenever Mariah was around, Randy would catch his eyes following her. He would stand a little straighter and laugh a little louder, but in vain. Mariah maintained her professional demeanor and gave him nothing else. Whatever frustrations were building up inside of him, he had no choice but to keep his distance.

What Robert didn't know was that Mariah more often than not warmed herself in Randy's bed.

'He thought I was a lesbian,' she giggled one night as they lay apart, waiting for the sweat of passion to dry on their bodies.

'You're kidding!'

'What an egotist! I guess it was the only explanation he could come up with for my lack of interest.'

'He's not used to women turning him down,' Randy felt obliged to explain. 'Very few do.'

'Maybe that's his problem,' she observed. 'He's always had everything too easy.'

'I guess you could say that,' Randy had to admit. 'As a matter of fact, I can think of only one other woman in the last thirteen years who refused to give him a tumble.'

'Who was that?'

'She was a secretary. Her name was Maggie Holden, and damned if she didn't look just like Julia Roberts. She distracted the hell out of him.' Randy chuckled. 'It was really funny sometimes, watching him around her, preening like a peacock. But he was old enough to be her father and I honestly think that was the way she saw him.'

'What became of her?'

'Who knows? She was there one day and gone the next. That happens more than you might think in D.C. A lot of people just can't handle the pressure. It was a little weird, though, because when she went, she really went. She never called, never even came back to clean out her desk. When Mary Catherine finally packed up her stuff and took it around to her apartment, her roommate said she'd gone home to Utah.'

'It sounds like maybe it was the senator she couldn't handle,' Mariah said. 'There were some women, you know, who refused to put up with sexual harassment even then.'

'I don't believe it went as far as sexual harassment,' Randy protested. 'I think all he did was flirt with her.'

'Perhaps she didn't see it that way.'

'Well, whatever, it was too bad. I think she could have had a career in Washington, if she'd wanted it. She wasn't only a knockout, she was damn smart.'

'Well, based on my own personal experience,' declared Mariah, 'I'd say that the senator can be very persistent when he wants to be and he doesn't handle rejection very well.'

'I'm sorry about that. Do you want me to talk to him?'

'No, of course not.' She laughed. 'I'm a big girl. I can take care of myself. But I suppose you should know – I elected to tell him a small untruth.'

'What sort of small untruth?'

She shrugged. 'I told him I was married.'

'Why did you do that?'

'I thought it would shake him loose for a while.'

Randy sighed. 'As you've probably figured, Robert needs a lot of … exercise,' he explained. 'We've been keeping him on a very short leash.'

'He's not a baby, for heaven's sake,' Mariah snapped. 'He's fifty-four years old. Isn't it time he learned how to control himself?'

'He is what he is.'

'Well, if a little lie keeps him from hitting on me,' she said with a yawn, 'that's all I care about.'

Randy reached out and pulled her into the warm circle of his arms. 'Maybe someday that won't have to be such a lie,' he murmured.

Mariah snuggled against him. 'Maybe, someday,' she said, already half asleep.

By the end of March, Robert was steamrolling toward a first-ballot nomination. With his eye fixed on the June 2 California primary, he returned to San Francisco for a two-week round of politicking. Janice Evans had long since left the campaign and gone back to New York to put together her segment on the man behind the candidate. It was scheduled to air a week before the primary.

'I'm doing my part to win you the nomination,' she told him over the telephone. 'So long as no one catches on why.'

'You're going to make one hell of a press secretary,' he replied, shifting in his chair and wishing she were in town because he'd already gone without for too long.

The Willmont campaign headquarters on Front Street was cranked into full gear. Although still two months away, winning the California primary, and winning it big, was considered essential to put Robert on top going into the convention. The suite of offices was filled to overflowing with teams of tireless volunteer workers, mimeographing dozens of press releases, licking thousands of contribution envelopes, and manning an intimidating bank of telephones.

Mary Catherine had arrived the week before, while the senator was still campaigning in Wisconsin. By the time he appeared at Front Street, on April 2, every last detail of his two-week stint had been arranged.

'Maximum exposure, minimum wear and tear,' she told him. 'It's a work of art, but I can't take the credit.'

'Why not?' he asked.

'Because the volunteer staff did it. One woman in particular, who's a whiz at organization. She put the schedule together, made all the reservations, prepared press releases for the locals at every stop, and now she's working on half a dozen different promotional packets.'

'Point her out,' Robert requested.

Mary Catherine scanned the busy work area. 'There she is, over there by the Xerox machine, the one with the dark hair and the designer dress.'

Across the room, the senator caught a glimpse of a neat, attractive woman who looked to be in her middle thirties. She was nothing at all like Mariah Dobbs – dark where Mariah was light, slender where Mariah curved – but there was something about the way she moved, something about the cool efficiency with which she worked that connected the two women in his groin.

'She could be useful,' he murmured.

'Forget it,' Mary Catherine told him. 'She has a very successful career and no long-lasting interest in politics. And in case you've got something else in mind, she's also very married.'

'What kind of career?'

'Have you seen a book called *Tapestry*?'

Robert shook his head.

'I have,' Randy said. 'Pictures and poems about the Southwest. It was impressive, as I recall.'

'*Tapestry* is one of a whole series of books that she

and another woman have done about America,' Mary Catherine noted.

'They're the same two who did *Dichotomy*,' Randy added. 'You know, the book on D.C. that everyone was raving about a few years ago.'

Robert did remember that one. Elizabeth had had it out on the coffee table for months.

'She's a photographer?'

'No. She's the poet.'

'What's she doing here?'

'I guess poets must be voters, too,' Mary Catherine said with a shrug. 'She wandered in one day and said she had some free afternoons, and you were the first politician to come along who wasn't afraid to tell it like it is.'

'Wait a minute,' Robert said with a sudden frown. 'Do I know her? I think she looks familiar to me, but I can't seem to place her.'

'I can,' Randy told him. 'If I'm not mistaken, she was at the groundbreaking ceremony back in December. In fact, I'm pretty sure she wanted to say something to you that day, but then I guess she changed her mind.'

'I must have made quite an impression,' the candidate replied, flashing one of his famous grins and standing up a little straighter.

Karen had been working for the senator's campaign for three months. She spent Tuesday and Thursday afternoons promoting a man she had every wish to see chewed up into tiny pieces and spit out, and the sheer perversity of it all made her smile while she worked.

'I need to do this,' she told Ted the night before her first day at Front Street. 'Don't ask me why, I just need to do it.'

'I *have* to ask you why,' he protested.

'I'm not sure I can explain it,' she replied. 'But this is a man who almost killed me and certainly changed my entire life – and I don't even know who he is. Natalie said that maybe a man who destroyed at twenty-three could have learned to build at fifty-three. I want to find out if he has.'

'Surely there's another way,' he argued.

'I can't learn the things I need to learn about him from reading articles and watching interviews,' she declared. 'I know it might sound crazy to you, it does a little to me, but I need to know who he really is, from up close. I have a right to know who he really is.'

The Xerox stopped grinding out copies and Karen bent down to pick up the stack. Straightening up, she turned in the direction of the collating machine, only to collide with a navy-blue suit. Pages scattered in all directions.

'I'm terribly sorry,' the suit said. 'Here, let me help you.'

Robert scrambled to gather the errant papers. Up close, he could see she was perhaps a bit older than he had first thought, but certainly no less attractive.

'We haven't met,' he said. 'I'm Senator Willmont.'

'I'm Karen Doniger,' she replied, amazed at how calm her voice sounded.

He put out his free hand and, while it took all the courage she could muster, she took it.

'I understand you're something of an expert on America,' he declared.

'I beg your pardon?'

'Your books.'

'Oh,' she said in some confusion. 'I didn't realize you were familiar with my work.'

'To be perfectly honest, I'm not. My staff is.'

She allowed herself a slight smile at his ingenuousness. 'From a certain, very limited perspective,' she conceded, 'I suppose you might say I'm an expert.'

'Your perspective could be very useful to me,' he said. 'Maybe we can find time to discuss it.' He still had hold of her hand.

'Maybe,' she returned, disengaging her fingers with apparent unconcern.

It was a noncommittal answer to a non-question. The opening gambit had been played. He returned the stack of papers he had collected with a dazzling smile.

'I'll look forward to it,' he promised, caressing her with his eyes exactly as he had on a December night so many years ago.

seven

'Y ou didn't forget that I'm going over to DeeDee's for dinner tonight, did you?' Amy asked at breakfast the following Tuesday. 'I have to help her study for the history exam.'

'No, I didn't forget,' Karen replied, putting a bowl of cereal in front of her stepdaughter, and thinking how easy her transition to San Francisco had been, after all.

'I've got that meeting with the supervisors tonight,' Ted said. 'It's bound to run late.'

'That's okay,' Karen replied with a smile. 'Contrary to popular opinion, I can handle an evening on my own.'

'Are you sure?'

'Of course I'm sure. In fact, if they ask you to join them for dinner after the meeting, go ahead. A little hobnobbing with the politically lofty can't hurt.'

'Okay,' Ted replied with a smile. Ever since she had

gone to work for the Willmont campaign – a decision he wasn't entirely easy about – the ins and outs of politics seemed always on her mind.

Karen spent a long time in the shower, washing her hair, applying a deep conditioner and pampering her body with rich moisturizing lotion. When she came out of the bathroom, snuggled inside a thick terry-cloth robe, she spent a long time in front of the big picture window that offered an ever-changing panorama of the Pacific Ocean right from her own peach-and-aqua bedroom, and gave her a whole new perspective on water.

She did busy work in her office for an hour. Nancy had already made two trips to San Francisco and had planned her last for late July. Once the photographs for their new book, *Reflections*, were selected, Karen would be swamped, but until then, there really wasn't much to do, and she went upstairs with plenty of time to prepare for her afternoon in the Willmont camp.

Left to her own devices, she would have whiled away the rest of the day in front of the picture window, watching the freighters and tankers go by, watching the seabirds swoop down around the fishing boats, watching the undulating water stretching all the way out to the horizon. But, she conceded with some reluctance, she had other things to do.

She hung her robe on the back of the bathroom door, peered into her closet, and pulled out a simple navy silk pleated dress with long sleeves and white trim. She added low-heeled navy pumps and transferred her wallet and keys and makeup case into a navy handbag.

It was one more magnificent Bay Area afternoon as

she backed the Volvo out of the driveway and headed downtown. The sky was radiant blue, the breeze was soft, and the temperature was in the high sixties. She parked in a garage half a block from the campaign headquarters and stopped at a little coffee shop on the corner for a container of fresh orange juice, which she sipped on the way up in the elevator.

'Am I glad you're here,' Mary Catherine greeted her the moment the doors slid open at the twelfth floor. 'The senator wants a press reception set up for tomorrow afternoon, complete with promotional stuff. Randy sent over some notes. Can you work them up?'

'I'll get on it right away,' Karen promised. 'What's the topic?'

'A woman in San Jose asked the senator why we burn crops, leave grain to rot in silos, and pay farmers not to farm when there are millions of people starving in America.'

'That sounds like a reasonable question to me,' Karen observed.

'That's what *he* said – so now he's hell-bent to make a campaign issue out of it.'

It was seven-thirty by the time Karen had selected the appropriate boilerplate and reworked Randy's notes into readable prose with the help of the user-friendly Macintosh on her desk. The rest of the volunteer staff had long since disappeared. If nothing else, she mused, her experience here had banished the dread of computers that had kept her clinging to a pad and pen all her life. She typed the final period, printed out a fresh copy, and headed for the Xerox machine.

'How are you doing?' Mary Catherine asked.

'Almost done,' Karen told her.

The administrative assistant glanced through the copy. 'Say, this is good,' she praised. 'Very good. I think you've just created your first position paper.'

Karen chuckled 'And I thought that political pundits had to ponder those things forever.'

'You'd be surprised,' Mary Catherine retorted. 'Can I help you finish up?'

Karen shook her head. 'There's not that much left to do. Besides, my family has deserted me for the evening, so there's no reason why I can't stay and get it done.'

Mary Catherine smiled. 'I really don't know what we'd do without you,' she said.

By the time Karen finished the Xeroxing and turned to the collating machine, it was almost eight.

'I thought the senator might stop in,' Mary Catherine said, purse in hand. 'But I guess he decided not to. So I'm going to go find myself a Scotch and sandwich. Care to join me?'

'No, thanks,' Karen replied. 'I've a few more things left to do here and then I think I'll just head on home.'

'In that case, I'll see you tomorrow. Just close the door when you leave. It locks automatically.'

The clatter of the collator was too loud, some twenty minutes later, for Karen to hear the outer door open and close, so the senator took her completely by surprise.

'Do I pay you enough to work these hours?' he asked.

'Probably not,' she replied, noting that he was alone, with neither Randy Neuburg nor the private security detail following in his wake.

'Where's everyone?' he inquired, looking around.

'Gone home.'

'Except you.'

'Except me, for about five more minutes. Mary Catherine decided you weren't going to come in this evening.'

'I wasn't,' he said. 'It was a last-minute idea. I thought of it after I gave my shadows the night off.' He grinned. 'But I guess I'm safe enough for one evening. Anyway, all that constant scrutiny tends to get to you after a while.' He peered over her shoulder. 'Is that the stuff for tomorrow?'

'Yes,' she replied, inching a step away.

'Good. I wanted to get a look at it.'

'Help yourself,' she murmured.

He leaned against the collator and flashed his famous smile down at her.

'You know, I've been meaning to find the opportunity to tell you how much we appreciate your dedication to the campaign. How much *I* appreciate it.'

'It's for a worthy cause, isn't it?' she said obliquely.

'Look,' he said, checking his wristwatch, 'why don't you let me buy you a drink or something, to thank you for all your time and effort.'

'That's not necessary.'

'I know, but I'd like to do it anyway,' he pressed. 'Besides, there's your unique perspective on America that we were going to talk about, remember?'

Karen snapped off the collator and began to staple the press packets together.

'Thanks,' she said, 'but I really have to get home.'

She finished the stapling and carried the kits over to the long worktable beside Mary Catherine's desk, knowing he was watching her every move. She was out of the building, into the parking garage and behind the wheel of the Volvo before she could banish the sensation of his eyes on her body.

She shook her head, impatient at her foolishness, and twisted her key in the ignition. Nothing happened. She tried again, and again nothing happened. The engine refused to turn over.

'Just what I need,' she groaned, popping the hood and climbing out of the station wagon, although she knew next to nothing about cars and realized it was highly unlikely that she would recognize any kind of problem.

'What's the matter?' Robert asked.

She couldn't believe he was standing there and wondered if he had followed her.

'My car won't start.'

'Let me see.'

Before she could protest, he had slipped into the Volvo and was turning the key. There was no response. He tried wiggling and thrusting and pumping, but his efforts were in vain.

'It's not the battery,' he said with assurance. 'But it might be the starter.'

'What does that mean?'

'If it's the starter, it means you'll have to leave the car here until morning and then get it towed.'

'Damn,' she muttered.

'Can your husband come get you?'

Karen checked her watch. 'He won't be home yet,' she sighed. 'He's at a dinner meeting.'

'Well, don't worry about it,' he said with a reassuring smile. 'I can drive you home.'

'Oh, that's not necessary,' she declared. 'I can take a taxi.'

'Nonsense,' said Robert firmly. 'I won't hear of it. After all the hours you've put in on my behalf, it's the very least I can do.'

Karen looked at him for a long moment with an expression he couldn't define.

'Well, all right,' she said finally, 'if you're sure it won't be an inconvenience.'

'Not at all,' he replied with a smile. 'Maybe we can even stop on the way and have that drink. I really do have a lot of questions to ask you.'

She couldn't think of a polite way to decline. 'We could go across the street,' she suggested, referring to a popular bar on the corner that she felt certain would still be busy at this hour.

'Done,' he said.

Over three Scotches, a bucket of steamed clams, and the constant interruption of political supporters glad to find him unencumbered by a wall of security, he encouraged her to talk about her books and experiences, inserting a question every now and then. Karen found herself describing the special characteristics of New York, Atlanta, Houston and Tucson without even realizing she had noticed them.

It was ten-thirty by the time they returned to the garage. They tried the Volvo again but it was useless. So they moved on to Robert's black Mercedes, parked just a few spaces away.

He opened the passenger door for her, making sure the pleats of her navy blue dress were safely tucked in before he closed it again with a firm click and went around to the driver's side.

Despite the three Scotches, which usually had a numbing effect on her, Karen's heart began to flutter as he steered the Mercedes out of the garage and she realized she was now more alone with him than she had ever been before. Part of her couldn't believe she was here, even as she knew that in the peculiar twists and turns of fate it was inevitable. It was a testimony to how far she had come that she was able to sit there without dissolving into a cowering, mewling blob.

They spoke little. At that hour, traffic was light and he took advantage of it. He drove with speedy assurance straight up California Street, veering around whatever vehicles they encountered, left and right and left again, before taking the Presidio Transverse into Golden Gate Park, the most direct way to St. Francis Wood ever since the Embarcadero Freeway had been damaged by the earthquake two and a half years ago.

It might have been his driving, or the Scotch, or the realization of what she was doing, but suddenly her stomach began to churn with ominous intent.

'Please,' she gasped. 'I think you'd better pull over. I'm not feeling very well.'

'What's the matter?' he asked.

'I'm sorry,' she said, 'but I think I'm going to be sick.'

eight

It was halfway between dark and dawn when Arthur Gertz trotted down the steps of his house, jogged across Lincoln Way, and entered Golden Gate Park.

Streetlights cast a faint yellow beacon into the mist as the solid night sky began its slow dissolve into the distinguishable gray shades of morning. The phosphorescent digits on his sports watch told him it was not quite five o'clock.

It certainly wasn't Arthur's idea of fun to get up an hour early every morning and go running around the city like some health nut. He had just gotten tired of listening to Essie's nonstop nagging.

'You're fifty-six years old, Arthur,' his wife had harassed him for a year. 'You're overweight and out of shape. Overweight, out-of-shape men drop dead of heart attacks at fifty-six.'

For his fifty-seventh birthday, she gave him a warm-up suit.

'What's this for?' he asked.

'So you should live to be fifty-eight.'

But it was rising before five in the morning that was going to kill him sooner than anything else, he grumbled to himself as he jogged along.

Arthur was a certified public accountant in one of those big firms that merged so often he sometimes didn't know the latest company name. He had spent his adult years organizing his life into neat sections – his job, his family, his stamp collection, his Tuesday-night bridge game, his Robert Ludlum novels. Jogging didn't fit into any of those categories, and Arthur was not a man who took easily to change.

But Essie left him no choice. She stopped serving red meat at home, eliminated dairy products from their diet, and bullied him into beginning a program of sensible exercise. To shut her up, he carved an hour out of the section of his life marked 'sleep' and plotted a daily route through the morning mists of Golden Gate Park that would take him exactly fifty-two minutes to complete, and he never deviated from that course by so much as one yard.

On this particular Wednesday morning, however, he was looking to shorten his route by seven minutes. Last night at the bridge table, he had made a stupid mistake that cost him the rubber. He agitated over it so much afterward that it took him an extra twenty minutes to fall asleep. As a result, he awakened twenty minutes late.

He made up one minute by selecting the jogging shoes that fastened with Velcro. Then he calculated he could make up four minutes by not washing his hair, three minutes if he didn't floss when he brushed his teeth, and five minutes by refusing a second helping of oat bran and skipping the obituary section in the morning newspaper. That left seven minutes, and it explained why, on this particular day, Arthur Gertz took a detour.

Instead of his usual run along Martin Luther King, Jr., Drive, around the Arboretum and down past the old Kezar Stadium, he opted for the shorter route up to Stow Lake and around Strawberry Hill.

Afterward, he couldn't remember what caught his eye, what turned his head in that direction, what made him take a second look, and then a third. He was only glad that he did.

She was lying half-concealed beneath a clump of bushes, bits of her clothing scattered around her. Even in the early light, he could see that her face was cut and battered, her lip split and bleeding, one eye blackened. He noticed an angry trail of bruises down her body.

She was slender but not young. He wondered how she had gotten there, what persuasion had drawn her into the park at such an early hour. Arthur could pretty much guess what had happened to her. He was sure she was dead. She lay so still and her skin was so pale that he actually jumped when she moved. It wasn't a big move, more of a shudder, really, and then he heard a low moan.

'Oh my God,' he muttered. 'Oh my God, she's alive.'

He turned every which way, hoping someone else would be in the park at this hour of the morning. But they were alone with each other. He crept closer and knelt down beside her.

'Take it easy,' he said. 'You're hurt, so just lie still. I've found you, I'll take care of you, you're going to be all right.'

Blue-gray eyes fluttered open to focus on him for a second or two and then closed again.

Arthur thought fast. He didn't know how badly she was hurt but he knew enough not to move her. If he hurried, he calculated it would take him roughly four minutes to get back to Lincoln Way, where he would at least be able to find a telephone. He stood up, stripped off his warm-up jacket and placed it carefully over her. It wasn't much, but it was better than leaving her the way she was.

'I'll be right back,' he told her, although he wasn't at all sure that she heard him. 'I'm going to go get help and then I'll be right back. Don't move. Just lie there nice and quiet until I get back.'

With one last look at her, he took off at a dead run.

'My name is Azi Redfern,' the short, redheaded Native American said to the woman lying motionless on the table in the curtained cubicle. 'I'm from the Rape Treatment Center and I'm here to help you in any way I can.'

It was less than fifteen minutes from the time the call came into the Center that Azi and a nurse-examiner reached the Emergency Room at San Francisco General Hospital.

'Is she conscious?' Azi had asked the resident on duty.

'Dazed, but conscious,' he replied.

'Anything serious?'

The doctor shook his head. 'A number of abrasions and lacerations, but no evidence of internal trauma. Her nose is broken, she's got a split lip and a black eye. The rest appears to be superficial, but she took quite a beating.'

The counselor nodded to the nurse-examiner. 'Let's go,' she said.

The resident pulled aside the curtain and allowed the two women to enter the tiny cubicle ahead of him.

'The doctor is going to treat you first,' Azi told the victim in a gentle, soothing voice. 'He's assured me that your injuries are minor and that you're in no danger. So try to relax as much as possible. Do you understand?'

The woman blinked once and closed her eyes.

When the doctor was finished, Azi touched the woman's shoulder.

'The nurse needs to examine you now,' she said, 'to collect as much physical evidence as possible.' The woman's eyelids fluttered and Azi quickly reached down and took hold of her hand. She smiled reassuringly. 'It's purely routine.'

When she was thirteen years old, Azi Redfern's father sent her from the reservation to an uncle in Santa Fe for a proper education. Three weeks later, her uncle raped her, the first of what became a weekly occurrence that lasted until she was seventeen, when she was awarded a scholarship to the University of New Mexico in Albuquerque.

She was too ashamed to tell her father, too ashamed to tell anyone, until she met a psychologist at the university who was able to help her deal with the pain and the anger. After college, she went on to become a counselor, knowing she could draw on her own experience to help other victims of sexual abuse.

Half an hour later, the nurse-examiner had filled a dozen or more plastic bags with swabs of vaginal secretions, slides of semen residue, pubic hairs, fingernail scrapings, torn underwear, what was left of a navy-blue silk dress, shredded nylon stockings, grass specimens, and blood samples. A female police officer had slipped into the cubicle to observe the examination. A police photographer had snapped twenty or more images of the battered woman from every conceivable angle. Azi still had hold of her hand.

'Why do you do all that?' the woman mumbled through her swollen, sutured lips, as she watched the nurse label each of the plastic bags and then gather them together into one large envelope, which she sealed and handed to the policewoman.

'It's what we call the chain of custody,' explained Kelly Takuda, one of the two uniformed officers who had responded to Arthur Gertz's frantic call. 'First we collect the physical evidence, then we seal it all up to make sure that no one tampers with it, then we have the police lab analyze it. Later, we can use this analysis to identify the person who assaulted you just as positively as if we had actually seen him do it.'

'Oh.'

The police hadn't found her purse or any identification on her person.

'Can you tell us your name?' Officer Takuda asked.

'Karen,' the woman said. 'Karen – Doniger.'

'Is there someone you would like us to call for you?'

'. . . .my husband.'

Karen gave the telephone number, and Kelly Takuda wrote it down and passed it to her partner outside the cubicle.

'Now,' she urged, 'can you tell us what happened?'

Karen took a tremulous breath. 'I felt sick,' she replied. 'I guess maybe I drank too much, or maybe it was the clams, but I felt sick. I asked him to stop the car.' Tears began to roll down her cheeks, stinging smartly when they reached her raw, swollen mouth. 'He pulled off the main road and then onto a side road, and I got out and started to walk around a bit and take some deep breaths, you know, so I'd feel better. And then, all of a sudden, he – he grabbed me and – and – and he was too strong and I couldn't get away from him.'

She was shivering now, choking on her tears and words and Azi pulled a blanket up around her and held her with an arm about her shoulders.

'It's all right,' she murmured. 'You're all right.'

'Do you know your assailant, Mrs. Doniger?' Officer Takuda asked. 'Can you identify him?'

Karen's head was throbbing. She tried to focus on the policewoman but saw only the uniform, and, with a small groan, she turned her head away. Kelly glanced at Azi, but the rape counselor shrugged and shook her head.

'I guess that's enough for now,' Officer Takuda said kindly. 'Perhaps we'll be able to get a more detailed statement from you later, when you're feeling better.'

The call came just before seven o'clock. Ted was so frantic by then that it was actually a relief to hear that Karen was only injured. He had spent much of the night talking to the police and calling every hospital in the city, afraid she might be dead. He reached the Emergency Room just as the two officers were leaving.

'She's had a bit of shock, Mr. Doniger,' Kelly Takuda said. 'And she's a little banged up. But she's all right, and the doctor says she can go home whenever she's ready.'

'What happened?' he asked.

'Why don't we let her tell you about it,' the policewoman replied diplomatically. There were just some things, she had long ago concluded, that belonged between a husband and wife, at least in the beginning.

Ted knew then, of course, like a knife plunging itself into his heart. There was only one kind of injury that the police hesitated to discuss.

Karen was still huddled beneath the blanket when he entered the cubicle. A redheaded woman was holding both of her hands and talking to her, too low for him to catch the words. He came up and put his hand on his wife's hair and smiled down at her. Tears of relief that she really was alive and even well enough to be sitting up filled his eyes.

'I was so worried,' he said.

'I'm sorry,' she whispered.

'No, don't,' he cried. 'It's enough that you're all right.' But he saw her eyes slip away from his and knew that she wasn't all right at all.

The redhead took the change of clothes that Ted had brought along and began helping Karen to dress.

'I'm a crisis counselor,' Azi said, after introducing herself. 'I've been here since the ambulance brought your wife in.'

He saw the angry bruises on Karen's thighs and, without either of them saying a word, he knew what kind of crisis counselor Azi Redfern was. The knife twisted itself deeper, and he wanted to scream and bash his fists into somebody's face, as someone had so obviously done to Karen.

'Thank you,' he murmured.

With some encouragement, Karen managed to stand up, but she couldn't seem to coordinate her legs well enough to walk.

'I'll get a wheelchair,' Azi offered.

'That won't be necessary,' Ted told her. He lifted his wife into his arms as though she were a feather and carried her out of the hospital.

The doorbell rang at two o'clock.

'My name is Lamar Pope,' drawled the giant of a man standing on the threshold. He was dressed in a western shirt and jeans, a leather jacket with fringe, and an exotic pair of tooled leather boots. He handed his card to Ted. It identified him as a sergeant for the Bureau of Investigations, Sexual Assault Division.

'Come in, Sergeant,' Ted invited hesitantly. 'My wife is resting. I don't know if she's up to seeing anyone yet.'

'I won't stay any longer than necessary, Mr. Doniger,' Lamar assured him. 'But we like to get the facts as fresh as possible, you understand.'

Karen was curled up on one of the pale-green sofas in the living room, inside a cocoon of fuzzy blankets. Azi had just brought her a fresh cup of tea.

'I'd sure like to get a statement from you, ma'am, if I could,' Lamar said after the introductions. 'To get the investigation going. Tomorrow or whenever you feel up to it, you can come down to the department and make it official.'

Karen looked up at him apprehensively. Azi, noticing, sat down beside her.

'They have women investigators in the division,' she said softly. 'We can request one, if you prefer. But you won't find anyone better than Lamar. He's not just a great detective, he's one of the most decent men I know.' She glanced up at him and he gave a short nod. 'Twenty years ago, his daughter was raped and murdered by a young man who got off because the prosecution didn't do its job right. Lamar's been involved in sexual-assault investigations ever since.'

The heavyset officer with the shock of white hair and bizarre cowboy clothes looked nothing at all like her memory of Michael Haller.

'I guess it's all right,' Karen consented.

Lamar sat down in the opposite chair and produced a pad, a pen, and a microcassette recorder from various pockets.

'This is so I don't forget anything,' he said, gesturing to the recorder. 'And this,' he said, holding up the pad and pen, 'is so that I have something to do with my hands. I'm trying to quit smoking.'

'Would you like something to drink, Sergeant Pope?' Ted asked.

'Well, sir, if that's tea your wife's having, I wouldn't say no to a cup if it was offered.'

Azi went to the kitchen to get the tea and Ted retreated to the study, leaving Karen and Lamar alone.

'I'm sorry about your daughter,' Karen murmured.

'I appreciate that, ma'am,' he drawled. 'I surely do.' He pressed the little red button on the recorder. 'Well now, suppose you tell me, in your own words and at your own pace, exactly what happened.'

It took Karen almost an hour to recall it all, from the moment Robert had approached her in the downtown parking garage to the moment he left her in Golden Gate Park. Lamar scribbled copious notes, stopping her every now and again to ask for a clarification or a further detail.

And through it all, the soft-spoken giant was kind and gentle and supportive.

'You're doing just fine, ma'am,' Lamar said when Karen began to falter. 'And we're almost through.

Now, you say that, after he forced you to have sex with him, the man got into his car and drove away, and just left you there?'

'I think so,' Karen replied. 'I mean, I guess he must have, because I was still there when the jogger came along. But I really don't remember very much about what happened – you know, afterward.'

'What kind of car was he driving?'

'A Mercedes. Black.'

'What was he wearing?'

Karen thought a moment. 'I think it was a gray suit with a little stripe in it, a white shirt and a gray-and-maroon tie. And black loafers with little tassels.'

'All right,' Lamar coached. 'You say you met him in the garage and he took you for a drink and then offered to drive you home.'

'He offered to drive me home first and then we went to have a drink,' Karen corrected.

'At any point in the evening, did he happen to tell you his name? Where he lived? Where he worked?'

Karen stared long and hard at the police investigator. He seemed so fatherly, with his white hair and careworn face. But behind the sympathetic blue eyes, she knew, was a keen mind. She wondered if it was also a fair one.

'He didn't have to tell me his name,' she said finally. 'I knew who he was. That's why I agreed to let him drive me home. I've been working as a volunteer at his campaign headquarters for three months. His name is … Robert Drayton Willmont.'

Lamar's left hand shot out and hit the stop button on the microcassette recorder. He sat there frozen with shock, wondering what the hell he had stumbled into, and why it had been his accursed misfortune to be the investigator on call this particular day.

There was no point in asking if she was positive of her identification. Obviously, she was. There was no point in asking if there were any political motivations behind her accusation. If there were, she would certainly not admit it. There was no point in asking her anything more at all until he had time to digest what he had already heard.

'I think that about does it,' he said finally. 'I will ask you not to discuss this with anyone until the department completes its investigation and decides how to proceed. Due to the rather special circumstances involved here, I think it would be wise if the press were kept out of this as long as possible.'

'I have no intention of talking to the press,' Karen declared with dignity. 'Or anyone else.'

Lamar dropped the recorder back into one pocket, stuffed his pad and pen into another, and hefted himself to his feet.

'I thank you for your time, ma'am,' he said. 'No need to bother your husband. I can see myself out.'

'Goodbye, Sergeant.'

Karen watched him go. Thirty years ago, it had been a fine, upstanding Harvard law student who had never been in any trouble. Now, it was a United States senator who was seeking the highest office in the land. Her word against his. And another male police investigator. She wondered if there was any justice to be had in the world.

It was evening. Ted had sent Amy off to spend the night with DeeDee because Karen didn't want her stepdaughter to see her the way she looked. Then he called Natalie.

'She won't admit it but I know she's in pain,' he said after a brief explanation. 'I need to go out and pick up a prescription the doctor ordered, but I don't want to leave her alone. Can you sit with her until I get back?'

'Of course I can.'

'I won't be long.'

Natalie knew her own remedy for pain. She took a full glass of brandy up to the bedroom.

'Drink,' she instructed.

Karen sipped the fiery liquid but it had little effect.

'Did Ted tell you?' she asked through swollen lips.

Natalie nodded. 'I can't believe it,' she lamented. 'I feel like this is all my fault. I didn't argue when you said you were going to join his campaign. I realize now I should have. I guess, way down deep, I wanted to believe he had changed. It just never occurred to me that this could happen twice.'

'Or me,' Karen said. 'That's why I got into the car with him. I thought, well, he's an important person now, he's certainly older, and he should be wiser, and besides this is 1992 and he's got so much to lose, he'd be crazy to try anything – so why should I be afraid?'

'What are you going to do?'

'I'm not going to do anything. It's up to the police to decide what they're going to do.'

'Talk about a bombshell,' Natalie murmured. 'Nobody's going to want to come within a hundred miles of this.'

'You and Ted and the investigator are the only ones who know who it was. If the police don't prosecute him, I don't want it going any further.'

Natalie groaned. 'I'm so sorry,' she repeated.

'Please don't blame yourself,' Karen said. 'It's not your fault. I'm an adult. Whatever I did, I did all on my own.'

Ted held her all night long, rocking her, caressing her. With Natalie's help, he had gotten some hot soup into her on top of the brandy, but she couldn't seem to get warm.

'I didn't tell them,' she said.

'You didn't tell them what?'

'About … about the other time. They would have thought me so stupid to let it happen again.'

'But shouldn't they know?'

Karen shrugged. 'It was so long ago, and it was my word against his. Besides, that was then and this is now, and it would only confuse things.'

He remembered the night, barely six months ago, when she had told him about her first encounter with Robert Willmont. He remembered holding her tight and promising her that he would never let anyone hurt her again.

He was sick inside because he hadn't been able to keep his promise. He couldn't understand what kind of man would brutalize a woman, then not even remember it and turn around and do it again. He had not been thrilled when Karen said she wanted to work for the Willmont campaign, but he hadn't argued all that strenuously against it, either. Not when she was sure it would be a positive step toward putting the past behind her. But now he wished, with the impassioned accuracy of hindsight, that he had objected.

'Save America!' was rapidly becoming a powerful slogan throughout the country, a heady concept that was rallying thousands to the cause every day – and the man behind it all had turned out to be nothing but a brutal rapist.

Ted Doniger was a gentle, caring man, a true Libra, who believed that sufficient good existed in everyone to balance out almost any bad. It was just that, as his father used to say, you had to look a little harder to find it in some. As hard as he now looked, Ted was unable to find sufficient good in Robert Willmont.

He stared into the darkness, choking on an unfamiliar anger that burned so hot inside him that, had he owned a gun, he knew he would have gotten up in the night and used it.

nine

It was a point with Lamar Pope that he never used elevators if he could help it. More a matter of innate impatience than any specific effort at exercise, he habitually walked up to the fourth floor of the Hall of Justice, the solid gray building that occupied a whole block of Bryant Street and looked so oddly out of place in the dismal neighborhood of warehouses, factories, and body shops.

This morning was no exception. Lamar climbed the steps, taking two at a time, and lumbered down the corridor to Room 436, where the Sexual Assault Division was located. Going directly to the rear of the shoulder-high partitioned space, he spent some minutes rummaging through the bottom drawer of his desk before making his way into the lieutenant's cramped office and dropping heavily into a chair.

It was eight-thirty on Friday and he had been sitting on his bombshell for almost forty-eight hours.

'You're not going to believe this,' he said.

Lieutenant Mike Perrone had been a policeman for twenty-three years and in charge of investigations for five. There wasn't a whole lot he wouldn't believe. Every day, as he got ready to leave for work, he told his wife he didn't know how much longer he could stand to stay in the Sexual Assault Division. Too many of the victims had begun to haunt his dreams.

'Lay it on me,' he invited.

'Okay,' Lamar nodded. 'I've got a woman who claims she was raped by Robert Willmont.'

'*Senator* Robert Willmont?'

'That's the one.'

Perrone, a medium-sized man with a barrel chest and a thin mustache, threw back his head and guffawed.

'You're right,' he cackled. 'I don't believe it.'

Lamar shrugged. 'The trouble is,' he responded, chewing the end of an unlit cigarette, 'it may just be true.'

The smile on the lieutenant's face slowly faded. 'The Prince of Pure? The squeaky-clean people's advocate? The trumpeter of "Save America!"?'

'Yep.'

'Well, I'll be damned. When? Where?'

'Tuesday night, Golden Gate Park.'

'Where's the report? I haven't seen anything about it come through. All hell hasn't broken loose.'

'I buried it,' Lamar declared. 'All things considered, I thought that was the smartest li'l ole thing to do until we knew where this was going.'

Perrone nodded. 'Okay, what have you got?'

'I've got her statement,' Lamar told him. 'I've got her physical condition. I've got all the stuff that the

Rape Treatment Center collected, including finger-nail scrapings – she says she scratched him pretty good. I've got a footprint at the scene. And I've got her positive identification.'

'Hell, this smells like a setup to me,' the lieutenant muttered. 'What is it – two months before the primary? Shit! That's a pretty timely coincidence.'

'The thought did cross my mind,' Lamar agreed. 'That's why I've been playing it so close to the vest. But I have to lay it on the line. I've spent the last forty-two hours checking her out. If she's got any political axes to grind, I can't find them. On the contrary, every-thing I've learned about her so far leads me to believe that she was honestly committed to Willmont's philos-ophy.'

'Christ,' Perrone breathed. 'You don't really think it's possible, do you?'

'Gut feeling?' Lamar asked.

'Yeah.'

'Anything's possible.'

'What do you want to do with it?'

'I think we've got enough for a friendly chat.'

'Well, make sure you cover our asses first, but good,' Perrone said. 'What have you done with the stuff?'

'I relabeled the RTC evidence. Now no one but me can find it. I listed the cast we made of a footprint at the scene under a John Doe. I took the report filed by the uniforms that answered the call and the medical report and the photographs that were taken at the hospital and lumped them all under an alias. I erased the mention of his name from my tape record. I guaran-damn-tee you this isn't going to leak until we're ready to make a move.'

'All right,' the lieutenant sighed. 'Let me look at the

report. If I agree with you, we'll call him in.'

If there was one thing Mike Perrone had learned in the last five years, it was that Lamar Pope was never wrong.

'He won't come in,' the investigator replied.

'Hell, I know he won't,' Perrone snapped. 'But we damn well gotta follow procedure.'

'I tell you, Hal, it's absurd,' Robert Willmont raged at his attorney over the telephone. 'The woman's a goddamn liar. This whole thing is a frame, can't you see that?'

'Then you have nothing to worry about,' Hal Sutton replied calmly. 'Besides, they just want to talk to you.'

'The hell you say. They're not going to haul me down there for one of their interrogations like I was some common criminal.'

'I'm sure we can arrange a compromise,' the son of the former senior partner of Sutton, Wells, Willmont and Spaulding said. 'I'll handle it. But first, you'd better tell me exactly where this is coming from.'

'She's a volunteer who works at headquarters,' the senator explained. 'Her car wouldn't start, so I offered her a lift home. We went across the street to a bar and had a few drinks and talked for a while. Then, on the way to her place, she got sick or something, asked me to pull over. She got out of the car and disappeared, so I got out, just to make sure she was okay, and the next thing I know, she's jumping me. I mean, she was worse than those crazy groupies who follow after rock stars. She was all over me, scratching and biting. Hell, I couldn't get away from her.'

'She was that strong, eh?' Sutton asked.

'Well, all right,' Robert admitted, 'maybe I didn't try

very hard. You know how it is, a little alcohol, the stress of the campaign, a woman throwing herself at you. So maybe my resistance was low – okay, she was a cold and I caught it. After all, I'm only human, and Randy's had me living in solitary confinement since December. But if she thinks she can get away with crying rape, she's got another think coming!'

'Don't worry,' Sutton assured him. 'Acquaintance rape is a very muddy charge and the hardest kind to prove. If it's not true, believe me, she won't get away with it.'

'But if it goes to trial, that alone will be enough to ruin me,' Robert argued, considering the big picture. 'I haven't come this far to be done in by some crazy person.'

'Well, you might consider pleading to a lesser charge.'

'Like what?'

'Maybe simple assault.'

'That's still a felony, and a felon isn't going to get elected President of the United States.'

'It's better than rape.'

'What if I just denied everything?' Robert suggested. 'Said I was never there and had an alibi to prove it?'

'I would never knowingly let you perjure yourself – or anyone else you may be thinking of involving in this,' the respected partner of Sutton, Wells, Willmont and Spaulding replied tartly. He and Robert were not exactly friends, but they had known each other for over twenty-five years. 'Besides, they're bound to have DNA evidence, at the very least, that can place you at the scene just as surely as an eyewitness from a foot away.'

'I've been in the inner circles long enough to know

that evidence can … disappear,' Robert said casually. 'All it takes is enough money and the right connections, and I've got both.'

'You've built your reputation on honesty,' his attorney reminded him. 'My advice would be to stick to that.'

'It was just a thought.' Robert sighed, wondering what good an honest reputation was going to do him in the middle of a maelstrom. 'So now what?'

'Let me sort things out,' Sutton said, 'and I'll get back to you.'

Lamar trudged up the steps of the Jackson Street house just after three-thirty that afternoon and pressed the bell. A faint melody of chimes sounded from somewhere inside, and a moment later an elderly man in black livery opened the door and, without so much as a word, ushered him into a room off to the left of the entrance foyer.

Three men awaited him in a richly appointed library of the type that Lamar had heard about but had never been invited to enter. He recognized Robert Willmont, of course. The second man was perhaps ten years older than the senator, not as tall but equally distinguished-looking, with a full head of silver hair. The third man was shorter, younger, thinner, with receding red hair and glasses.

'I'm Hal Sutton, Sergeant Pope, Senator Willmont's attorney.' The silver-haired man stepped forward but did not offer his hand. 'This is the senator's aide, James Randall Neuburg. And, of course, you know the senator.'

'Gentlemen,' Lamar acknowledged.

'I appreciate your cooperation in allowing this

meeting to be held here, instead of at Justice,' the lawyer continued smoothly. 'Discretion is vitally important in this instance for reasons you can readily understand.'

'I assure you that I would have preferred to meet the senator under very different circumstances,' Lamar responded in kind, but he wasn't one for social chitchat. 'So, with your permission, I suggest we get right to the matter at hand and get it over with as quickly and painlessly as possible.'

'Certainly, Sergeant.'

They sat down on facing sofas. Lamar pulled out his tape recorder. 'Do you mind, sir?' he asked with just the right note of deference. 'It helps me to remember.'

'Not at all,' came the senator's reply after a quick glance at his attorney.

'Thank you.'

'You know that I would be well within my rights not to make a statement at this time,' Robert declared.

'Oh, I know that, sir.'

'The only reason I'm doing so is because I want this whole thing to go away before it does some real damage.'

'I appreciate that.'

'All right, then, where do you want me to begin?'

It took less than twenty minutes for Lamar to obtain the senator's account of the events of Tuesday evening.

'I'm sure you understand,' the senator concluded, 'there could be any number of people out to get me. Someone in my position is always vulnerable. Was I foolish, under the circumstances, to succumb to a woman I hardly knew? Of course I was. But I assure you, foolishness is the only thing I'm guilty of. Now I hope this will be the end of it.'

'Well, sir, I can't exactly promise you that,' Lamar replied. 'Needless to say, your version conflicts somewhat with the lady's, and that means we'll have to do a little more investigating.'

'You certainly aren't going to take her word over mine, are you?' Robert asked with a sharp edge in his voice.

'It's not up to me, Senator,' Lamar told him. 'I just gather the information.'

'Well, who then?'

'Once my investigation is completed, it'll be up to the district attorney's office.'

The senator glared at Lamar. 'I don't believe this,' he snapped. 'Some deranged woman comes out of nowhere and tells a big fat lie, and because it involves someone respectable and important and very much in the public eye, you people jump all over it.'

In the background, Hal Sutton cleared his throat.

'Yes, well, what more can I say or do, Sergeant?' Robert went on in a more reasonable tone. 'What will it take to convince you that I didn't rape anyone?'

'Perhaps you'd be good enough to show me the clothes you were wearing on Tuesday.'

'My clothes? What the devil do you want with – ?' Robert began. 'Of course – you're looking for evidence that may support one story or the other. Well, I certainly don't know what my clothes can tell you that I haven't already told you, but you're welcome to them.'

He jumped to his feet and crossed to the door, yanking it open. 'Preston,' he barked at the aged man who waited in the hallway. 'Bring down whatever clothes I was wearing on Tuesday. Suit, shirt, tie, everything.'

'Shoes,' Lamar prompted.

'Yes, and my black loafers.'

The four men stood around looking uncomfortably at one another until the butler returned with the clothing.

'I'm sorry, sir, but the shirt has already been sent to the laundry,' he said, apologizing for his efficiency.

Robert shrugged. 'Then this will have to do.'

'In that case, sir,' Lamar requested, 'I hope you won't object to unbuttoning your shirt.'

'I damn well do object!' the Senator snapped. 'Who the hell do you think – ?'

This time it was the redhead who cleared his throat.

'Certainly, Sergeant,' Robert said stonily.

He ripped off this tie and undid his shirt. Four angry-looking red lines slanted down his chest.

'Yes, she scratched me, if that's what you're looking for,' he conceded. 'But I assure you it came out of her … exuberance, and not from any effort to fight me off.'

'Thank you,' Lamar said, gathering up the senator's clothing. 'I believe that's all I need for now.'

'What do you think?' Robert asked the moment the door closed on the police investigator.

'I think they'll probably charge you,' Sutton replied.

'Shit!'

'When they start asking for clothing and looking for scratches, it's a pretty good indication,' Randy agreed.

'But I didn't do it,' Robert protested.

'I think we could still plead it out,' Sutton advised.

'If he pleads to anything,' Randy declared, 'it ends his political career right there.'

'Maybe so, but it might keep him out of jail.'

'No,' Robert sighed. 'The only chance I've got is to be cleared in open court.' He turned to his aide. 'Get Dobbs on this. Let's turn it into a cause célèbre. A real civics lesson that will prove to the whole country that the system does work.'

'What if it doesn't?' Randy asked softly.

'Of course it will,' the senator assured him. 'Don't forget – this is my state, my town, my people. No jury here is going to convict me of something I didn't do.'

At nine forty-five on Monday morning, Jay Agar, the Deputy District Attorney for the City of San Francisco, walked resolutely down the third-floor corridor of the Hall of Justice and stopped at an office barely larger than a moderate-sized closet. A window with a broken blind overlooked the freeway and took up most of one cracked beige wall. The scarred desk took up most of the floor space.

Agar rapped on the open door to catch the attention of the woman inside.

Teresa Maria Yacinta Escalante, hands down the best ADA he had ever had the good fortune to work with, glanced up from the stack of files in front of her. She was a black-haired, black-eyed beauty with very white teeth that flashed when she smiled. She was smiling now.

'I heard you coming,' she admitted. 'But I was hoping you would pass right by. Just look at this desk. I can't possibly handle a single other thing for the next two months.'

'I'm sorry, Tess,' Agar sighed, dropping a folder on

her desk. 'You don't know how sorry I am.'

Tess flipped the folder open, knowing it had to contain something big because he hadn't even bothered to pose his usual questions about her weekend. She scanned the pages quickly and her already large eyes grew even larger.

'This is a joke, right?' she charged. 'Like in April Fool's?'

'No joke.'

Tess frowned. 'You mean, someone is really accusing Robert Willmont of rape?'

'So I'm told.'

'*Senator* Robert Willmont?'

Agar sighed. 'He's the only one I know.'

'Why me?' she protested. 'You usually grab on to all the biggies. Why aren't you grabbing on to this one?'

'The Stepaner case,' Agar reminded her. 'I can't tell the judge in the middle of a triple murder trial that I'm sorry but something else has come up.'

He didn't bother to mention that the Stepaner case was a notorious one, bound to enhance his reputation, while this one was clearly destined to be a no-win situation, whichever way it went.

Tess leaned back in her chair, her brow furrowed, and tapped her pen against her left palm.

'It doesn't make sense. Willmont's got to know there's a goddamn microscope trained on him,' she observed shrewdly. 'He's just about got the nomination sewed up. Why would he risk it? Does it strike you that the timing here may be just a little too perfect – that this might be a setup?'

'Sure.' Agar shrugged. 'But it doesn't matter what I think,' he said. 'The DA is afraid it's too solid to ignore. What you think is up to you.'

'Why me?' she repeated.

'Because you're honest, non-partisan, and the best – and everyone knows it. If I put anyone else on this, both sides would cry foul.'

'But I'm already over my head.' She gestured to the mountain of paperwork on her desk.

'I know, and I'm willing to let you lay off as many of your other cases as necessary. Needless to say, this one gets top priority.'

'No kidding,' she grumbled.

'Look, will it help if I tell you that you've got Lamar on this one?' he coaxed.

'Don't try to butter me up,' retorted Tess. 'I wouldn't touch this case without him and you know it.'

Tess Escalante and Lamar Pope were a team, the best ADA in San Francisco and the best sexual-assault investigator in the country.

The beefy ex-Texan brought a degree of dedication, intuition, and sensitivity to his work that surprised everyone but Tess, and kept him digging after most others would have given up. On more cases during the last five years than Tess cared to remember, she knew she would have been dead in the water without him. But even with Lamar Pope in her corner, the last thing Teresa Maria Yacinta Escalante wanted to do was go after a United States senator – especially this one.

She wasn't any more or less political than any other assistant district attorney whose career hung on the reelection of the administration that employed her, but neither was she blind to what was happening in America. She liked the things Robert Willmont was saying, although the majority of her colleagues considered him too radical.

The daughter of migrant workers who had escaped the border patrols to live and die stooped over the crops they were lucky enough to pick, Tess could see the writing on the crumbling wall of America. What both surprised and pleased her was that she was apparently not alone, judging from the impressive number of primary victories that the senator from California was piling up.

There had never been so much as a hint of a shadow over Robert Willmont's private life, which meant that either the public relations pabulum being fed to the people about him was accurate, or he was very discreet. Tess considered Edmund Muskie and the forged letter that was his downfall, Geraldine Ferraro and her husband's business affairs, Michael Dukakis and Willie Horton, and the more recent flap over Bill Clinton and Gennifer Flowers, and she couldn't stop the specter of dirty tricks from looming large in her mind.

'All right, go on and get out of here and let me do my job,' she said, waving Agar off. 'But you're going to owe me for this one. Boy, are you going to owe me.'

She read through the folder again, this time studying the preliminary police report, Azi Redfern's account, and the two statements made by Karen Doniger. Then she looked at the police photographs. Finally, she read Robert Willmont's account of the event. By the time she finished, Lamar Pope stood in the doorway to her office, filling it up.

'So who are you voting for in the primary?' she asked.

'I don't vote in primaries,' he drawled. 'I've been a registered nonpartisan my whole life.'

Tess chuckled. He was the only one in the office who could get away with wearing jeans and fringe to work.

The cowboy with the college education, she thought, as she shoved the folder away from her and looked squarely at him.

'How did you ever get Willmont to make that statement?'

Lamar lowered his bulk into the chair across the desk from her. 'He offered. He said he wanted the truth to be known right up front.'

'Well, what do you think?'

'I'm not sure yet,' the investigator admitted. 'With the primary just around the corner, I can't figure out why the man would be so stupid.'

'More or less the same thing I told Agar,' Tess agreed.

'Are you thinking it could be a frame?'

Tess sighed. 'I don't know what I'm thinking – except that right now I wish I'd never left Salinas.'

ten

Mary Catherine sat at her desk in the gathering dark, the outer door of campaign headquarters safely locked. She had sent the staff home the moment the story broke, the moment Robert Willmont had been arrested on charges of sexual assault and battery, the moment he had been escorted downtown to be fingerprinted, photographed, and booked, the moment the office had begun to be bombarded by the media.

'I'm sure it's all just some horrible mistake,' she assured the wide-eyed workers who stood in a daze as they watched the first telecasts from outside the Hall of Justice and saw a behemoth in cowboy clothes conducting their beloved senator inside. 'You know, one of those cases of mistaken identity. By tomorrow, I'm sure it will all be cleared up, and everyone will be right back on the job.'

But in her heart, her bones, or whatever it was that

had deftly guided her through forty years of politics, she knew better.

She told the flood of reporters she had no official comment, but as a woman who had known the senator for over a decade, she personally could not believe there was any merit to the charges.

'What can you tell us about the alleged victim?' they cried.

'Nothing,' she said. She had been warned not to talk about Karen Doniger, not to the media, not to anyone.

'But you do know her, don't you?'

'I'm sure the senator will have a statement for you in the next day or two,' she replied.

Then she politely ushered them all out, locked the door and turned off the telephones.

Mary Catherine had no idea why her most valued volunteer had cried foul, but she could not bring herself to believe that this was a question of assault and battery. She knew Robert Drayton Willmont was far too desirable a man to have to resort to forcing a woman to accommodate him.

Still ... Karen Doniger didn't seem either unbalanced or the type to let herself be used as a political pawn. On the contrary, she was bright, competent, and to all appearances perfectly normal – in fact, just the kind of woman who was likely to appeal to the prurient side of Robert Willmont. Not that it really mattered, Mary Catherine reasoned. Whether he was found guilty or innocent, he was going to be politically dead in the water. The Moral Righteous would turn away from him like so many stampeding cattle, and even the thinking segment of the population would, in the backs of their minds, remember the old saw about where there's smoke – there's likely to be fire. The administrative assistant, who had to all intents and purposes grown up in Washington, D.C., knew that the stain of accusation would never wash off.

They had met at Jackson Street on Saturday – Robert, Randy, and Mary Catherine – to work out a contingency plan should worse actually come to worst.

'I can't believe this,' Robert had fumed. 'The woman practically rapes me, and *I* may end up being arrested. Maybe *I* should charge *her.*'

'We don't have time to waste on anger,' Randy suggested mildly. 'We have to decide how to handle the situation. You have three scheduled appearances this weekend. Do you want to go public now with your side of the story? Do you want to claim political motivations on her part?'

Robert turned on Mary Catherine. 'What do we know about her?' he growled.

'We know she's attractive, accomplished and efficient,' the administrative assistant replied. 'She's married, she has three stepdaughters and two step-grandchildren, and she writes popular poetry.'

'What does her husband do?'

'He's an architect,' Mary Catherine told him. 'In fact, he's *the* architect on the China Basin project.'

Robert's eyes narrowed thoughtfully. 'Can we bring any pressure to bear there?'

'I think it's too late for that,' Randy said.

'Why didn't I just deny the whole damn thing and tell everyone to go to hell?'

'As your attorney already advised you,' his aide told him, 'that kind of bluster wouldn't have worked very well.'

'Why not?' the senator shot back. 'It sure worked for Clarence Thomas.'

'Clarence Thomas was judged by his peers, in every sense of the word,' Mary Catherine declared with more than a touch of cynicism. 'You won't be that lucky. You're going to be judged by the voters.'

Robert sagged against his seat. 'Needless to say, I've been in touch with all of my top campaign advisers, every one of whom has counseled me to brazen it out. But the two of you are still my best political weather vanes. What do you think?'

'First,' replied Randy, 'you keep your mouth shut for the time being, and carry on as scheduled. You don't want to open any can of worms unless you have to.' He had spent over two hours on the telephone with Mariah, discussing strategies and probabilities.

'I agree,' Robert said.

'Second, we hire the best damn private detective agency in the country to find out every last thing there is to know about Karen Doniger.'

'Mary Catherine, get on that,' Robert directed.

'Done,' she said. She already knew the right firm to contact.

'Third, if and when it becomes necessary, you admit to a very foolish mistake – cry stress, cry exhaustion, you can even cry temporary insanity, if you like. Voters love to forgive repentant sinners when they sound sincere, so you'd better sound sincere.'

'I *am* sincere.'

'Fourth, you suggest that this is nothing more than a political frame; since you are clearly about to capture not only the nomination but the election as well, someone needed to find a way to stop you. But be careful you don't make the issue a partisan one. In this case, it would be wiser to hint that it could have come from either side, not to mention the auto industry, the NRA, and a few foreign countries who are heavily dependent on American aid.'

'I like that,' Robert said. 'I like it a lot.'

'Fifth, if it comes to trial, you call in every marker you can to push for an early date. Who knows, if we can expedite matters and win a fast acquittal, we might still be able to salvage something.'

'What do you mean *if?*' Robert barked. 'Of course I'll be acquitted. I'm innocent, damn it.'

'Sixth, for however long it takes, you and Elizabeth are joined at the hip.'

The senator shifted uneasily. 'To be honest, I don't know how that's going to go over with her. We haven't been especially … close lately.'

'Well then, we'd better have her in and find out,' Randy declared. 'Because without her we don't have a prayer.'

Elizabeth Willmont had spent the afternoon at the beach with Adam, where she delighted in her son's agility with his new surfboard. She returned with glowing cheeks to find Robert and his two associates anxiously awaiting her.

'I understand you wanted to have a word with me,' she said, floating into the library.

'We need your help,' Randy said simply, before Robert could respond.

Elizabeth smiled. She had always liked Randy Neuburg. Even at forty, he retained a boyish charm that was direct, unaffected, and appealing.

'Has this anything to do with all the closed-door meetings that have been going on around here the past couple of days?' she inquired.

Genuinely startled, Randy turned to Robert. 'Doesn't she know?' he demanded. 'Haven't you told her?'

'Know what?' Elizabeth asked.

'I didn't really see the point,' the senator replied uncomfortably. 'I mean, you know, unless it turned out to be necessary.'

'It's necessary,' Randy retorted. He strode across the room and took Mary Catherine by the arm. 'We're going to take a walk around the block,' he said meaningfully. 'We've been cooped up in here all day and it's time to stretch our legs. We'll be back in half an hour.'

When they returned, the glow was gone from Elizabeth's cheeks. Her eyes were narrowed and her chin was set. On the table beside her were a glass of water and her pillbox.

'If you thought this would come as a surprise to me,' she said coolly, 'you were wrong. In fact, I knew it was only a matter of time before his promiscuous ways caught up with him. Of course, I always thought it would be something like gonorrhea or AIDS, which is why I've refused to sleep with him for years. But don't worry. I'm his wife, and for better or worse, I'll stand by him. I'll even lie through my teeth in court, come to that.'

Then, with as much dignity as she could muster, she stood up and left the room.

What a woman, Randy marveled to himself. She had known about the senator all along and kept her silence. In a time when wives were divorcing their husbands for a good deal less, Elizabeth had been able to focus on the big picture. She was stronger than he had suspected, despite the vagaries caused by the pills, and he was now confident that, however messy things might get, she would stick.

She must want to be the First Lady a whole lot more than anyone realized, Mary Catherine mused with increased respect, knowing that, if she herself had been married to the good senator, she would have long since kicked him out of more than her bedroom – White House or no White House.

Robert cleared his throat. 'Naturally, I won't hear of her saying one word publicly,' he said. 'Unless, of course, worse comes to worst.'

Worse came to worst on Monday, April 13, at two o'clock in the afternoon, when Lamar Pope met the senator at his home, presented him with a warrant for his arrest, and escorted him down to the Hall of Justice.

Mary Catherine sighed deeply. She knew she ought to be doing something other than sitting there in the office in the dark. Pack some of her things, perhaps, or make arrangements for a flight back to D.C. But she didn't move. She went on sitting there because she was sixty years old and it was too late to pick up and start over again.

There would be no more bright-eyed idealists to teach, to guide through the political quagmire, to cultivate and mold. No, it was time to take her prudently managed savings and retire somewhere.

A little after eight o'clock, the elevator doors slid open and closed and she heard the sound of a key fitting into the lock on the outer door. It was the sound she had been waiting for.

Randy came in and snapped on the lights. 'I thought

you'd be here,' he said wearily. 'But why in the dark?'

'It seemed suitable,' Mary Catherine replied. 'Where is he?'

'At home. Hal had everything arranged. The booking, even the arraignment. I left them at Jackson Street. The preliminary hearing is set for the twenty-third.'

'That's pretty fast, isn't it?'

'We would have opted for tomorrow, given the chance.'

Mary Catherine nodded. 'How is he?'

'Incredulous ... confused ... outraged,' Randy reported. 'About the same as I would be, if my whole life suddenly exploded in my face.'

'Does he know?'

Randy shrugged. 'On some level, I think he knows. But he'll never admit it. He's sure he'll beat this thing and that the people will rally behind him.'

'Voters have done crazier things, I suppose.'

'I suppose.'

'The media's having a field day,' Mary Catherine said wearily. 'He has to make some kind of statement.'

'He's going to call a press conference for tomorrow,' Randy told her. 'He wants to get his side of the story to the people while the woman is still hiding behind anonymity.'

'What does Hal say?'

'He says it can't hurt.'

'I'll set it up.'

'Make it before three,' Randy directed, 'so we can catch the national newscasts.'

Even in the midst of disaster, her last protégé was in charge – the dedicated aide, the political engineer who had almost made a dream come true. Mary

Catherine peered at the man she had nurtured and taught so well for so many years.

'How are *you*?' she asked gently.

'Numb ... angry ... frustrated.' He sighed. 'We were so close.'

'What will you do?'

He thought for a moment. 'Go back to practicing law, I guess. Get married. Have a life.'

'That sounds pretty good to me.'

'Damn it, though, it just isn't fair,' he raged. 'That somebody can come along and ruin someone else's whole life, just like that.' He snapped his fingers for emphasis.

Mary Catherine hauled herself to her feet and picked up her purse. 'Come on,' she said. 'Let's go get drunk.'

eleven

The lights in Tess Escalante's third-floor office had burned well into the night for a week, until less than twelve hours remained before she would present her evidence at the preliminary hearing, and ask that Robert Drayton Willmont be bound over for trial on charges of sexual assault and battery. Even though she normally had weeks instead of days to put a case together, she felt she was prepared.

At the start, she had resented Jay Agar for dumping this hot potato in her lap, but now she was forced to admit that her interest had been piqued. Regardless of her position as prosecutor, the ADA had been fully prepared to dislike the alleged victim and to disbelieve her story, if only because the man Karen Doniger had accused of rape was the man whom many, Tess among them, truly believed to be the last hope of a desperate country.

The whole staff watched the senator's press conference, the day after his arrest, and it served only to strengthen Tess's convictions.

'As some of you still may not know,' he had said, looking straight into the camera and holding tight to his wife's hand, 'I was charged yesterday with rape.'

His face openly showed both fatigue and stress.

'Did I have sex with the woman in question?' he went on, carefully avoiding the use of her name, as he had been instructed. 'Yes, I did. I'm not going to lie to you. I knowingly broke my marriage vows, and I have no excuse for that, at least none worth offering you. But did I rape her? *No, I did not.* Our encounter was mutual and brief and we parted on what I believed were amicable terms.'

As a silent affirmation, Elizabeth Willmont moved half a step closer to her husband.

'How do you defend yourself when a woman cries rape?' he asked. 'How do you call her a damn liar without sounding like a cad? How do you convince anyone that, while you may have behaved stupidly, you did not behave criminally? How do you suggest that the timing was too perfect – that, because of who you are and what you stand for, someone would plot to discredit and disgrace you?'

Despite themselves, a ripple ran through the collected attorneys who sat watching with Tess.

'There are those who are saying that my candidacy is dead,' he declared. 'Certainly, if a jury of my peers convicts me of this heinous crime, they're right. But I believe in the system. I believe that America is still a country where truth matters and the innocent are acquitted. And if it is, then I will be acquitted.'

Behind the senator, members of his staff lifted their heads a little higher and stood a little taller.

'Now, I could request that my attorney employ the type of tactics that would delay this matter for years,' the candidate continued, his voice rising oratorically. 'But instead, I have instructed him to expedite it, to pull every string and call in every favor to get my case before the court as soon as possible, so that I may be freed of this stigma and allowed to return to my life's work.'

He paused unblinkingly for five full seconds.

'There are those who think that candidates for high office should be heros, saints, even gods,' he concluded in a more normal voice. 'But the truth is, most of us are just men – vulnerable, fallible, very human men, doing the best we can with the tools we're given. And that's exactly who I am and have always been – just a man who believes that he can help his country get through a terrible time. I know of no way to convince you to give me the benefit of the doubt until this awful business is behind me and my innocence is established. I can only hope that you will.'

Tess sat staring at the screen long after it had gone blank.

'He should have been an actor,' one of the ADAs said with a chuckle.

'Nah,' replied another. 'The last thing we need is another actor in the White House.'

'But you've got to give him points for style,' said a third.

'How about you, Tess?' someone asked. 'What do you think?'

'I think he's a very smart man,' she replied.

Guilty or innocent, he had done absolutely the right thing. He had put his case before the public himself, with dignity and alacrity, and more than anything, Tess

Escalante wanted to believe him.

But after only one meeting with Karen Doniger, it was clear that the alleged victim was no one's political ploy, no mental case who manufactured events, no eccentric in search of notoriety. In fact, just the opposite seemed to be true.

'I don't really want to be here,' the woman declared after the formalities, her words slurring softly through her stitched lip.

'Then why are you?' Tess asked bluntly.

'Because Azi convinced me I had to at least come and talk to you,' she replied, nodding to the RTC counselor beside her.

'Yes, I did,' the Native American confirmed. 'I told her it shouldn't matter that the man who raped her is somebody big and important, because, as big and important as he might be, in the eyes of the law he's no bigger and no more important than she is.'

'I agree with that,' the ADA said.

'Is it true,' the woman asked, 'that I can refuse to testify?'

'Yes,' Tess told her, 'that's your right. And if you exercise it, the charges against the senator will be dropped and the case will be closed. Of course, if he actually committed the acts you claim he did, he will then be free to go out and commit them again.'

'I know,' the woman whispered, and Tess saw a haunted look come into her eyes.

'I don't want to deceive you,' the ADA said. 'A rape trial is very often every bit as vicious and as humiliating for the victim as the original assault. Is that what you're afraid of, that you might not be able to stand up under the pressure?'

'I don't know,' came the reply. 'Maybe, if I thought

he would be convicted, I could convince myself that anything was worth it. But to tell you the truth, Miss Escalante, I don't think he'll be convicted, and I don't want to go through an ordeal that will surely devastate and maybe even destroy my family and my life for nothing.'

'I happen to think we have a very strong case against him, Mrs. Doniger,' Tess assured the woman. 'Why don't you think he'll be convicted?'

Blue-gray eyes looked straight into black ones.

'Because men like that are never held accountable for what they do,' the woman declared. 'What they want, they take. What they can't buy their way out of, they lie their way out of. There are still a lot of people in this world who don't really believe that a woman can be raped, that she can be held down and kicked and punched and forced to have sex. Even with all the evidence in the world against him, it will still come down to my word against his, and he's an elected politician who can do a lot of good for this country. Who am I?'

Tess eyed the woman thoughtfully. One of the things that made the ADA so very good at her job was her talent for objective evaluation. Despite her strongest-held beliefs, she was able to interpret every piece of evidence, every scrap of testimony, every glance, every nuance with unbiased clarity.

'He did it, didn't he?' she breathed, feeling her heart sink to the bottom of her stomach.

'Yes, Miss Escalante,' the woman said clearly. 'He did it.'

'Then Azi is right. It doesn't matter how important he is. No one is above the law and he *can* be held accountable.'

'Perhaps you believe that,' the alleged victim agreed. 'But I watched enough of the Willie Smith trial to know better.'

'I see.' Tess nodded with understanding. 'And you're afraid I might turn out to be as inept as you apparently feel Moira Lasch was?'

'It was clear, even to the experts, that the defense didn't win that case,' the woman said. 'For whatever reason, the prosecution gave it away. Now, I have nothing against you, Miss Escalante. I don't even know you. But I have children I care a great deal about and a husband whose work depends on public acceptance, and I've even enjoyed a bit of success in my own right. I can't afford to have happen to me what happened to Patricia Bowman. I don't think I'm as strong as she is. And even if you believe in me one hundred percent, you aren't going to be representing *me* in the court-room, you'll be representing the people. If you lose, what does it really matter to the people? But I'm branded a liar, an adulteress, or worse, for the rest of my life.'

The ADA sighed. 'All right,' she said, 'I'll grant you the system isn't perfect, but it does work.'

'I don't doubt the system works,' countered the alleged victim. 'I doubt that justice is always served.'

'For most people it is.'

'Perhaps. But Robert Willmont isn't most people.'

'Mike Tyson was convicted.'

'Yes,' the woman conceded. 'But I think he may have been convicted more because he was black than because he was guilty.'

'I'm good at my job, Mrs. Doniger,' Tess said. 'Very good. I do my homework. I don't make many mistakes. I don't go into court unless I'm convinced I can win.

It's true that you can never totally predict which way a jury will jump, but my conviction rate happens to be a pretty decent seventy-three percent.'

The alleged victim looked over at the RTC counselor.

'I've known Tess for five years,' Azi said. 'And even though, technically, she won't be representing you, I don't think you could be in better hands.'

'More importantly, Mrs. Doniger,' the ADA added, 'if you don't agree to testify, if we have to drop the charges and let him walk, it's as good as saying that what he did to you is okay. Do you really believe that what he did to you is okay?'

There were tears in the blue-gray eyes as the alleged victim studied her hands, considering the truth of those words and agonizing over her decision. It seemed like a lifetime before she looked up at Tess.

'My name is Karen,' she said.

The accelerated pace dictated by the defense resulted in Tess's having to lay off every other case in order to prepare for this one. Now, on the eve of the preliminary hearing, she was going through everything one more time, looking for flaws, loopholes, contradictions, anything that might cause a failure to secure an indictment.

'I thought I'd find you here,' Lamar drawled from the doorway. 'Piling on the overtime.'

'Just a formality,' she assured him. 'We've got more than enough for probable cause. What about your end?'

Lamar flopped into the chair across from her. 'You know, every time I take on one of these investigations, I see it as a giant jigsaw puzzle. And I know that, as soon as I put all the pieces together, the picture will come clear. It's what keeps me interested in the process. Only, in this puzzle, there's a piece missing.'

'What do you mean?'

The big man scratched his right ear. 'I don't rightly know, it's just this feeling in my gut that I'm missing something somewhere.'

Tess had learned to trust her investigator's gut. 'Like what?' she pressed.

'Like this whole thing doesn't make any sense to me,' he sighed. 'Because I believe Karen Doniger. I would stake my reputation on the fact that she's telling the truth, that what happened to her happened exactly the way she says it did.'

'So?'

'So my gut says that Willmont just may be telling the truth, too.'

'Well, they can't both be telling the truth.'

'That's the point,' Lamar agreed, 'isn't it?'

'You know,' Tess mused, 'there are some men who really don't understand the word '*no*,' or, more pre-cisely, they don't believe it can apply to them. For whatever reasons, they think of themselves as above rejection, which frequently makes them incapable of accepting it. It's possible that Robert Willmont is one of those men.'

'Maybe,' Lamar said, but he wasn't convinced.

'Look, the way Hal Sutton is rushing us, you haven't had enough time to do your usual thorough investiga-tion. We'll get our indictment tomorrow, and then I'll make sure you have enough time to pursue your elusive missing piece.'

'You like Karen Doniger, don't you?' he asked.

Tess nodded. 'Yes,' she answered. 'I do like her. A

lot. There's something terribly vulnerable about her, and yet very brave. There's a lot of pain there and you can almost see inside her as she struggles to deal with it.'

'Yes, I sensed that about her,' Lamar agreed.

'She's such a private person, too, and I know this public invasion is going to be as dreadful an experience for her as the assault was, whatever the outcome.'

'That's the part I hate the most.'

Tess smiled. 'I do believe you like her a bit yourself.'

'She's a real lady,' Lamar declared. 'And the truth is, you don't get to meet too many ladies in my line of work. It's just that …'

'I know,' Tess finished for him. 'There's a piece missing.'

PART EIGHT
1992

There is no such thing as justice –
in or out of court.

— *Clarence Darrow*

one

The Honorable Oliver Wendell Washington was suffering from an acute case of gastritis. In fact, he had been suffering from just such attacks every single day since he learned that he would preside over the trial of *The People* v. *Robert Drayton Willmont*.

'Why me?' he groaned to his wife as he made his second dash of the morning to the bathroom.

'Because you're a judge, I expect,' Thelma Washington reminded him through the bathroom door. 'And someone obviously thought you were the right judge for the job.'

'I wish I was a janitor,' moaned the former Stanford University law professor.

'You do not,' she chuckled. 'You're just as pleasured as pie to be a judge.'

'No, my *mama* is pleasured as pie,' he corrected her. 'It was her dream. She had it in her head from the day I was born that I was going to be a judge. That's why she named me Oliver Wendell – so I'd never forget.'

'And you've done your mama proud.'

'You don't understand,' he grumbled. 'I'm up for reelection in November. If I make one mistake in this trial, lean too far in either direction, I can kiss Mama's dream good-bye forever and probably send her to an early grave.'

'Early?' Thelma scoffed. 'She's eighty-eight, if she's a day.'

'Maybe if I just lie down for a minute or two.'

'If you do,' Thelma declared, 'you're going to be late to court – and *that'd* be a mistake.'

'If I called in sick right now, before jury selection starts, they'd find someone to replace me.'

Thelma wagged her head. 'I declare, I think I'd see a yellow streak running down your back – if your skin wasn't so black.'

'But it's the truth,' he insisted. 'Look at me. I can't get more than ten feet from the john.'

'Oliver Wendell,' his wife admonished in a voice that brooked no nonsense, 'now you stop all that whining and be about your business. You're a fair and impartial judge and everyone in this town knows it. That's why you were given this case. And you're going to do fine. But, just in case, I'll pack the Kaopectate in with your lunch.'

Department 21 of the Superior Court, Criminal Division, was referred to by those who worked at Justice as the Glass Courtroom. Positioned at the end of the inner third-floor corridor, it resembled the other courtrooms in modest size and unimpressive style, with its center aisle, its gallery of uncomfortable flip-down spectator seats, its yellow wood paneling and

Naugahyde chairs right out of the 1950s, and its California bear anchored beside the Stars and Stripes. And like all the courtrooms in the row, it was windowless. The one significant difference, and hence its sobriquet, was the ominous bulletproof partition – two thick panes of tempered glass bonded to fine wire mesh – that separated the spectators from the proceedings.

'Isn't that a bit overdramatic?' Lamar observed when Tess told him where to meet her.

'I guess no one wants to take any chances on some weirdo with a water gun slipping through,' she said with a shrug.

But now, as the ADA threaded her way through the milling throng in front of Department 21, Lamar was nowhere to be seen. It was Thursday, June 4, two days after Robert Willmont had won the California primary with a resounding eighty-two percent of the vote. All things being equal, the race for the nomination was over.

'Hey, Tess,' a reporter yelled. 'What do you think your chances are of convicting the next President of the United States?'

'About the same as any other citizen,' she replied with a professional smile.

'How can you do this awful thing to such a fine man?' a woman in a faded housedress cried.

The ADA didn't bother to respond to that. She showed her badge to the armed guards at the door and slipped inside the Glass Courtroom.

It was twenty minutes to nine. The left side of the gallery was already filled with members of the media and other interested parties. In less than half an hour, the seats on the right side would be taken by prospective jurors and the process of selecting the twelve, plus two alternates, who would decide this case, would begin.

Tess was wearing what she described as her jury suit – a classic gray gabardine with a gently fitted jacket and a slim skirt that was just short enough to attract the men but not short enough to distract the women, and expensive enough to establish the credentials, but not the extravagance, of a confident professional.

She laid her briefcase on top of the table to the right of the center aisle, closest to the jury box – which wasn't really a box but two rows of chairs, the second row raised one step above the first – and began to pull out the various files and folders she would need, arranging them neatly in front of her.

The past month had been busy, to say the least. Not counting the preliminary hearing, the ADA had been in and out of court half a dozen times on motions, during which the judge had denied a motion to dismiss, upheld a motion to expedite, denied a motion to exclude, upheld a motion to disclose, and denied the application of Court TV to produce what would surely have become a summer spectacular.

All in all, Tess felt she had come out even. She settled down in her chair and opened one of the files. In it were the names of two hundred registered voters who had been summoned for jury duty during this calendar quarter and would be available for this trial, and it was this list of names that had occupied her overworked staff for the better part of two weeks. Finding out who they were and what they did and how they lived and what they thought was as crucial to a verdict as building the case.

As the jury-selection process began, the ADA would

be searching for the right combination of men and women who would best be able to judge the testimony and weigh the evidence, and every scrap she could learn about each of them would help her in making that determination. While one or two staunch conservatives wouldn't hurt her cause, and a Bible-thumper, a couple of radical feminists, and a senior citizen might help, the best she could hope to get were twelve open minds.

There were three specific things Tess looked for when she questioned a prospective juror – eye contact, straight answers, and the ability to listen. Karen was right about there being people who would refuse to believe that a woman could be raped, no matter what, and Tess was always on the alert to spot them.

Next to her own judgment, the ADA most trusted Lamar's. The beefy cowboy would slouch in the chair next to hers, with his arms crossed over his belly and his leather-tooled boots sticking out from under the table, and pretend to doze. But each time she returned to her seat, a piece of paper would be waiting with either an 'aye' or a 'nay' scrawled on it.

Tess glanced at her watch and then over her shoulder. Lamar usually beat her into court – it was not like him to be late. In the five years they had worked together, she had come to rely on him, much like a security net, to catch her should she fall. An anxious frown crossed her face.

Hal Sutton chose that moment to enter the courtroom, flanked by a striking brunette in a Chanel suit, a good-looking African-American who reminded Tess of the guy on *L.A. Law,* and a stocky man with a shiny head and brand-new wing tips that creaked with every step. Covering all the bases, she thought, the frown becoming a wry smile.

In addition to being a formidable trial attorney, Hal Sutton was a smooth, attractive, impeccably dressed man who belied approaching retirement by keeping himself in excellent physical condition. He was referred to, around Justice, as the Silver Fox. Male jurors envied him, female jurors fantasized about him. Robert Willmont couldn't have made a better choice.

Sutton gave Tess a cordial nod as he and the others arranged themselves around the defense table to the left. Sitting by herself, Tess felt a little like David going up against Goliath, and she looked around again for the giant who was supposed to be on *her* side.

A few minutes later, the first group of some forty potential jurors filed into the courtroom. Tess heard them shuffling into their seats but she didn't turn around. It was a superstition of hers – not to speculate about them as a whole, but one at a time.

At exactly nine o'clock, Robert Willmont appeared, dressed in a neat dark suit, a crisp white shirt, and a conservative tie. Accompanying him were his wife in tailored taupe, his mother in lavender lace, a slight man with thinning red hair, freckles, and glasses, and a middle-aged woman with gray hair wearing a black dress that was far too warm for the season.

The senator took great care to seat his aged mother in the first row of chairs behind the bulletproof window and give his wife a kiss on the cheek before he joined Hal Sutton at the defense table. The block of jurors took it all in. Tess smiled to herself. The show was on.

At ten minutes past nine, the bailiff stepped to the front of the courtroom and began his speech.

'All rise,' he intoned.

There was a general scraping of chairs and rustling of clothing as everyone stood.

'Department 21 of the Superior Court of the City of San Francisco is now in session. Case number 458-026, *the People of the State of California* versus *Robert Drayton Willmont*. The Honorable Oliver Wendell Washington presiding.'

With that, the door to the left of the bench opened and the former Los Angeles prosecutor, former San Francisco attorney, former Stanford law professor emerged. Swathed in his robes, the judge looked half again his already considerable size. His intelligent brown eyes revealed a mixture of resignation and discomfort, and his usually shiny black face had a definite gray tinge to it.

'I apologize for my tardiness,' Washington mumbled after clearing his throat. 'Are the People ready, Miss Escalante?'

'The People are ready, Your Honor,' Tess said.

'Is the Defense ready, Mr. Sutton?'

'Yes, Your Honor.'

Washington nodded to the bailiff. 'You may call the first name.'

The bailiff rotated a small black cylinder several times before reaching in and pulling out a slip of paper.

'Agnes McFaddan.'

A tiny woman in her seventies scrambled out of her seat and made her way to the jury box. Tess found the name on the list – unmarried, librarian, registered Democrat.

The ADA stood up, took a deep breath to quell the butterflies that always took flight inside her stomach during the first stages of a trial, and approached the woman.

'Good morning, Miss McFaddan,' she said with a pleasant smile. 'How do you feel about being here today?'

The woman considered for a moment. 'About the same as I felt all the other times.'

'How was that?'

'Proud to do my duty, sad to have to sit in judgment on a fellow human being.'

'And how many juries have you served on?'

'Four in my lifetime.'

'Do you remember what those cases were about?'

'Of course I do. It's not something you can forget so easily.'

'Tell us about them,' Tess invited.

'Let's see, one had to do with a young man accused of robbing a liquor store. There were three eyewitnesses – we had to convict him. Another was about a drunk driver who killed a little boy. I'm afraid we had to convict him, too. The third was about a man who was supposed to have plotted to kill his wife, but the prosecution didn't convince us he had done any such thing. And the fourth was about a woman who shot her ex-husband when he broke into her house. We acquitted her.'

'What do you think this trial is about?'

'I *know* what it's about,' Agnes McFaddan declared. 'It's been in all the newspapers and on every television channel for weeks now, hasn't it? Why, CNN devotes half an hour to it every single evening, it's that important. This trial is about rape.'

'And how do you feel about rape, Miss McFaddan?'

'I think it's a crime,' the prospective juror replied.

'And I rank it right up there next to murder and kidnapping.'

'And how do you feel about the defendant?'

A big smile broke out across Agnes McFaddan's face. 'I think he's a fine man, and a fine senator. I'm sure he'll make a fine President.'

'I don't think there are many here today who would disagree with you on that,' Tess conceded. 'But the question is, would you be able to put aside your high regard for him as a politician and vote to convict him of the crime of rape if the evidence presented was overwhelming?'

There was another pause as the elderly woman pondered her response. Then she looked straight into the ADA's eyes. 'It would make me sad,' she said, and sighed, 'but I guess I'd have to, now wouldn't I?'

'Thank you, Miss McFaddan,' Tess said with a flash of white teeth. 'I have nothing more.'

She turned to sit down and was delighted to find Lamar sprawled in the chair next to hers. On the table in front of her was a folded piece of paper with the word 'aye' scrawled across it.

The bald, stocky man in the creaky wing-tip shoes was named Andrew Cardigan. He was one of an emerging breed of analysts whose advice on jury selection was being taken very seriously by defendants able to afford the high price tag.

He sat to the left of Robert Willmont, with his own stack of profiles in front of him, and continually passed notes across the senator to Hal Sutton and his assistants. In addition, two of Cardigan's associates were stationed in the spectator section of the small courtroom, monitoring the responses of the jury pool and keeping constant, muffled radio contact with Cardigan by means of transmitters on their lapels and tiny receivers in their ears.

'How long have you lived in San Francisco, Mrs. DeMaio?' Hal Sutton asked a twenty-three-year-old newlywed.

'All my life,' the young woman replied. 'The only move I ever made was when I got married. Then I went from my father's house in the Sunset District to me and my husband's place on Potrero Hill.'

'Do you know much about this case?'

She shrugged. 'Only what's been on the news.'

'Have you formed an opinion, as a result of what you've seen on the news, about the guilt or innocence of my client?'

'No.'

Andrew Cardigan slipped an urgent note down the table to Sutton's black assistant, who glanced at it and then audibly cleared his throat. Sutton turned around and took the note, read it, stared for a moment at Cardigan, then turned back to the young woman.

'Let me rephrase. Have you formed an opinion, based on anything at all, about the guilt or innocence of my client?'

'Look,' she replied. 'Two years ago, my baby sister was raped on her way home from school. He came up to her as nice as you please, telling her she reminded him of his own little girl, and then he dragged her into Sigmund Stern Grove and raped her. She was eleven years old, for God's sake. So, as far as I'm concerned, if a woman says a man raped her, he raped her.'

'Did you vote in the primary on Tuesday, Mr. Hiltz?' Tess asked a gangly garage mechanic in his thirties.

'Sure did,' the man replied.

'Mind telling us who you voted for?'

'Sure don't. Voted for the senator over there and proud of it.'

'Why?'

'Because he's not like them other shysters that make big promises just so's they can get themselves elected and then conveniently forget them the very next day. He may be rich, but he knows how to speak for the workin' slobs like me.'

'And what do you think of the crime the defendant is charged with having committed?'

'Crime? What crime?' Hiltz asked. 'I don't see as it's a crime to give a dame what she's askin' for.'

'Are you a feminist, Miss Chu?' Sutton inquired of a pretty young dental hygienist.

'If you're asking me whether I believe that men and women are equal, yes, I do. Even though my family comes from a country that doesn't yet comprehend that, my father always treated my mother with great respect.'

'Do you think adultery is a crime?'

Elaine Chu though for a moment. 'A moral crime, yes, but I wouldn't know about it being a legal one.'

'Would you be more likely to convict a man of rape if you knew he had committed adultery?'

'I wouldn't convict a man of rape,' the dental hygienist replied, 'unless I was convinced he had raped.'

'Do you believe that a woman has the right to say no to a man, Mr. Barstow?' Tess asked a forty-two-year-old computer software salesman wearing a polka-dot tie.

'Yes and no,' he replied. 'If she says it right up front, yes, absolutely, and a man ought to respect that. But if she leads him on, teasing him and getting him all excited and everything, and then up and thumbs her nose at him, well, I'm not so sure that's right, either.'

'Would you be able to listen to the evidence presented with an open mind?'

'I think so.'

'And do you think, after hearing all the evidence, you would be able to render an impartial verdict in this case?'

'Yes, I would,' Brian Barstow said.

'For a while there, I didn't think you were going to make it,' Tess said to her investigator over hamburgers in the Flower Market Café shortly after noon.

'I may be on to something,' Lamar told her.

She stopped in mid-bite.

'Something usable?'

'Don't know yet,' he said. 'Got some more digging to do.'

'I can go it alone if you need the time,' she offered.

He shrugged. 'I have a meet set up but it's not until later. I'll stick.'

'How are we doing?' Robert asked his team at the end of the day.

'I think we're doing great,' Cardigan said. 'Those people love you. For the life of me, I can't understand why the DA didn't ask for a change of venue.'

'Tess Escalante is smart,' Sutton replied. 'She wants everyone to believe that her case is so strong she can beat us right here in the senator's backyard.'

'Is it?' Robert asked.

'Let's not kid ourselves,' Sutton said. 'If we can't find some kind of motive in this, her case is going to come across as pretty damn convincing.'

Robert turned to Mary Catherine.

The administrative assistant sighed. 'I'm sorry. The detective agency I hired is top drawer all the way, strictly ex-FBI. They've got over a hundred people out there digging, but so far they haven't turned up a thing.'

'Why don't you tell them they don't get paid if they don't get results?' Robert snapped in frustration.

'What *do* we know about her?' Randy asked.

Mary Catherine opened a pitifully thin folder. 'She's fifty years old. She was born and raised in Great Neck, Long Island, New York. Her father's a retired dentist, her mother's a housewife. The parents moved to Florida seven years ago. There's one sister who lives in Boston, the husband is an attorney, they have two children.'

'Anything there?' Robert asked.

'No. He's an estate planner, no particular political affiliation.'

'Go on.'

'She went to college, didn't graduate. On the fringe of the counterculture back in the late 1960s, early 1970s. Hung with a group of anti-war, popular-cause types. Held a series of nondescript jobs. Managed a posh Manhattan art gallery for a while. Married an architect in 1981, a widower with three children. Received some national recognition for a series of photographic essays on America.'

'What about her partner?'

Mary Catherine shook her head. 'The photographer is her sister-in-law. Nothing there.'

'Why didn't she graduate from college?' Randy asked.

The administrative assistant flipped through the pages. 'Let's see. I remember there was something about an accident. Yes, here it is. During her junior year, she was involved in some kind of accident and pretty badly injured. The hospital records are no longer available, lost or something, they said, but people who were there around that time seemed to remember it was an automobile accident. She spent several months in the hospital and then, apparently, she had a couple of years recuperating at home. Just decided not to go back to school after that, I guess.'

'No political ties?'

'None.'

'No mob connections?'

'None.'

'What about her history with men?'

'Other than an old college boyfriend in Maine who told our detective to go to hell – and her husband, of course – the agency hasn't been able to find a single solitary man who can so much as lay claim to having kissed her.'

'Where does that leave us?' Robert asked.

'With Snow White incarnate,' Randy said. 'But only if you believe in fairy tales.'

'Keep digging,' Robert instructed.

Jury selection took the better part of two weeks. In the end, the prosecution and the defense were able to agree on five men and seven women, Agnes McFaddan, Elaine Chu, and Brian Barstow among them, and two female alternates, who would decide the fate of Robert Drayton Willmont. Both sides congratulated themselves. Both sides predicted success.

two

'How are you holding up?' Tess asked, a matter of hours after the jury was sworn in, the day before the trial was to begin. The ADA had arrived at the Doniger home in St. Francis Wood to find a swarm of reporters had taken up residence on the front lawn.

'I've been working on the new book as much as I can,' Karen replied, shutting the door quickly against the barrage of rude questions that followed Tess inside. 'It keeps my mind off things. I don't go out very much and I try not to watch television.'

It was barely a month before the convention, and Mariah Dobbs was making the most of every opportunity to portray Robert Willmont as a pilloried savior – although, granted, a savior with a slightly tarnished halo.

Each day, after court, the senator would stop on the steps of the Hall of Justice to tell the media how deeply sorry he was to have broken his marriage vows and, in so doing, allowed some vague and nameless villain to take advantage of his momentary weakness. Always by his side were his wife and his son and his mother.

'My boy is innocent of this vicious allegation,' Amanda Drayton Willmont would declare whenever anyone inquired. She was eighty-four now and palsied, but her voice was still strong and clear. 'If you ask me, this is all the work of people who are afraid of their fat pocketbooks if my Bobby is elected President.'

'I know the enormous stress my husband has been under,' Elizabeth Willmont said on a national morning talk show, looking lovely in pink. 'I know how difficult it can be for someone to resist temptation when he's pushed himself past the point of exhaustion. I've forgiven his transgression, and I hope the country can, too.'

In addition, much of the media – not an institution known for maintaining its neutrality one minute longer than was deemed absolutely necessary – had flocked to the side of the senator, screaming outrage and crying 'dirty tricks' in chorus with the majority of the public. Every night, it seemed, another prominent commentator was coming forth to proclaim the candidate and denounce the alleged victim.

'It's probably best that you don't watch,' Tess agreed.

Karen picked up the morning newspaper. 'Unfortunately,' she said with a sigh, 'I haven't stopped reading.'

The three-inch headline read: 'Volunteer Accuses Senator of Rape – Trial Begins Tomorrow.' The accompanying article contained just about everything but her weight and bra size.

'I'm sorry about that,' Tess apologized, 'and about

the mob scene out front. But I assure you, the leak didn't come from our office.'

'I know that,' Karen replied, recalling the personnel files that were kept at the Willmont campaign headquarters. 'It was bound to get out, sooner or later. Actually, I'm surprised they waited as long as they did.'

The stunned, skeptical, supportive telephone calls had begun well before seven o'clock California time.

Laura called from Boston. 'It was all over the news this morning,' she confirmed. 'Your name and everything. I couldn't believe it. It's so weird, having them talk that way about my own sister. Is there anything I can do?'

'We've been following the story for weeks, of course,' Jill Hartman proclaimed from her summer home on Shelter Island, 'and we were all positive it was a political setup. We never dreamed it was you.'

'It's incomprehensible,' Arlene Minniken Slarsky, the Scarsdale psychologist, ex-Floridian, ex-roommate drawled. 'Let's face it – on the surface, Robert Willmont is an absolute dreamboat who could probably have any woman in the world he wants just by snapping his fingers. It makes you wonder why someone like that had to resort to rape.'

'A private detective came snooping around here, looking for dirt,' Peter Bauer told her. He had taken his father's company beyond every expectation and now sat at the forefront of computer electronics. He and his wife had five children and four grandchildren. 'I sent him packing.'

'Thank you for calling,' Karen said. 'It means a lot.'

'Look,' he added awkwardly, 'I have three daughters. Each in her own special way has helped me realize how badly I behaved back then. I know I can't ever make it up to you, but if there's anything I can do, please, let me know.'

'Why did they have to say it was you?' Gwen exclaimed indignantly the moment the twins had gone down for their naps. 'They had no right to say it was you right out in the open like that.'

'I guess they thought they did,' her stepmother sighed.

'I'll be there tonight,' Jessica declared during a coffee break from her summer job as a hematology intern at a Denver hospital. 'I've got everything all arranged, so don't argue.'

'Are you sure you don't want me to come out?' Nancy pressed. 'I can at least answer the telephone and the door and keep the press off your back.'

'We're with you, dear,' Ione assured her.

'Hang in there, girl,' Demelza instructed.

Then the call came from Palm Beach.

'Are you satisfied now?' Beverly Kern demanded. 'Your father's had a heart attack.'

Leo had had two small coronaries in the past five years. The doctors recommended bypass surgery, but the seventy-eight-year-old retired dentist didn't trust their judgment. He was trying, instead, to get his wife to cut cholesterol out of their diet.

'How is he?' Karen asked.

'Well, I suppose he'll live,' her mother conceded, 'no thanks to you.'

'Tell him I'm pulling for him.'

'Why are you doing this?' Beverly moaned. 'At your age, for heaven's sake, you should know better. You were always a good girl. How could you even think of doing such a dreadful thing to us?'

'I'm not doing anything to you, Mother,' Karen replied. 'I'm doing what I have to do for me.'

'But what will people say?'

'Is that really what's most important – what the neighbors will think?'

'You may not realize it, but we live in a very small community down here,' Beverly said. 'I can't go anywhere without meeting someone I know. The phone's been ringing off the hook all morning.'

'About me?'

'Well, they ask about your father, of course, but I know that's not why they're *really* calling.'

'Give Daddy my love.'

'You're ruining this family and that's all you have to say?'

'Tell him I'll call him soon.'

The line went dead.

'She was just upset,' Ted said reassuringly. 'She was probably worried about your father.'

'Don't make excuses for her,' Karen replied as she hung up the phone. 'She's been that way her whole life.'

'Everyone's been really terrific,' she murmured now as she poured a cup of tea for Tess. 'Well, almost everyone.'

The two women were seated at the table in the

breakfast room, at the back of the house, away from prying eyes.

'Don't let it get you down,' the seasoned ADA told her. 'We've still got a long way to go.'

'What about the jury?'

'About average, I'd say. One Asian, two blacks, two Hispanics, two Jews, one born-again Christian, one Irish Catholic, two WASPs and an atheist. Four Republicans, eight Democrats, and they're split right down the middle as far as blue collar/white collar. I think it's a good enough mix not to make for bias on either side.'

'So then,' Karen said with a big sigh, 'tomorrow's the day.'

'Not to worry,' the ADA replied. 'We have a strong case.'

'I just hope I don't let you down,' Karen murmured.

Tess smiled in spite of herself. Oddly matched though they were, the two had become close. It amused the ADA that Karen had begun their relationship by fearing the system would let her down, and now she worried that she might fail the system.

'If you tell it like you told it to Lamar and to me,' Tess reassured her, 'you'll do just fine.'

Karen sighed and her gaze slid out the window. Ted had taken the afternoon off and he and Amy were out working in the garden, a small walled space at the back of the house, protected by a locked gate from the prying eyes and insensitivity of the press.

'Have you ever been married, Tess?' she asked.

'Once,' the ADA replied, 'for about forty-eight hours.'

'*Two days?*'

Tess half-shrugged. 'It was a long time ago.'

'How long?'

The attorney sighed. 'We met in college. It was one of those cases of instant magic. You know, bells ringing, feet never touching the ground. His name was Eddie – Edward Parker Hilliard. I was there on full scholarship. He was there on full parentship. For three years, neither of us dated anybody else, and the day after graduation, we eloped. It was foolish, I suppose, but so romantic. We dreamed of having a little apartment and going to law school together. Then we came back and told our parents the glorious news.'

Karen listened intently. Other than an occasional story about her family's stoop-labor life, Tess never talked about her past.

'My parents were thrilled,' she went on. 'They really liked Eddie. But the Hilliards – well, that was a different story. They were furious. You see, they had no intention of allowing their son to contaminate the bloodline. They tried to buy me off, but I wouldn't hear of it. Next they tried to buy my father off, with more money than he would earn in his entire lifetime. To his credit, he told them to go to hell. Then they threatened to pull strings and have my scholarship to law school revoked, and finally, they swore they would disinherit Eddie and see to it that he never went to law school, either.'

Here, she paused for a chuckle, but it held no humor. 'I was feisty even back then. I said we didn't need their dirty money, that we loved each other and we could make it on our own. But I guess Eddie wanted to be a rich lawyer more than he wanted to be a poor husband. Anyway, the next day, his parents began the annulment process and I never saw him again. End of story.'

'And since?'

Tess tossed her head. 'Too busy to look, I guess.'

'I was almost forty when I married,' Karen reflected. 'I liked my husband but I wasn't in love with him. He just happened to be the one who was there when I realized it would probably be my last chance. We had a pretty bad time of it, you know, a lot of conflicting expectations, but now – now I don't know what I'd do without him.'

Tess leaned forward and pressed Karen's hand.

'It's going to be okay,' she promised.

The doorbell at St. Francis Wood rang at eight o'clock that evening. Karen was in the kitchen with Amy and Jessica, finishing up the dinner dishes. She heard Ted open the door and then there was a flurry of muffled conversation before the door slammed shut. Drying her hands, Karen started out of the kitchen and bumped into Ted coming to get her.

'There are some people who'd like to say a few words to you,' he said, unable to conceal the big grin on his face. 'I didn't think you'd mind.'

Ever since the press had descended on them, Ted had been her shield, letting no one but Tess, Lamar, and the Shaffers through the door. Curious, Karen took several steps past him and looked down the hall.

'Hi, kiddo,' Mitch Rankin greeted her. He was still a bear of a man at fifty-nine. 'If we'd known how popular this address was, we'd have come a lot sooner.'

'Now don't be upset with us, dear,' Ione urged, a gray Peter Pan at fifty-eight. 'We just had to come.'

'We figured you could use some friendly faces out

here in West Hostile,' Demelza added. At sixty-nine, her once thick black hair was now thin and white and she kidded about how it had taken the ravages of colon cancer to trim her figure down to gaunt.

'The truth is,' Jenna said, her arm linked in John's, 'we needed a vacation.' Jenna had kept her carrot-colored hair and her baby fat, even into her forties, and John looked even more like Sherlock Holmes now that his face was creased from half a century of living.

'I think it's nothing short of amazing that it never occurred to me to come to California before this,' Felicity declared, still straight as a stick at fifty-two, still the dancer.

'We're already camped out at Campton Place and we're staying for the duration,' Mitch concluded, referring to one of San Francisco's finest hotels. 'And we won't hear another word about it.'

Ted came up behind Karen and squeezed her shoulders. 'I think they mean it,' he whispered.

The pillars of her shaky past, she thought, the stalwart Sullivan Street set, who had always been there to defend her, protect her and support her, were still lining up behind her without question, without judgment. Tears crowded her eyes.

'I'm so glad you're here,' she cried.

'We have it all planned,' Ione told her as they settled themselves on the pale-green sofas that faced each other across the living room. 'We're going to court every day and do our best to remember everything that happens. That way, when you put together what each of us saw and heard, we're bound to come up with a pretty complete picture.'

'Not necessarily objective, mind you,' Demelza conceded, 'but complete.'

'Then, after court, you'll all come here for dinner,' Karen announced, glancing at Ted for confirmation. 'It won't be too much work and it'll give me something to do.'

'Amy and I will make sure it's not too much for her,' Jessica put in. 'She won't let us go to court.'

'Certainly not,' Karen retorted. 'I won't have you being hounded by the media any more than you already are.'

The doorbell rang again at nine-fifteen.

'Now, don't say a word,' Nancy Yanow ordered, pushing her way past the tactless mob of reporters and shutting the door firmly in their faces. 'So I'm a month early – you won't even know I'm here. I can bunk in the sunporch or on the sofa or anywhere there's a horizontal space, and I'm not leaving. If you think for a moment I'd go back out there, you're crazy.'

Karen hugged her sister-in-law and closest friend, who had grown even rounder with the passing of time.

'As long as you brought your camera,' she said, 'it won't be a total loss.'

'Of course I did.' Nancy grinned, her asymmetrical eyes twinkling. 'You didn't think I'd come all this way just for you, did you?'

Ted disappeared into the kitchen, returning with a tray of glasses and two bottles of champagne.

'I was saving this for after the verdict,' he said. 'But I think we should drink it now.' He popped the corks and poured. When everyone had a glass, he raised his own. 'To justice,' he said.

'To justice,' everyone else echoed. 'To convicting the bastard.'

'Yes, indeed,' Karen murmured, taking a small sip. 'To justice.'

* * *

The clock ticked past midnight. There was little more the defense could do. They had spent a thousand hours and hundreds of thousands of dollars trying to find the answer, but no answer had been found, and they had run out of time.

The senator sat at his desk in a pool of lamplight, spinning a paper clip on the end of a pencil. Randy was slouched in a chair across from him. The campaign offices were dark and silent.

'Feels like a funeral in here,' Robert observed wryly.

'Oh, I wouldn't dig the grave just yet,' Randy said buoyantly.

'I'm not.' The senator chuckled. 'I just figured everyone else was.'

'Not quite,' Mary Catherine said from the doorway. She was holding three glasses and a bottle of champagne.

'What's that for?' Robert asked.

'Two months ago, if you'd asked me,' she replied, 'I'd have said that not only the campaign but your whole political career was over. But I must have been reading from the wrong script because, despite this whole mess, here you are, with practically the whole country rallying behind you, one step away from the nomination. All that's standing between you and the White House is an acquittal.'

What a fickle world it was, Robert mused. Not that long ago, a politician had been crucified for a harmless little peccadillo in Bimini, and now here *he* was – being forgiven. He wanted to believe it was because he was a more important person, but he knew it had more to do with the sorry state of the nation.

'And if the voters believe you're telling the truth,'

the administrative assistant added, 'why shouldn't the jury?'

'She's got a point,' observed Randy. 'Even though we couldn't find a plausible reason for the woman to cry rape, it's still all going to come down to her word against yours.'

'That's right,' Mary Catherine confirmed. 'And you can bet the prosecution will have a pretty hard time trying to convince anyone that a man like you would have to use force.'

'Then let's drink to an acquittal,' Robert suggested.

Mary Catherine poured the champagne and the three of them raised their glasses, the click of touching rims echoing through the silent suite of offices.

'To the acquittal,' they toasted.

Lamar Pope did some of his best thinking just before dawn. He rarely slept more than four hours a night anyway, and even then his restless dreams were filled with images of Darcy, his bright, beautiful little girl.

He had never stopped blaming himself for her death. Because back then, being a cop was his life, all he thought about, all he needed. Being a father had come a distant second. Even after his wife died, leaving him alone with a twelve-year-old he hardly knew, it didn't change anything. He always meant to spend more time with her, get to know her better, but somehow the weeks, months, years slipped by and he kept putting it off. Until it was too late.

Then he learned about her after she was gone, from other people who had taken the time to know her and make a place for her in their lives.

'She was an angel,' they said. 'We were blessed to have known her.'

'She loved you so much and was so proud of you,' they told him. 'And she always knew you were there, looking out for her.'

But he hadn't been. Instead, he had been out looking for some sleazy stool pigeon the night she was raped and beaten to death.

He spent the weeks after the funeral stumbling around in a drunken stupor, knowing that, if she had meant little to him when she was alive, she meant everything to him now that she was dead. Around the time he sobered up, the punk who had brutalized her walked.

'The motherfucker has an airtight alibi,' the homicide detective who handled the case told him. 'Of course we know it's bogus, but we can't break it.'

Lamar nodded calmly. 'Mind if I take a look at some of the files?'

'Shit, no,' the detective said. 'If it was my kid that had been offed like that, I'd sure want a peek.'

The files told Lamar that the punk was a rich college kid, a football jock, and that his team had lost a crucial game the evening Darcy was murdered. The alibi had come from several of the punk's teammates, who swore he had been with them the whole night.

Lamar put the files away. Then he began to probe. It didn't take him long to learn that the punk had been involved in three other incidents – one in El Paso, one in Lubbock, and one in Abilene – over the past two years. None of them had resulted in anything as compelling as a death, but each time the punk had been arrested and then released, either because the charges were mysteriously dropped or because he was provided with an airtight alibi by his friends.

Darcy's father began to watch and wait. He was in no

hurry, he knew his opportunity would come. It took seven months, but sure enough, the punk made his last mistake.

On a spring night, in the middle of final exams, the football jock took another high school girl for a ride into the desert west of Amarillo – another high school girl who was too drunk or too naive to know what he had in mind.

Lamar heard her screaming as he braked to a stop behind the red Corvette. He was out of his car in less than three seconds, his gun already in his hand and aimed at the punk's head. He never thought twice, he just pulled the trigger.

The girl was too frightened and too grateful to wonder how Lamar happened to be there. She just clung to him and sobbed. He wrapped her in a blanket and drove her home. Then he went down to the station to report the killing.

Once the girl told her story, he was exonerated of any wrongdoing. No one seemed to care why he was in the middle of the desert in the middle of the night. They were only grateful that he was. He even became a bit of a local hero.

Amarillo had been good to Lamar for more than forty years. He could have stayed, but he left. Too many memories of too big a failure made him pack and go. He never remarried. He knew he had nothing to give a woman. And although it was clear to him that he could never be anything but a cop, he intended to be a different kind of cop.

For the twenty years since Darcy's death, Lamar had concentrated on putting puzzles together, special kinds of puzzles having to do with only one kind of crime, until there was no one better at it.

Now, as the hands on his wristwatch inched toward six, he stared one last time at the scribbled notes in front of him. Page after page, hiding a hint here, offering him a clue there. He had crisscrossed the country three times in the past six weeks, digging, probing – doing what he did best. Finally, it had come down to two sheets of paper, one culled from a report filed by a deceased New York police investigator named Michael Haller, the other scribbled during a reluctant conversation with a Dr. Stanley Waschkowski from New Hampshire. Lamar placed the two sheets side by side on his kitchen table and sat there looking from one to the other.

'I'll be damned,' he muttered slowly.

He knew the defense would never figure it out. After all, they were investigating Karen Doniger, not Robert Willmont. He was the only one who was investigating them both. He also knew there was nothing he could do about what he had discovered. And he was honest enough to admit that there was probably nothing he *would* do, even if he could. It was enough just to know he *was* right. And he *was* right. He knew it inside – by the little click he always felt when the missing piece of a puzzle finally fell into place.

three

The inner third-floor corridor at the Hall of Justice was packed. Media representatives from every corner of the country milled around with literally hundreds of curiosity seekers who had been disappointed by the space limitations in the Glass Courtroom.

Under pressure, Judge Washington had agreed to a closed-circuit TV setup wired to an adjoining courtroom where the media overflow could follow the proceedings. The curiosity seekers were out of luck.

Tess Escalante and her staff assistant, a plain, spare woman with a photographic memory named Anne Jenks, made their way through the crowd.

'I knew this was going to be a circus,' the ADA yelled above the din. 'But I never expected anything like this.'

Lamar was waiting for them inside.

'I've got something interesting for you,' he announced. 'Unfortunately, it's FYI only. You can't use any of it.'

'Show me,' Tess said.

He pulled out a sheet of paper he had drafted less than an hour ago and handed it to her.

'It seems our senator may not be the human saint that he and his PR people would like the world to believe.'

'Where on earth did you get this?' she marveled as she scanned the page.

'Don't ask.'

Tess smiled briefly. It was his standard response. She stared at his scrawled notes. She was the only ADA in the department who could decipher his handwriting.

'His father paid off the one in college?'

'Yes,' Lamar confirmed. 'She agreed to talk to me, but only in private. She's married now, with a family, and she won't come forward.'

'And this one?'

'I had a hunch.' Actually, he had researched every sex or seemingly sex-related crime in the city of San Francisco for the past thirty years. 'I was able to track down two of her old neighbors. They said he was a regular visitor, three or four nights a week. She used to tell everyone she and her Bobby were going to get married. The neighbors said they would have gone to the police when she died, but they were told it was a suicide. Besides, they didn't believe for a moment that such a nice young man could have had anything to do with her death.'

'What about this reporter who went to jail?'

'She claims she was framed because she had secretly taken some pictures of them together. Of course, I've only got her word for it, but part of her story checks out – her apartment *was* broken into the week before she was arrested and nothing of any value was taken. I talked to the D.C. police, and they confirmed that it was an anonymous tip that led to her arrest on drug and prostitution charges.'

'The old anonymous tipster.'

'Yeah. She maintained that someone called and set up an interview for her in that particular hotel room, but she didn't know who the caller was. That, plus a known dealer who had also gotten a mysterious phone call and two kilos of crack the police found under the sofa pillows, put her away.'

The ADA chuckled. 'I bet she'd just love to testify.'

'Hell, yes, but it wouldn't help us. She says he certainly liked sex but she never said he raped her, so there's no relevance. The relationship she says she had with him is hearsay, and she's a convicted felon. He could deny everything and come out smelling like a rose. Not to mention that Sutton would cry foul before she ever opened her mouth.'

Tess knew her investigator very well. 'What have you got,' she asked, 'that isn't on here?'

'Well, there was something about an assault when he was in law school,' Lamar replied casually, reflecting on those last two pieces of paper he had studied so late into the night. 'But our boy flatly denied culpability and no charges were ever filed.'

'Another payoff?'

'Who knows?'

'So, what do you think we're dealing with here, an innocent bystander or a slimy bastard?'

Lamar looked around the almost full courtroom. 'Rumor has it he's been doing a certain TV journalist on and off for the past ten years. Left side, second row, aisle seat.'

Tess glanced at the attractive brown-eyed blonde with the highly recognizable face and sighed. 'We won't get any help there, for sure.'

'You'll just have to rely on the strength of your case,' Lamar said, 'and trust in the jury's better instincts.'

'I always do,' Tess agreed, slipping the sheet of paper into her briefcase. 'Still, I wouldn't have minded a slight edge. After all, it's his town, his people, his whole damn country, and that doesn't exactly put the odds in our favor.'

'I'm sorry I couldn't get you more,' Lamar said.

'That's okay,' she told him with a toss of her shiny black hair and a twinkle in her dark eye. 'I'm at my best when I'm the underdog. It's just that I'm even better when I have an ace up my sleeve.'

Like some macabre wedding party, the family and friends of Robert Willmont gravitated to the left of the spectators' gallery, unofficially designated as the defense side, while Karen Doniger's supporters arranged themselves on the right.

Janice Evans sat in the second row, directly behind Elizabeth Willmont and Amanda Drayton Willmont. In front of them, through the bulletproof glass partition, she could see Robert sitting quietly among his impressive entourage of attorneys and advisers.

Her piece on his campaign, which was first yanked by the network and then hastily revised to reflect recent events, had aired a month ago.

'Get on out there and do a follow-up,' her producer told her. 'Your segment pulled a bigger share than the fucking Super Bowl. So, whichever way the trial goes, we're bound to top our time slot.'

'I'm sure he'll appreciate all your care and concern,' Janice observed wryly.

The producer shrugged carelessly. 'To the extent that he's salable, I care a whole lot.'

'You know this is clearly a case of political sabotage,' the reporter insisted. 'Forged letters are passé – sex is the weapon of the 1990s.'

'If you're right,' the producer said, 'you'll be able to name your price in this industry.'

Janice was on a plane to San Francisco two days later.

Now, as she studied the faces of the twelve jurors and two alternates that filed into the courtroom and took their seats, she wondered if it were possible that they might find him guilty, might actually believe the ridiculous lies of some frustrated, rejected, middle-aged woman? They looked so pompous sitting there, puffed up like peacocks with their own importance. Janice wondered what they were thinking, indeed whether they were thinking at all. She wished she could have five minutes with them to set them straight.

'Can't you see what's happening here?' she would shout. 'Can't you see there are evil forces at work, determined to keep him out of the White House at any cost? Look at him! Isn't it obvious that he doesn't need to assault used-up old women when he's got vibrant young ones lined up for the privilege of being fucked?'

She smiled to herself. Perhaps the last part wasn't exactly appropriate. Especially after all the efforts of Smoeller and Dobbs to promote Robert as a devoted family man. It was ironic, mused Janice, when those in the know knew that he probably made it with every halfway decent-looking woman under the age of forty who crossed his path.

Take the prosecutor, for example. That was one he wouldn't miss were circumstances otherwise. She was a knockout in an Hispanic sort of way, and she knew how to dress. Her slim burgundy suit with matching pumps breathed competence and confidence, and the thin gold chain around her neck added exactly the right touch of femininity.

Power dressing, as it had come to be called, was something the New York newswoman knew a great deal about, and with a sinking heart she realized that an attorney who was sharp enough to wear an outfit like that into court was probably sharp enough to destroy Robert Willmont.

Across the aisle, Felicity Gravois was studying the twelve faces just as intently as Janice Evans.

'They look pretty ordinary,' she remarked to Demelza.

'Most people do,' the Demion Five co-owner commented.

'But are they bright enough to know the truth when they hear it, and not be taken in by the rich and famous?'

'I certainly hope so.'

'Do you really think there's a jury in this city that would convict him?' Mitch Rankin asked his wife.

'Look at the prosecutor,' Ione replied. 'The one in the smashing burgundy suit. I'd say she knows what she's doing.'

'Maybe,' Mitch cautioned. 'But the defense attorney doesn't look like any slouch either.'

Ione's response went unspoken because the bailiff stepped forward at that moment to make his speech, those present scraped to their feet, and the Honorable Oliver Wendell Washington, in his flowing black robes, swept into court and took his seat on the bench.

It was one minute past nine o'clock on Thursday, June 18. The trial of *The People of the State of California* v. *Robert Drayton Willmont* had begun.

'I will remind the gallery that there are to be no outbursts or demonstrations of any kind,' Judge Washington intoned from his side of the bulletproof wall. 'You are guests of the court and as such can be removed at the whim of the court. I will also remind everyone – members of the media, in particular – that guests of the court are prohibited from taking photographs during these proceedings or using any kind of recording devices.'

There was a general shifting in the gallery as everyone glanced around at everyone else and then settled down. Judge Washington clasped his hands in front of him and nodded to the prosecutor.

Tess pushed back her chair and stood up.

'Good morning, ladies and gentlemen,' she addressed the jury. 'My name is Teresa Maria Yacinta Escalante, and I represent the People of the state of California.'

Her voice was melodious and clear and carried easily to every corner of the room.

'That's why this case is called *The People versus Robert Drayton Willmont*. When a crime has been committed, it is up to those who represent the People to collect every possible scrap of evidence, examine even the most minute detail, and analyze every available piece of information to determine who may have perpetrated that crime. Only after we have done all that to the best of our ability do we come here, to a court of law, to ask a select group such as you to tell us how well we've done our job.'

She stepped out from behind the table.

'There was a time, not all that long ago, when the courts of our country refused to recognize such a thing as rape. When people actually believed that if a man took advantage of a woman it was because he either had some preordained right, or because she had asked for it. Thank God that time is past. Thank God our courts are now willing to prosecute those who rape, and thank God there are juries brave enough to convict them. Because there are few crimes in this world as heinous as rape, and fewer still as heinous as acquaintance rape.'

The ADA walked slowly toward the jury box.

'It's one thing, ladies and gentlemen, for a woman to be pulled into a dark alley and assaulted by a total stranger. We can get our minds around that. We can say he was a maniac and she was an innocent – and that makes the crime clearly definable and the circumstances acceptable to most of us. But it's something quite different to be assaulted by someone you know, perhaps even admire, but certainly trust – to put yourself innocently into the hands of such a person and then to be betrayed in such a vicious and violating manner.'

Tess glanced casually toward the defense table.

'That's the distinction that the courts don't always make. That there is more than one kind of rape, and that each must be viewed and evaluated separately. That's the distinction that you are going to be asked to make here. It is the People's position that just because a woman goes to a bar with a man she knows – sits and drinks with him and even agrees to let him drive her home – does not mean she has agreed to have sexual intercourse with him.'

She looked directly into the eyes of each of the jurors.

'There have been some celebrated trials concerning this very issue recently, with juries who, comfortable or not, dutifully considered the facts and delivered their verdicts. Now, it's your turn. There are no eyewitnesses here, as there rarely are in such circumstances, and so the People's case will come down to two things: credibility and evidence. Whose story will you believe, and what proof will sway you?'

The ADA nodded slowly.

'I think the credibility of the victim will be obvious. And the evidence will show, beyond a reasonable doubt – no, beyond a shadow of a doubt – that Robert Drayton Willmont raped and beat Karen Doniger on the night of April seventh and then left her, like so much garbage, in the middle of Golden Gate Park. It doesn't matter who his family might be or what high office he seeks. All that matters is that he did it. *He did it*. And if those of us who represent the People weren't absolutely sure of that, we wouldn't be here today.'

With a small nod, Tess walked back to the prosecution table and sat down.

'Way to go,' murmured Mitch on the right side of the gallery.

'Shit,' Janice Evans mumbled on the left.

Judge Washington gestured to the defense and Hal Sutton rose to his feet.

'My name is Hal Sutton,' the Silver Fox began. 'But that's not very important. What's important is that I am the attorney who represents Senator Robert Drayton Willmont. In fact, that's all that's important here.'

He glanced over at Tess.

'The assistant district attorney says it doesn't matter who my client is, or what high office he seeks,' he went on. 'I say that's exactly what matters. In fact, that's what this case is all about. And it's one of the oldest stories in history. Let a man be brave enough to stand up and say: "Come with me, I know the way," and immediately there are those, too frightened or greedy to follow, who must plot to destroy him. Two thousand years ago, such a man died on the cross.'

'Wonderful,' Demelza muttered under her breath. 'So now we've got Jesus Christ Willmont on trial here.'

'Ladies and gentlemen,' Sutton continued smoothly, 'if you understand anything at all about this proceeding, you must understand that, were Robert Drayton Willmont not exactly who he is, were he not running for the highest office in the land, there would be no cry of rape here, there would be no trial, there would be no slander to this honest and decent and hard-working man who has spent the last fourteen years of his life in the service of his country.'

He put his hand on Robert's shoulder.

'Yes, my client admits to having sex with Karen Doniger. He is, alas, not God, merely one of His imperfect sons. But the fact is, it was *she* who encouraged *him*, *she* who seduced *him*, *she* who took advantage of *him* – morally weakened as he was by stress, fatigue, and Scotch – not the other way around. And then, surprise of surprises, she cries rape. What does that say to you, members of the jury? What does that suggest about the frightened and the greedy?'

He paused for a moment to let his words sink in.

'Senator Robert Drayton Willmont is a devoted son, a devoted husband and a devoted father,' he went on. 'His family sits in this courtroom today as testimony to that. And he has been a devoted public servant, too. His election and reelection to both the Congress and the Senate, and his overwhelming victories in this year's presidential primaries are testimony to that. Does it seem plausible that such a man, on the brink of his greatest achievement, would risk it all on a momentary exercise?'

He pressed Robert's shoulder lightly and the defendant got to his feet.

'Take a good look at him, ladies and gentlemen. A son of one of San Francisco's founding families, a true beacon of hope in our country's time of crisis, a man of wealth and stature and intelligence and charisma, who has chosen to dedicate his life to his country. Is this a man who would have to resort to rape?'

He held his client motionless for a full fifteen seconds before allowing him to retake his seat.

'The evidence to which the assistant district attorney refers,' Sutton concluded, 'will indeed show that Senator Willmont and Karen Doniger were intimate. That they had a few drinks together at a downtown bar and then drove to Golden Gate Park, where they got out of the senator's car and engaged in sexual intercourse. My client does not and has never denied that. But it's a far cry from consensual copulation to rape. And that, despite what the prosecution will attempt to make you believe, my client did not do.'

'Right on,' murmured Janice Evans on the left side of the gallery.

Across the aisle, John Micheloni shifted uneasily in his seat. 'He's damn good,' he muttered to Jenna.

four

Tess took a sip of cold coffee and stretched her aching back muscles, swearing for the umpteenth time that the city had better get her that posture-perfect chair she had been requesting for over a year now before her spine became permanently bent.

All in all, however, she had to admit that there was little to complain about. The first two days of the Willmont trial had gone well.

Arthur Gertz began the case for the prosecution and his testimony was every bit as effective as she had anticipated it would be. The precise, yet emotional recounting of his pre-dawn jog and his grim discovery at Stow Lake set a chilling scene that had enormous impact on the jury, an impact that Hal Sutton's brief cross-examination was unable to dissipate.

Next, Officer Kelly Takuda's dispassionate testimony had fixed two things in the jury's mind: that Karen Doniger had been found semi-conscious in

Golden Gate Park and that all indications were that she had been the victim of a brutal assault.

'Officer Takuda,' Sutton had inquired when Tess finished her direct examination, 'was it possible to tell from anything at the scene, or even from the condition of the woman herself, who initiated the sexual activity?'

'No, sir,' the witness responded. 'There was nothing to indicate how it began. All that was discernible was the result.'

'So it's entirely possible then,' Sutton pressed, 'that what you found at Stow Lake on the morning of April eighth was not the result of an assault, as you previously described, but the result of a consensual sexual act that might have been performed more, shall we say, exuberantly than most?'

The policewoman considered for a moment. 'Anything's possible, I guess – but it's not probable.'

'But is it possible?' Sutton drilled.

'I suppose so.'

'Thank you, Officer Takuda,' Sutton said resuming his seat. 'That's all.'

'Officer Takuda,' Tess said on redirect. 'How many incidents relating to sexual violence have you personally investigated in the past six months?'

'About forty,' Kelly replied.

'And last year?'

'Maybe a hundred, a hundred and ten.'

'Then based on your experience, having dealt with perhaps as many as a hundred and fifty such investigations in just the past eighteen months, when you reached Stow Lake on the morning of April eighth, was it your conclusion that the semiconscious woman you found there, bruised and bleeding, had participated in a consensual sexual encounter?'

'No, it was not,' the policewoman confirmed. 'My conclusion was then, and is now, that she was the victim of sexual assault and battery.'

'Just one more thing, Officer Takuda,' Tess concluded. 'Do you think it's possible – not probable, mind you, but possible – that the sky will fall tomorrow?'

'Objection!' shouted Hal Sutton.

'Miss Escalante,' Judge Washington admonished, 'you know better than that.'

'Withdrawn, Your Honor,' Tess conceded with a contrite smile. 'I have nothing more.'

The Rape Treatment Center nurse-examiner's testimony, detailing the procedures she used to collect the evidence and the precautions she took to keep the chain of custody intact, closed out the second day of the trial. She was a solid witness in the prosecution's case, confirming that everything she had observed during the course of her examination was totally consistent with forced sex. Sutton had been unable to dislodge her.

Now it was Friday night and tomorrow would begin the third day of the trial. While the court was not usually in session over the weekend, pressure by the defense for a speedy resolution had caused Judge Washington to adjust the schedule. Officially, he explained the Saturday session as an effort on the part of the court to have the proceedings concluded and the jury dismissed by the July 4th holiday.

Actually, Tess was pleased. She planned to put the police lab technician on the stand in the morning, and his testimony and cross-examination would probably last the entire day. Tess would have him go over each item, each piece of Karen's clothing, each grass stain and dirt smudge and blood smear and trace of semen. Next, she would have him detail his examination of Robert Willmont's clothing, the tear in his jacket, the split seam in the trousers, and whatever stains, smudges, smears and traces had been found on them. Finally, she would have him produce the highly technical, dreadfully boring but absolutely essential DNA evidence.

If all went well, the jury would retire to the Sheraton Hotel with two vital facts to mull over until Monday morning: first, the DNA unequivocally placed Robert Willmont's semen inside Karen Doniger's vagina and mouth; and, second, the condition of her clothing as well as the traces of blood in the vaginal smear clearly indicated that force had been used.

The ADA stretched again and stood up. Through her window, she could see a steady stream of headlights along the freeway, weekend traffic heading out of town. All those people with somewhere to go, she mused, unmindful that the biggest theatrical of the decade was being played out right here at home on the stage of the Glass Courtroom.

What had begun for her as a dubious duty had become a crusade. From a distance, Robert Willmont seemed a bright promise, but up close, he had lost much of his shine. There was something about the combination of humble contrition and angry indignation he portrayed to the outside world at every opportunity that rubbed Tess the wrong way and made her even more positive of his guilt.

'We're going into court with the strongest case I've seen in years,' she continued to assure Karen. 'And let me tell you that I've won verdicts with a great deal less.'

'I trust your judgment,' Karen said.

'What?' She chuckled. 'You've found new faith in the system?'

'I never doubted that the system works,' Karen corrected her. 'What I said was that there can be a big gap between the system working and justice being served.'

It was true more often than Tess liked to admit.

She remembered that now as she finished the last of her preparations for tomorrow's session, snapped off her desk lamp, closed the door of her office, and made her way down the third floor corridor toward the elevator. She had meant what she said about the case being strong, but she also understood the vagaries of a jury. No, understood wasn't the right word. She had never been able to understand juries, she had just learned how to work with them.

'You sound tired,' Mariah Dobbs said from the New York end of the telephone line on Sunday night.

'I guess I am,' Randy admitted from his studio apartment in the Marina district. 'And lonely.'

'You do understand why I can't be there with you, don't you?' she asked.

'Sure,' he sighed. 'You've got other clients who need you.'

'Exactly,' she agreed, although the real reason had more to do with distancing herself and her firm from Senator Willmont's unfortunate circumstance. 'There's really nothing more I can do for him at this point, anyway. It's in the hands of the jury now, and I have no way of influencing them. But if he's acquitted, you can count on my being around to launch a media bombardment that, come November, will dump him right at the door of 1600 Pennsylvania Avenue.'

'Two months ago, I wouldn't have given him an ice cube's chance in hell,' Randy admitted.

'Neither would I,' Mariah agreed, thinking that, despite the primary victories, she still wouldn't.

'It was your honesty gambit that saved him,' the aide told her. 'If he hadn't done the mea culpa bit right up front, and thrown himself on the mercy of the people, he'd be dead in his political grave by now.'

'The voters love him and they want to believe in him,' she conceded. 'So they're willing to give him the benefit of the doubt – until the jury comes in.'

'I sit in court and watch them,' Randy told her, 'and try to figure out what's going through their minds. I used to think it would take millions of people to decide whether we went to the White House or not, but now it's all come down to twelve – five men and seven women – who are going to make us or break us.'

Mariah chuckled. 'Interesting choice – the White House or the Big House. That's the fat and the lean of it, the up and the down, the yin and the yang.'

'Don't,' Randy groaned.

'How are things really going?' Mariah asked.

'Not great,' he admitted. 'The lab expert was on the stand yesterday. All the DNA stuff was very technical and dreadfully boring. I saw several of the jurors yawning, and it almost put me to sleep. But I've got to admit, the physical evidence is pretty damning.'

'What does the senator say about that?'

'He says he has no idea how any of it happened.'

'He'd better have more to say than that when he gets on the stand,' the public relations expert suggested. 'What does the lawyer think?'

'Hal keeps things pretty much close to the vest,'

Randy told her. 'If you press him, he says to wait until we have our shot, but between you and me, I think he's worried.'

'And the candidate?'

The aide paused. 'To be honest, I don't think he worries about anything,' he said. 'He just assumes that things will work out the way he wants them to.'

five

The surgical resident who treated Karen's injuries in the Emergency Room of San Francisco General Hospital was first to take the stand on Monday morning. He painstakingly detailed and categorized each of her bruises and abrasions, the number of stitches taken in her lip, the setting of her broken nose.

'Your Honor,' Tess said, 'I would like, at this time, to introduce People's exhibits sixty-six through seventy-two, and ask that they be presented to the jury.'

'I must renew my objection, Your Honor,' Hal Sutton exclaimed. 'The prosecutor has already elicited volumes about the physical condition of the alleged victim. The photographs add nothing new.'

'On the contrary, Your Honor,' Tess argued. 'Hearing about a broken nose or a split lip or a bruised thigh is not the same as actually seeing it.'

'The prosecutor knows full well, Your Honor, that

those photographs are deliberately inflammatory.'

'Mr. Sutton is correct, Your Honor,' Tess agreed, 'if you look at them from his client's perspective. But I want the jury to look at them from an objective point of view.'

'Objection!' Sutton stormed.

'That will do, Miss Escalante,' Judge Washington said. 'The photographs are admissible. Objections overruled.'

Tess handed the jury one picture at a time, presenting the entire group with an opportunity to take a good look. It pleased her to see most of the jurors wince.

'Now, Doctor,' she continued, when the last grisly image had been passed around, 'are the bruises you've described, the injuries shown in these photographs, the kind that you would expect to find from consensual intercourse?'

'No, Miss Escalante, they are not.'

'How would you describe them, then?' she pressed.

'I would describe them as being completely consistent with the use of force.'

'Thank you, Doctor.'

'Tell me, Doctor,' Hal Sutton asked. 'Is there any way to tell whether or not all of these bruises were inflicted by the defendant?'

'No, not specifically.'

'For example, isn't it entirely possible that the split lip or the broken nose might have been caused by bumping into a tree in the dark, or tripping and falling face down onto the pavement?'

'There was certainly no indication of that.'

'Could the injuries have been so caused, Doctor?'

'I suppose they could.'

'Thank you,' Sutton said. 'That's all.'

'Where is he going with that?' Anne Jenks whispered in Tess's ear.

'Wherever his limited options will take him,' Tess replied.

After the lunch break, Lamar Pope took the stand. He spent the balance of Monday and much of Tuesday detailing his interviews with both the alleged victim and the defendant, referring frequently to his notes.

From him, Tess elicited testimony relating to, among other things, the footprint found at the scene that matched the senator's loafer and the scratches on the senator's chest that matched the skin scrapings taken from under Karen Doniger's fingernails. Then the topic turned to Karen's missing handbag.

'As part of your investigation, Sergeant,' the ADA inquired, 'did you have reason to search the defendant's car on the afternoon of April tenth?'

'I did.'

'What, if anything, did you find?'

'I found a navy-blue handbag with identification and other items in it belonging to Karen Doniger.'

'Did the defendant offer any explanation for why the handbag was in his car and not with Karen Doniger?'

'No, he did not. He seemed surprised to see it there. Apparently, it had slipped between the seats and he hadn't noticed it.'

'Thank you,' Tess said. 'Nothing more.'

'Was Senator Willmont cooperative in your investigation, Sergeant Pope?' Sutton asked.

'Yes, he was.'

'Did he answer the questions you put to him to the best of his ability?'

'Yes, he did.'

'Did he decline to answer any of your questions?'

'No, he did not.'

'Did he deny having been with Karen Doniger on the night in question?'

'No, he did not.'

'Did he deny having sex with her?'

'No.'

'Now let's go back to those scratches for just a moment, Sergeant,' Sutton invited. 'Did Senator Willmont give you any explanation as to how he had gotten them other than you have already testified?'

'Yes,' Lamar replied, consulting his notes. 'He said they were the result of passion, not resistance.'

'Now, about the handbag.'

'Mr. Sutton,' Judge Washington interrupted, feeling a gastric attack coming on. 'It's already well into the afternoon. I know I'm tired of sitting and I can only assume that the jury is, too. If you are planning a lengthy cross-examination, and all indications seem to be that you are, may I give you every opportunity to complete it in the morning?'

'Certainly, Your Honor.'

'We're getting nowhere, aren't we?' Robert asked on the way back to Jackson Street.

'Evidence is just evidence.' Sutton shrugged. 'It's all in how it's interpreted. And you know as well as I do that it's never really interpreted until the very end.'

'But those photographs,' Robert groaned. 'I saw the shudder when the jury looked at them. They make me come off like I'm some kind of monster. Do you think they retouched them to make her look worse?'

'No, I don't think so.'

'Well, I don't remember her being that banged up. I may have gotten a little rough with her – hell, she asked for it. But I don't remember her looking anything like that.'

'The pictures certainly didn't help our cause,' Sutton agreed.

'At first, you know, I just assumed that no one with any common sense would buy her story,' Robert confided. 'I mean, who would believe that a United States senator running for President would deliberately go out and rape someone? But I was watching the faces of that jury today. Some of them looked like they wanted to lynch me.'

'Well, don't despair just yet,' Sutton said calmly. 'We haven't had our turn yet, you know.'

It was the same thing he always said. In the past, his words had been able to soothe Robert, but now they began to grate on him. Sutton was a longtime associate, but after all, what real difference would it make to him if he won or lost this case – he would still get his million-dollar fee, he would still be free to practice law, and he would even find a way to remove whatever tarnish might rub off on his spotless reputation.

The candidate sighed, knowing it was too late now to wonder whether he had been wise in his choice of attorney.

'Dr. Linderman,' Tess inquired on Wednesday afternoon, following the completion of Lamar's cross-examination and Azi Redfern's virtually unchallenged testimony, 'what is your primary work?'

'For the past three years,' Philip Linderman, the

respected Berkeley psychiatrist, replied, 'I've been involved in a research program dealing exclusively with the psychology of rape.'

'Will you please describe this program for the jury.'

'In the first part of it, we selected a random sample of four hundred and fifty convicted sex abusers and, through interviews, therapy sessions, and testing techniques that were formulated specifically for the program, we tried to develop a psychological profile that would help in the identification of potential rapists.'

'Would it be fair to say then that, as a result of your work in this program, you've become a recognized expert in this area?'

'Yes, I think it would be fair to say that. I have presented no less than half a dozen papers on the subject, both nationally and internationally, and I am a frequent contributor to the *American Journal of Psychiatry*.'

'Your Honor,' Sutton broke in. 'Defense is willing to stipulate to Dr. Linderman's credentials.'

'In that case, Doctor, tell us,' continued Tess, 'have you indeed developed the definitive psychological profile of a rapist?'

'Yes, and no,' he answered.

'Please explain,' the ADA invited.

'Well, we found we were unable to develop one basic profile because, as it turns out, there are several.'

'Several, Dr. Linderman?'

'Yes, Miss Escalante. One profile concerns what people generally think of when they hear the word 'rapist' – the total stranger who pulls a woman into a dark alley. There is another profile that deals with the domestic violator – the husband, the boyfriend, the father, the step-parent, the older brother. And a third profile concerns what we have in recent years come to call the acquaintance-rapist – the man who knows, and is known by, his victim – who already has a relationship of some sort with her, be they friends or neighbors or co-workers.'

'So what you're saying, Doctor, is that your research has determined that there are several distinct types of rapists who commit distinctly different types of rape.'

'That's correct,' Linderman confirmed. 'Even though the crimes have a violent orientation and lead to more or less the same conclusion, defining one in terms of another would be like trying to make applesauce out of oranges.'

'Will you please describe for the jury how the profiles you developed for the stranger-rapist and the acquaintance-rapist differ?'

'Certainly,' the psychiatrist replied. 'We determined that the stranger-rapist requires anonymity and his actions stem from deep-rooted anger, low self-esteem, and emotional impotence. He hates women, he sometimes hates the whole world, he certainly hates himself, although he frequently believes just the opposite. His purpose is to control his victim, to dominate and degrade her, as he feels dominated and degraded, and in the only way he can – sexually. For him, rape is not about sex, it's about violence and intimidation. It's about the release of his anger on someone who isn't strong enough to repel him, which represents a reenactment of some ongoing relationship of his own, where he is the weaker party. In other words, it's about the acting out of his unexpressed rage toward someone he *does* know on someone he *doesn't* know and, therefore, someone who is safe for him to attack. It makes him feel temporarily potent. But the feeling is short-lived and, like a narcotic, once it wears off, he must rape again to get it back.'

'Are there any patterns to this type of rapist?'

'Frequently. His victims, for example, may all look alike if he is deliberately choosing women who resemble the real object of his anger – his mother, a female employer, a girlfriend who rejected him. Even if they don't look alike however, there will usually be something that connects them – blond hair, a style of dress, a profession. Often, he may use the same ploy to find each of them, riding a specific bus, or shopping in a certain market. He will tend to use them the same way, make them do the same things, threaten them with the same weapon, or tie them up in the same fashion. He may say the same things, using the same or similar words. He may have one particular outfit that he wears every time he goes out to rape. He sees it as his protection; in a way, his suit of armor.'

'Nice guy,' Mitch murmured on the right side of the gallery.

'But not our guy,' Ione replied.

On her side of the aisle, Janice Evans turned to Randy, who was now sitting beside her. 'Where is the prosecutor going with this?' she whispered. 'None of it applies here.'

'I'm sure she has her reasons,' Randy replied dully.

'Now, Dr. Linderman,' Tess pursued, 'tell us about the acquaintance-rapist.'

Hal Sutton rose to his feet. 'Your Honor, while this is surely most enlightening, I fail to see the relevance.'

'Miss Escalante?' Washington queried.

'We believe it's essential to our case, Your Honor,' the ADA replied, 'that the jury be able to distinguish between one type of rape and another, and between one kind of rapist and another. One of the defense's primary thrusts has been to ask, "Why would someone like Senator Willmont need to resort to rape?" As though all women should just naturally fall at his feet simply because he's rich and attractive and politically powerful. I think I have every right to try to blow that theory out of the water.'

'Although that argument might better have been made during rebuttal, I'm inclined to allow it,' Washington said. 'Objection overruled.'

'Once again, Dr. Linderman,' Tess went on smoothly, bridging the interruption, 'will you describe for the jury the last profile you developed?'

'The acquaintance-rapist is a different breed,' the psychiatrist said. 'Unlike the stranger-rapist, he's not necessarily motivated by low self-esteem. He generally likes women, although he rarely respects them, and he may even go out of his way to be charming and attentive. He flirts and woos and convinces himself that any woman he singles out should be honored to accommodate him simply because of who he is. He wants the woman he rapes to know him, because he wants her to be impressed with his facade – his name, his looks, his background, his job, his home, his income and, by extension, his sexual prowess. He has two delusions: one is that all women find him irresistible; the other is that he's entitled to take whatever he wants. It's strictly a power play for him. We call it the "Me-Tarzan-You-Jane" syndrome. He pursues until she succumbs. But when he comes across a woman who doesn't succumb, he views his violation of her as just part of the game. He was raised on the concept that all women want to be taken – by force, if necessary.'

'Now *he* sounds familiar,' Demelza murmured under her breath.

'That's where she was going,' Randy muttered under his breath.

'Dr. Linderman,' Tess asked, 'are there any general parameters for this profile?'

'Some,' the psychiatrist replied. 'In our program, we found that the acquaintance-rapist tends to be more highly goal-oriented and professionally successful than the stranger-rapist. Like the stranger-rapist, he is usually the product of a dysfunctional family environment, but where the stranger-rapist is himself frequently the victim of incest or physical abuse, the acquaintance-rapist tends to be the victim of either parental overpampering or neglect. In a number of cases we studied, we found that the acquaintance-rapist had learned how to manipulate women at a very early age.'

'Is there any kind of discernible pattern to this type of rapist?'

'I call it more of an anti-pattern,' the psychiatrist replied. 'Where the stranger-rapist will plan ahead, and generally very carefully, the acquaintance-rapist rarely plans ahead. He is much more likely to be motivated by the moment and act on impulse. He might go to a party or a bar with the idea of finding someone to have sex with, but he doesn't set out to rape the woman. In macho terminology, he's going to hunt, pursue, and conquer.'

'Conquer?' Tess interjected. 'As in war?'

'Sexual dominance was once considered an acceptable form of victory in battle. There's a famous painting that depicts that attitude. It's called *The Rape of the Sabine Women*.'

'Victory in battle,' Tess echoed.

'Your Honor,' the Silver Fox protested. 'Is my client now being accused of ravaging an entire nation?'

'Point taken, Mr. Sutton,' Washington said. 'Miss Escalante, may we confine ourselves to the matter at hand?'

'Certainly, Your Honor,' the ADA conceded. 'So, Dr. Linderman,' she continued, turning her back to her witness, 'our typical acquaintance-rapist is super-macho, spoiled, fancies himself irresistible, and goes out looking to conquer?'

'That pretty much covers it. Of course, he doesn't necessarily go out on the prowl. He might be interested in someone who lives in his neighborhood or works in his office, and then he might simply wait for the right opportunity. Again, however, he would never consider what he intends as rape, because he assumes any woman would happily submit to his advances. It's only when she resists his attentions, when his manipulations fail, that the deep-rooted anger which motivates him flares up and he resorts to violence.'

'Gotcha!' Jenna breathed.

'Shit,' Randy sighed.

'The key to the acquaintance-rapist,' the psychiatrist summarized, 'is that he is generally attracted to the woman he ends up violating. What he can't accept is that *she* might not be attracted to *him*. Starting usually with his mother, women have always done his bidding, so he has every reason to expect this one will, too. If she resists, he tells himself she must be playing hard to get. In the end, it isn't that he intends to rape – it's that he's psychologically unable to accept rejection.'

'In your opinion, Dr. Linderman,' Tess concluded,

'and as an acknowledged expert, does anything in the profile you've described excuse the acquaintance-rapist's behavior?'

'Absolutely not. Once the woman says no, even if the man doesn't believe her, if he then forces her into compliance, he is guilty of sexual assault, Miss Escalante, no matter what he tries to tell himself, or anyone else.'

'Thank you, Doctor,' said Tess. 'I have no more questions.'

'Did I hear you correctly, sir?' Hal Sutton inquired. 'Did you say that, even though a man may sincerely believe he is participating in consensual sex, you believe he is guilty of rape?'

'If the woman resists, yes.'

'I assume that's a medical opinion, not a legal one, or are you also an attorney?'

'No, Mr. Sutton. I'm just a psychiatrist.'

'Well then, as just a psychiatrist, Dr. Linderman, how do you account for all the women we hear about who resist a man because they think they're supposed to, not because they really want to? Women who need to have men dominate them sexually in order to overcome what used to be considered a gross lapse in morality?'

'Thirty or forty years ago, perhaps, there might still have been women who reacted like that,' the psychiatrist conceded. 'Today, I doubt there are more than a handful.'

'But suppose we're talking about a woman who was raised back then, Doctor – say, a woman raised in the 1950s who still remembers the tenets of her upbringing?'

'Objection,' Tess called. 'Calls for speculation. How

can Dr. Linderman be expected to speak for women raised in the 1950s?'

'He's been accepted here as an expert on the psychology of rape, hasn't he?' Sutton argued. 'Did the prosecution mean to stipulate that his knowledge was restricted to one specific decade?'

'You're still asking him to be a mind reader,' Tess persisted.

'Hardly,' the Silver Fox responded silkily. 'I'm simply asking him to speak from the depths of his considerable experience.'

'Objection overruled,' Washington said. 'You may answer the question, Doctor.'

'I suppose such behavior patterns could continue up to the present,' the psychiatrist replied reluctantly.

'Thank you, Doctor. Now tell us, as part of your extensive research, have you worked at all with alleged victims of rape?'

'As a matter of fact, the second part of our study is devoted to victims, and we are currently working with a group of women whose attackers were both convicted and acquitted.'

'Let's talk specifically about those women in your study who exhibited significant injuries as a result of what they claimed were acquaintance-rape encounters, injuries not unlike those being represented in the case now before this court.'

'What about them?'

'Was one of those women named Marion Healy?'

'Objection, Your Honor,' Tess interrupted. 'Relevance. What does one particular research subject of Dr. Linderman's have to do with the matter at hand?'

'I assure the court that I will make the connection,' Sutton said smoothly.

'I'll allow it,' the judge declared.

Tess murmured something quickly to Anne Jenks in the seat beside her, but the staff assistant already had her eyes narrowed in concentration.

The Silver Fox turned his back to his quarry. 'Now, Doctor, I repeat, was one of your research subjects a woman by the name of Marion Healy?'

'Yes, I believe so.'

'And during the course of your interviews with her, what did you learn about the circumstances of her alleged rape?'

'How did you get access to my files?' snapped Linderman.

'I don't know that I had,' Sutton replied blandly. 'The case is a matter of public record. My staff may well have learned about Miss Healy from some other source. Again, Doctor, what did you learn?'

'She admitted that she had encouraged the man to have rough sex with her because that was the way she needed it, and that it was only when she saw how badly bruised she was, and after the man refused to pay for her medical bills, that she changed her mind and reported the incident as a rape.'

'Nevertheless, an innocent man was convicted and sent to jail, wasn't he, Doctor?' Sutton demanded.

'Your Honor!' Tess protested.

'Mr. Sutton!' Washington barked.

'May it please the court,' Sutton argued. 'This expert witness has been called to the stand to give us his learned opinions about rape. I think I have every right to ask him to present both sides of the story to the jury. Prosecution opened the door by referring to the research program, and by basing her witness's expertise in the field on it.'

The judge sighed. 'I think he may have you there, Miss Escalante.'

Tess shook her head in disgust.

Anne Jenks picked up a pen and began to scribble on a piece of paper.

'Again, Dr. Linderman,' Sutton pressed, 'Marion Healy, whose bruises described in court appear to be somewhat similar to those of the alleged victim in this case, later admitted that she had participated in, and even solicited rough consensual sex, did she not?'

'Yes, Mr. Sutton.'

'Thank you, Doctor. That's all.'

'Thank God he was able to get that part of it in,' Mary Catherine murmured from the seat on the other side of Randy.

'I don't think the judge should have allowed any of that,' Felicity grumbled.

Anne Jenks slid a scribbled sheet of paper over to Tess, who looked at it and jumped up.

'Dr. Linderman,' she said on redirect. 'You mentioned earlier that there were four hundred and fifty men in your research program. How many women were there?'

The psychiatrist pulled a notebook from his jacket pocket and flipped through the pages.

'Seven hundred and ten,' he replied when he found the right page.

'And how many of those seven hundred and ten women were the alleged victims of acquaintance rape?'

Linderman peered again at his notes. 'Three hundred and forty-two.'

'And how many of those three hundred and forty-two had been injured in some way by their attackers?'

'Forty-eight.'

'All right, in how many of those forty-eight cases did the victim later admit to falsifying the charges?'

'One.'

'Was that one Marion Healy?'

'Yes, it was,' Linderman confirmed. 'And I'd like to say something about that, if it's all right.'

'Certainly,' Tess invited.

'Marion Healy is a disturbed woman who may or may not have been raped. But the man who was first convicted of the crime and then later released when she changed her story is currently serving a twenty-five-year sentence in a Nevada prison for sexual assault and battery.'

'Thank you, Doctor,' Tess said. 'That's all.'

'That's enough,' Janice groaned.

'Way to go,' Mitch exulted.

'What hat did you pull that rabbit out of?' Tess whispered to Anne Jenks.

'I remembered seeing something about it in the Nevada newspapers a while ago,' whispered the staff assistant, who seldom forgot anything she had seen or read or heard.

SIX

At ten minutes past nine the following morning, Tess got to her feet.

'Your Honor,' she said clearly, 'there are a number of character witnesses I had originally intended to call before the court, but in compliance with the defense's expressed wish for a speedy resolution to this matter, we will present just one more witness. The People call … Karen Doniger.'

With a collective gasp, everyone was suddenly alert. People were sitting up, twisting in their seats, eyes trained on the double doors at the entrance to the courtroom. It was what they had all been waiting for. They had been hearing her name for weeks now, but for many of those present, including the jury, this was the first time they would actually see the alleged victim in person.

A photograph of her, taken from the dust jacket of *Tapestry*, had been splashed across the front pages of

some of the seamier newspapers, and had even managed to creep onto a few respected television channels,
but Robert Willmont's accuser had held no press
conferences, made no public statements, and allowed
no interviews. *Hard Copy*, *Inside Story* and *A Current
Affair* had all been turned away with their hundred-
thousand-dollar checks still in their pockets.

The doors opened and, with a watchful deputy on
either side of her, Karen entered the courtroom. She
paused for perhaps five seconds on the threshold
before she squared her shoulders, walked straight
down the aisle, looking neither to the right nor the
left, and marched resolutely through the bulletproof
opening toward the witness box, wedged, as it was,
between the judge and the jury.

She was wearing a silk suit in a deep mauve color
and an ivory Victorian-style blouse with the traditional
high lace collar. At her throat was an opal cameo that
Natalie had given her to wear for courage, and on her
wrist was a new gold bracelet created by Felicity that
Ted had given her.

Jessica had styled her stepmother's hair back off her
face, while Amy kept bringing up fresh pots of tea.
Nancy had pressed her suit. And Natalie had fussed for
over an hour, choosing just the right shade of stockings and appropriate pair of pumps.

'Nothing too spiky,' Nancy warned. 'She should
look conservative.'

'And nothing too bright,' Natalie agreed. 'We
wouldn't want her to appear flashy.'

Everyone took a hand in her makeup, giving her
a little more rouge and a little less mascara and
then deciding on a soft-pink lipstick and pale eye-
shadowing.

And all the while, Karen stood in front of the full-length mirror and wondered who the woman was who looked back at her. The swelling had gone down around the nose and lip, and the ugly bruises had all but faded, but the cheekbones seemed too prominent, there was something disconcerting about her eyes, and the set of the jaw was new and unfamiliar.

Yesterday, when she had ventured out into the garden for a breath of fresh air, she discovered that a rude reporter had scaled the wall.

'So how does it feel to take down the greatest man in America?' he yelled at her.

Fortunately, Nancy was there to take a broom to him, sweeping him away like a speck of dirt, but Karen was left wondering, for perhaps the thousandth time, if she were doing the right thing.

'. . . your right hand,' the bailiff had already begun. 'Do you solemnly swear that the testimony you are about to give before this court is the truth, the whole truth, and nothing but the truth, so help you God?'

'I do,' Karen said, her voice clear and firm.

'State your name.'

'Karen Doniger.'

'State your address.'

She gave the number of the house and the name of the street in St. Francis Wood.

'Be seated.'

The chair took her by surprise. It was deep and almost too comfortable for such a formal occasion. She was still settling herself into it when Tess stood up and walked toward her.

'Good morning, Mrs. Doniger,' the veteran ADA said with courtroom cordiality, tempered by an encouraging smile.

'Good morning,' Karen murmured, sitting up straight and folding her hands in her lap.

'To begin at the beginning, tell the court how you came to be working for the defendant's political campaign.'

'One of the things I've done a lot of over the last ten years is move around the country,' Karen replied, remembering to look at the jury as often as possible, as Tess had coached her to do. 'I've never been very political. I mean, I vote, but not for any particular party, only for a candidate if I like what he or she seems to stand for.'

'As many of us do,' Tess murmured.

'I was raised to believe that the United States was the greatest country on earth, but in some of the places I've lived, it would have been impossible not to see that something was going very wrong with the American Dream.'

'An opinion shared by many,' the ADA suggested. 'Please continue.'

'It bothered me a lot, but I didn't really know what I could do about it. After we moved to San Francisco, I became aware that Senator Willmont not only saw what was happening to the country, but believed he knew exactly what to do about it. When he announced his candidacy, I thought – this is something I can do. I can work for someone who understands the problems and might even be able to solve them.'

'So you volunteered at the Willmont campaign headquarters?'

'Yes, two afternoons a week.'

'What did you do there?'

'In the beginning, I stuffed envelopes and ran the Xerox machine and made telephone calls, all the usual volunteer things. But one day, they were rushed for a press release and no one seemed to know what to do, so I just took the material and sat down and wrote something. After that, they started asking me to write more releases and promotional kits, and I even wrote a position paper on hunger. In fact, that's what I was doing when … when … well, that night.'

'Suppose you tell us, for the record, what it is that you do, and why the campaign staff would trust you to write so much of their material.'

'Well, I don't really know if it was a big factor, but I'm the co-author of a number of pictorial books on America. My partner takes the photographs and I write the accompanying poetry. Some of the staff members had seen my books, so I guess they assumed I knew how to write.'

'Your last book, *Tapestry*, was highly acclaimed, wasn't it?'

'Yes, it was,' Karen confirmed. 'It was by far our most ambitious project.'

In the third row on the right side of the spectator section, Nancy smiled, and Ted, sitting beside her, squeezed her hand. Demelza looked over her shoulder and winked.

Meanwhile, Tess had taken several steps back toward the prosecution table before she stopped and turned.

'Mrs. Doniger, how many times have you been married?'

'Once,' Karen replied.

'And how long have you been married to your husband?'

'It will be eleven years this November.'

'Have you ever, during that time, had an affair with another man?'

Even though Tess had prepared her for the question, Karen felt herself color. 'I was thirty-nine years old when I got married, Miss Escalante,' she said with dignity. 'And, unbelievable as it may seem, I never had an affair with another man before my marriage and I have not had one since.'

'A thirty-nine-year-old virgin?' Janice Evans murmured. 'I bet there's one hell of a story in that.'

Beside her, Randy shifted uncomfortably.

'Now, let's turn our attention to the night of April seventh,' Tess suggested. 'Why were you at campaign headquarters so late on that particular evening?'

'I was working on a position paper, the one I mentioned before. The senator had decided to make hunger in America a campaign issue, and he wanted some material ready for a press reception the next day. My daughter was spending the evening with a school friend and my husband was going to be out for dinner, so I was able to stay until I was finished. The senator came in a few minutes before I was ready to leave.'

'Was anyone else there?'

'No. His administrative assistant was there earlier, but she had already gone. I was alone in the office when he arrived.'

'Tell us what happened.'

Karen carefully recounted the details that had led up to her accompanying the senator to the bar across the street.

'How long did you stay at the bar?'

'About two hours, I think. Long enough for each of us to have three Scotches and share a bucket of steamed clams.'

'What did you talk about?'

'We talked about my books, mostly. When we could.'

'What do you mean?'

'Well, the bar was pretty crowded and people wouldn't leave him alone. They kept coming over to the table. But he seemed to take it all in stride, so I guessed it was like that wherever he went.'

'When you could talk, what besides your books did you talk about?'

'He talked about the campaign for a while, about how well it was going, and about how hard it was to have to be on the road so much, and how lonely it was, and how glad he'd be when it was all over.'

'Anything else?'

'I don't remember anything else, specifically.'

'All right, what happened after you left the bar?'

'We went back to the parking garage and got into his car and he started to drive me home. The most direct way to get to my house is to go through the park. That's exactly what we were doing when I got sick.'

'You got sick?'

'Yes. I don't know whether it was the Scotch or the clams or what, but all of a sudden I got sick to my stomach and I asked him to stop the car for a moment.'

'Did he?'

'Well, he said he couldn't do anything on the crossover, but he'd stop the first chance he had. I thought he meant after we left the park, but, when we got to the traffic light, which is less than a block before you come out of the park, he suddenly turned left onto Martin Luther King Drive. I said I had to get out and walk a bit, but he said that if I was going to be sick I should have privacy, so he turned up the little road to

Stow Lake and stopped there.'

Here, Karen paused. Her heart had begun to race and her breath was starting to come in little gasps.

'Would you like to take a brief break before we get to this next part?' Tess invited.

'No, that's all right,' Karen replied, sucking air deep into her lungs. 'I'm okay.'

'Are you sure?'

'Yes,' Karen said more firmly. 'I'd rather keep going. I'd like to get through this before I lose my courage.'

'All right,' Tess agreed. 'Tell us what happened after he stopped the car.'

'I got out and started walking around a bit, taking some deep breaths to settle my stomach, and then there he was, right behind me. I must have jumped a mile. I didn't even realize he'd gotten out of the car.'

'Did he say anything?'

'He asked me if I was going to be sick. I told him if I could just walk around in the fresh air for a minute or two I'd be okay, at least until I got home.'

'Did you?'

'Yes. Then I started back toward the car. He was leaning against the hood. I told him I felt better and I thought it would be okay to go. I opened the car door but he said he was in no hurry and I should give it a little longer, just to make sure. He said his car was still new and I guess he didn't want to take any chances. So I walked around the car a couple of times and then he came up very close behind me. He asked me if I was cold and he took off his jacket and started to put it around me, but I told him I wasn't cold and I sort of moved away a little. But he said I was shivering and he wanted to be sure I stayed warm in case I was coming down with something, and he was right next to me, and when I tried to get away, he … he grabbed me.'

Nancy felt Ted stiffen in the seat beside her. She slipped her arm through his and held on tight.

Across the aisle, Elizabeth Willmont took a deep breath and thought about taking Adam to the beach.

'Tell us what happened then,' Tess urged softly.

Karen blinked back hot tears. 'I tried to push him away, but he was too strong, and then he kissed me. He said he'd been wanting to do that all evening, and he could tell that I wanted him to. I told him he was wrong, that I was happily married, and that … I wasn't interested in him in that way, and all I wanted to do was go home. I tried to pull away, but he just laughed and held me tighter. He said he knew a come-on when he saw it, that I'd been flirting with him all night, and just begging for it.'

'Begging for it?'

Karen nodded. 'I told him he was crazy, but I guess that was the wrong thing to say because he sort of went wild. He slapped me so hard that I fell against the car. When I tried to get up, he started yelling that I'd be crazy about him by the time he finished with me, and then he … he dragged me off the road and threw me down on the ground.'

Tess waited calmly while her witness fumbled around in her purse for a handkerchief and dabbed her eyes.

'We can stop for a bit, if you need to,' she offered, but Karen shook her head. 'All right, then, tell us what happened next.'

In fits and starts, Karen described in agonizing detail how the defendant had torn aside her dress and stripped off her panties, and how he had then forced himself into her. As almost everyone in the courtroom squirmed uncomfortably, she told how he had laughed at her protests, and how she had managed to reach out and scratch him, and how he had reacted by hitting her again and pinning both her hands beneath her.

In his seat two rows behind the defendant, Randy squirmed with the rest of the gallery and tried not to listen to the words that damned the California senator with every syllable. This woman, whom he had first admired through her work, and then liked for her dedication, and now wanted to despise because of her betrayal, was clearly having a devastating effect on the jury, on the entire court. Even the judge looked queasy, and the typically acerbic Janice Evans was silent beside him.

Randy was a closet romantic who had waited until he was forty to fall in love. Raised to respect women, he knew in his soul there was no place for the kind of violence that Karen Doniger was describing. He had no illusions about the world being a perfect place, but he still had some illusions about the people he knew and had chosen to follow.

Robert Willmont could be inconsiderate, Randy knew, and even downright nasty when the situation called for it, but that was a far cry from the vicious animal this woman was making him out to be. He wondered what silent forces had gotten to her with their evil message.

He had offered to testify himself.

'I've known the senator for fifteen years,' he told Hal Sutton. 'No one has been closer to him. Let me tell the jury that he just couldn't do the things they're claiming.'

'Have you spent every minute of every day of those

fifteen years with him?' Sutton asked.

'Well, certainly not *every* minute,' Randy had to admit.

'Then you can't help,' Sutton said kindly but firmly. 'If we need character witnesses, we'll go to one or two of his colleagues in the Senate, or a couple of his supporters on the Supreme Court, or the mayor or the governor or several of his more influential backers here in California. No offense, but I'm sure you understand.'

Randy understood. But it didn't help his anxiety as he squirmed in his seat and steeled his heart against the respectable middle-aged woman who seemed determined to cut his friend and mentor up into a messy pile of pieces.

'I tried to fight him,' Karen was continuing, tears dripping slowly down her cheeks, 'but he was just too strong. I was crying and choking and gasping for breath, and he kept telling me how much he knew I'd enjoy it, and how long he'd been waiting for this opportunity. But I'd only met him a few days before. And then, just as, well, just as he was, you know … concluding, he gave this strange kind of laugh and he said, "It was only a matter of time, Mariah, until you gave me what I wanted."'

Randy Neuburg's head snapped up.

'He called you Mariah?' Tess queried. 'Not Susie or Sally, or even Elizabeth, but Mariah?'

'Yes.' Karen nodded. 'I'm certain. It was Mariah.'

Janice Evans turned to the senator's aide and chuckled. 'Has Bobby been fantasizing about the human iceberg?'

But Randy wasn't amused. He gripped the arms of his chair until his knuckles whitened and a hard knot formed in his stomach. Two rows in front of him, separated from him by a bulletproof wall, Robert Willmont didn't move a muscle.

'Do you know anyone named Mariah, Mrs. Doniger?'

'I believe the senator has an adviser by that name, but I've never met her.'

'An adviser … I see.' Tess nodded. 'All right. Let's pick up right after he called you Mariah.'

'Well, he kept saying how I'd probably never had it so good before,' Karen said in a choked voice. 'And then he – he said he knew exactly what I wanted next.'

'Did you know what he meant?' Tess asked.

'I didn't at first,' the witness gulped. 'But then I did.'

Under the ADA's guidance, Karen tremulously recounted how the senator had pushed himself into her mouth.

'He said that was the way he liked it best. And he said … he said he was sure I'd like it just as much as he did.'

On the right side of the gallery, Ted Doniger groaned.

On the left side of the gallery, Elizabeth Willmont barely concealed a gasp.

'What happened then?' Tess asked.

'I gagged,' Karen replied. 'And I guess I must have bitten him or something, because he yelled and pulled away. Then he said he'd teach me to play games like that, and he punched me in the face with his fist. The next thing I remember clearly, a man in a jogging suit was putting his jacket over me.'

'Thank you,' Tess said. 'Well done,' she whispered.

The ADA walked over to the prosecution table and

leaned on it for a moment with her back to Karen. Then suddenly she straightened up and whirled around.

'Mrs. Doniger, did you at any time during that evening, in the garage, at the bar, or in the car, give the defendant any indication that you wanted to have sex with him?'

'No, I did not,' Karen declared. 'You see, I *didn't* want to have sex with him, so why would I have given him any reason to think that I did?'

'You did not consent?'

'No, Miss Escalante, I did not consent.' The response was quick and emphatic.

'You did nothing at all that could possibly have been construed that way?'

'Nothing. Unless having a drink with him and agreeing to let him drive me home means I gave him some kind of implicit permission to do what he did to me.' Karen looked up at the judge and then over at the jury and finally turned her eyes on Tess. 'Did it?'

The seasoned ADA considered her witness for a moment. The question had come as a surprise, but it was perfect.

'No,' she replied. 'I don't believe it did.' Then she, too, took a deliberate moment to look around, at the jury, at the gallery, at the defendant. 'And I would hope that there is no one in this courtroom who does.'

'You did just fine,' Ione said during lunch at Campton Place. 'You answered every question as well as you could, and it was obvious, at least to everyone in the gallery, that you were telling the truth.'

The moment Judge Washington called the noon

break, two deputies had escorted Karen and her entourage out a rear door where Ted had a limousine waiting. They chose the dining room at Campton Place because it was quiet and exclusive and there was no better food to be found in the city. But Karen just picked at her plate.

'Truth is a very elastic thing,' she murmured, 'that can be stretched to mean whatever people need it to mean.'

'I was watching the jury,' Demelza said. 'They were just as appalled as the rest of us.'

'I was watching the defendant,' Jenna said. 'He sat there through the whole thing like he was made of stone.'

'What did you think of Karen Doniger's testimony, Senator?' a reporter called as Robert and his party made their way down the front steps of the Hall of Justice.

'It was quite emotional,' the senator replied calmly, holding his wife's hand, 'quite theatrical, quite calculated, quite inaccurate.'

'Do you have any idea why she's trying to smear you?' someone sympathetic to the candidate inquired.

'She certainly hasn't confided in *me*, if that's what you're asking,' Robert said. 'But I think it's very sad when a woman is as unhappy, as frustrated, and as desperate as she must obviously be to have involved herself in such an outrageous and malicious lie.'

'She sounded awfully convincing.'

'Not to me.'

'What about the jury – do you think they believed her?'

Robert flashed one of his brilliant smiles. 'I think

the jury is smarter than that, don't you?'

'Will your attorney be able to discredit her?'

'For what I'm paying him,' the senator said, chuckling, 'I sincerely hope so.'

But it was a different story, fifteen minutes later, in the Sutton Wells conference room on Front Street.

'She buried me, damn it,' Robert cried, 'and I had to sit there and listen to her do it.'

It was a last-minute strategy session with Sutton and his associates to make sure they were prepared for the afternoon's cross-examination. The candidate insisted on being present at all such meetings.

'I won't lie to you,' Sutton conceded. 'She was a very compelling witness for the prosecution.'

'Compelling? It was an Oscar-winning performance. Can you trip her up?'

Sutton shrugged. 'I'll certainly try. There are a few soft spots in her story that I think we can expose.'

'Why do you think the prosecution quit so soon?'

'I think it was just a clever maneuver to turn our haste back on us,' Sutton replied. 'Escalante was trying to send a message to the jury that her case was so strong, she didn't need to waste time with character witnesses.'

'Is it?' Robert inquired bluntly.

'Let's just say it's not time to worry yet,' Sutton assured him. 'Don't forget that we have a few compelling things on our side. We have your reputation, which, until this little … lapse, has been spotless. We have the Drayton name, which carries enormous weight in this city. And we have the total lack of motive for you to risk your whole career in such a frivolous way. In the final analysis, it won't be evidence or expert witnesses, but credibility, that will decide this case, and

I think it's fairly accurate to say that your credibility in this community is rock solid.'

'Mrs. Doniger,' the Silver Fox inquired as the afternoon session began, 'you said that, on the night in question, you worked late at campaign headquarters to finish a project that the senator needed for the following day; is that correct?'

'Yes,' Karen replied after a three-second pause. Tess had coached her to wait that long before answering, in case the ADA wished to object.

'Were you expecting the senator to return that evening?'

'No, not necessarily.'

'Were you perhaps taking longer on the project than you might have because you were hoping he would return?'

'No.'

'Whose idea was it that your daughter spend the evening with a friend?'

'Hers.'

'Whose idea was it that your husband have dinner out after his meeting?'

'I guess it was mine, but that was only because – '

'So, would it be fair to say,' Sutton interrupted her smoothly, 'that you were prepared, as early as that morning, and before you knew anything at all about the position paper, to stay late at campaign headquarters?'

'No.'

'He's twisting it all around,' Jenna complained. 'He's trying to make it look like she was planning to get raped.'

'That's his job,' Mitch told her.

'The man is just about to earn his fee,' Mary Catherine murmured.

'Returning to your earlier testimony,' Sutton went on, 'you said you were motivated to join the senator's campaign because you believed he might be the only man who could help solve America's problems; is that correct?'

'More or less.'

'Was there any other reason?'

'I don't understand.'

'Well, let me rephrase my question. Did you consider the senator handsome?'

'I suppose he's handsome.'

'Did you find him charming?'

'Yes, he appeared to be charming.'

'Were you curious about the senator personally, what the man behind the politics was really all about?'

'On some level.'

'You were attracted to him, then?'

'Professionally, perhaps. Not personally.'

'Didn't you ever fantasize about what he might be like when he, say, took off his clothes?'

'No.'

'Or what it might be like to have sex with him?'

'No.'

'So, according to your testimony, the senator was handsome, he was charming, you were curious about him, you thought enough of him to spend two days a week working for his election – but you weren't the least attracted to him?'

'No.'

'The man's a genius,' Janice Evans observed.

'Why doesn't the prosecutor object?' Felicity cried.

'To what?' Demelza sighed. 'He has every right to try to discredit her.'

'Let's move on now to the parking garage,' the Silver Fox proposed. 'You claim you couldn't get your car started; is that correct?'

'Yes.'

'You said you were about to look under the hood when the senator came along?'

'Yes.'

'You said you thought he might have followed you?'

'Yes.'

'Were you hoping he would follow you?'

'No.'

'Where was his car parked?'

'Several spaces away from mine.'

'Then is it possible that he was simply going to his own car when he saw you in trouble and offered to help?'

'It's possible.'

'When you couldn't get your car started and the senator graciously offered to take you home, why did you agree?'

'Because he was insistent and I didn't want to appear discourteous.'

'But if you hadn't wanted to go with him, you could have refused and taken a taxi, couldn't you?'

'As I said, I didn't want to appear discourteous.'

'Whose idea was it to go to the bar across the street?'

'To go to a bar was his idea. To go to the one across the street was mine.'

'Do you frequently go to bars with men and drink three Scotches in the course of a two-hour conversation?'

'No.'

'But you did on this particular occasion?'

'Yes.'

'And the next day, after you accused my client of raping you, when your husband had a towing company come to collect your car – what did they find wrong with it?'

'There was a loose wire.'

'Not a dead battery?'

'No.'

'Not a faulty starter?'

'No.'

'Just a loose wire that anyone could have reached under the hood and pulled free – anyone, that is, who might have wanted an excuse to be in the garage when the senator came for his car?'

'I know absolutely nothing about cars, Mr. Sutton,' Karen declared. 'I have no idea how the wire came loose.'

'All right, let's go back to your quite extraordinary statement that you had never had an affair with a man before your marriage. That was your testimony, wasn't it?'

'Yes.'

'A remarkable thing in the 1970s, Mrs. Doniger. You're to be commended. You were practicing safe sex before anyone knew there was a deadly reason to do so, weren't you?'

The gallery tittered.

'Objection, Your Honor,' Tess said in disgust. 'Mr. Sutton's attempt at humor demeans this proceeding.'

'I agree,' the judge snapped, smacking his gavel sharply at the gallery and scowling at the defense attorney.

'Withdrawn,' the Silver Fox demurred. 'During the years of 1969 through 1977, Mrs. Doniger,' he asked instead, 'where were you living?'

'On West Twelfth Street in New York City,' the witness replied.

'Were you at that time familiar with a section of New York known as Greenwich Village?'

'Very familiar. I worked there and I had very good friends who lived there.'

'These friends, did they live on Sullivan Street, by any chance?'

'Yes.'

'Will you please tell the court something about the living arrangements of these friends?'

Karen considered the attorney for a moment. 'Like a great many people at the time,' she said finally, 'and for economic reasons as much as anything else, they had what you would probably call a commune.'

'A commune – where several unmarried people of mixed sexes shared the same apartment?'

'Objection,' Tess called. 'Where's the relevance?'

'Your Honor,' Sutton argued, 'this morning, Mrs. Doniger testified to having had no sexual relationships before her marriage. I'm simply pursuing that line of inquiry.'

'Objection overruled,' Washington said.

'Again, Mrs. Doniger, this particular commune – was it shared by both men and women?'

'Yes.'

'How many men and how many women?'

'Different numbers at different times,' Karen replied. 'The lease was held by a woman who allowed friends with no place else to go to come and stay as long as they liked.'

'Would you describe these friends who came and stayed as having been part of a counterculture? What were commonly referred to as "hippies"?'

'Yes.'

'Did these hippies who came and stayed engage in sexual intercourse with one another?'

'Sometimes.'

'In fact, didn't the bedroom of that apartment contain wall-to-wall mattresses?'

'It was a small apartment. There wasn't enough space for all the separate beds they would have needed.'

On the right side of the gallery, Ione shifted in her seat. 'Where did he get all this?' she hissed.

'From the ex-roommate, I'll bet,' Demelza muttered.

'Or the ex-landlord,' Mitch growled.

Across the aisle, Janice Evans sat forward. 'Maybe not so lily-white, after all,' she murmured.

'But it was quite common for two or three or even four different couples to – er – make intimate use of those mattresses at night?' Sutton pursued like a bloodhound.

'Yes.'

'And, from 1969 to 1977, you visited at the Sullivan Street apartment quite frequently, did you not?'

'I did,' Karen confirmed. 'As I said, they were my friends.'

'And how often would you spend the entire night there?'

'Sometimes once, perhaps twice a week.'

'Once or twice a week – you stayed the night at an apartment where unmarried couples were openly engaging in sexual activities?'

'Yes.'

'And yet you want this court to believe that you never had an affair before your marriage?'

Karen glanced at Tess. A small smile tugged at the corner of the ADA's mouth, but the Silver Fox missed it.

'What made those people so very special to me, Mr. Sutton,' the witness responded serenely, 'and the reason why I spent so much of my time with them, was that they never pressured me into doing anything I didn't want to do.'

'And you want the jury to believe that you spent night after night in a room full of mattresses and never once participated in any of the activities that were going on all around you?'

'The jury doesn't have to believe me,' Karen said. 'Most of the people from Sullivan Street are sitting right there in the gallery. Why don't you ask *them*?'

As though it had been rehearsed, five spectators on the right side of the aisle rose silently to their feet. The jury craned their necks to get a good look at the prosperous-looking middle-aged group.

'I'm sure that won't be necessary,' Sutton murmured as smooth as satin. 'I think the jury already has the picture. Now, suppose we turn to the night in question, the night of April seventh.'

For the rest of the afternoon session, the Silver Fox probed and prodded, searching for ways to exploit a weakness, highlight a contradiction, uncover an inconsistency.

'So,' he concluded at the end of the long day, 'after admitting you considered the senator handsome and charming, after arranging to work late at campaign headquarters that night, after making sure you were in the parking garage when the senator arrived, after suggesting that you go to the bar across the street, after consuming three Scotches, after thinking up an excuse to get the senator to stop his car in a remote part of Golden Gate Park, you still expect this jury to believe that the defendant raped you?'

'Yes, Mr. Sutton,' Karen retorted. 'Because he did.'

'I have nothing more for this witness,' the defense attorney said with a dismissing wave of his hand.

Tess Escalante stood up and addressed the bench. 'The People rest, Your Honor,' she declared.

'Did we make a dent?' the defendant asked after court.

'Hard to say,' Sutton replied in his taciturn way.

Robert sighed. 'Maybe trying to make her out to be some middle-aged, sex-starved groupie wasn't the right approach.'

'Without a clue as to her motive, what other choice did we have?' the attorney argued.

'I know,' the senator conceded. 'I'm just wondering how effective it was.'

'Juries can be hard to read,' Sutton reminded him. 'But don't sell them short. We've planted the right seeds, and as long as there aren't any last-minute surprises, I'm sure some of them will take root.'

'What kind of last-minute surprises?'

'Someone who can corroborate her story in some way.'

Robert gave a short laugh. 'I don't think you need to worry about that. Besides, if the prosecution had unearthed an eyewitness, we would already know about it.'

'Then it's just her word against yours,' Sutton said

agreeably, 'and the jury will hear your word last.'

'You were sensational,' Ted told her that evening. 'So calm and collected. It was almost as though you knew the defense attorney was going to ask about Sullivan Street.'

'I didn't,' Karen admitted, 'but Tess did.'

'He was sure barking up the wrong tree. Trying to make the jury think you set it all up. But I guess if I were the defense, that's exactly what I'd do – see if I could put the jury off-track by giving them other possibilities to think about.'

In Tess's dream, a perfect spring day was marred by the incessant whiz of a bumblebee that hovered around her head. In reality, someone was leaning on the door buzzer of her Russian Hill flat.

Tess opened her eyes and glanced at the clock radio on her nightstand. The ghostly green digits told her it was almost three o'clock. She climbed out of her canopy bed and stumbled toward the door, wrapping her fluffy chenille robe around her as she went.

'Who is it?' she yawned as she pressed the intercom.

'Lamar,' said the box.

Tess pushed the button that would spring the outer release and unlocked her door. 'This had better be good,' she cried when his bulk appeared in the hallway. 'Do you know what time it is?'

'Make some coffee,' the investigator suggested.

He was always amused at the way she lived, in a world of lace and ruffles and 'froufrous,' as his mother used to call them, when her professional facade was so tailored. Neat Victorian sofas and small Edwardian tables and a froth of chiffon at the windows. A company of stuffed animals, fresh flowers, a Persian carpet. She was the complete opposite of the police investigator, who flaunted his outrageous western attire and lived like a Spartan.

'Coffee?' she echoed.

He nodded. 'I want you wide awake for this one.'

It wasn't often that Lamar Pope appeared at her door in the middle of the night. Tess padded into the kitchen. Five minutes later, they were seated in her living room with their hands wrapped around steaming mugs of instant coffee.

'What? You expected percolated on such short notice?' she grumbled when Lamar grimaced over the first gulp. 'Now, tell me why I'm sitting here with you at this ungodly hour when I should be sound asleep so that I can be bright-eyed and bushy-tailed in court at nine o'clock?'

'I'm on to something,' he said, setting his mug down and fumbling in his jacket pocket for his notepad. 'I've been talking to a woman named Margaret Smith of Provo, Utah.'

'So?'

'It seems Mrs. Smith once worked as a secretary for Robert Willmont.' Indeed, he had painstakingly tracked down every female employee of the defendant, from his days at Sutton Wells to the present. 'In 1984, a year and a half into the senator's first term, she claims he raped her and then told her if she ever said a word about it to anyone he'd not only deny it – and who would take her word over his? – but he'd see to it that she never worked in Washington again.'

'Tell me I'm not dreaming,' Tess implored, any idea of returning to sleep forgotten.

'Wait – it gets better,' Lamar declared. 'She says he

then sat down and wrote out a check for two hundred and fifty thousand dollars, right on the spot, and told her it would be good only if she got permanently lost.'

'Two hundred and fifty thousand?' the ADA gasped.

'Yep.'

'So she got permanently lost.'

'You guessed it. But first she went to a hospital. The doctor had to make a report, so of course the police came around. She told them she'd been raped but that she didn't get a good look at her assailant. Hell, between a quarter of a million dollars and little assurance of a successful prosecution, she figured she'd take the money and run.'

Tess shrugged. 'It's beautiful, but it's nothing more than her word against his.'

'Not exactly,' Lamar corrected with a slow smile. 'It seems she took a copy of the hospital record – made up some excuse about needing it for her own doctor, and then, before she cashed the check the senator gave her, she ran it through a li'l ole Xerox machine.'

'She still has it?'

'Yep. Tucked away nice and safe for a rainy day.'

Tess's eyes widened. 'Will she testify?'

Lamar nodded, neglecting to mention the hours it had taken him to persuade her. 'She's been following the trial and she's ready to help you nail the bastard. She's been married the last five years and only just got around to telling her husband what happened. But he's obviously a good guy because he's behind her one hundred percent.'

'Did you check everything out?' Tess asked, hoping she already knew the answer.

'Sure,' Lamar nodded. 'I got onto the hospital in D.C. she said she went to. Don't ask how, but I tracked down the police officer she said she talked to. I called a couple of people I know who were on Capitol Hill around the time. And I just woke up a former congresswoman from Connecticut. I didn't want to come to you until I was sure that everything checked out. As far as I can tell, it does.'

'How soon can she get here?'

'She can be on a plane in the morning.'

There was a shrewd glint in the ADA's black eyes as she considered her options. Lamar could almost see the wheels whirling inside the razor-keen mind.

'No,' she said slowly. 'Call her and tell her to pack her bags but not to come out until Tuesday night. Then tell her to call my office on Wednesday – make sure it's after nine o'clock but before noon – and leave a message for me. Tell her to say something about having information that may pertain to this case.'

'I know that glint,' Lamar observed. 'It means that what you've got in mind may be slightly left of ethical.'

'Just slightly,' Tess conceded. 'Sutton's got a lineup of witnesses that will probably take us through Wednesday, and if he's as smart as I think he is, he'll play his ace last. He's going to count on the senator's charisma to win over the jury, and I'm going to play along. I'm not going to reopen the People's case – I'm going to keep Mrs. Smith for rebuttal.'

Lamar nodded. 'I like it.'

A satisfied smile spread across Tess's face. 'In fact, I'm going to do everything I possibly can to help the good senator put the noose around his own neck.'

seven

Just as Tess had predicted, the defense paraded a staggering array of technical, psychological, and character witnesses past the jury which lasted through the following Tuesday, and included a Harvard pathologist, an Oxford psychiatrist, the mayor of San Francisco, two female members of the House of Representatives, two notable United States senators, a justice of the Supreme Court, and even a famous entertainment personality who had been flown in from Hollywood for the occasion.

The two congresswomen, who testified to having worked closely with the defendant in a number of capacities, described the senator as a dedicated public servant who had never treated them, or any other woman, to their knowledge, with anything but the utmost respect. The Harvard pathologist assured the jury that the mountain of physical evidence presented by the People was not nearly as conclusive as the prosecution believed and was clearly open to other interpretation. On the basis of a twenty-minute interview, the Oxford psychiatrist pronounced the senator emotionally stable, mentally alert, well-focused, and not the least bit inclined to violence.

Tess's cross-examinations were perfunctory.

Finally, on Wednesday morning, Robert Drayton Willmont was called to the stand.

'There is no one in this court, or in this state, or probably even in this country, who doesn't know who you are, Senator Willmont,' Hal Sutton began. 'But I think it would be appropriate for you to tell the jury something about the man behind the public face.'

'I'd be happy to,' Robert replied.

And so the first hours of the defendant's long-awaited testimony were spent in congenial commentary about his background, his family, his work, his personal values. He wasted little time in telling the jury that he was a devoted son, a proud father, and a loving husband.

'I've been my mother's strength and support ever since my father died,' he said. 'I still tuck her up in bed at night every chance I get.'

In the gallery, Amanda Drayton Willmont wagged her head in agreement.

'My boy Adam is going into eighth grade in September,' Robert boasted. 'He's already almost as tall as I am – and at least twice as smart.'

Sitting beside her mother-in-law, Elizabeth Willmont wondered where he had found the time to notice.

'My wife and I are going to celebrate our silver wedding anniversary in October,' he said brightly. 'She's given me twenty-five wonderful years and the best home a man could ask for – and I'm afraid I was ingenuous enough to promise her the White House in return.'

A faint ripple of amusement ran through parts of the gallery. A faint smile was all Elizabeth could muster.

'My family has always meant everything to me,' Robert expanded. 'Elizabeth, especially. It's true what they say, you know, about there being a smart women behind every successful man. I've been exceedingly fortunate. Elizabeth and I are very close. We understand and respect each other. We discuss every important decision before I make it, we examine every action before I take it. She's my motivation, my inspiration. Without her behind me, believing in me, supporting me, I would probably still be an associate in my father's law firm.'

With a palsied hand, Amanda reached over to pet the daughter-in-law she had always resented.

Next, Robert praised his elementary and high school teachers, proclaimed his good luck to have attended the two finest universities in the country, waxed eloquent about his decade and a half in public service, and then spoke at length about his decision to run for President.

'I believe in America,' he declared. 'I believe in an America where people will work together to ensure that the greed of today doesn't impoverish the children of tomorrow. An America where the middle class can have a fair shake instead of always being made to bear the burden of the rich and the profligate. Even though I was born into money – no, *because* I was born into money – I was not only able to see where many of the problems were coming from, I could see practical ways to fix them. And it was clear to me that only as President of the United States would I have a real opportunity to implement my solutions.'

'He's making a goddamn campaign speech,' Mitch grumbled. '"Forget that I raped a woman, folks. I'll put money back in your pockets."'

By the time the Silver Fox elicited the desired response to a final preliminary question, Judge Washington was ready to call for the noon break.

'Clever,' Tess observed to Anne Jenks. 'Sutton is going to make very sure that his direct examination doesn't end until we adjourn for the day. That way, the jury will get to take the defendant's uncontested words to bed with them.'

'Why didn't you object to all that irrelevant patting himself on the back he was doing?' her assistant asked.

But Tess just smiled. 'Because I want the senator to have every possible opportunity to hang himself.'

'Will he?'

'He already has,' the ADA replied serenely. 'Oh, by the way,' she added, almost as an afterthought, 'notify Judge Washington's clerk at the end of court today that we might be presenting a rebuttal witness.'

'I can take care of that right now, if you like,' the efficient staff assistant offered.

'No,' Tess said firmly. 'At the end of court today.'

The afternoon session began promptly at one-thirty.

'Will you tell the court, in your own words, Senator,' Sutton requested without further preamble, 'what really took place on the night of April seventh?'

Robert turned toward the jury with a look of sincere regret etched into his handsome face, and throughout his recital the aquamarine eyes fastened on first one and then another of the five men and seven women who would be deciding his fate.

'I came home to San Francisco at the beginning of April to make some speeches, to raise some money, and to get out among you, and listen to what you had to say,' he began. 'After three very strenuous months of campaigning, I found myself physically, mentally, and emotionally drained. This city is where I was born and raised, it has always been the fountain of my strength, and it will always be the place I'll come home to.'

Here, he took a deep breath and slowly let it out.

'On April seventh, a woman from San Jose asked me why this country destroys so much of the food it produces when there are Americans who go to bed hungry every night. I'm ashamed to say I didn't have a very good answer. But I decided, then and there, that our agribusiness policy had to change. We talk a lot about the sad state of the economy and health care and education, but we are all suddenly silent when the conversation turns to a child crying in the night because his stomach is empty, or an old man sleeping on a park bench because he has no place else to go.'

The jury shifted a bit under the direct aquamarine gaze.

'I realized that these issues could no longer be shoved under a rug and I directed my staff to prepare a start-up document that I could use as the basis for serious change.'

'Someone should tell him he's already won the California primary,' Mitch muttered.

'Look at that,' Janice Evans murmured to Randy. 'He's got the jury by the tits and balls.'

'I returned from San Jose at about eight o'clock that

evening and made the unfortunate mistake, as it turned out, of letting my security people go. They'd been working very hard and I thought they deserved a break. It was afterward that I decided to go down to the office to get a look at the press material my staff had prepared.'

He reasoned it wasn't necessary to mention that his mother had already retired for the evening and the big house on Jackson Street was empty and depressing.

'Mrs. Doniger was at the office and she had obviously spent a great deal of time putting the information together. On the spur of the moment, I invited her out for a drink as a simple expression of appreciation. When she refused, I didn't argue. I took a copy of the packet she had prepared, read through it to make sure it was accurate and complete, put it in my briefcase, and left.'

'Were you aware that Mrs. Doniger had already left the office?' Sutton inquired.

'Yes,' Robert replied. 'She had said good night, and asked me to lock the door on my way out.'

'Did you go directly to the parking garage?'

'Yes, I did.'

'For what purpose?'

'For the purpose of getting into my car and going home.'

'What did you find when you reached the garage?'

'I found Mrs. Doniger having trouble with her car.'

Robert's account of the following few moments did not differ substantially from the testimony Karen had given.

'What happened then?'

'We went to a bar across the street for a drink.'

'She seemed in no hurry to get home?'

'No.'

'And how did she seem at the bar?'

'She was very animated and she seemed quite impressed by all the people who stopped by the table to wish me well. She laughed a lot and I remember she brushed her leg against mine several times.'

'Did this continue once you left the bar?'

'No. As I recall, she didn't have very much to say at all, once we were in the car. She sat very close to the door. Then, as we were crossing the park, she suddenly said she was sick and asked me to stop the car. I was driving in the left-hand lane and I couldn't very well stop in the middle of the road, so I said I'd pull over as soon as we were out of the park. But she said she couldn't wait that long.'

'She said she couldn't wait until you left the park?'

Robert nodded. 'I thought she was going to be sick any second, so I did the only thing I could. I turned left onto King Drive. I was about to stop the car when she said that, if she was going to be sick, she wanted more privacy, so would I please drive on a little further. When I came to the road that goes up to Stow Lake, she told me to turn there. I must have driven several hundred yards before she said it was all right to stop.'

'*She* asked *you* to drive up to Stow Lake?'

'Yes, she did,' Robert asserted with a sincere glance at the jury. 'Then she got out of the car and disappeared. I waited for perhaps five minutes, and then, when she didn't come back, I naturally got a little worried, so I got out and went to look for her. She was over by some bushes and she looked like she was shivering, so I took off my jacket and put it around her. But then she laughed and said she wasn't cold, the fresh air had fixed her up just fine, and it was such a great night, she thought it would be fun to go for a walk around the lake.'

'A walk around the lake?'

'That's what she said. I said that sounded nice but I really had to get home and I started back to the car. But just as I got there she comes flying out of the dark and she's all over me – she actually had me pinned against the hood. And she starts telling me how she's been dreaming of this moment ever since she first saw me, and that she just couldn't stand it any longer, to see me and not be able to have me, and no one ever had to know, it would stay between the two of us because she wouldn't want her husband to find out any more than I would want my wife to.'

'Are you telling this court that Mrs. Doniger approached *you*?' Sutton asked slowly, deliberately. 'Suggested intimacy to *you*?'

'Approached me? She attacked me,' Robert declared. 'I swear to God – and this court – it was all her idea.'

'But you didn't resist?'

The senator sighed deeply. 'I wish I could say I did. How I wish I had. But no, after my initial surprise, I didn't resist. I'm not normally much of a drinker and I'd had three highballs, I was exhausted and I hadn't slept in days. No, I'm ashamed to say, I didn't resist. She dragged me off into the bushes – she was like a tiger, ripping at her clothes, tugging at mine. And she kept crying things like "Hurt me, hurt me," and "The rougher you do it, the better I like it." Then she scratched me down the chest to prove the point. And all the time she was moaning and groaning and saying things like "You're irresistible. You're incredible. You're fantastic. I've never had it so good."'

'Can you believe this garbage?' Ione hissed.

'Anyone who knows Karen knows how ridiculous it is,' Jenna retorted.

'Sure,' Demelza observed. 'But the jury doesn't know Karen.'

Janice Evans leaned toward Randy. 'I can certainly testify to the senator's irresistibility.'

'What happened then, Senator?' Sutton pressed.

'I … well … I wasn't able to respond very well at first, because of the fatigue and the Scotch and all, but she said she knew how to get me going, and then she started performing oral sex on me.'

Here, Sutton urged his client to provide explicit details, while the jury shifted in their seats, the women trying not to look too embarrassed, the men trying not to look too interested.

'After a while,' Robert concluded with a properly chagrined expression, 'what she was doing began to work and I achieved an erection. As soon as that happened, she said something like "Great, let's go!" But she wasn't exactly as ready as she led me to believe.'

'What do you mean?' the Silver Fox inquired.

The witness replied in even more graphic detail. The jury continued to look uncomfortable. So did the senator.

'I tried to tell her it wasn't working, but she wrapped her legs around me and wouldn't let me stop. Finally, I managed to penetrate her and then, before I knew it, well, it was over.'

'You climaxed?'

'Yes.'

'Did she?'

'She may have – I don't know. I don't think so.'

'Was she upset by your … quickness?'

'She didn't seem to be. I apologized, rather profusely, as I recall, but she just smiled and said it was exactly how she expected it to be.'

'Then what?'

'I got up and put on my clothes and said it was time to go, but she didn't move. She said she thought she'd stay for a while and maybe take that walk around the lake. I told her it was getting late, but she said she didn't want to see her husband just yet, or maybe she didn't want him to see her, I don't know. I explained that I couldn't wait around, I had to get home. But she waved me away and said it was all right, she would find a taxi when she was ready. I tried to argue with her, I really did. I even tried to grab her to force her into the car, but she pulled away from me. I mean, I didn't want to leave her there all by herself in the park in the middle of the night, but she wouldn't listen. She just ran off. I tried to find her, but she was either gone or hiding. So, finally, I got into my car and left.'

'A real gentleman,' Felicity drawled.

'He never apologized to *me* for coming too fast,' Janice muttered under her breath.

'Senator Willmont,' Sutton continued, 'you saw People's exhibits sixty-six through seventy-two, the photographs taken of Mrs. Doniger when she was admitted to the hospital on the morning of April eighth. I ask you now, under oath, are you responsible for the injuries depicted in those photographs?'

'No, I am not,' Robert stated emphatically. 'She encouraged me to be rough with her, she said that was the way she liked it, but I never did any of those other things.'

'She looked perfectly all right when you got into your car and drove away?'

'Well, her clothing was torn a bit, mostly by her own doing, I might add, and there may have been a few bruises on her arms and legs, but that was all.'

'Then how do you account for what we saw in those seven photographs?'

'I can't. It was horrible, how she looked, all beat up that way. But I swear she didn't look anything like that when I left her.' Here, Robert turned and faced the jury. 'I made a mistake, I admit it. Unfortunately, it was a big mistake, and I'll spend the rest of my life regretting it. But I'm not a sadist, I'm not a maniac, I'm not a pervert – why would I do such a thing to anyone?'

'Senator Willmont, did you rape Karen Doniger?'

'No, I did not,' Robert replied, again looking straight at the jury. 'I engaged in consensual sex with her – at her suggestion – no, at her insistence.'

'Did you, in the course of that intimacy, beat her, slap her, punch her, and leave her, barely conscious, in Golden Gate Park?'

'No, I did not beat her, slap her, or punch her, and she was fully conscious when she insisted that I leave her in Golden Gate Park.'

'Do you know of any reason why Karen Doniger would claim that you did these things to her?'

'No,' Robert admitted. 'She seemed like a very nice person. Maybe she was afraid to tell her husband the truth. Maybe she was being manipulated by some political group. I don't know. But I do know that she lied to this court. I'm a candidate for President of the United States, for God's sake. Why would I deliberately risk destroying my chances of being elected by raping and beating a volunteer worker on my own staff? It just doesn't make any sense.'

'Thank you, Senator,' Hal Sutton said. 'I have nothing more.'

'Ready?' Janice Evans called.

She stood on the steps in front of the Hall of Justice, straightening her skirt and buttoning her jacket, and then running a quick hand over her hair to smooth it down in the gusting wind.

'Ready,' the Minicam operator replied.

'Ready,' the engineer echoed.

'Okay, roll.'

The cameraman hit the button.

'I'm standing in front of the Hall of Justice here in San Francisco,' Janice said in her best on-air voice, 'where not just the fate of Robert Drayton Willmont is going to be decided, but perhaps the fate of America, as well. A few short months ago, the remarkable senator was a rising political star, streaking toward a first-ballot nomination. Now, rather than the voters, his political career will depend on just five men and seven women who, very soon now, must choose a side in what is perhaps the most celebrated he-said/she-said controversy of our time.'

She began to walk slowly down the steps, into the camera.

'But whose side will they take? That's the question that has the entire country glued to the evening newscasts and embroiled in endless arguments. No cameras have been allowed inside Judge Oliver Wendell Washington's courtroom, and the outside world has heard only filtered accounts of the proceedings from those who are witnessing this high drama. I've been sitting in the gallery, peering through the ominous bulletproof shield that separates the spectators from the participants, trying to separate fact from fiction. It's a monumental task, and as each day unfolds, I wonder, more and more, how the jury will be able to do it.'

Janice stopped at the bottom of the steps.

'Okay, that's a wrap for here,' she told her crew. 'Let's pack up and get over to Jackson Street.'

'I've never heard such a load of crap,' Mitch declared in the cab they had squeezed themselves into to get over to Campton Place. 'Not even back when the politicians were still trying to defend being in Vietnam.'

'And the jury was just eating it all up,' Felicity said.

'Because, deep down in their hearts, they want to believe him,' Demelza observed. 'They want any excuse to acquit him.'

'The sad truth is,' Ione commented with a sigh, 'you don't have to know how to govern to get elected in this country – you just have to know how to lie.'

The senator sat next to his wife on a rich leather sofa in the dignified Willmont library that had been his father's favorite room, the unblinking television lights illuminating every wrinkle, every blemish.

'One might be able to fool a live audience,' he said wryly, 'but it's impossible to lie to a camera, isn't it?'

'Were you thinking of lying?' Janice asked from the sofa facing him.

'No,' he replied simply. 'I was just wondering why so many people think they can get away with it.'

The newswoman crossed her ankles, licked her lips,

and nodded to the half dozen technicians.

'The last time we spoke, Senator Willmont,' she began in her on-air voice, 'you were planning for your future to be decided by the majority of voters in this country. How do you feel now – about it being decided by a handful?'

'Sad,' Robert said thoughtfully. 'Sad for my family and sad for America, that such an outrageous charge was allowed to be brought into court in the first place. But I also feel confident – confident that this jury is not going to let itself be taken in by so blatant an attempt to smear me.'

'Then you think you'll be acquitted of all charges?'

'I believe in the system,' the senator replied. 'I believe that the innocent are protected under the law. I believe the jury will exonerate me.'

'Even though your story of being attacked like a tiger by a middle-aged woman half your size sounds awfully far-fetched?'

'But that's the whole point, isn't it?' Robert exclaimed earnestly. 'The truth is too bizarre for me to have made it up. If I were going to lie my way out of this, I assure you I would have come up with something a lot more plausible.'

'If you are acquitted,' Janice observed, 'you will in all likelihood receive the nomination for President. Do you think you'll be elected in November?'

Robert considered for a moment. 'I think so, yes,' he said with the confidence of a man who has never learned to accept rejection.

'Even though you're a confessed adulterer?'

'I believe I may be elected in part *because* I confessed, because I didn't deny it or try to lie to the people. I came right out and admitted my mistake, whopper though it was. There are precious few perfect people in this world, Miss Evans, and I'm obviously not one of them. There'll be some pure souls who will feel they have to turn away from me, but I hope that most of the people will respect me for being honest about my imperfections.'

'If you are acquitted, will you sue Karen Doniger for character defamation?'

'Why?' Robert sighed. 'The verdict is all that matters to me. I have no interest in humiliating the woman or her family any further. My only hope is that they use whatever money I would have won from them in a lawsuit to get her the psychiatric help she so desperately needs.'

eight

'Senator Willmont,' Tess began on Thursday morning, the thirteenth day of the trial, 'I would like to go back over certain portions of your testimony from yesterday, if you don't mind.'

'I don't mind, Miss Escalante,' the senator responded with a pleasant, confident smile.

'Beginning with your glowing tribute to your marriage.'

Robert produced a boyish grin. 'I could probably talk forever on that subject.'

'I don't think forever will be necessary,' Tess replied. 'I'm interested only in the basics of your relationship with your wife. You testified yesterday that you and she discuss every decision before you make it and examine every action before you take it; is that correct?'

'Yes, I said that. Yes, it's correct.'

'Did you and your wife discuss your having sex with Karen Doniger before you had it?'

'Well, no, of course not,' Robert replied. 'As I said, it was a spur-of-the-moment thing.'

'Does that mean you would have discussed it with her had it not been a spur-of-the-moment thing?'

The senator sighed. 'Had I stopped to think about what I was doing that night, Miss Escalante, I wouldn't have done it. So there would have been nothing to discuss.'

'Does that mean you and your wife have discussed your intent to commit adultery on less impulsive occasions?'

'Objection,' Sutton called. 'What does it matter what he does or doesn't discuss with his wife?'

'Your Honor,' Tess argued, 'the defendant testified that he discusses everything with his wife before the fact. I'm simply trying to determine if he was telling the truth when he made that statement.'

'Your client opened the door himself, Counselor.' Judge Washington sighed. 'Objection overruled. But you're skating on thin ice, Miss Escalante. Be careful.'

'Yes, sir,' Tess agreed, returning to the witness. 'One more time, sir: Have you ever discussed with your wife your intent to commit adultery?'

'I was referring, of course, to political issues when I made that statement.'

'Then the decision of whether to commit adultery is not one you discuss with your wife, but one you make on your own?'

'I don't think that's what I said.'

'I beg your pardon,' Tess said politely. 'What did you say?'

'I said this was an isolated incident,' Robert retorted.

'By "isolated," do you mean that it was the only time

you had committed adultery, or the only time you didn't have the opportunity to discuss it beforehand with your wife?'

'You're twisting my words,' the witness objected.

'I certainly wouldn't want to do that, Senator,' Tess murmured. 'So, let me rephrase my question. Have you ever discussed infidelity with your wife?'

'There has never been cause,' Robert Willmont declared.

'What does that mean, Senator? Are you testifying that, aside from your untimely encounter with Karen Doniger, you have never been unfaithful to your wife?'

'I'm saying that I made a mistake, Miss Escalante. One I will regret for the rest of my life. I hurt my wife, I embarrassed my family, and I disappointed a lot of good people who believe in me. I can't begin to say how sorry I am.'

'For what, Senator?' the ADA inquired. 'Are you sorry you raped Karen Doniger – or just sorry you got caught?'

'Objection!'

'Miss Escalante,' the judge admonished.

'I withdraw the question, Your Honor,' the ADA conceded. 'Prior to the night of April seventh, Senator Willmont, had you ever been unfaithful to your wife?'

'Objection!' Sutton complained. 'Prosecution is badgering the witness.'

'Your Honor,' Tess argued, 'this man has painted himself into a Norman Rockwell example of marital devotion and we seek only to confirm or deny its validity. The defense tried its best to portray Karen Doniger as a counterculture nutcase who hunted down the defendant like a predatory animal for no apparent reason. Shouldn't I be allowed the same opportunity to suggest that Robert Willmont is a man of insatiable appetite who wants what he wants, and is not above taking what he wants, by force, if necessary?'

'She has a point, Counselor,' Washington suggested. 'Besides, you could have made a pre-trial motion to exclude prior behavior. You didn't.'

'Because it wasn't necessary, Your Honor,' the Silver Fox explained. 'Everyone knows that the senator is above reproach.'

'Then your client has nothing to worry about, does he?' the judge declared. 'Objection overruled.'

'Prior to April seventh, Senator,' Tess repeated, 'had you ever been unfaithful to your wife?'

Randy Neuburg and Mary Catherine O'Malley exchanged worried glances, Janice Evans slid an inch or two lower in her seat, and Elizabeth Willmont sat frozen, afraid that her carefully composed mask might crack.

Across the aisle, the Sullivan Street set held their collective breaths, and those on both sides of the gallery leaned forward just a little so as not to miss a syllable.

'I have a beautiful and loving wife,' Robert replied. 'Prior to April seventh, I had no cause to be unfaithful to her.'

A sibilant sigh floated across the courtroom.

'That was slick,' Randy murmured.

'The man's a born politician,' Mary Catherine agreed.

'He didn't answer the question,' Felicity protested.

'You noticed,' Demelza observed.

'Hardly a direct response, Senator,' Tess suggested. 'But then, I suppose we'll have to chalk it up to your having been in Washington for so long.'

'Your Honor!' Sutton complained.

The ADA shrugged. 'Sorry.'

'Don't abuse the court's tolerance, Miss Escalante,' the judge suggested.

'I'll try not to, Your Honor,' Tess acquiesced, pausing a beat. 'Who is Mariah?' she asked the defendant suddenly.

Randy held his breath.

Robert stiffened slightly. 'If you mean Mariah Dobbs,' he replied carefully, 'she's a media consultant.'

'Someone you've had, or hoped to have, an affair with?'

'Certainly not.'

'I see – she's just someone whose name you happened to cry out at the height of passion, for no particular reason?'

'Your Honor!' the Silver Fox complained.

'Yes, Mr. Sutton,' Washington agreed. 'Move on, Miss Escalante.'

'Yes, sir,' Tess conceded. She took two casual steps away from the defendant. 'Not including April seventh, Senator Willmont,' she asked in a clear voice, 'how many other women have you raped?'

'Objection!' the defense attorney exclaimed.

'It's all right,' Robert declared, forestalling the judge. 'I don't mind answering the question. *Including* April seventh, Miss Escalante – none.'

'None, Senator?' Tess parried. 'You mean that you never in your life had to force a woman to have sex with you? They all came to you willingly?'

'I believe they did,' the witness replied. 'I wasn't exactly a monk before my marriage. Like most young men, I sowed my share of wild oats, and I assure you that the lovely young ladies in question, who shall naturally forever remain nameless, were all quite willing.'

'They all freely participated in consensual sex, just as you claim Karen Doniger did?'

'Yes,' Robert assured her. 'They did – just as Mrs. Doniger did.'

'To sum up then, Senator: Prior to April seventh, you had never been unfaithful to your wife and, to the best of your knowledge, you have never raped a woman. Is that your testimony?'

'It is.'

Tess smiled, the slow smile of a cat who has cornered a mouse.

In the gallery, Randy frowned uneasily.

The ADA spent the rest of her cross-examination going over the details of the night of April seventh, but her questions were now mostly routine. She already had everything she needed. The rest was just for window dressing.

'How long did you stay at campaign headquarters after Karen Doniger left?'

'I'd say about fifteen minutes.'

'And you said that, while you were there, you read the promotional packet she had prepared?'

'Yes.'

'How large was that packet?'

'Perhaps twenty pages.'

'Would it surprise you to know that the packet in fact contained almost forty pages?'

'I guess it could have.'

'Are you a speed reader, Senator?'

'No, but I can scan pretty quickly when I know what I'm looking for.'

'So it is your testimony that you spent about fifteen minutes in the office, reading, after Karen Doniger left?'

'Yes.'

'Were you in any particular hurry to leave?'

'I was tired, but not in any particular hurry.'

'Not too tired to invite Mrs. Doniger out for a drink?'

'That was a spur-of-the-moment gesture.'

'Yes, so you said. So, even though you weren't rushing to get anywhere, you scanned almost forty pages of what you yourself considered to be a vital document and still managed to be at the parking garage in time to help Karen Doniger with her car?'

'I had no way of knowing she would still be there.'

'What would you say if I told you that the log in the lobby of your office building lists Karen Doniger as having signed out at eight-twenty-five that evening, and lists you as having signed out at eight-twenty-nine?'

'I would say that I don't recall what time it was. In fact, I don't normally sign the log at all.'

Tess picked up a thick ledger and approached the bench.

'Your Honor, at this time, I would like to introduce into evidence People's exhibit seventy-five, the log book from the building where the Willmont campaign offices are located.'

Sutton jumped up and came over to authenticate.

'No objection,' he sighed. The log was genuine. His own signature was featured prominently on many of the pages.

'So entered,' Washington said.

'You're correct about not signing the log that night,

Senator,' Tess said. 'The doorman has become accustomed to doing it for you, and I'm prepared to call him as a rebuttal witness, if necessary.'

The defendant and his attorney exchanged glances.

'In the interests of time, Your Honor, defense will stipulate,' the Silver Fox said.

'In that case,' Tess continued, 'kindly read to the jury the first entry pertaining to you on the night of April seventh.'

'It says that I arrived at eighteen minutes past eight.'

'And the second entry?'

'It says I left the building at eight twenty-nine.'

'So, according to this log, and even assuming you took the express elevator to the twelfth floor, you could not have remained in the office, reading, for fifteen minutes after Karen Doniger left, could you?'

'I guess not,' Robert conceded.

'In fact, you left immediately after her, didn't you? Probably by the very next elevator.'

'I wasn't really paying attention. I certainly wasn't following her, if that's what you're getting at.'

'No, of course not,' Tess murmured, taking the log from him and placing it on the evidence table.

'How tall are you, Senator?'

'Six feet two.'

'How much do you weigh?'

'About two hundred and fifteen pounds.'

'Would you say you were in good physical shape?'

'Fairly good. As good as a candidate on the road six days out of seven can be, anyway.'

'And yet you say that a five-foot-six-inch, one-hundred-and-ten-pound woman pinned you against the hood of your car?'

'Yes.'

'You then say that this unbelievably strong, although small, woman dragged you into the bushes and demanded that you perform sexual acts on her and abuse her in the process?'

'Yes.'

'And you obliged her?'

'I'm not proud of it, but yes, I had sex with her.'

'And you bruised her?'

'She begged me to be rough with her. I may have bruised her slightly.'

'Slightly? You consider a black eye, a broken nose, and a split lip that took seven stitches slight?'

'I don't recall doing any of those things.'

'And you also claim she scratched you, and that it was from passion and not an attempt to fight you off?'

'Yes.'

'And these scratches, were they hard enough to dig into the skin on your chest and cause actual bleeding?'

'Yes.'

'Did it hurt?'

'I suppose it did.'

'Yet you did nothing about it? You didn't cry out, you didn't protest, you didn't slap her, you didn't pin her hands beneath her to keep her from doing it again?'

'No.'

'You just went right on doing whatever it was you were doing?'

'Yes.'

'And after you had this consensual sex, you simply got into your car and left her there, in the middle of Golden Gate Park, in the middle of the night, with her clothes in shreds, her nose and lip bleeding and no visible means of getting home?'

'I never saw any blood,' Robert protested. 'And I would have taken her home. I didn't want to leave her there. She insisted.'

'She needed medical attention, she was practically naked, her purse was in your car so she had no money for a taxi, or even a telephone call, and yet you want this jury to believe that she insisted on staying where she was?'

'I know it sounds crazy now, but yes, she did.'

At ten minutes after two in the afternoon, Tess finished her cross-examination of the defendant and returned to her seat with a nod to Lamar Pope, who stood at the rear of the courtroom.

'Senator Willmont,' Hal Sutton redirected, 'did you rape Karen Doniger on the night of April seventh?'

'No,' Robert declared. 'I did not.'

'The defense rests,' the Silver Fox said.

'Miss Escalante?' Judge Washington inquired.

Tess stood up. 'The People have one rebuttal witness, Your Honor. We call Margaret Smith to the stand . . .'

Sutton looked at his client. The senator shrugged and shook his head.

'. . . Margaret Holden Smith.'

In the second row of the gallery, Randy and Mary Catherine looked at each other in surprise. At the defense table, Robert Willmont blanched.

'Stop her,' he hissed at his attorney. 'Whatever you have to do, stop her.'

'Uh – may we approach, Your Honor?' Sutton cried, jumping quickly to his feet.

Washington nodded and covered his microphone with one hand as he gestured the two attorneys forward with the other.

'What is it, Mr. Sutton?'

'Defense has had no prior notification of this witness. The name does not appear on any of the lists we received. We object to her testimony being presented.'

Tess swallowed a smile. 'I apologize for the short notice, Your Honor, but I wasn't even contacted by Mrs. Smith until yesterday, after court had begun. As soon as possible, after receiving her message, I had my associate notify your clerk about the existence of a potential rebuttal witness. But, until I had the opportunity to interview her in person, which wasn't until late last night, I couldn't be sure her information was relevant.'

'The assistant district attorney is correct, Counselor,' Washington concurred. 'We did receive notification. She did follow procedure.'

'Then, at the very least, Your Honor, I would want a continuance,' the Silver Fox argued, entirely unsure of his footing, 'until defense has had the opportunity to take the witness's deposition and then has had time to study it and conduct a thorough investigation of its own.'

'And just how long would you anticipate this taking, Counselor?' the judge asked.

'I would think it might take two or three weeks at a minimum,' Sutton estimated.

'Somehow, that's what I thought you'd say.' Washington sighed. 'Miss Escalante?'

'It's July the second, Your Honor. Even two weeks would put us past the convention, and I seem to recall that the reason I had barely two months to prepare for this case was because defense wanted a resolution before July thirteenth.'

'She has a point, Counselor,' the judge acknowledged.

'May I have a moment to confer with my client, Your Honor?' the defense attorney requested.

Washington nodded.

Tess kept her face carefully blank.

'What the hell is going on?' Sutton demanded with his lips to his client's ear. 'I'm operating blind here. Just how far do you really want me to go with this?'

'As far as you have to,' Robert declared.

'We're not going to be able to exclude this witness's testimony. Escalante went by the book. The best we can get is a continuance that will take us past the convention. What can this Margaret Smith do to you?'

Robert looked at his attorney for a moment. 'She can bury me,' he said.

'My client seeks a continuance, Your Honor,' Sutton said, returning to the bench.

'In chambers,' declared Washington, advising the jury and sweeping from the courtroom. 'Now, what's this all about?' he demanded as soon as the door had closed.

'The senator realizes that a continuance will take us past the convention,' explained Sutton, 'but he feels his rights would otherwise be compromised.'

'What have you got, Miss Escalante?' asked the judge.

'The senator said, under oath, that prior to April seventh he had never been unfaithful to his wife and had never in his lifetime raped anyone,' Tess responded. 'Mrs. Smith is prepared to rebut both statements.'

'Hearsay,' snapped Sutton.

'Not exactly,' corrected the ADA. She turned to the judge. 'I believe you know me better than that, Your Honor. I've never had a case come back on me.'

The judge nodded slowly.

'Besides,' Tess continued, 'had I had the proper length of time to prepare my case, defense would have had all the time necessary to prepare its cross.'

Washington sighed. 'Both the district attorney's office and my office did everything in their power to expedite this trial, Counselor,' he told Sutton, 'in order to get you the speedy resolution you not only requested, but demanded. So I'm not particularly inclined to grant you any lengthy delay. But I'll tell you what I *will* do – I'll allow Miss Escalante to present her witness and then, if you wish to take the long weekend to prepare your cross-examination, you may do so. However, I intend to have this case wrapped up and sent to jury by the middle of next week. Do I make myself clear?'

'Yes, Your Honor,' both attorneys replied.

'Then let's get on with it.'

'You can't let her testify,' Robert hissed when Sutton returned to the courtroom and resumed his seat.

'I can't stop her,' the Silver Fox hissed back. 'But we have the weekend to plan a rebuttal.'

Maggie Holden Smith, looking even lovelier than Randy and Mary Catherine remembered, walked to the witness stand and took the oath.

'Mrs. Smith,' Tess began, 'will you tell the court how you came to be acquainted with the defendant?'

'I worked as a secretary in Senator Willmont's office

in Washington, D.C., from January to June of 1984,' the rebuttal witness said in a naturally husky voice.

'Did you enjoy working there?'

'For the most part. The job was exciting, the pace was incredible, and there were really important people coming and going all the time that, before then, I had only read about in newspapers or seen on television.'

'This was important to you?'

'I graduated Brigham Young University with a degree in political science and all I wanted to do was work in Washington. I was twenty-two years old and full of ideals, and this was my first exposure to the world of power and politics.'

'You said you liked your job, for the most part. What part of the job didn't you like?'

'I didn't like it much when the senator was there.'

'Why not?'

'Because he used to hang around my desk a lot, making comments that embarrassed me.'

'What sort of comments?'

'Oh, things like how distracting I was to have around, or how he wished he were single when he looked at me, or how he could be arrested for what he was thinking when I walked across the room. Things like that.'

'Did you take these remarks seriously?'

'I thought he was probably kidding, but it made me very uncomfortable anyway.'

'Did you discuss how you felt with Senator Willmont? Did you ask him to stop?'

'Heavens, no. I was just a kid, all on my own in the big city, and I really needed my job. I was afraid if I said anything to him I might get fired. But after a while I got up enough courage to tell his administrative assistant. She said that was just the way he was and I should try not to let it bother me. But she must have seen how upset I was because she promised she would talk to him. I guess she did because he stopped doing it for a while.'

In the gallery, Mary Catherine nodded slowly. She remembered the lovely young woman almost in tears, and the senator's shrugging off her remonstrations with a laugh.

'Then what happened?'

'About a month or so later, it started again, only it got worse. Even though I wasn't his personal secretary, he would ask me to bring him coffee or files or something, and then when I came into his office he would stare me up and down. He said he'd like it better if I wore low-cut clothes because it would show off my bosom, and he wished miniskirts were still in style so he could see more of my legs.'

'When the senator made these remarks, weren't you able to just laugh them off?'

'I come from a very conservative, very religious family, Miss Escalante, where making remarks about such matters just isn't considered decent. He made me feel like I had no value as a person, and it was humiliating.'

'What did you do?'

'I started looking for another job.'

'Did you find one?'

'I had a final interview with a congresswoman from Connecticut scheduled for the third Wednesday in June. She really liked me and I think I would have gotten the job.'

'Your Honor, I fail to see any relevance in a

discussion of Mrs. Smith's employment history,' Sutton objected.

'If the court will allow me to proceed,' Tess rejoined, 'I'm sure it will find this witness's testimony to be entirely relevant.'

'Objection overruled,' Judge Washington decided. 'But let's get to the point, Miss Escalante.'

'What happened on the day before your final interview with the congresswoman from Connecticut?'

'The senator's secretary was out sick,' Maggie replied, 'and the senator asked me to stay and retype a paper he had written. I didn't really want to, but he promised it would only be for an hour or two and I didn't know how to refuse without sounding like a real idiot, and I needed the overtime anyway, so I agreed. But he kept making changes and I had to keep retyping, and it was almost ten o'clock by the time I was finished. He offered to buy me dinner, in appreciation, but I said it was too late. So then he offered to drive me home. He said it was the least he could do.'

In the second row on the right side of the gallery, the Sullivan Street set began to look at one another with growing anticipation and Ted sat up a little straighter in his seat.

Across the aisle, Randy felt the cold knot that had been occupying the pit of his stomach begin to tighten. Beside him, Mary Catherine sat like a stone.

'Did you accept his offer?' Tess inquired.

'Well, it *was* late,' Maggie replied, 'I was tired and the buses weren't very reliable at that hour. Besides, he hadn't been offensive during the evening, and I didn't want him to think I was rude, so yes, I let him drive me home.'

She shivered and clutched at the arms of her chair.

'Would you like a glass of water?' Tess asked gently.

The witness shook her head. 'I'm okay,' she said in an uneven voice. 'It's just hard to talk about, even after all these years.'

'Take your time.'

Maggie took a deep breath and let it out slowly. 'I lived in Alexandria, which is about forty-five minutes out of the city, and when we got there he asked if he could come in and use the bathroom, being that it was such a long drive back to Rock Creek Park, where he lived. The apartment was a mess. My roommate had just left for vacation and half her wardrobe was left where she'd dropped it and I didn't really want to invite him in. But how do you tell a United States senator that he can't come in and go to the bathroom because your roommate's closet is all over the floor? So I let him in and then I just waited by the front door to let him right out again. But when he came out of the bathroom he was taking off his jacket and untying his tie and he said, "You can close the door – I'm not planning on leaving just yet."' The former secretary took another deep breath. 'And then he raped me.'

A startled gasp rose up from every corner of the packed courtroom and met the echo of Margaret Holden Smith's words.

'Your Honor, I object to this totally uncorroborated testimony!' the Silver Fox cried.

'Sit down, Counselor!' Oliver Wendell Washington barked. 'You'll have your chance to cross-examine.'

'Senator Robert Willmont raped you?' Tess pressed the witness.

'Yes,' Maggie confirmed. 'He told me I had been asking for it for months, teasing him, enticing him with my sexy dresses and phony modesty, and it was time to end the game. He forced himself on me, and when I tried to resist – tried to scream – he beat me, slapping me with his open hand and punching me with his fist. When he finished with me, he got up and straightened his clothes and told me maybe it would be better if I didn't come back to work at his office. I told him I had no intention of coming back. I told him I was going to the police.'

'What did he say to that?'

'He laughed. He said I could do whatever I wanted but he would deny everything, and who did I think the police would believe – a respected United States senator or a nobody sexpot who thought she could sleep her way to the top? Then he started to leave, but right at the door he stopped and came back. He said, on second thought, he didn't want there to be any hard feelings between us, and then he sat down on my sofa and wrote out a check for two hundred and fifty thousand dollars.'

'The defendant wrote you a check for a quarter of a million dollars?'

'Objection!' Sutton called. 'Witness is testifying to material not in evidence.'

'Sustained.'

Tess walked over to the prosecution table and picked up a sheet of paper. 'Your Honor, at this time, I would like to introduce People's exhibit seventy-six, a Xerox copy of a bank draft, number 8038, drawn on account 331-020-665, dated June 20, 1984, in the amount of two hundred and fifty thousand dollars, written to Margaret Holden and signed by the defendant.'

'Objection!' Sutton cried. 'Best evidence, Your

Honor. There's no proof that any such check ever existed. This Xerox could be a forgery, or it could be an altered version of a check relating to an entirely different matter.'

'This is *not* best evidence,' Tess agreed. 'We would much prefer that the senator provide us with the original.'

There was a hurried conversation between defendant and attorney.

The Silver Fox sighed. 'I'm sorry, Your Honor. It seems that, like most honest, hard-working people, the Senator does not keep personal records for longer than the seven years required by the IRS. Whatever checks he may have written in 1984 have been destroyed.'

'Then I ask the court to accept this photocopy in lieu of the original,' Tess countered.

'Approach,' Washington barked, covering his microphone. 'I assume you have precedents, Miss Escalante?' he asked.

'Yes, Your Honor.'

'Okay, into chambers.'

The judge suspended proceedings with a bang of his gavel. A well-armed Anne Jenks followed Tess and the defense contingent out of the courtroom. Ten minutes later, when they reappeared, Tess had a slight smile on her face and Hal Sutton was trying to conceal a scowl.

'I'm going to overrule the objection,' Judge Washington declared for the record, as his bowel complained. 'Subject to controverting testimony or presentation of the original check, the photocopy will be entered into evidence.'

'Exception!' Sutton snapped.

'Noted,' Washington snapped back. 'You may continue, Miss Escalante.'

'Where did this copy come from, Mrs. Smith?' Tess asked as the trial continued.

'I made it,' the witness replied. 'When the senator gave it to me, he said it would be good only if I left Washington immediately and never said a word to anyone about what happened. He said if I didn't, he would see to it that I never worked in Washington again, and that my family would be ruined, too. He said he had the resources and the power to do that.'

'What did you do?'

'I'm ashamed to say I took the check. I was scared to death. After all, he was a big important man, and I figured he was probably right. Who was going to take my word over his after I'd let him drive me home and then let him into my apartment late at night? All he would have to say was that I consented. How could I prove I didn't? But I wanted to have something, just in case he changed his mind and tried to hurt my family anyway. So, right after he left, I went to an all-night store where they had a Xerox machine, and I made the copy. Then I went to the hospital.'

'Your Honor, at this time, I would like to introduce into evidence People's exhibit seventy-seven, a copy of Margaret Holden's hospital record on the night of June 20, 1984.'

Sutton took a perfunctory look at the document and shrugged. 'No objection.'

'What injuries, if any, did you suffer that night, Mrs. Smith?' the ADA asked.

'I had a black eye, a fractured cheekbone, multiple bruises and two crushed ribs.'

In the gallery, Mary Catherine silently began to cry.

'Your Honor, the hospital record just entered into evidence will show that Margaret Holden did indeed suffer, and was treated for, those injuries on the night of June 20, 1984.' Tess turned back to the witness. 'Did you talk to the police?'

'Yes. The hospital said they had to call them. But I was so scared that I told the officer I didn't get a good look at the man who raped me.'

'And then you left Washington?'

'Yes. The very next day. I went home to Utah. I didn't call anyone before I left. I didn't even go back to the office to clean out my desk. I was so embarrassed. I knew how I looked. I didn't know how to explain.'

'You kept your silence for eight years,' Tess observed. 'Why are you breaking it now?'

'Out of guilt, I think,' Margaret Holden Smith replied. 'And because he can't hurt me anymore. When Sergeant Pope found me, I'd been following the story in the news, and all the time I was thinking, if I'd been stronger back then, if I'd stood up to him instead of taking his dirty money and running away with my tail between my legs like a kicked dog, maybe Karen Doniger wouldn't have had to go through what she did.'

'Objection!' Sutton exclaimed.

'Sustained. Confine your answers to only those facts in evidence, Mrs. Smith,' Washington advised.

'I have no more questions, Your Honor,' Tess said.

Tears were running down the witness's cheeks. 'It wasn't fair, Miss Escalante – all I ever wanted, my whole life, was to be a part of the process and work in Washington. I was good at my job. I was learning. I could have gone places. It wasn't fair that he was allowed to take that away from me.'

'No,' Tess agreed. 'It wasn't.'

'Why the hell didn't you tell me?' Sutton snapped later that evening.

'I didn't think it was that important,' Robert said.

'Not that important?'

'It was her word against mine – how was I supposed to know the cunt would make a copy of the check?'

'Is what she said true? Did you rape her?'

'Of course not,' Robert dismissed the idea. 'Why would I have to rape anyone? So maybe I got a little rough with her, but that's all. She'd been coming on to me for months, with her tight clothes and her holier-than-thou attitude. She wanted me to take her home that night. She was clearly giving me the message. So I gave her what she wanted. I only wrote the check because it was my first term in the Senate and I didn't want any problems.'

'You should have been honest with me, Robert,' his attorney declared, massaging his temples. 'Then maybe I could have prevented this. At the very least, I could have moved to exclude past behavior.'

'We couldn't do that,' the senator reminded him. 'We needed to be able to discredit Doniger, remember?'

'Except that it didn't quite work out that way, did it?' Sutton retorted. 'Instead, Escalante set a trap and we walked right into it, like a pair of first-year associates.'

'The bitch,' Robert mumbled. 'So now what do we do?'

'We can argue irrelevance, we can try to discredit, we can attempt to paint this Margaret Smith as the whore of Capitol Hill, we can move to exclude, but I don't know. I'm very much afraid the prosecution has established perjury.'

'Okay, maybe I made a mistake,' Robert admitted. 'Maybe I should have told you about Maggie. Maybe I shouldn't have been so cavalier on the stand when Escalante pressed me about the infidelity issue. But what happened back then has nothing to do with this case. I didn't rape Karen Doniger, Hal. Believe me, she asked for it.'

'That may be,' the Silver Fox said, 'but I'm no longer sure I can convince the jury of that.'

Sutton spent most of Monday trying to undo some of the damage that Maggie Holden Smith had done. He called for a mistrial. Judge Washington denied. He tried to have the witness's entire testimony stricken. Again, Washington denied. He tried to discredit her story. He harped on her refusal to identify her assailant to the police. He suggested that the senator might have had cause to interpret her actions as provocative. He even went so far as to speculate that she had asked the senator to drive her home that night, instead of the other way around, and perhaps even invited him into her apartment in an attempt to further her career. Then he sought to intimate that she had set the whole thing up as a blackmail scheme. Finally, he dredged up a handwriting expert who was willing to testify that it was possible the Xeroxed check was a forgery.

It wasn't clear whether his effort had any significant impact on the jury, but the media, which had since April been overwhelmingly sympathetic to the senator, were suddenly scrambling like cockroaches in a bright light.

nine

Closing arguments were presented on Tuesday.

Sutton argued eloquently and vigorously that his client was simply the innocent victim of political sabotage. It didn't seem to matter that he had been unable to prove this theory with direct evidence and sworn testimony, and he played on the socio-economic climate of San Francisco to hammer his point home.

'The one man who can make a difference,' he declared, 'the one man with the vision to change this country for the better – that man cannot be allowed to survive. Why not? Because he's the only real threat to the superwealthy who, thanks to twelve long years of incompetent government, have gotten America right where they want it – with the poor getting poorer, and the rich getting richer. One man stands in their way. Robert Drayton Willmont. A rich man who refuses to play their self-serving little games. And how better to rid themselves of this very real threat than to have a woman cry rape!'

In the gallery, Amanda Drayton Willmont nodded.

Mitch grinned. 'It's a downright conspiracy.'

'Cry rape today, ladies and gentlemen,' Sutton exhorted, 'and the whole world stops to listen. The images it conjures up are lurid and loathsome. A woman entices a man into a compromising situation and then claims he took advantage of her. How does he defend himself without sounding like even more of a heel than he would had he actually done the deed?'

'He's a heel, all right,' Jenna murmured.

Elizabeth Willmont sat beside her mother-in-law. She had swallowed a handful of pills during the noon recess and now she was twelve years old again, basking in the glory of a Denver summer.

'There are people walking among us who just could not let this man become President of the United State,' Sutton said, looking directly at each juror. 'They are people who will stop at nothing to preserve what they have, at the expense of the rest of us. And they found a way to destroy him, didn't they? They found a middle-aged ex-groupie who would agree to cry rape.'

The attorney paced back and forth for a moment.

'Could it have happened the way Karen Doniger said it did?' he wondered aloud. 'It could have. After all, she had to concoct a believable story, or there would have been no case. But couldn't it just as well have happened exactly the way the defendant said it did? Couldn't he have been drawn innocently into the middle of an insidious plot? Of course he could have.'

Sutton nodded sagely.

'And that's why they didn't stop there. No, they couldn't risk that you might be smart enough to see through their little scheme. Not when, despite their dirty trick, the candidate was still out there piling up victory after victory in the primaries, with the nomination almost in hand. They realized that one woman might not be enough to do the foul deed. So what did they do? They went out and found themselves another woman – a disgruntled ex-employee who harbored a grudge against her former employer, who waved a piece of Xerox paper around that was conveniently eight years old and about as legitimate as the forger who probably wrote it, and they convinced *her* to cry rape, too.'

The Silver Fox wagged his head as though it were all just too overwhelming.

'Can Robert Drayton Willmont survive *two* pawns bent on destroying him? Are they going to win, after all? Is our country destined to have four more years of disastrous leadership? Will we have to stand by and watch while America is bled dry by the greedy until there's nothing left to save? If you convict this man of a crime he did not commit, that's exactly what will happen. They will win and the country will lose.'

Sutton peered intently at each of the jurors in turn. 'Ladies and gentlemen of the jury,' he said solemnly, 'it's up to you.'

'Amen,' the defendant's mother breathed.

Demelza scowled.

With one deep sigh that seemed to bear all the weight of the world, the Silver Fox reclaimed his seat, just as Tess Escalante rose from hers in rebuttal.

'Sinister cliques? Insidious plots? Scare tactics?' she cried scornfully. 'I think the defense attorney should have been a mystery writer. The key to a good mystery is the ability of the author to misdirect the reader. Boy, have we just been misdirected.'

'Amen,' Demelza said.

The defendant's mother scowled.

'To hear the defense tell it,' Tess continued, 'Robert Willmont is a bona fide saint, sent to us to save the world, who just happened to be in the wrong place at the wrong time. Who just happened to invite Karen Doniger out for a drink. Who just happened to show up in the parking garage four minutes after she did. Who just happened to insist on taking her home. Who just happened to drive his car to a remote area of Golden Gate Park. Who just happened to have sex with her, break her nose, split her lip and blacken her eye.'

The ADA shook her head in disgust.

'Never mind that the defense was unable to provide one shred of evidence that Karen Doniger was manipulated by any political motives. They want you to take their word for it anyway, on faith. Well, let's separate the facts from all that fiction, ladies and gentlemen. Let's make sure we have it perfectly clear. Robert Drayton Willmont is a rapist – and the worst kind of rapist, too. The kind who builds trust and then betrays. The kind who not only forces himself sexually upon defenseless women, but who likes to beat up on them, as well.'

Tess allowed a visible shudder to run down her slender body.

'The facts of this case were clear from the moment Karen Doniger spoke them, no matter how hard the defense attorney tried to contort them. But even if there remained a flicker of doubt in the most stubborn of minds, Margaret Holden Smith had to have doused it. Because if the defendant did not rape these two women – who have never met and have never spoken to one another – how then did they manage to come up with almost identical stories? The answer is painfully simple. They couldn't have. Robert Willmont raped both of them, exactly as they said he did, and that's the sad fact of it. He's a rapist, ladies and gentlemen. The great hope of America is a rapist. As brilliant as he may be politically, that's how warped he is personally. And that's the only sinister plot at work here.'

Amanda Drayton Willmont clutched her handbag to hide her anger.

Felicity clutched her handbag to keep from clapping.

The crafty ADA sighed deeply.

'But why would he have to resort to rape, this United States senator and presidential candidate who, on the face of it, has everything? This matinee idol who walks along the path of life with women literally dropping at his feet? That was the one question that I wrestled with, the one thing that I couldn't understand, until I heard the testimony of Dr. Linderman. If ever a man fits his psychological profile of an acquaintance-rapist, one who sets out to seduce and ends up choosing to violate, it's Robert Willmont, a man used to taking what he wants – even when it's not offered.'

Now it was Tess's turn to pace.

'This isn't about political intrigue, ladies and gentlemen of the jury, about secret cliques out to seize America for themselves. This is about one two-hundred-and-fifteen-pound man overpowering one one-hundred-and-ten-pound woman in the middle of Golden Gate Park – and you saw for yourselves the graphic and gruesome results of her resistance.'

Now it was Tess's turn to look each juror in the eye.

'Robert Drayton Willmont raped Karen Doniger, despite his background, despite his position, and despite the extent of his exposure. Why would he be foolish enough to risk it? Perhaps that's the simplest question of all – *because he thought he could get away with it*. Because he thought that his looks, his charm, his power, and his money would protect him from things that ordinary people like you and me are held accountable for every day. Look at him. Payoffs, perjury, denial, coercion – those are the ways of his world. What he can't lie his way out of, he'll try to buy his way out of.'

Tess didn't think Karen would mind her borrowing the line. She raised her left arm and jabbed her finger in the direction of the defendant.

'Sitting over there is a man who thinks he's above the law,' she declared. 'Ladies and gentlemen of the jury, tell him he's not.'

Oliver Wendell Washington took almost an hour to charge the jury, making sure that he walked the fine line of neutrality without a slip. He was known as a by-the-book judge, and by the book he went. By the time the five men and seven women retired to consider their verdict, there was no doubt in their minds about what they could and could not do. It was four-thirty in the afternoon.

Robert Willmont went home and closeted himself in the library. Randy Neuburg did not go with him. Mary Catherine O'Malley went to her apartment on Telegraph Hill and began to pack. Hal Sutton went to his office and sat at his desk, staring into space as he waited for the telephone call he knew would not be long in coming.

Tess left word with Anne Jenks that she could be reached at the Donigers' home in St. Francis Wood.

'I want to be in the courtroom for the verdict,' Karen announced. 'I have the right.'

The ADA nodded. 'I suppose you do,' she said. 'But what if it doesn't go our way?'

'I can handle it,' Karen replied. 'I just want to be there. I need to be there.'

'I'll be with her,' Ted said. 'We'll all be with her.'

Everyone was at the house, preparing for the vigil without knowing how long it would last. Felicity and Ione were cooking. Amy and Jessica were setting the table. Demelza was sitting quietly in the study. In the laundry, Jenna was ironing the simple beige dress Karen had chosen to wear. Mitch was pacing nervously up and down the living room. John was fixing drinks. Nancy was outside, talking with the reporters who still lingered on the front lawn.

'They've certainly changed their tune,' she observed with a chuckle when she came back inside. 'They were actually polite.'

'How long does this sort of thing normally take?' Jenna wondered as they seated themselves at the table.

'I've learned never to try to second-guess a jury,' Tess replied as the salad was passed around. 'They could be out a day, they could be out a week.'

'If he's convicted, will he go to prison?' Amy asked.

'Yes.'

'For how long?'

'Maybe for the rest of his life.'

'What makes it so complicated?' Felicity asked.

'There are two separate charges that the jury must deal with,' the ADA explained. 'The charge of sexual assault, which is the rape, and the charge of battery, which is the beating. All twelve jurors must agree on each count.'

'You mean, they could find him guilty of the battery but not the sexual assault?'

'Yes. They might decide that Karen contributed to the rape but was in no way responsible for the beating.'

'You mean, just because she had a few drinks with him and let him drive her home?'

Tess sighed. 'As hard as you try to read the people you put on a jury, you never really know how they'll react. You also have to consider the dynamics of the group and what kind of peer pressure will be brought to bear.'

'I served on a jury once,' John said. 'Not a big case, like this one, and I remember how two of the jurors squared off against each other and tried to force everyone else to take sides.'

'What happened?' Amy wanted to know.

'They hung the jury.'

'Can that happen here?' Jessica asked Tess.

'Anything can happen,' the ADA had to admit.

'But it's not going to,' Ione said, bringing in a huge pan of lasagna. 'It might take the jury a while, but I watched them and I know, in the end, they'll get it right.'

The telephone rang at ten minutes past seven.

Karen sat beside Ted in the third row on the right side of the gallery, her hand tightly clasped in his. From the corner of her eye, she could see Elizabeth Willmont across the aisle. Whichever way this went, she felt sorry for the woman. Beyond the glass partition, the defendant sat calmly in his chair, waiting.

The courtroom was bursting. Every inch of space that was not taken by friends and relatives was filled with reporters. The closed-circuit television camera next door had been fine for the trial, but everyone wanted to be on the scene for the verdict.

Tess stared at the jury, trying to read something in a stray glance or a shift in position. The five men and seven women sat silent and unmoving, with their eyes on the judge.

'Has the jury reached a verdict?' Washington intoned.

'Yes, we have, Your Honor,' replied Brian Barstow, the computer software salesman and elected foreman.

'How do you find?'

A sudden stillness fell over the entire courtroom as those with and without any vested interest strained to hear.

'On the count of battery,' the foreman read from the slip of paper in his hand, 'we find the defendant ... guilty as charged.'

From every corner of the gallery, there was a sharp intake of breath. Karen's hand tightened in Ted's.

'On the count of sexual assault,' Barstow continued, 'we find the defendant ... guilty as charged.'

'So say you all?'

'So say we all.'

The courtroom exploded. Reporters scrambled to get out, everyone wanting to be the first to file the story, the first to get it on the air. A number of Willmont supporters wailed in protest, even as the small contingent of Doniger allies shouted in glee.

Robert sat as though paralyzed, stone-faced with disbelief and rage, oblivious of his attorneys, who were
reassuring him of an appeal; of his wife, who rose and
quietly left the courtroom; of his mother, who was
unable to grasp what had happened. He was oblivious
of everyone, even the two bailiffs who took up positions behind him.

Hal Sutton was on his feet demanding that the
verdict be set aside, even though it was clearly nothing
more than a formality. Judge Washington was futilely
banging his gavel, shouting over the din as he thanked
and dismissed the jury and set the sentencing for
September 14 at 2:00 p.m.

It was over.

Karen felt so weak she wasn't sure she could stand.
In all her dreams, she had not dared to hope that this
moment would ever come, and now it was here – after
thirty years of anguish, it was here. So she stayed where
she was and savored it for a time, closing her eyes and
letting it wash over her like a gentle rain. And Ted put
his arm around her and sat wordlessly by her side.

She didn't see Robert jump from his chair, knocking
it over in the process, or push past the startled bailiffs
as he stormed up the aisle. She was aware of him only
when he stood in front of her, his aquamarine eyes
glaring down at her.

'Why, goddamn you?' he insisted. 'Why?'

A cold winter night came into focus in Karen's
mind, a night when she could do nothing – and
merged with a mild spring night a lifetime later, a
night when she could do anything. She saw the clump
of bushes by Stow Lake, as much like Central Park as
she could find. She saw her face, as bruised and
bloodied as she felt she needed to make it. She saw a

soul that was shattered finally made whole again.

There were any number of times during the past few months when she felt her confidence slipping and doubted she would get away with it. But in the end she was strong enough to pull it off and the irony of it did not escape her. Thirty years ago, she had told the truth, and was not believed. This time, *he* had told the truth, and was not believed. She couldn't remember now how the idea had come to her – to frame him for the crime he had already committed – but it didn't matter. All that mattered was that she had succeeded.

An eye for an eye, the Bible said. So be it. As he once took from her the thing she wanted most in the world, now had she done the same to him, and she felt no remorse.

She looked up at him, her blue-gray eyes calm, her conscience clear.

'December 22, 1962,' she said softly.

Warner Books now offers an exciting range of quality titles by both established and new authors. All of the books in this series are available from:

    Little, Brown and Company (UK),
    P.O. Box 11,
    Falmouth,
    Cornwall TR10 9EN.

Alternatively you may fax your order to the above address. Fax No. 01326 317444.

Payments can be made as follows: cheque, postal order (payable to Little, Brown and Company) or by credit cards, Visa/Access. Do not send cash or currency. UK customers and B.F.P.O.: please send a cheque or postal order (no currency) and allow £1.00 for postage and packing for the first book, plus 50p for the second book, plus 30p for each additional book up to a maximum charge of £3.00 (7 books plus).

Overseas customers including Ireland please allow £2.00 for postage and packing for the first book, plus £1.00 for the second book, plus 50p for each additional book.

NAME (Block Letters) ....

....

ADDRESS ....

....

....

☐ I enclose my remittance for ....

☐ I wish to pay by Access/Visa Card

Number ☐☐☐☐☐☐☐☐☐☐☐☐☐☐☐☐

Card Expiry Date ☐☐☐☐